Darkness of Order

Lyndie Swedersky

Book 2 of the Alecien Series

W & B Pbulishers
USA

A-Argus Better Book Publishers, LLC

For information:
A-Argus Better Book Publishers, LLC
9001 Ridge Hill Street
Kernersville, North Carolina 27285
www.a-argusbooks.com

ISBN: 978-0-6159046-4-1
ISBN: 0-6159046-4-5

Book Cover Art and Design By
Samantha Tarkington
And
Kate Rhodes

Printed in the United States of America

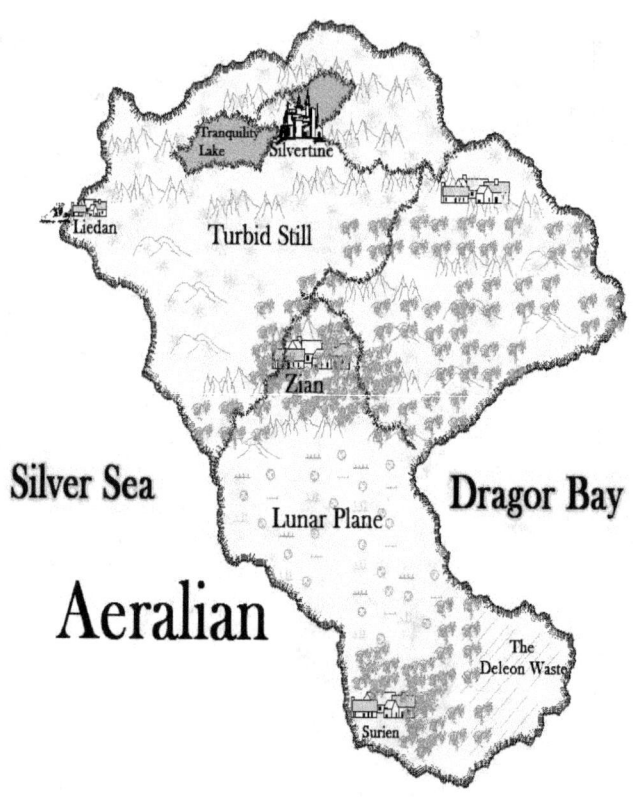

Silver Sea

Dragor Bay

Aeralian

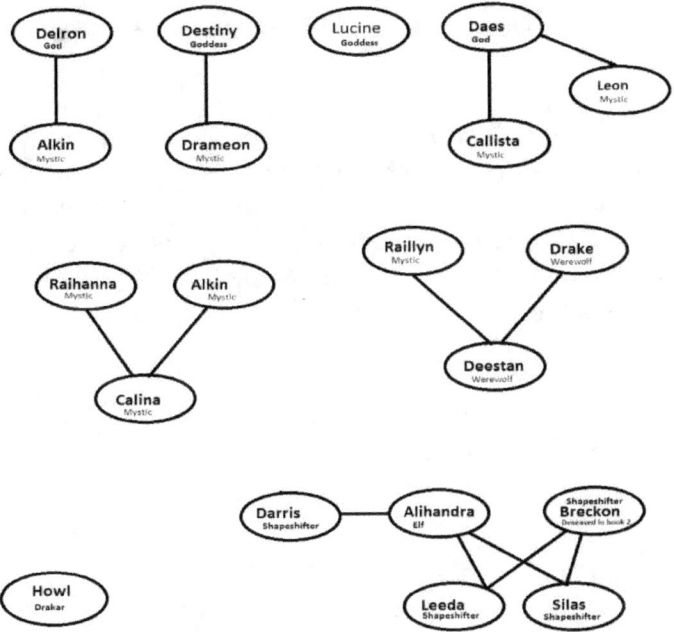

~Dedication & From the Author ~

*I would like to say thank you to everyone who has sup-
ported me through the years. I truly am happy to see these
characters and their story come to life. Thank you Samantha
Tarkington, for late nights of editing and the endless giggles,
as well as drawing Raihanna! Kate Rhodes, thank you so very
much for coloring, you are amazing! You two really gave her
life!*

*Lastly thank you the reader, because without you their
story would never be lived!*

The Alecien I knew has changed so much, and the passage of time for our kind is meaningless. I cannot even remember exactly how much time has passed since the first mistake. Only that it has been nearly two-hundred and fifty years since her death. There were so many mistakes that day...

Walking the old chaotic streets that were once peaceful, filled me with dread. The old ways have died, and paved way to the new, but the new ways are a path of darkness and destruction. As long as the mortal races of Alecien continue on this path, balance will never be restored, and the old ways will be lost. The Gods who created the world, surely cry over the destruction and downfall here.

When the blood of the Elders began to spill, and the first books and scrolls were burned, the old races fled, seeking shelter across the Silver Sea. The Ancient races that remained were destroyed because of their power, their history lost.

Only the common races stayed and fought. For what? The world they knew was lost to them, the blood that was spilled was too strong and the repercussions irreversible. Even now, there are few who remember its beginning and those that do, do not speak about it.

The beginning of the war was marked by the slaughter of an innocent. Desperately she tried to make things that had gone astray right, and by doing so lost her life. Her blood is on my hands and forever will be, but no one remembers that. No one remembers that it was the slaying of the Werewolves Den Master at the hands of the Vampires that sparked the first catastrophe. Numerous magic users, Mystics, Drakar, and Dragons alike had been slain from this hatred. They were the first to die, but not the last.

Balance must be restored but at what price? I am fearful to reckon with these sins.

~Drameon~

Intro ~ Alkin

Never in my wildest dreams did I think things would turn out this distressing. Raillyn's limp body lay in my arms as we walked the dark halls of The Keep. Already I was dreading what I had to do.

I was careful to ensure there would be no chance of her becoming an undead Vampire, so the halls were emptied before our arrival. Hunter wanted Raillyn to remain alive. He wanted her power, and to have her assist him in his plan. However none of this was his plan.

From here on out no one, other than a select few, would know or intervene with this. As I walked towards the Alchemy Wing in the Vampire's Keep, I went over what would come. I knew I had to work quickly, the task at hand would be difficult. As I walked, Hunter was met by a few of his Elite, Ash, Thierry, and Aurielle, following just paces behind us.

Glancing at the familiar dark stone halls, lined with exquisite red, black, and blue colored tapestries, ornate carpets, and more, I couldn't help but smile. Hunter himself did not want to deal directly with Raillyn. Instead, he chose me to do this task.

The dark demeanor of the spell was enough to collapse anyone, I had cast it on her myself. Regretfully, I allowed the darkness to overtake her, abusing the bond we shared between us. Upon entering the living, things had moved fast. Aurielle grabbed the baby out of the sling and held her with disgust. Snarling at her in anger, I was sure to prove I meant what I had said earlier. Aurielle recoiled a little, she knew not to hurt the child. I had threatened her over the past few weeks, but still it made me nervous. Trying to calm my temper, I began going over the many spells that would be used. Inwardly I couldn't help but smile, finally we were on the right track.

Reaching the door, Hunter held it open. Gently I carried Raillyn in. The extensively large room is nearly pitch black. I had been here many years ago in a similar situation. I shook my head and tried to chase away that thought. It was another time and a much different situation.

Pausing a moment I let my eyes adjust. A small magic light glowed on the empty wooden table' two crystal coffins lay a few feet away. Darkness filled the space of the empty room making it much bigger than it seemed. My footsteps echoed in the vastness as I went in. Gently I laid Raillyn down on the simple wooden table. I wanted to reach out and brush her hair aside, kissing her forehead, but I couldn't with Hunter here. So I disregarded the temptation. Turning I checked my components that were laid out on the smaller table beside me. Vials filled with herbs, iridescent liquids and objects of nature lay scattered across its surface.

Glancing at Raillyn, I knew very little time remained. Her magic was strong, and she would not be subdued by my spell for long. I had already pushed my luck and used other means that Hunter was not aware of to ensure her submission. Biting my lip, I was sure in the future I would get an ear full about what I've done. For now though, I just prayed this worked.

Double checking, I ensured everything was in its place before I began reciting the ritual. The spell would sever the bond of her mind and soul, displacing all she knew, and all she was. This darkened art was a powerful necromantic spell, beyond anyone else's capabilities in The Keep. Regretfully, Raillyn would die in this act and be reborn anew.

My companions stood silently and unwavering as I worked. The subtle light from the nearby table reflected off of their retinas, causing them to glow an eerie rust color. As my power began to grow inside me, my own non-reflective eyes began to glow crimson.

Working quickly, and quietly, Ash and Thierry handed me the necessary components from the small table. Carefully I measured the herbs before crushing them in the small stone pestle and mortar. Next, I added them to the iridescent liquid, with a few side components. Slowly I began to mix them until they became a sticky tar like substance, smelling of soil. Then I place it on Raillyn's wrists, ankles, and forehead.

Immediately I order everyone out of the room, pausing only a moment to slow my work. I needed to concentrate. Knowing if I faltered this next step all would be lost, and my master would have my head—in addition to my sanity. I had to separate the conscious mind from the unconscious one, and then remove it. This would ensure that the new body would live but equally ensure that the conscious mind could be altered.

Reaching out with my dark arts, I placed my hand atop her forehead and called to her soul. This was a critical point and I knew if I faltered now she would be lost to the world forever. Her bright blue essence met my hands as I gently pulled the pure energy upright and out of her once living body. It fluctuated in my hands as if it protested. Much like her mind and body struggled against one another in Death's Realm. It was hot, then cold to the touch.

Reaching out along the mental link she had ignored, I tried to soothe her soul. My essence reached out to comfort hers and calm it. Tentatively holding her spirit close, we make our way towards Death's Realm. All seems calm as I enter into its icy waters. My eyes meet the thin greenish grey fog, hampering my vision.

It's not a normal fog. Not the kind that creeps into an early morning harbor and casts clouds upon the shore. It's a different substance that thinly veils the realm. I was vulnerable here. I knew Delron would be keeping his eyes open to anything suspicious. But that's not what concerned me; I needed to be more wary of other Necromancers, than of my father.

This was the realm of the Gods themselves and the only place this spell would work. A place that amplified the art of Necromancy, and blood magic. Scanning the icy waters surface, for any threats, I continue the spell. It's here I begin to gather all of Raillyn's living knowledge into a small orb.

Pulling at her mind through our unique link, I gather her living memories, that I do not want her to know or see, into the orb. Like a key easily turning a lock, my magic seals it. Gently I place the orb containing everything about Raillyn, afloat on the icy waters. I stand and watch for a moment as it disappears into the fog beyond. Momentarily, grief crosses my mind. For the time being she is dead.

Anxiety peaks within my soul, as the bonds between us breaks. My chest hurts and aches, and my heart feels as if it is torn from my chest. For a moment, I fall into the icy waters of Death's Realm, gasping for breath. My eyes sting as a few stray tears run down my cheek.

Desperately I try and steady myself, my soul feels empty and dark thoughts cloud my mind. Forcefully I take a few deep breaths, my mind and body fight against me. Physically I want to fall into the waters of Death's River and die alongside her. Mentally though, I know everything is alright, and that it will all be fixed later. Still, my body cannot overcome the shock and separation from my mate.

Sweat runs down my face and into the icy waters below, mixing with my tears. For a moment, the water around me begins to boil from my struggle. My vision hazes as my magic pours out of me in a red fog. *Now is not the time for this!* I tell myself, forcing my body upright.

Stiffly I go to my feet, my body feels leaden and slug-gish. Shaking I close my eyes and think of her, my rock, my love, and my everything. *Gods, I love her and would do any-thing for her...*

Closing my eyes I take a few steady breaths, finally con-trol returns. My body accepts what my mind has been telling it. That everything will be made better through this act. Hold-ing Raillyn's remaining life essence, I move on.

Twisting, turning, and manipulating it, I begin to bundle her soul into a bright blue ball. Holding the fiercely glowing orb up to eye level, I slowly examine it. Turning it over in my hands, I feel the erratic shift in temperature, a fascinating change between hot and cold. Its power radiates through my body like a static charge; it knew everything, even though Raillyn herself wouldn't understand till later. This little thing was her very life essence, and magic. This was all she was, her very soul, and it would animate the new body.

Holding it close, I turn and leave Death's Realm to finish my work in the living. When I emerge I close my eyes, my emotions quiver once more. Fear begins to build up inside me. Slowly I draw my dark demonic blade, knowing what had to be done next. I needed to concentrate and not allow myself to be distracted from my task. For a moment, I can't help it.

Glancing one last time at her body, I pause momentarily to take in her soft features. Her leucistic skin has lost the red glow of life and now lay ashen. Even her lips no longer look as bright as they should. A tear escapes my eye knowing what I have done. *None of this should have happened, I should've never had to kill her.* Slowly I lean down and brush my lips against hers, sorrow fills my heart. Then I regrettably shrug the emotions aside and begin my work.

With the blackened blade, I cut away skin, tissue, bone, blood, and hair, how much I will not say. Each piece I cut away of Raillyn is placed in a concoction I had created months earlier. This will be the basis to recreate a perfect copy.

In the end, a disfigured body remains. My heart aches as I quickly place a light healing spell on it and slip her into the first crystal coffin. Sealing it tightly, it pulses brightly before going dim once more. Spelled with Ancient magic, the crystal will preserve and slowly heal the body, in a sleep like state. With a small gesture of my hand, I send the coffin to my true master. What he chooses to do with it, I do not know.

Turning quickly I draw my attention back to the second part of my work. Two critical steps remained. First I had to finalize the body. Thankfully the remaining crystal coffin would do this for me.

Completing the body would be the easiest. Carefully I placed the concoction, created from the bits and pieces I collected from her body, into the coffin. In addition, the construct body would need elements of nature, soil collected from the shores of Tranquility Lake near Silvertine—across the Silver Sea—a dash of magic, and blood, my blood. This would not only complete the spell but link me, the caster, to her, my creation. In turn, it would allow a weak link to be formed between us until a stronger one could be created later. Placing these three ingredients into a small hole at the top of the crystal coffin, it immediately begins to glow deep blue.

Next part, inserting memories for Raihanna. Hunter and I had worked late into the night for several months to ensure they were perfect. He insisted she have some over others. In the end, I carefully choose her emotions, feelings, and friendships. Never, would I allow him to have full control over her.

When she awoke I would be her mentor, and lifelong friend, always trusted, and her partner in all of Hunter's work. It was the least I could do. Hunter would remain as her Uncle. She would be programmed to follow his orders, as any of his Elite would, as well as agreeing in the current plan to bring destruction into the world.

As far as Deestan, she would be allowed to raise her as her own. These memories were easy. She would believe that Deestan had been taken from the Werewolves, and placed into her care. An easy fix to an already complicated situation. Lastly, adding the basic knowledge of Mystics, and their magic would serve us best. So we implanted fake memories of growing up under my watchful eye, as well as Hunter's. Learning the arts of fighting, and magic. However, some of them were not fake, but only I knew what were real. They were lost memories from before her time with Chaimh. Memories, from when she was young that I had painstakingly choose and shared so she would remember.

These were to be placed into the body and soul, giving her a new existence in the Vampire world. A mixed existence, if you could call it that. Of what should have been, and what was.

With the crystal coffin glowing bright blue and creating the body, adding the remaining soul fragment and memories to the mix was easy enough. Carefully I dropped them into the small opening and watched.

Lights illuminated the once dark room. You could see a distinct body forming from the grey solution within. One last task remained. It was from my true master, someone who was more powerful than Hunter, but who was not allowed to have an unmitigated hand in many of the events.

I reached into my cloak and pulled out a simple black Mythril box. It was spelled with God-magic that I could not unlock. If Hunter knew I was influencing "his" creation he would be furious, but then again, this was never really "his" plan.

I smirked slightly as I held the box in front of me. It seemed to have sensed the magic from the coffin and quivered. Before falling apart in my hand, slipping between my fingers like grains of sand. The magic within flew out, and spiraled upwards in a blue prism of colors then shot down, entering the coffin.

Suddenly, the coffin and room dimmed as an earth shattering sound was heard. The crystal coffin split and shattered open. Pieces fell to the ground just as rocks falling from a quake. What it revealed was the newly formed body that started to breath.

Raillyn was gone and in her place laid Raihanna. Raihanna's features were much like Raillyn's, the facial structure remained the same, but her hair was a deep auburn with reddish highlights illuminating it. It hung in loose ringlets around her head and down her back.

Deep down I knew she would act differently when she was around me than anyone else. It was our unique link that tied her soul to mine a link I was thankful could never be fully severed. In the end, she was mine, and mine alone. Everything I did was for her. Even though she would never admit it to herself, it was the truth. Even now I couldn't deny how much I loved her.

Caressing her silky locks I brought one up to my nose and smelled her sweet scent. Honeysuckle, vanilla, and thyme, a scent I couldn't eradicate, even with the change. One that still made my heart flutter.

On the outside, she could be mistaken for a twin, but with the magic, she was a polar opposite. She had memories of a life living, and growing up in the Vampire's Keep. Training in the dark arts of necromancy, death, and blood magic. Raihanna was the very thing Raillyn had fought so hard against and now she was Hunter's most prized Elite warrior.

The Keep ~ Raihanna

Night in The Keep was dangerous to those who were living, or those who did not have the brains to avoid certain areas. This was the time when the Vampires would gorge themselves on their victims. The cellar level of The Keep was not as administered as the upper levels.

My Uncle Hunter allowed his Gentry to indulge themselves there as long as they kept within their bounds. This meant their endeavors were kept in the cellar, or out of view. His word was the law. Anyone who disrespected him, or disobeyed, was killed. So most of us kept our mouths shut and did as we were told.

The Keep itself was an extravagant two-story black chateau that contained a lower level, including a dungeon. The main level, or ground level, was where the Gentry resided while Hunter and his Elite resided in personal chambers on the second floor. The lower chambers and cellar were underground.

Once you descended the stairs from the main level, turning down the left hallway would lead you to the library, alchemy rooms, and other studies. While going right would lead you further into the ground, and down a hall towards the cellar, a place of blood and mayhem.

The cellar was a series of tunnels carved from the very rock and ground the Keep sat on; little rooms dotted its vast system. Unlike the cellar, the lower levels were where we Elite did most of our work. Magic, such as imbuing items, studying, and growing herbs, were just a few of the things we did there. The infirmary was near an underground garden that held various plants, both helpful, and poisonous.

My Uncle leads our small group of Elite warriors that are separate from the guard. It is our job to carry out his duties that lie outside The Keep's life. These duties include a compilation of tasks set forth by Hunter to bring our God fully into the world.

Hunter told us our people once worshipped all the Gods. But that was long ago before the war broke out. It's common knowledge in The Keep that the Werewolves cast the first stone. They attacked and slayed our leaders. Many races fled the bloodshed, taking their beliefs with them. For us, only one deity remained. Daes the God of destruction, and chaos was the God evil Vampires worshipped. Daes was a feared God. Vampires, Demons, and races of evil would pay homage to him by sacrificing their victims in ghastly rituals. It is said that Daes despises anything living unless it lives to serve chaos, and the undead.

Amongst the races of Alecien, Daes is an un-liked God, only a few who choose to follow him do so within our lands. We hide it so well that races outside our rule still believe we follow Delron, the God of Death. Delron didn't care whether or not people were changed into Vampires, as long as it was not against their will.

Our magic lay in the dark arts. We had powerful Necromancers working for us, as well as the use of dark blood magic. The Necromancers who remained living worked on creating undead, using their power to bring souls back into a dead corpse, animating it, and being able to control it. While the undead Vampires uses their blood magic, a powerful art that uses blood as power, manipulating the person's magic to the will of the caster. All blood holds power, the stronger the individual, the stronger the power within their veins. This was the key to our magic.

I and my five comrades are Hunter's Elite. We are executioners in our land, and law in The Keep. Even though we don't deal directly with the laws, people fear crossing us. We erected totems that in turn open portals into the demon world. This is where we had acquired some of our stronger soldiers.

Sadly, recently—though this has not been the case—the last portal we had was torn down by the Werewolves over two years ago. Our forces have been growing weaker by the day.

It has to be stopped. Between the Demons and Vampires we have under our control, we're hoping a new portal will help us. This new portal shall be the last one before we bring Daes into the world. That's the plan anyway.

This morning, though, I had my own priorities. While lying in bed, the sun touched a curly lock of my deep auburn hair, illuminating its reddish hue. My thoughts wander to the not so distant past. A few days ago a growing need was slowly creeping throughout my body. One minute I went from slashing my latest victim to bits, to feeling like I wanted to cry. Even now that not so distant day disgusts me.

It was a typical morning; the sun was high in the sky, past noon. Birds flew about tending their young in the early summer heat. Alkin, Ash, and I left to gather more blood for the coming summer feast.

Approaching a small hut, I smelled the scent of several Humans within. Sending Ash in to gather them up, I knew he would have no problems. That's when I sensed the stuttering.

For a moment, my mind blanked, my vision became choppy. A lump formed in my throat as bile threateningly built up within. Briefly I saw Ash exit the hut with a man and a woman.

Static filled my ears as I heard her frantic screams. It only added to the choppy stuttering. Never had I remembered feeling like this. The scent of pine filled my nose, and turning to look at Alkin only made it worse.

When I turned back around, the woman was on her knees. Ash held her down, his hand around her neck as his other hand kept the man at a good distance. She continued to scream, my head hurt, and my body began to ache. Fire spread from the depths of my stomach and ignited every cell in my body.

The screams continued. I couldn't stand her wails any longer. With my mind stuttering, I drew my dagger. Wanting to silence her, I slit her throat. Blood flew from the force of my blow and splattered on nearby trees. It poured from her wound and down her front, covering the ground in front of her in a pool. The man screamed and shied away, horrified by the sight. Quickly Ash brought his dagger across the man's neck and spilled his blood.

Smiling, I saw Ash release our victims and pull out the bottles. As Ash filled them, I turned and met Alkin's eyes. He seemed upset, and for a moment my mind stuttered again and remorse filled my mind. Like glass breaking on stone, my demeanor broke. I was so sure about this mission, gathering blood for the feast, and now I felt sick about what I had done. *Why was I faltering?* Reaching towards Alkin I told him to take me home.

That was two days ago, and today I would not only upset my Uncle, but Alkin, as well. The growing need inside me indicated only one thing. I wanted a child. No one in The Keep could grant me that, and the few who could wouldn't. Deestan had grown fast and was often sad that there were no other children to play with. I found it hard to raise her and show her I loved her, when I was always away. Often it resulted in me bringing her items to keep her happy. I wanted her to have a playmate more than anything else, and no one would stop me from getting it.

In passing, I've only mentioned this to Alkin. He had been my friend for years now and had trained me in the Mystic arts. Recently, we had become closer than just mentor and apprentice. He had become like family to me. He was the only Mystic I had met before, and I was glad he worked for my Uncle.

After pestering Alkin about the issue, he often chased the thoughts away by telling me it was a terrible idea, and that it would only land me in trouble. Regardless of what he said I still could not shake the feeling that I was letting my daughter down. She was the only child in The Keep, and I desperately wanted to give her a playmate.

So, in the darkness of the early morning, I slowly crept from my bed. Padding my bare feet across the floors cold surface to my dresser, I quietly pulled out simple clothes. Black linen pants, and a deep brown tunic. I wanted to appear as harmless as I could. Many of the older races north in Alecien knew who the Vampires, and their warriors were, and I did not want to be recognized.

As I dressed in the darkness I thought of my plan, I would leave, go north, and hopefully find someone to my liking. Someone equal in power to give me what I wanted.

This task would be difficult; a common Human or Half-breed would not do, I wanted a strong magic user. If I had no luck in the northern region of Alecien, I would travel from Kerin Port, across the Silver Sea, to Liedan in Aeralain, and try my luck there. I hoped this would not happen.

The Vampires were frowned upon in Aeralain, and often slain by Shadow Walkers. Even though I'm not technically a Vampire, I carry the distinct scent of vampirism on my skin from living in The Keep. It would take a few weeks at the very least before the scent would naturally disappear. Sandalwood however, could mask it, for a short while. So, for the time being, I choose to use it.

As I silently slipped out my door, my eyes met absolute darkness. I steady myself by reaching out, and gently touching the wall on my left, allowing it to guide my way as I walked in darkness till I reached the main den. A soft glow could be seen from the base of the main door. Magical lights slightly illuminated the den. Their soft glow was just enough for me to walk towards the door, and not trip on any furniture. Just as I reach out to grasp the handle, a hand tightly grabbed my wrist.

Immediately the darkened room was lit, and in a flash I could see Alkin's face. Quickly, he pulls me away from the door, in short whip-like action he nearly tosses me to the floor. Unconsciously I reach for my dagger with my free hand. Turning to confront me his face was expressionless, but inside I could feel his emotions shift between anger, and grief.

"You would raise your dagger against me?" He asked. It was a lapse in judgment on my part; I had let my instincts take over. Angry I released the dagger from my grasp, dropping it back into its sheath. "You know I would win, I am centuries older than you, and I'm more proficient in my magic, unlike you, my little poppet." Alkin said.

As soon as I released the dagger, Alkin released my wrist. "I will not let you travel north in hopes of acquiring what you want."

"How-" I asked, a bit baffled. For a moment, my stomach burned.

He ignored me, and began pacing the room, "What happens if there are no magic users that are to your liking, what then?" Alkin asked tartly as he crossed his arms in front of him and blocked me from the door.

"If I find no one up north, than I will just take a boat across the Silver Sea. There are plenty of Ancients there. One of them would do just fine. So either you let me leave freely now, or I will leave on my own later." I stated while trying to shoulder my way around him. He blocked my path once more and pushed me into the nearby wall.

"You will not leave!" He snarled in a furious tone, before addressing the situation calmer. "If you do so, you will not come back alive, and you know it. You reek of Vampire and the Shadow Walkers will kill you for it. The very idea is asinine. I'd alert Hunter before allowing you to leave freely." Alkin stated as he tossed me backwards further into the room.

I was furious, and beyond mad, and knew I would get no help from him. Luckily I knew that if I infuriated him enough he would leave, giving me the few moments I needed to escape. I quickly debated my choices, before it struck me. Suddenly I knew the one thing that would infuriate him the most.

For a moment, I allowed the burning sensation to overtake me, igniting every cell in my body. It was the first waves of my cycle. A shift occurred as my scent changed accordingly. Smiling, I rivaled in it momentarily before going to Alkin.

His nostrils flared, I knew he was taking in my scent. A thought crossed my mind, *would he even be able to resist if I let this continue?* Never had I hide my true self from Alkin, he could read me inside and out, so what was the point? For a moment I didn't feel like myself, I was thrilled and excited with this new power.

Going to him, he fidgeted nervously. Smiling deviously I reached out and placed my hand on his cheek, he seemed to melt into me. Never before had I had this power over him, he was like putty in my hands, and I enjoyed it. Leaning forward I gently brushed my lips across his.

"I will carry through with this asinine plan whether you help me with it or not." I said before turning, and going towards the door once more.

Alkin stood momentarily stunned, either unsure of what I said, or unsure how to react. I felt nothing from his mind until the mental wall went up. Turning, and facing him I was suddenly filled with fear. Never in my life had I been frightened like this. It bubbled inside me, causing me to withdraw, like creatures frightened of light. At this moment Alkin frightened me more than anything, he was the light that I shied away from.

A sudden click of anger, before he threw up the mental wall, signaled his rising power. It gave me a moment to react before his spell hit me. Turning towards the door I knew I would not make it; there was no time.

Alkin built up his magic in a red haze that enveloped me, and twined around my body like a giant snake. Its rope-like texture dug into my skin as I fell to the floor. Not wanting to appear weak I tried to stifle the cry that echoed in the room. Twisting, and turning I attempted to loosen its hold on me.

Regardless of how much I struggled to break free, I knew it was futile, he was my mentor, and I was his student. This spell was stronger than anything I had worked with, as of yet.

Even though Alkin had blocked me from his emotions and immediate feelings, I could clearly see it on his face. In that instance I regretted saying what I had said, and how I acted.

His ever-changing eyes glowed red as he approached. A wicked smile spread across his face. I knew if I was forbidden to leave, he would be my best chance for what I wanted.

Kneeling down he pulled on the red ropes and brought me to my feet. I refused to let him know how he frightened me, and blocked my own emotions, hardening my face into a mask of determination. Almost slamming me against the wall, Alkin took me aback, slowly he closed his eyes. Leaning forward he inhaled sharply, before releasing me from the magical ropes, and lowering his walls.

Once again I could feel a wave of emotions hit me, at first it felt like a jumbled mess, which gave way to calmness. Then one word changed everything, "Fine." He said subtly, before leaning forwards and kissing me deeply. I stood stunned.

Time ~ Alkin

It had been well over three years since I last spoke to my true master, and remembering back to when I last contacted him had me troubled. It was shortly before Raihanna's asinine idea, an idea I had reluctantly agreed to help with. One that, as I watched my daughter laugh and run about with her older sister on the meadows edge, chasing iridescent fireflies, I don't regret.

Smiling I watched Callina twirl and dance amongst the tall grass as Deestan did the same. Her black hair twirled around her head and her Elvin-like features. I was thankful she did not inherit any of my Demon features. Mainly, dark peach-colored skin. Instead, her skin was more like my father's, as well as her mother's. Deestan still held her bright copper hair, green eyes, and elf-like face.

Hunter still to this day suspects nothing. He knows she is a pure Mystic, meaning both parents are Mystic, her ever-changing eyes proved this to be true. Yet, he does not know she is mine, and that is how I prefer to keep it. Even after Raihanna carried Callina, we had stayed the same—she was my student, and I was her mentor. Even then, an inescapable bond had formed between us, one that she tried to pass off as more of a fancy. Whether she knew it or not that bond was stronger, and it made me smile, knowing I had family in her.

Even though it had been so long since I last spoke to my master, I was not surprised. The Ancient races, the ones who truly had lived well beyond a couple hundred years, felt time meant nothing. Most of the Ancient races could live over a thousand years or longer, as long as they weren't killed. It was a treasure that Alecien had lost during the war. I myself was well over nine-hundred years old, rivaling my whelp of a student.

It felt strange being here again. Walking the same old halls of The Keep, which I had walked well before the war, and seeing how much had changed. How much was lost...

At the beginning of the war, so much of the old ways had been destroyed, burned, stolen or scattered to the wind, causing Alecien's history to be rewritten. Nothing of the old ways survived the war's relentless nature. I had smirked to myself the first time I heard how the Vampires believed they were created.

In a sense yes they were right, they had retained enough knowledge to know a God had a hand in it, but the exact God was wrong. Their creation, as they think, began when they tampered with an ancient blood magic spell and accidentally summoned Daes the God of destruction. They were given a reward for performing such an immense spell—immortality— and in exchange they were told to bring darkness into the world. They believed Daes was the God of destruction, chaos, and darkness. In a sense, they are right, but it's really Delron who rules deeper in that area.

The true story of their creation is much darker than what they know. Once Vampires had been Shadow Walkers, living, breathing, and nurturing; but that had been before the first renegade broke off from their race. That one renegade went south beyond the Lunar Plane of Aeralain to the Deleon Waste, a place where Demons lived. He made friends with the Demons and learned their dark ways, and the hated blood magic. With this knowledge, he learned necromancy and slowly began walking in Death's Realm, an act that was taboo in the Shadow Walker world. He became proficient in the darkened magic of our world and, when he realized he could progress no further due to his blood, he decided to abolish it.

While walking in Delron's land that day, he began a destructive spell, one that would turn his living body into a hatred shadow. They had the power to cause destruction if released in the living world. Delron had sensed this magic and went to investigate; immediately he caused a mortal wound to the Shadow Walker, causing him to slowly bleed out in the realm of the dead. Before the last drop of blood left his body, and fully killed him, Delron stopped his death.

"You are so bent on destruction and chaos? I shall grant you this wish." Delron said in a haunting tone.

Delron took his soul and his last bit of mortal blood, paying the immense blood price for the ancient spell. In exchange, Delron granted him immortality and left him with the cold blood of death.

No longer did his heartbeat or warm blood run his veins; instead his heart stilled. What Delron did not mention was that blood no longer empowered him; instead it became his only source of nourishment.

When he was cast out of the realm of the dead, the newly created Vampire tried to harness the blood power, and found no source of magic in the blood. This infuriated the Vampire, and when he reached for Death's Realm once more, to speak to Delron, he found nothing. No longer could he travel to the realm of the undead; instead he was banned from it. So the Vampire turned against his old kin, bringing those who had a darkened soul to his side, and caused havoc in his wake.

As time went on, his hatred died, and the newly created Vampire race traveled across the Silver Sea and learned to coexist in Alecien. Only the Vampires who resided in Aeralain, or those who brought about their own destruction, were slain. Regardless of, how well they behaved, the Vampires were still a shunned race, an abomination to the Ancient races. Their race had become proficient in blood magic, and the dark arts and death was never far from their doorstep.

Suddenly, the subtle nudge of a Mystic call was felt in my mind. Immediately I turned my attention towards it and accepted the message that accompanied it. My true master's voice entered my mind, "I wish to speak to you", I sighed momentarily, *the time has come*, I thought to myself.

I called the girls back from their games and immediately took them to The Keep. The walk was short since we were just outside the walls. Two guards, clad in black plate armor, stood watch over the large wooden gates. This was the main entrance to the small village surrounding The Keep. As I walked the darkened streets, I kept the girls close. The Vampires were not only heartless but ruthless to the living.

Some drunken Vampires spilled out of a nearby door and fell into the streets. A group passed us, and pleas were heard from a woman, who was brought to the village as a late night snack. I closed my eyes to the terror the village wrought and pulled the girls closer. I understood why the Ancient races disagreed with the Vampires' ugly ways, and wished I could have a say in the matter concerning my family.

As we neared The Keep itself, a hand reached out of the darkness, grabbing Callina by the wrist, pulling her towards the shadows. Quickly I tightened my grip, and thrust Deestan behind me as Callina let out a blood curdling scream. Calling my darkened shadow blade, I slashed inches in front of her hand, severing the Vampire's clean off. It landed in a bloody heap in the dirt below. His wails and screams echoed through the loud streets, mixing with the cries of human victims. Quickly I dissipated the blade and scooped Callina into my arms. Taking Deestan by the hand, I rushed them into the safety of the nearby Keep.

Here, things were calmer. Hunter had full authority within these walls, and those who were allowed entry knew if they crossed him, it would mean their death. So luckily most of the Gentry and other Vampires left the few living who resided here alone. Deestan looked at me concerned. Placing a finger to my lips, I led them swiftly through the quiet halls, trying not draw unwanted attention to us. Callina's muffled cries continued and echoed off the stone walls.

I couldn't help but shake my head, displeased at what The Keep had become. Once a place full of decorative portraits, colorful tapestries, and elegant rugs was now a barren cold pit. I tried hard to hide my displeasure from the girls, but they both noticed. Looking at Deestan made me wonder, I knew her lineage, and worried what we would do with her in The Keep once she shifted. Hopefully she would not be here when those years hit. Hopefully she would be home where she belonged. As long as everything went as planned, anyway.

This is what the Gods wanted, not just myself, or my master. For now, however, she would remain here.

Finally, we rounded the corner to the stairs. They would lead to the second floor, and Raihanna's chambers. I continued to pull Deestan along as we entered the dimly lit stairwell. At times, I had found several of the Elite causing trouble in the darkened shadows here, but thankfully tonight all was quiet. We hustled along and stopped at Raihanna's door. Quietly I spoke the words that would grant us access, and shoved the door open, pushing Deestan in before tightly shutting it behind us.

"Callina, you need to stop. You are safe, child, back in your mother's chambers. All is well." I said in a gentle tone, trying to quiet my daughter down as I placed her onto the floor. She sat down and sniffled.

Deestan lately had become a little mother to her sister, and often took up comforting her and doting on her while Raihanna was away. She knelt down and brushed her sister's messy black hair back. "Alkin's right, you're ok. That Vampire didn't get you. Alkin would never let that happen." She said as she wiped away Callina's tears.

Before I could say another word, Nora, the girl's nursemaid came in. "Is everything ok, Master Alkin?" She asked in a quiet tone.

I knew I had to watch what I said and did in front of the Vampires, so I replied carefully. Already I was pushing my luck, lately. "Everything is alright Nora. We just had a bad run in with one of the village folk. He frightened Callina is all. Thankfully the girl did not get hurt. I can't say the same about the other guy." I said smiling cockily.

Nora smirked at my words. She was different, she was not the normal Vampire, I painstakingly convinced her to come and attend the girls. She agreed and left Silvertine, disguising her scent with magic, and vials to assist me with their care. No one was the wiser, and I was thankful for that.

"I have business to attend, so please take care of the girls until Raihanna, or I return. Under no circumstance allow them to leave The Keep." I threatened, even though I knew Nora was very diligent in her task. I still felt uneasy in The Keep, even after nearly ten years here.

Quietly I slipped into the icy cold halls. I was thankful Raihanna kept such warm chambers. Most of the Elite, held old Shadow Walker rooms, where fireplaces were used. Though some of the Elite choose not to use them, Raihanna always kept hers lit during the colder months.

I shook my head once more at The Keep. The warmness no longer was felt in the halls as it once had when the Shadow Walkers tried to live here with the Vampires. Instead, it was like the lifeless body of the Vampires themselves, an empty shell, cold, and stale.

The Keep overall was no longer whole either. The other towers, chambers, and areas had been destroyed during the war and replaced by the wretched village outside. I still could not believe the ruin the Vampires left to the once magnificent Chateau. In the end, only the main building stood. Shaking my head in displeasure I opened a darkened portal and walked through it.

My true master stood in the center of a large den. Exquisitely sculpted rafters hung from the ceiling, and equally beautiful artwork hung from the walls. It was a huge relief from the Keep's bareness. Bookshelves lined not only the walls but dotted the room, along with various deep red chairs. A large mahogany table sat in the center, near a fireplace. Dragon and Phoenix carvings twined up its legs.

He smiled at me as I met his eyes. High cheek bones, Elvin-like ears, all stood out against his long silver hair, and ever-changing eyes.

"Hello Drameon." I said while bowing slightly to him. "Sorry for the delay, we had a small run-in with a Vampire, but it was quickly taken care of." I said while smiling, and standing back upright.

Drameon nodded his head as he took a seat in a nearby chair, and motioned for me to do the same. "So how does it go in The Keep? Anything important happen lately? It seems that the Vampires have been rather quiet, and I find that unsettling." Drameon questioned while he folded his hands under his chin.

I shook my head in reply. "Not much has been going on lately. Hunter has been trying to recoup from the attack on the portal six years ago. It's only been recently that he has spoken about creating a new one." I said matter of fact.

Life in The Keep has been mellow recently, council meetings have been uneventful and rather boring. The only troubling council meeting we had was right after the portal fell. It seemed like it took months for everything to calm down, the meeting—which was set for the next day—was still held, but it was strenuous. Accusations had been thrown around by all the races, Half-breeds, Werewolves, and Vampires alike. The Shapeshifters had left, disappearing as the Wolves once had so long ago.

"Raihanna is well, I hope, and you have had no issues with her?" My master asked interrupting my thoughts.

I sighed knowing this would be a touchy subject. "She has been well, and Hunter has been keeping her busy. She is just as ruthless as ever, and Hunter enjoys that. Lately, he's been having her gather ingredients for creating the totems for the new portal, as well as harvesting potent blood." I said remembering how much blood was needed from both human and magic users alike in creating the staves. "I did have one minor issue, a little over three years ago." I began. "Raihanna got a terrible idea stuck in her head and tried to evade me."

Drameon looked at me puzzled and concerned. "What sort of idea? There is nothing wrong with her, is there?" He asked, suddenly jumping to conclusions.

This subject was not only touchy but unsettling. I didn't want to explain to him that she began brooding. I shook my head as I felt his anger increase momentarily. Typically Drameon was extremely careful and never allowed his emotions to show.

"No, she is fine, she began brooding and wanted to give her daughter a playmate is all." I said trying to judge how to proceed. Either unsure how to answer or waiting for me to continue, Drameon sat listening, and waiting. "She was willing to travel to Aeralain in order to find a magic user who would suit her purpose." I said, rather annoyed and irritated. "After numerous attempts to keep her in The Keep, and countless arguments, it was becoming hard to contain her and keep her, home. In the end, she gave me an ultimatum. Either I help her in her plan, or she would leave. I knew she was serious." I said smiling inwardly while watching Drameon for his reaction.

His thoughts were fully blocked from me; he sat and listened, his ever-changing eyes displayed the colors of his mood. Momentarily, before closing them, they flashed red with anger. I knew he was considering my act, and trying to justify it.

When he opened his eyes again, they changed accordingly once more. This time not giving away his inner most emotions. "You and Raihanna have a child?" He asked.

"Yes," I said in response.

Drameon took a deep breath, and sat back in his chair, he gazed at the ceiling, and rafters. "And what is your affection towards each other after this act?" He asked in an authoritative manner.

"Just as it always is, she is my pupil, and I am her mentor. Only recently has that began changing, but we both knew she would. I hate having to keep my family there, and I cannot wait for this to be over." I said allowing my emotions to show, so he would see I spoke truth.

Drameon stood and walked around the room, deep in thought for a moment before continuing. "I understand. Still, everything must go accordingly. Raihanna is too large of a pawn in this game to lose her now to pettiness. We have worked for too many years to get her into The Keep. She has to stay there." Drameon said annoyed. "You know what will happen if we fail, and you know it would not only mean our end but the end of Auran as well." Drameon spoke carefully as if even his own home had prying ears. "This is too important for a mistake. We cannot fail, I still pray that this will work." He said, saddened. "Go, just ensure everything stays according to plan, and only deviate if the need is great. I can see this was unavoidable, and can understand why it happened."

I bow one last time to my master and old time friend, before opening a portal back to The Keep.

Drameon

As I watched Alkin leave I lean back in the red velvet chair, and take a deep breathe. I could see how it had come to Alkin assisting Raihanna, but it still bothered me. Raihanna was cunning, too cunning at times; and if she truly tried, she could have easily evaded Alkin, and left. However I was thankful he had a link to her, their bond.

From the last talk I had with my old friend, I learned that Raihanna had excelled in her Mystic training. I had to warn Alkin to be sure she didn't find the Ancient spells that were more destructive than most. I feared her power.

We needed her alive, and not getting herself killed by spell or Vampire. She had become such a vital piece in this century's oldest puzzle. Now we had all the pieces coming together just right, and it needed to stay that way. I myself had to continue forward with care, I had taken too much time in my ploy for it to be diverted now. Even the Werewolves would fall unknowingly into place in this larger game of chess.

New Land ~ Raihanna

As the light from the newly risen sun shone through my curtains, I awoke, and remembered what today was. We had been talking for weeks about this outing. Today was finally the day that we would survey the outcrop of land in the Northern Hills, just south of Issia.

We needed this new portal. I had been able to bring soldiers into Alecien since the destruction of the last portal, but not nearly enough for our plan. A new portal would ensure easier access to more troops.

As I laid my feet down on the rug below, I looked around my room. The bed sat near a mahogany wardrobe that lay in the corner, a small mirror sat on top of it. Rubbing my eyes wearily, I walked over towards it and looked at my face.

My pale skin held a touch of redness from the bitter chill in the air. Sleepily, I ran my fingers through my dark auburn curls tousled around my face and over my shoulders. I tried to fix its disarray before pulling out my blackened armor from the drawers below. Running my fingers across the black surface, magic danced over the material, vibrating slightly to the touch. My fingers tingle with its power and dance with a lightning sensation. Checking the straps for durability, I pulled the armor over my head and fasten the clasps. Looking in the mirror one last time I ensured my red amulet, my Uncle had given one to each of us, was around my neck.

The necklace, I was told, was from the God Daes, giving us the power to create portals. We could use it for quick travel, as well as communicate mentally with each other. The portals we created could only go to places where we had been already, and even then it was shaky unless you knew the area well. I looked around my room once more before leaving, ensuring all was in place, and that I wasn't forgetting anything.

After I made sure all was well, I went to the door and into the hall.

I was thankful I had one of the larger chambers in The Keep. I had lots of room for myself and my daughters, with plenty of space to spare. That was good because I had been housing Alkin for a few years now while I studied under him. It only made sense, since he had become the girls tutor, as well as being Callina's father.

The four bedrooms near the eastern edge of the chambers were connected to the large hall leading into the main den. This was the center room, and was connected to the main hallway that led further into The Keep. The main den also held a stairwell that went down to a lower den, my small study.

As I followed the hall towards the main den, I traced my fingers against the cold stone wall; lightly I brushed one of the many brightly colored tapestries adorning the walls surface. I had spent many years collecting these treasures. Some were found in the lower levels of The Keep and dated back to before the war, while the others I had retrieved from the outings Hunter had sent me on.

Entering the den, I noticed it was empty; a fire still charred in the fireplace from the night before. The stairs in the far corner were dark, but the curtains were pulled back allowing for the morning sun to shine in.

The girls must have awoken first and walked themselves down to the dining hall. Before leaving, I picked up several books that were scattered across the floor. Deestan was probably reading to Callina again last night. She was always teaching her little sister everything she was learning.

After they were placed neatly on the nearby table, I left my chambers and entered the main hall. Several servants and maids were already hard at work tidying up the place. I knew my personal maid would be attending my chamber before too long.

Walking the halls, most of The Keeps servants avoided eye contact, keeping their heads down unless addressed. These Vampires were human before they were turned. They were weak, only created to serve the stronger people of our race. Most were full or half-breeds, Elves or Fae before being turned.

The halls were chilly this morning as if within its walls winter had set in early. The hall's dark stone surface gleamed as I walked its length; nothing hung from the walls, and the floors were bare. Rune symbols lit up certain doors and hall-ways, indicating their purpose. This level of The Keep was kept extremely nice, and clean. The lower levels were not al-ways this way. One would not be surprised to find blood now and again splattered across the wall or floor, from an un-known victim in the night.

Rounding the last corner I approached my destination, and pushed open the door. All was quiet as I entered the din-ing hall. My comrades sat on the far end of the table adorning the center of the room, they spoke quietly amongst them-selves.

I noticed my daughters; Deestan with her tousle of gold-en hair, and pale skin, sitting in one of the blue chairs along the exterior of the room and Callina, her sister sat beside her. She had her father's Elf like features, black hair, and the ever-changing eyes of a true Mystic while her skin matched her sister's, and my own. Deestan had her nose in one of the many books I had given her the night before, and as I ap-proached her she read to Callina.

"See, you can summon water with your magic, and force it to swirl upwards out of its source. Or gather it into a ball and toss it." She said to her sister.

"Learning much?" I asked her while leaning down to kiss both of them upon the head. Deestan's emerald green eyes met mine momentarily as she smiled, before returning to her reading.

"I just don't see why I have to study so much, I want to learn how to fight, and use swords." Deestan said between sentences.

But before I could reply, the main door opened and my Uncle strolled in laughing, as he came into the room. His stout figure walked towards my companions slowly. My Uncle's sandy hair, wispy and thin, clung to his head where he kept it slicked back to hide the spots of missing hair from years of battles. His often black-red eyes glowed brightly when he was eager about a new plan, and today this was the case.

"Child you must learn all about Alecien and its history so you and your sister can one day sit on the council. Your heritage is very important, and it would be a dishonor if you did not learn everything about the land where you live and its happenings," he said as he walked towards Aurielle, Ash, and Thierry, a few of his Elite.

Looking at Deestan, and Callina I agreed before going to join them. Ash looked over at me, smirking as I came to stand near him. He stood a good two feet taller, and was rather mysterious. Even though he was one of my right hand men—and a good friend—I still knew very little about him.

His pitch-black hair was pulled back loosely while his deep brown eyes glowed slightly red in color against his Elfin like features. His good friend, Thierry, whom he called his brother, was slightly shorter. He had a stockier build. His straight deep-brown hair gently brushed his shoulders and his greenish-red eyes glowed as his listened to my Uncle.

Glancing towards Aurielle, my sister, she smiled eagerly. We resembled each other slightly, her ebony hair hung straight and normally was kept back out of her face, while her deep-brown eyes held the red tone of a typical Vampire. She had been turned years ago while I choose to remain living. Smiling back at her I listened to Hunter.

"As you know I need you four to survey the land around the Northern Pass. We need an area that no one disturbs and is secluded with no ease of access. I think the Northern Hills will be a good place. With all the snow, they don't get too many visits there." Hunter said while pacing the floor. "Just keep out of sight and report back with your findings." He said, taking his leave back into the main hall.

We all nodded in unison, and I took my seat at the table while breakfast was placed around us.

For the living, the food consisted of fruits, vegetables, nuts while various breeds of bottled blood were also included for the undead. Not many Vampires ate food, but some considered it to be a hobby, and did so for entertainment. Some preferred the taste while it did nothing for their bodies. Their true nutrition lie in blood that was acquired from nearly all corners of Alecien.

Unlike the Shadow Walkers—who drank blood for power—Vampires drank to sedate their hunger. The weaker the blood the shorter one could go between feeding, and the stronger the blood the longer one could go.

As we sat, we talked in light about the situation at hand. "I hope we find someone to play with, on this trip." Aurielle said, while popping a grape into her mouth, and grinning.

I looked at her with disregard but as well as authority. "Hunter doesn't want any trouble. We have to proceed quietly, so no one suspects anything abnormal in the area." I said, taking my place as one of their leaders. Within the Elite Ash, Alkin, and I were Hunter's top warriors; we often lead the others since we were the strongest.

Aurielle rolled her eyes at me haphazardly as she got up to leave. I looked at Ash who often helped keep the others in line. His brows furrowed, I could tell he was not happy. He closed his eyes and shook his head at Aurielle's display.

"I'll go talk to her." Ash said, as he got up and followed her into the hall. "Meet us in the stables." His voice echoed as he left.

Sighing, I nodded in reply, and after kissing my daughters goodbye, I left to grab my items. I needed my sword, which I typically did not wear unless I left The Keep, and a few other items. Even the simple task of going into town resulted in me adorning my weapons since many hidden dangers lurked there. Anywhere outside The Keeps walls was not safe unarmed.

As I entered my chambers, Alkin sat in a chair in the main den. His ever-changing eyes looked at me as I closed the door while his long chestnut hair fell over his face. I smiled slightly, knowing I could never be rid of him. He smiled back at me, as I felt the subtle pull of his emotions indicate his mood.

"I was told to meet you here, and accompany you." He said, placing his book on the table and standing. "Also I brought you this." Indicating towards the other chair, where a new blackened chestplate sat. "Hunter said it was better than the one you had, and told me to bring it here."

Perplexed I went over to inspect it, the chestplate was flexible, and yet I could tell its durability was beyond the typical skills of our smiths. "Where did it come from?" I asked while unbuckling my old one. Alkin quickly came over to assist me, his fingers danced over my waist as he unclasped the bindings.

"Hunter did not say; probably from one of the other areas he visited recently. He said he wanted to bring more back for his other Elites. Either way, the craftsmanship on this is far superior to ours. Hunter stated that no one other than you, his wonderful niece, should wear the first piece." Alkin said while smiling.

In recent years, my Uncle heavily relied on Alkin. He had become his personal adviser, and our ally. From what I knew, Alkin had come to us from the Demon lands when I was just a child. I was told, as time went on, my Uncle was quick to realize that he was not a Demon. That he also possessed necromancy, and was actually a Mystic. He was a rare breed and became my Uncle's prized soldier. Thinking back to my earlier days made me smile. I still remembered when he took me to Aneross Peeks and let me play in the snow.

Snow was a rare sight in our region, we were too close to the Himar dessert for it to stick. I was young, probably no older than three, and was in tears because the first light flakes had disappeared after mere minutes. Crying, something I only did around Alkin, I begged to see more snow.

Gently he brushed my hair aside, and pulled me into his arms, without any words he carried me through a portal. When it dissipated, we stood at the foot of a towering mountain range. Icy crags loomed high above us, there mighty appearance brought both fear and wonder to my young mind.

The white peaks were high, higher than anything I could imagine, and seemed to touch the clouds. Smiling I turned, and darted into the freezing snow, it was colder than Death's River, but I didn't care. Laughing I made snowballs and playfully tossed them at Alkin.

After getting hit with a few he chuckled, and tossed some back, eventually we were both covered in snow. Even then he was a good friend to me. Who knew our relationship would progress as I grew.

Later, when we began working side by side, he taught me how to tie our magic together. Alkin was proficient in the Mystic ways as I was only just learning. With my Uncle's permission, Alkin took me as his pupil, and began teaching me more about our kind. I learned that Mystics were one of the Ancient races and that very few remained on this side of the Silver Sea. As I learned, I began to excel in ranks myself. Soon I had joined Hunter's Elite. Hunter was proud on how fast my capabilities had grown with Alkin's help.

As I grew, he taught me about blood bonds, an art I knew a little about from my lessons with the Vampires. Forming a blood bond was as easy as exchanging blood between two people. With Vampires, it created a sire bond between master, and underling. The master would give orders, and the underling would have to obey.

This was not a large problem with the Elite since most of the Vampires serving my Uncle wanted the same outcome. I knew that Shadow Walkers had created blood bonds between people they loved, and people they worked with. This gave them an advantage of being able to track those people with magic, following the special magical signature, created when sharing blood.

While Mystics had a similar reason to Shadow Walkers, our way was more similar to the Drakar, the Dragon-touched race. Their race was similar to Mystics, both created by the Gods specially.

Mystics and Drakar shared blood to form a more powerful bond between two people. One could locate the other as long as spells were not preventing them from being found. Magic could be intensified with spell twining, spinning two people's power into one, while emotions, ideas, or memories could be passed between one another. Often a long lasting friendship was formed.

After the lesson, I had begun questioning him more about blood bonds if there were side effects, or anything dangerous about them. The most dangerous thing with these types of bonds was the emotional attachment that formed.

Once formed these ties were unbreakable and last for the rest of one's life. Forming such bonds that intensified emotional attachments were unheard of in The Keep. The Vampires were a race driven by need, not by emotions. It was enough to stop my questioning, it wasn't enough to stop Alkin though. During my younger adult years, he often mentioned, nonchalantly, the idea of taking me as his mate. Never going into full detail how that was done, I cringed at the thought.

Not that Alkin wasn't handsome or anything, but because I had a reputation to uphold, and taking a mate would make me appear weak in the eyes of some. However, not long after I stopped asking about the blood bonds, Hunter commanded Alkin and I to form one. Panicked, I went to my Uncle and demanded he rethink his command. That only landed me with a bloodied lip and bruised face.

Neither Alkin or I wanted any emotional ties to anyone. But, we had no choice if we were to continue working for Hunter, and to remain in the Elite we would have to obey. So the bond was formed, and a small leaf pattern dotted my left shoulder, and chest, running down across my heart.

Placing the mark was simple enough; however, it did lead to unintended situations. It started innocently, Alkin said it would be easier to form the bond if we connected, physically and mentally. So gentle kisses and soft caresses were exchanged between the two of us. However, that changed and like wildfire it grew. In the end, I took him to my bed.

At first I was fearful I had become his mate, still to this day he never fully addressed the issue, or explained. But, after a few days I was thankful things got out of hand. I was the youngest Elite, the most inexperienced, this simple act placed me more on the Vampires level, and proved I wasn't weak. That was six years ago, just days after the portal fell.

Overall the bond was an adjustment I had to learn to deal with, and at first, I couldn't even bear to touch him. I would feel overwhelmed with emotions, almost as if I was trying to swim in a lake, but I was drowning just below the surface. Eventually, I learned to control it, only letting my guard down temporarily when I wanted another child. That had brought on feelings, and emotions neither of us were prepared for.

A little over three years ago, after giving Alkin the ultimatum, he told me to travel north to Issia, and that he would report me missing to Hunter. We both knew that Hunter would send him to retrieve me, and bring me home. In this way, Hunter wouldn't have a clue who the father was. So after Hunter sent him out to find me, we met up in the Issia tavern. He seemed reluctant, and blocked his mind from me, but slowly that changed. I had known what I wanted, and required.

Determination crossed my face as I wrapped my arms around him. Smirking he pulled me closer and ran his fingers across my waist. The link we had created, erupted in a scattered array of overwhelming affection, and happiness. I was breathless by the emotional bond we shared. It mixed, and twisted with the need he had to please me, and give me what I wanted. My mind shattered, and stuttered as instinct took over.

Neither of us had chosen to take lovers in The Keep, and maybe this was why. The bond we shared went deep, and even though I felt he was hiding memories of unease from me, he was not hiding his emotions. Even the first time, when we established the bond wasn't this forceful. This overwhelming feeling was earth shattering, and inescapable.

He was nervous and uneasy, but his need mixed with mine and created a hurricane inside both of us. My body burned, like lava ready to explode out of a fiery volcano. I felt his body shake with anticipation as we stripped each other of our garments.

He was hundreds of years older than I was, and through our link I had know he took various lovers over the years, but they never meant anything to him. None of them were Mystic, and he never cared for them. Now however, that was changing, he was committing himself to me, in a way, by giving me a child. Tied up in the intense feeling of closeness, magic, and power I gave him my ultimatum once more.

"If you will not help me with this then I will find another to do so." I said as he closed his eyes. I felt him battle inner demons. Ones who screamed at him, and told him this was wrong. Still I don't understand why...

Suddenly his resolve came to a final decision. The already consuming emotional need and overall touch intensified as his nails dug into my hips, causing me to cry out. My warm blood ran down my legs, and onto the ground. He knew what he had done, and so did I. He had marked me as his mate. Deep down no matter how much I wanted to fight it, I knew there would only be him. The thought of taking someone else to my bed brought on repulsive feelings of disgust. I only felt comfortable with Alkin. As my mind accepted what happened, he kissed me deeply. It was as if I was swimming in an inescapable sea of raw magic, one that we didn't surface from for several days.

Thinking back to that day I'm thankful Mystics only brood once every three to five years. It would be awful if we were like the more common races, and had a monthly cycle. Even now, those emotions flared once in awhile but never amounted to anything. However I knew my time was running out, how much longer I had I didn't know, and he wouldn't tell me. I knew he could smell it on me as it approached, and he had a better sense of when that would be, than I did. Due to it both of us were careful to not let our true emotions show.

Deep down though I knew he did feel a sort of love for me, one that I shared. We both respected each other, and our position in The Keep. Maybe one day we would be able to safely pursue what we felt for one another, and the situation we had created with Callina. But for now that was not possible. However, I had grown fond of Alkin, he had become more than a mentor to me, he had become my family.

Even now as Alkin helped me strap the sides of the new chestplate, and I couldn't help but smile fondly. My Uncle had given this to me, not only because of my position in the Elite, but also because I was his niece. Yet unintentionally, he had already given me an even greater gift, my friendship with Alkin.

In a way, I was half tempted to lean down and kiss his head, instead however, I resisted the urge and waited patiently. Only Alkin had the privilege to see me for me. Everyone else saw a hardened warrior, uncaring, and unwavering.

His fingers tickled my sides briefly as he fastened up the last clasp. Meeting my gaze, I stepped away from him. Twisting a little, and leaning down, I could tell the armor allowed me to move and flex. I was sure in battle maneuverability would be easier than with full plate armor, that the men wore. Pausing I lightly touched the armor, my fingertips glowed blue and tingled slightly. There was magic weaved into the metal, I was impressed with the piece. It felt like it was imbued with a powerful force, that strengthened its wearer, something I was eager to try.

Suddenly a chime echoed in the room. It was a call from one of the Elite, in this case, my sister and our team.

"Time to go." I said while I grabbed my sword. Alkin followed as we entered the main hall, and walked towards the stables.

Our horses were creatures of darkness, they were Death Steeds and their appearance was quite gruesome. They had open sores with bits of rotted flesh across their body. Often their black coats were covered in a gleaming bloody sweat. Some were more gruesome than others. Unlike the other Death Steeds, my horse appeared to be an ordinary black horse at first glance. It had a sheen coat, and blood-red eyes. However, it sweated blood.

The Northern Hills ~ Raihanna

The icy wind blew across us as we climbed, and scaled the Northern Pass. It was a place few journeyed, and fewer survived. The steeds' split hooves and ability to never go lame allowed them to endure the grueling conditions. They easily maneuvered over rocky crags, like sure footed mountain goats. Necromantic spells protected us as we climbed. We felt no cold, nor the stinging pain from the harsh winds or bitter temperatures. Finally, we reached the outcrop Hunter had spoken of, and dismounted, tying the horses to a single pine.

"I'm going on ahead to survey." Ash said as he and Thierry disappeared around the rocky slope north of us.

"Just hurry up." Aurielle said, "We have to report back tonight and I don't want to be stuck here longer than needed." All the while she was kicking the snow around her feet.

Alkin laughed slightly and shook his head.

"I guess it's the best place since it's so far from civilization, but it's barren and opaque, and this whole trek has been annoying." No sooner than I spoke the words, a presence was felt behind us.

Someone was charging a spell. Its statically charged energy was aimed at us. Unknowing if this enemy was living or dead, I began to conjure a counter spell, a phantom fire Dragon. The effects of it would engulf them in a large torrent of flames, incinerating them on contact.

Suddenly a bright arch of light lashed out towards us. Alkin grabbed for mine and Aurielle's wrists, quickly porting us away from our current spot. This was a skill we had practiced many times before. Atop a nearby rock, out of visibility, we scanned the snow for our attackers and spotted them a few feet away from the rock we perched on.

Glancing at my hand, and extending my arm, I watched the flames leap out as I released the spell's deadly force. It took the shape of a Dragon creature and spiraled in the air towards the attacker. Fiery claws and teeth formed as it made its way towards them. Aurielle readied her long, ebony, silver-handled bow. The Dragon slashed at the attackers. Narrowly it missed the three figures that stood in the snow near the mountains edge.

I was annoyed. Immediately I adorned my hood that would stay in place by magic and keep me hidden in its shadows. Jumping from the rock I landed yards away from the figures. Calling upon my magic I summoned my darkened blade and smiled at my victims.

They appeared to be soldiers, of which breed I could not be sure of at this time. The first was easy to dispose of. I caught him off guard as he ran towards me haphazardly. My blade caught the man across the back as I stepped sideways dodging his blades downward sweep. As soon as my blade exited his back I quickly brought it upwards, back across, severing his head in the process. Blood sprayed the pure white snow, and alerted the other two remaining men of the threat they now faced. I saw them take a defensive stance as I jumped out of reach, and landed a few feet away. The snow around me melted to the ground, from the touch of my magic.

A few feet away I saw the two remaining soldiers, back to back with each other. The larger of the two had a magic shield up, that was repelling the arrows Aurielle shot at them. "Stop your useless onslaught of arrows, it isn't doing anything. I will handle them stay out of this!" I mentally yelled to my sister.

Aurielle's arrows ceased, and both men looked around bewildered. The larger one turned and met my gaze; agitation filled his eyes. Even under the hood he seemed to know what I was. As the wind picked back up I was able to smell what they were, *Werewolves,* I said mentally to my sister and Alkin. Their foul scent was easy to distinguish from other races. They held the musty smell of fecal-ridden dirt.

I smiled as I approached, targeting the smaller guard. I would remove him first. It was intriguing to see someone who knew us, even though this was becoming more frequent. It was always fun to "play" with them, and keep them alive till last.

Walking, blade in hand, I allowed it to dig into the snow, and created a perfect bloody line. The man, who recognized me as an Elite, boldly charges forward in an all or nothing attack. It was anticipated. Quickly I jumped over him to attack the smaller man, who remained unprepared.

The hilt of my blade caught him square in the back bringing him to his knees, he groaned as he fell forward. Still smiling, I walked around towards his front. While the larger man suddenly stopped and turned around, he realized too late what was happening.

As he ran at me once more, I brought my blade down on the smaller soldier. He screamed in pain as my black blade severed his shoulder bone and torso nearly in half. My blade was sharper than any metal forged. It was constructed of pure magic, and did not need a forge to strengthen it. I stepped sideways as the man fell, an empty look filling his eyes. His spirit left swiftly and entered Death's Realm.

The larger man turned and charged me furiously. My pulse quickened with the excitement, and I couldn't stop myself from grinning. Wolves were easy to read when they were angered.

With a harsh clatter of blades, I blocked his incoming attack. Our swords rang out and echoed off the snow-covered peaks. Again he swung at me, this time low. Smirking I jumped over his sword and slashed at his head. He ducked, and I missed him by a hair's length. In the midst of our duel, I notice an emblem insignia on his breastplate. This wolf wasn't just a nobody, but part of the royal guard. He was quicker, faster, and more skilled, than the other two I had already disposed of. It seems I'd slightly underestimated this one. This was a seasoned warrior, not like the other two whelps.

Swinging in one swift movement, his blade changes directions in a sweeping blow directed at my midsection. Quickly jumping back I narrowly get out of way as the blade whistles past, missing my armor by mere centimeters.

Now it was my turn. No sooner had my feet touched the ground than I lunged towards him once more. Aiming my sword towards his knees, I hoped to disable him and bring him down swiftly. He parries my attack, and instead I land a blow along his greaves. My sword struck the metal armor with such a force I could only imagine that it vibrated his kneecaps. Thankfully I kept going, and easily slid off the greaves, striking the soft tissue underneath. Blood sprayed the white snow covering it in a red splatter.

In swift retaliation, the guard swung his blade once more. This time he did not miss, I was moving forward too fast to change directions. In one fluid motion, his blade swept across my chestplate, slightly knocking me back. The magic imbued in the armor crackled, and sparked as the blade made its way across my front. Contact with his blade caused sparks to fly off my armor as a blue lightning rippled across its surface. His wild eyes met mine in shock as he backed away as if unsure how to proceed.

Momentarily I stood my ground, both of us were a bit taken aback. Never in my life had I heard of armor that did such a thing. Glancing down I noticed a slight scratch across its surface. I cursed under my breath. The fact that he managed to get close enough to graze my breastplate, infuriated me. I wanted to end him now.

However, before I could respond a familiar presence soothed its way into my mind, calming my thoughts and making itself known. "Not this one." Alkin said mentally to me as he suddenly blocked my path. I was so distracted I hadn't even noticed the newly created portal that he was appearing out of.

The hot rush of adrenaline and anger that built up from the battle was aching to be released. A fool had managed to slide past my defenses, and I wanted to remind him that he was nothing more than a lowly dog, who manage to get a single solitary cheap shot. Enmity radiated down to my fingertips causing the sword in my hand to quiver. For a moment, Alkin's interruption stirred a new found feeling of resentment in me.

Regardless, I stopped my attack, letting the man back away slowly and looking extremely perplexed. He shook his head, seemingly trying to regain his composure. Slowly his hand went to an amulet that hung around his neck, he raised it up, almost into the air. I felt the subtle shift of magic indicate he was calling someone. In that moment, Aurielle joined us, prepared for another attack.

The three of us stood our ground as he stood his. A few feet behind him, smoke began swirling out of a center point, creating a large blackened mass. Suddenly another man appeared, out of the newly opened portal. The man did not attack; instead he quickly grabbed the guard, and re-entered the blackened mass. As they disappeared within its folds, in turn did the smoke, leaving nothing behind.

Furiously, I threw off my hood. My anger coursed through me as a staticy inferno. Gathering energy in my fist, I threw it towards the rocky cliffs. The whole mountain seemed to groan from the blow.

"Why did you stop me?" I yelled at Alkin. "You will pay for this intolerance." I continued in my rage.

"Oh, will I?" He questioned, raising his eyebrows and nearly putting his nose to mine. "That man was none other than Saibal, Captain to Lord Drake and his Werewolves." Alkin stated and backed off just as Ash, and Thierry returned. "Hunter wants him alive, girl!" He snarled, trying to put me back in my place.

Ash and Thierry seemed aware of what had happened. I expected Alkin, or Aurielle had called them back, and told them of the events mentally. Still angry, I stormed off in the direction of the horses.

Strange Events ~ Saibal

Garion brought me back to the castle by teleportation. When I arrived I was met by Lord Drake, and Briar. Immediately careful hands lowered me onto the ground.

"Saibal, your leg. What happened?" Drake questioned as I heard Briar tell a maid to fetch Luca, the Castle's doctor.

"I went to the Northern Hills to help train two of the new recruits in the colder weather. While I was there, I ran into a group of Elite." Momentarily I cringed in pain and took a deep breath. "One took great note of us and attacked. It killed my men, and then came after me. But that Demon stopped the battle. So I took advantage of it, and had Garion fetch me."

"What? We haven't seen the Elite in years, why are they returning all of a sudden?" Drake spoke softly, his tone still forceful.

"But that's not all." I said while closing my eyes momentarily to the pain. "When I actually landed a hit on the armor, my blade reacted to it, just as our blades react when it comes into contact with Mythril Armor." It was all I could manage to say. A gray haze filled my eyes, before slowly turning my world black.

Drake

Just as quickly as Saibal lost consciousness, an even more unsettling gut feeling began to creep into existence. Our race was the only known race in Alecien to possess such armor and weapons. Only among the wolf clan was it such an advanced art, and a well-kept recipe.

"Drake," Briar said, breaking my train of thought. Luca and her assistant Leece entered the room.

With the help of two guards, Saibal was moved to the infirmary, leaving Briar, and I to ourselves.

"Briar, we must talk, let's find Droggen," I said while standing and walking towards the hall door.

Briar followed closely as we walked down the red carpet. Approaching the throne room, we found Droggen already making his way there. He paused when he saw us.

"There you two are, we have important business to attend to..." He started to say, but I held up my hand, interrupting him.

"It can wait, follow me." I said walking towards the small den just south of my quarters.

As we entered the room, Droggen asked. "What is the meaning of all this?" while looking at Briar and I.

Before speaking, I ensured the door was completely closed. "We must call Drameon, now. Saibal returned today without the troops he was training. They were attacked by the Elite." I stated. Droggen gave a worried look. Not waiting for a response, I used the blue stone amulet that hung around my neck to send a call out to Drameon.

He had given me several of these over six years ago after the fall of the last portal and Raillyn's disappearance. I had a gemcrafter from the local Den place them into various Mythril necklaces. The amulets had been the easiest way to contact Drameon.

We didn't have to wait long. A grey billowy fog crept from what appeared to be a center point. It flowed out in a circular clouded mass. As the grey smoke dissipated, Drameon stepped out revealing his long silver hair, shining with hints of red in the light. His ever-changing eyes met mine.

Wasting no time we went over the events that had transpired with Saibal, and what he had told me about the armor.

"Drameon, explain to me how this is possible. My people are the only ones able to smelt Mythril on Alecien. Where did they get the armor?" I questioned him flatly. The possibility that the Vampires had found more allies, as strong, or possibly stronger than ourselves was troubling.

"The material is not usually used with other races here. However, there are other races in the world that can melt it down, but they are long gone from Alecien. It's a possibility that the Elite are recruiting members from across the Silver Sea." Drameon said while pacing deep in thought.

"In addition Saibal mentioned that a Demon was there. I suspect it was Alkin since he's the only Demon I know who works with the Elite."

Drameon paused as he listened to my words, a look of concern crossed his face. "Perhaps you are right, I don't know of any other Demon who works with them. This is troubling news to hear, with the council meeting just hours away." Drameon paused as if pondering his next move. "Perhaps I may accompany you to this meeting?" He asked, meeting my eyes.

A look of surprise crossed my face, Drameon could not interfere with the happenings going on. He was a Demigod, and was not allowed to interfere in the events of our world. However, I felt that maybe he could at least sense the situation.

"Perhaps it wouldn't be a bad idea." While we lacked evidence to prove anything, we were pretty sure it was Hunter leading the Elite.

So it was agreed, Drameon would join us at the next council meeting. If past events were suddenly reopening, then having allies with us would be better than going at it alone. Leaving the small den, we made our way towards the southeast corner of the castle, where we would make a quick stop to the infirmary.

"How is he, Luca?" I asked while Drameon, Briar, and I entered the infirmary.

Luca shook her head, "He will live, it seems that he was more affected by the blade's magic than anything else. He'll remain unconscious for a day or so, but he should be better within the week." Luca said in a chipper tone as she mixed more herbs.

Drameon stepped forward and laid a hand a few inches away from the wound. "May I try and trace the magic?" He asked while his hand began glowing green in color.

Over the last few years, I had learned that Drameon often didn't wait for permission. While he asked out of common courtesy, he was a typical Demigod and often took things into his own hands. I noticed this often made it difficult to not fully interfere.

After Raillyn's disappearance Drameon decided it was best that we knew more about who he was. He explained that Raillyn had known in part that he was more than a typical Mystic, and she was right. Even though Mystics and Demigods were so similar they had one difference. Their lineage. Drameon's mother was Destiny, one of the Goddess' that created our world, his father was another Demigod born from a different God, making Drameon extremely powerful and not a true Mystic. This is how my people understood it.

I nodded my head, knowing if anyone could trace the magic he could. As a green light pulsed over Saibal's wound, I was hoping that tonight's meeting would reveal even more to this new mystery.

As the light faded Drameon sighed. "I am not sure if I will be able to trace this or not. It is quite powerful and dark. For now let us go to the council." He said while turning towards the door. Briar and I followed as we went to meet the council.

Council ~ Drake

Walking the familiar halls of the council, I couldn't help but think that it had been years since we had attended an actual meeting. In fact, the last time had been just after Raillyn's disappearance. Many events had occurred since then, and walking the halls once more brought about those memories.

After the portal was destroyed and I brought Alihandra and her people to my castle, we awaited Raillyn's return, but she never came. Eventually, Garion went to seek Delron who relayed the events that happened. Raillyn and Deestan had been taken by Hunter and the Demon. I was furious, and would have stormed The Keep if Briar and Garion had not stopped me. With all the chaos occurring, Leece and Luca had pulled out their potions, and herbs to sedate those who needed it. I was one of them.

When I had awoken, I was calmer. Even then, I had a gut feeling Hunter was leading the Elite, and I wanted revenge. But, Drameon was there after I awoke. Since we had no direct evidence we could not hold Hunter accountable. Bringing it up at the council meeting only caused more issues rather than help.

Hunter lied. I could see it in his face. He deceptively portrayed to the council alarm and concern, causing everyone to believe he was sincere and only wanted what was best. I was seething in my seat, with my hands gripping the rail in front of me. My anger rose to the point that I felt like jumping down to confront him. He stood with two of his cloaked elders reassuring everyone that he would assist us. Everything he said was all lies.

Prior, Drameon had stepped in and cautiously warned me not to do anything rash. If Hunter did have Raillyn alive, lashing out at him might spell her death. Left between a rock and a stone wall, I couldn't do anything other than play his game. At least, for the time being.

It was not just my people who suffered; the Shapeshifters were also grieving. After the death of Lord Breckon, and loss of the Shifter Princess Leeda, Alihandra pleaded with the Goddess to have their kingdom removed from Alecien just as we had done so many years ago.

They feared their kingdom would not be able to rebuild after the death of their king and removal of their heir. Shortly after they left Alihandra had discovered she was with child. Months later a healthy baby boy was born and appointed heir of the Shifters. Since Shifters didn't allow queens to rule alone, a new ruler was put into place until the boy grew into adulthood. It was Drameon who had suggested one of his Shifter friends. So Darris was placed in charge, and kept an eye on the situation, ensuring no harm befell them.

Drameon stated that this situation was becoming very similar to the one before the war and even though he did not impart any details he said to be careful. The Vampires were gaining numbers fast, and in turn Alecien was not as safe as it had been prior to the portal.

Many people had become prey to the Vampires. No longer were they as concerned about keeping the peace, and remaining civil. Once the Vampires were courteous and would ask to take blood for nourishment, often only taking a little. Now, however, this was becoming less and less; the Vampires took what they wanted when they wanted and did not care of the consequence. Chaimh and Drameon often spoke about the monstrosities in The Keep.

This was the first clue that things were going very amiss. It became the new norm after Raillyn's abduction. I often wondered if Raillyn herself had fallen victim to this endeavor, but Drameon doubted it.

Drameon said Hunter's history goes back almost a hundred years… When he turned forty he allowed a Vampire to turn him, by removing his mortal blood and replacing it with the tainted Vampire's. Lillian had said that even growing up as kids Hunter was different, but he never scared her. He was just dark in nature, and when he turned she didn't think any-thing of it. Later however, after they acquired Raillyn, his be-havior became erratic. He often threatened the girls about a beating if they disrespected him. Lillian had said he was all bark and no bite, but Chaimh believed otherwise.

It was Raillyn who proved her father true. Drameon said she was young, and that Chaimh relayed the events to him when they met in the library years later. Raillyn was given a task outside in the woods. She meditated, trying to calm her magic and mind, to focus it better. However, Hunter found her, and his eyes were wild with hunger.

Slowly he made his way towards her, but she ran for the house. Against a full grown man, let alone a Vampire, her tiny seven-year-old body could not outrun him. He grabbed at her and sunk his teeth deep into her neck. As the blood drained from her body, Chaimh could only assume what happened from what Raillyn had told him. Her magic took full control of her in an effort to save her life. A brute force of power con-sumed Hunter in a blue electric bolt.

He dropped her, and she ran charged with her natural Mystic magic towards the house. Her agility and speed matched Hunter's. As she raced into Chaimh's arms, Hunter suddenly stopped dead in his tracks. Lillian was exiting the house and Chaimh drew upon his Necromantic magic to de-fend his daughter. He left without a word, and from that day forth Hunter was not trusted nor welcome in their house again. Lillian even stopped being able to trust her own brother and often felt fear from him at every council meeting. Her anxiety was bad enough to cause her to stop attending them all together.

Today's meeting, however, was unavoidable, it was an important one. With all the issues the Elite had caused, many other races in Alecien wanted to withdraw from the council and leave Alecien, as so many had done before the war. To-day would define the course of action on whether or not the council would continue meeting, or allow each race to run on its own accord. And personally I believed that should not be the case. At least with the meetings other races had a vague knowledge of what was going on around them. Even the Shifters would attend today.

Upon entering the council room, we took our seats in the regular area. The candelabras illuminated the room while the sun beamed through the windows. Looking towards my right I noticed that Alihandra and Darris were already seated not far from us, in the Shifters normal spot. Darris looked at Drameon questioningly, before smiling and nodding. He had sat next to Briar and I and waited, knowing his appearance might stir unease from all around who knew who he was.

Shortly, Hunter entered the council room accompanied by the rest of his elders and a few remaining Vampires, who sat on the lower levels. The Vampires I vaguely recognized, but Alihandra seemed ready to jump out of her seat at the sight of them. Drameon also took note.

While they took their seat, Hunter stood in the center of the room, ready to begin. Hunter's greasy brown hair was slicked back in a distasteful manner as he began to speak, the council door opened once more. Another Vampire entered the room, their face was turned down, but obviously it was a female. Auburn curls hung around a small frame. Momentarily she turned, bowing to Hunter before quickly taking her seat. Then she began looking around the council room. Her appearance was haunting. She resembled Raillyn, but she was distinctly not Raillyn. I glanced at Drameon who equally seemed shocked by the sight of her.

"Do not be deceived. Necromancy rolls off this one. She's not Raillyn." Drameon said mentally to Briar and I.

Hunter smiled briefly at her as she sat in Raillyn's old spot before he began the meeting.

"Ladies and gentlemen I am pleased to see that you have all made it. We have had many eventful happenings since our last gathering. And I must say it has been a very rocky and disturbing time for all of us." Hunter started off. "Looking around I see we have a few new faces, Darris it's wonderful that you were able to step in and assist the Shifters during this time. It's such a depressing matter when a kingdom loses not only its King but its heir as well." Hunter continued as his eyes drifted around the room and stopped at Drameon. "And what brings you here in attendance to our little meeting, Demigod?" He spoke with slight distaste in his tone.

"I was unaware I was unwelcome in such a place, seeing as I have free reign to come and go as I please as long as I don't toil in your events. I find them most interesting, to say the least. How you lesser beings move around, and make decisions the way you do." Drameon said countering Hunters remark with detest.

"Ah yes you're right, you can come and go as long as you do not interfere. As I hope that is the case here. Sit, and listen to our meeting, if you must." Hunter said while he turned back, and began going over the events which had occurred.

The menial topics he had brought up did not surprise me. We had a slew of crops that were planted, and there were lesser races that had moved onto other lands. Territories would be expanding depending on who withdrew today, between those who choose to stay.

Each race was allowed to speak their thoughts on whether or not council meetings should proceed to join or if each race should be left to their own accord. Most races opted for staying together, and those that choose to leave would be allowed to do so with no consequence. Only a few half-breeds, Elves, Fae, and Humans remained in Alecien, while the more widespread races tended to be the Vampires and Werewolves, since the Shapeshifters had temporarily left the world. The remaining races, the older ones, had left long ago, and we had lost track of many of them. Only hearing about a rare visitor, or rumors now and again.

Our race had nothing new to say, we would not speak up about Hunter or the Elite again without proof. The Shapeshifters agreed and would not speak up either. Both Darris and I nodded in agreement to stay, when we were asked if our race would stay or go.

When the Vampires-appointed speakers took the stage, I noticed that Alihandra was displeased. Aurielle and Ash took center stage. "We stand for the Vampire race, and we believe that it is best to continue meeting with anyone who wishes to meet." Aurielle spoke. "More so…"

"More so you are a liar and a cheat dear sister!" Alihandra spoke. "Where the hell have you been and why the hell are you helping Hunter?" She asked as a hush fell over the crowd. Darris quickly grabbed her arm and tried to pull her back into her seat. Alihandra tried to bat him off, to no avail.

"Hush," he said while pulling her down. "I know you have conflicts with your sister but this is neither the place nor the time for this behavior." Darris said hushed.

Drameon disagreed, he had known Chaimh's family for too long, and he knew the situation which Alihandra spoke of. He stood up, interrupting Alihandra before more could be said. "I must agree with the Shifter Queen in this case. Aurielle you did betray your own family in order to join the ranks of the Vampires, when you could have easily just said what you wanted, and done so without betrayal." Drameon said while smiling.

"I said…" Hunter started to say. But Aurielle held up a hand for him to still his tongue.

"No, he's right. I need this to get out, and to be properly dealt with. You see people, my father and mother didn't approve of my decision on this matter. They wanted me to go and train to become a priestess. I however did not want to. I wished to join my Uncle whom I love dearly. Since I was denied it when I spoke up about it, I decided to stage an event where it would be perceived as if I had died. This allowed me to have free access into my Uncle's world. So that is what I did." Aurielle spoke softly, matter of fact, Drameon nodded his head, and I supposed she spoke truth on this matter.

"So, getting back to agreeing that the council should continue to meet…" A new voice said and took center stage. "Peace needs to remain in place for the remaining races that wish to help uphold it." The lady with auburn hair said.

"Raihanna, yes you're right." Aurielle stated, she backed up and allowed her to continue wrapping up the Vampires end of the agreement and the end of the meeting itself.

As Raihanna spoke, I could tell that Drameon had spoken true. Even though she seemed so similar to Raillyn, she spoke very differently, and seemed to be a much darker person. The very essence that flowed off her was perplexing and unfamiliar. Her power seemed to flow freely while at the same time seemed restricted somehow as if she was holding it at bay. I wondered if she might be one of Hunter's Elite soldiers.

After the meeting, we went to speak with Alihandra who was still carrying on about Aurielle, but in a quieter tone. "Drameon, I did not expect you to be attending the council." Darris said as he accompanied Alihandra towards the Wolves' seats and the stairs.

"I did not expect to attend myself, but after the events recently I was unsure of what else to do in making sure things would go smoothly." Drameon said while whispering a silent spell, and placing two fingers upon Darris' forehead.

Darris seemed unsurprised by it, and gave Drameon a worried look, understanding crossing his face. I assumed Drameon had magically relayed the events that had occurred with Saibal and the Elite.

"This is troubling news, but let us not speak further of it here." Darris said as we descended the stairs to the main level.

We saw Hunter, and his Vampire group standing around talking with many of the other leaders. "Lord Drake, Briar." Hunter spoke as we walked towards the door trying to leave. Drameon remained with us, but Darris and Alihandra took their leave while they could.

"I'm pleased to see you decided to attend and stay with us in the council." Hunter said making small talk. Aurielle smiled behind him and slightly bowed her head.

"Well someone has to keep an eye on everything, ensuring the peace is kept intact." I said while returning a smile.

Raihanna stood a few feet away talking with Ash, and another Vampire, she glanced at me momentarily. Her ever-changing eyes met mine, and I knew at that moment she was a Mystic. Shaking her head she came over towards Hunter. "Hunter, I take my leave, I have other business to attend to." She said, while walking swiftly behind him towards the door.

"Wait, child." Hunter said grabbing her elbow before she got too far. "You need to broaden your knowledge of the races who are in peace with us. Please let me introduce you to these fine people. This is Lord Drake, Briar, and Drameon." Hunter said while pointing to each of us.

Raihanna didn't hide her displeasure about the situation and gave Hunter a bedeviled look. "Fine," she said while smiling. "Raihanna." She said tartly while reaching out to shake each of our hands.

The magic that emanated from her was just as I expected, it felt like any Necromancer's magic, but it held the subtle tune of something else. As soon as she was done shaking hands she left, shaking her head in disapproval as she did so. We immediately excused ourselves from Hunter's company and bid him farewell. Turning his back on us, he picked up where he left off with the small group of council members he'd been talking with. Relieved, we left through the same door Raihanna had, moments ago. However, as we closed the door, and began walking down the hall, I was perplexed. Raihanna was nowhere in sight.

Suddenly Drameon laughed slightly. "Whatever you are thinking, I would not try anything with me, child." He said while turning around, facing Raihanna, who stood to the left of the door we had just exited.

Raihanna smiled, she appeared to have a different agenda, and instead charged Drameon. We stood behind waiting for his queue in this new event, unsure on how to proceed. We had not fought with Drameon let alone catch a glimpse of how he fought.

As Raihanna moved with breakneck speed, she began charging an energy ball. I wondered if she knew Drameon was a Demigod, or if she even cared.

Drameon moved with equal speed and as soon as he met her, he dissipated the spell she was casting. Raihanna, realizing her folly, immediately leapt backwards towards the ceiling above. Her feet lightly touched the corner as she glided over him and off the adjacent wall, this time with a blade in hand.

I heard Drameon sigh, and pull his own blade out as he shouted at us to back up. Drameon moved faster than I had seen anyone move before. Raihanna followed his movement easily and turned the direction of her sword to counter his new position. As she brought her own blade down towards Drameon's face, he quickly, and masterfully parried her attack.

His motions were as fluid and awestruck as the Elves of old. His sword swung around Raihanna's, then flicked it away as if it was nothing. Raihanna looked startled as Drameon brought his knee up, meeting her square in the stomach. I heard the breath leaving her lungs as she became a crumpled heap upon the floor. He rolled her onto her back, pinning her down, sword against her neck.

Raihanna laid there taking deep, steadying breaths. "What are you?" She said out loud.

"I could ask you the same thing, child." Drameon replied, just as the door to the council room opened once more.

Neither budged as Hunter walked into the hall. "Raihanna Whitervan!" He yelled. "Do not ruin any of our peace talks with your incessant power tests." Hunter said in a more subtle tone. "Drameon is a Demigod, he could destroy you in less than a heartbeat, and here you are provoking him."

Raihanna laid there, anger welling up in her eyes. "Fine." She finally said as Drameon removed his sword from her throat. Reaching down he grabbed Raihanna's arm, pulling her up. She pulled back furious, and I felt her power spike momentarily.

"Leave now!" Hunter yelled at her, halting her power charge.

With her eyes now red, Raihanna bowed, apologized half-heartedly for the incident, and left down the hallway. Hunter stood silently for a moment ensuring she obeyed then put on a humble face. "I am so sorry for the trouble, I will personally see to her punishment in The Keep. This will not happen again." He said angered but sincere while bowing at Drameon.

Drameon looked at Hunter, equally angered. "See to it that it doesn't. You know as well as I do that next time you will be out a minion." He gave Hunter a warning look before turning, and mentally telling us to move on.

Briar and I had not moved from our spot, Drameon's power had a resounding effect; its essence rang throughout the hall. The space in the small hallway still seem charged with conflict, and excitable energy. Words could not penetrate it. So we walked in silence till we managed to reach a different atmosphere, back in our own territory.

"What was that about?" I asked with an authoritative tone, directed at Drameon.

"That is someone you do not want to meet alone on the battlefield. If Hunter is behind everything that has been happening lately, then there is no doubt in my mind that she is one of the Elite. She's strong, stronger than she is letting on. She is probably one of his top warriors." Drameon said while he started to pace the floor.

I interrupted him. "I know she's not a Vampire, she's a Mystic, her eyes constantly changed colors with her mood, just like yours do." I said while he pausing momentarily to listen.

"No, she is not truly Vampire, she is Mystic. Her magic however, seems different..." Drameon pondered out loud as he began pacing once more. "Regardless, never try and face that one alone, or in your case together." Drameon said while looking at Briar and I. "I must go, I have been here too long, and I fear if I stay much longer I will toil where I should not." Drameon said and quickly bid us farewell, before creating a portal, leaving to other matters.

We however, were left to ponder, and debate about this girl being an Elite, or what part she played in Hunters plan.

Interval ~ Raihanna

After my attacking Drameon last night, Hunter refused to speak to me or include me in the new location of the portal. Since we had run into Lord Drake's people in the Northern Hills, we needed a new location. I was furious at my Uncle for keeping this information from me. I was one of his top soldiers, and never was I left out of anything.

Unfortunately, Hunter had made up his mind, and I was stuck at home. So I decided to spend some time with Deestan, and Callina who had completed their studies on Alecien. "Mommy what kind of new books will I get this time?" Deestan asked eager for something new to read.

Since I had encountered the Werewolves on the Northern Peak, and attended the council meeting, I decided Deestan would benefit from learning about their race, along with the Mystic race. I gave her almost twenty books this time. Some from the library in The Keep, and some were received from various vendors in our village that I had collected over the last week of my excursion.

Deestan was rather shocked at the amount of reading I had planned for her. "Are all those for her to read me?" Callina asked with an eager look on her face.

I nodded, and smiled in return, "Yes, baby, these are all yours. I haven't really read them all, but I believe since we are working closely with these people, you two would benefit from learning about them." I said as a tapping was heard from my main chamber door.

Almost immediately the girls started pouring over the books trying to decide which to read first. As I opened the door, Alkin stood holding even more books. "You had asked me to keep my eyes open for more books. I think the girls would benefit from these. I too kept the Wolves, and Mystic races in mind." Alkin said as he smiled, and placed another ten or so books in my hands. Some ranged from fairy tales from both races to more complicated spell books.

While looking them over, I gave him an odd look. "I thought at least if they studied some of the spell structures they could identify them, if and when they ran into these spells," Alkin said matter of fact.

I nodded in agreement, knowing it was probably a good idea.

"Plus, we can't have the girls only learning all the time. They have to read something fun once in awhile, hence the fairy tales." Alkin said as Deestan and Callina began acting out several fairy tales they had already heard from Alkin and I.

I couldn't help but smile, and shake my head in response. Even though Callina was young she was smart, and often picked up what her sister read her. In many ways, it frightened me to know my Mystic daughter was growing up and catching onto the world so much faster than her sister. Alkin assured me that it was normal, and all part of being a pure Mystic. We had tried to encourage play, but she often withdrew to books with her sister in tow.

"Also, before I forget, Hunter wants to see you." Alkin stated as he caught Deestan who jumped from a nearby chair. Callina raced around me pretending to zap her sister with energy balls. She wiggled and squirmed in Alkin's arms playing with her sister that he had to put her down. He rolled his eyes and smiled at their came. But, as soon as the girls heard Hunter's name they quieted down and returned to the books.

Deestan eagerly began looking over the fairy tales, stating that she would start on the spell books later that night. I laughed slightly and told them to behave while I was away, as well as to mind their maid. Then I turned to leave with Alkin.

As Alkin and I walked the halls in silence, I wondered if I would be allowed to work with my team once more. This included getting the portal up and ready before anymore events occurred that could stop us. Mentally reaching towards

Alkin's emotions gave no indication to the events occurring, he was mentally quiet.

Upon reaching Hunter's den, Alkin opened the door and allowed me to enter first. "I have done as you asked." Alkin said while taking his seat, and awaiting his next order.

I composed myself while entering the room. Hunter's den was dark. The shades were black and pulled shut. A large table lay in the center of the room, just a few feet in front of me. It was adorned with maps, magic lights and various bottles of blood. Wooden chairs sat not only around the table but around the room, as well. Darkened skins and silk tapestries hung from the walls. This den was one of Hunter's spare rooms connected to not only the main hall but to his main chambers, as well.

Hunter turned to face me. He wore his red amulet around his neck and played with it as he spoke. His beady eyes met mine, and he frowned.

"I am still immensely upset about your outburst at the council meeting. But you can make it up to me by meeting your group in the Fellshores, to the east. The marshy lands provide a perfect place for the portal to be opened up. Everyone has created their totem except for the summoning one. That, I would like you and Alkin to create together; combining your magic will enhance its strength. This portal will not be used for warriors. It will be used to ultimately call Daes into Alecien. So do not mess this up." Hunter spoke sternly as he looked at Alkin and I.

"However, before you leave, I have a list of components I would like you to acquire to use in the creation of this totem." Hunter said while handing me a parchment of paper. Most of the items on the list we had: ash wood, moonstone, nightshade, crimson leaf, and blood; the typical ingredients used in creating a summoning totem. In addition, rune stones that would be carved into the wood before imbuing it with magic.

I looked at my Uncle questioningly. "We have all these items." I stated, hoping for more answers.

He smiled in response, "Yes we do, but I don't want the typical items for this totem. No, I want more unique items."

My Uncle began to say as he walked around the table towards us. "I have already instructed Alkin to carve the runes along its width, and while he does so, I am sending you out to gather potent blood. I don't care what type it is, but it has to be stronger than what we have in The Keep." Hunter said as he paced the room.

"Afterwards, I want Alkin and you to mix the blood with your own, and imbue the totem in Death's Realm completing it. I have already instructed Alkin with the details. So you only need to worry yourself with getting the blood. For now, anyway. I will have your horse readied if you need it, or you can teleport, I don't care, but you leave immediately." His deep red eyes pierced my own as he spoke.

I nodded in agreement. If my Uncle needed stronger blood, I would find it for him.

I smiled in response. I was pleased to hear I could return with the others. I had begun missing my duties for my kingdom and its people. This small act would help us proceed further with taking over Alecien.

After Hunter dismissed us, he returned back to his maps and writings on the table. I left glad to accompany my friends once more. We walked in silence knowing we were not to discuss anything Hunter had relayed to us, at least not until we could ensure no one was eavesdropping.

Upon returning to my quarters, I glanced at Alkin before saying anything. "So what kind of blood does he want me to get, and where does he expect me to find it?" I asked trying to run over the different races remaining in Alecien. I knew most of the more powerful races had left. Very few visited Kerin Port, or the northern towns.

Alkin shook his head. "I would just go north and travel around Issia, Balone, and Kerin Port, I'm sure you will find someone in hiding up there." He said as he approached me. "Wherever you go, stay safe, and call me if you need any help." The tone in his voice said enough, he was concerned and wanted me to stay out of trouble.

For a moment, he pulled me into an embrace, hugging me, before gently laying a kiss on the top of my head. Part of me wanted to pull back, but another part wanted to stay, and relish in the feeling. Releasing me, he made his way towards the stairs, and the lower den.

"I have to get to work on these runes. Hunter has chosen intricate ones, and they will probably take me weeks to finish. Just be safe and stay on this side of the Silver Sea." He sighed.

I just nodded in response. I knew what lay across the Silver Sea, I had been foolish to think years ago I could travel freely over there and survive. The Ancient races that lived in Aeralain despised and hated the Vampires who resided in Alecien. Even those who worked with them and traveled there never returned.

As I watched Alkin descend the stairs, I went to retrieve my armor and items that I might need for the trip. I planned to teleport just north of the Shapeshifters' old region, putting me in the small town of Kaila. From there, I could take the mountain pass to Balone, or travel the road east towards Kerin Port. I hoped it would be easy to find a powerful blood source.

Before leaving, I found the girls in bed, reading together as they often did. I knew with attending Elite business Deestan, and Callina often stayed in the same room together. I was glad they were able to be there for each other, and that Alkin would be home with them. As I kissed them both goodbye, I noticed they were reading a nasty brown-looking book with silver bindings on it. I disregarded it and left them to finish their reading.

Before leaving to meet the others, I instructed the maids to fill my tub, and infuse it with sandalwood oil. I wanted to appear harmless to the villagers of the north, and carrying Vampire scent on me so heavily would not help my cause. The sandalwood oil would wash that away.

The North ~ Raihanna

I had chosen to travel along the road from Kaila towards Kerin Port in hopes of finding a potential blood source. I still reeked of sandalwood as I stumbled through the uneven dirt streets in the harbor region. I had already checked the local bars, and the port was the last spot I was checking before leaving once more.

Most of the races I run into had been human, or half breeds, either part Fae or part Elf, nothing that would possess strong enough blood. I was beginning to become agitated. Already I had spent a week to get here to search, and for what; nothing. Now I needed to move on to Balone, and hope to find someone there, but I knew my chances were slim if not impossible. I might have to travel further north into the Aneross Peeks to find any hidden villages that might harbor Ancients.

So I left the harbor area. It reeked of fish and was too crowded with the lesser races. Their close presence made me feel gross and icky. Quickly I located a merchant who I heard was planning on traveling to Balone. I knew I had to move on. Thankfully, the merchant had agreed to let me ride with him for the cost of a few gold. Since I knew the area was dangerous, and I should not spill anyone's blood before I accomplished my task I decided to pay the outrageous amount, and travel with his group.

It was frigid as I climbed into the back of the open wagon. I knew winter was beginning to set in, and with that the snows would come. I was thankful that we wouldn't have many issues because the road was well traveled, and this close to the coast the snow was almost non-existent.

As we traveled further towards the mountains we had to trade out the wagon for a sled, and sleigh team. They would get us the rest of the way to Balone. Thankfully, the trip was quiet, and few questions were asked. I was able to keep quiet, and hide who I was or rather what I was.

Nearing Balone, we were greeted by a talkative guard. Before I knew it, he and the merchant were conversing in what seemed like harmless information. A mysterious house appeared in the middle of the night along a town road. It was said to be enchanted since it did not appear to be naturally built. Upon hearing this, I took note and listened.

The house was a tall, two-story stone structure that lay on the outskirts of the northern region of town. It was said that a magical sorcerer had conjured it up in the middle of the night for his dark rituals.

As I listened to the stories of this new occurrence I couldn't help but wonder if maybe this house belonged to one of the Ancients. That would be too good to be true, but since it was my only lead it was worth investigating. The search for powerful Ancient blood had become tedious. I didn't want to have to spend more time here than needed stumbling around town blindly.

The guardsman was an older man sitting on a tired-looking draft horse. His face, worn and creased, gazed at me questioningly. Heavy eyebrows hooded quizzical looking eyes. "I would not go near it, my child. If an evil mage does in fact, live there then it would be unwise to venture so close. Don't you know that young maidens are always the first to be used in the dark arts?"

I almost burst out laughing. The idea of me being sacrificed was so ridiculous, so absurd. However, it gave me an idea. Smiling innocently I nodded. "Understandable, sir. I am just worried and wish to avoid such a horrid place." I said as meekly as I could.

The older guard chuckled to himself, his eyes were sincere and warm. "Oh, I suppose that is reasonable. I can see that you are a smart girl. Now, let me think." His voice was gruff, but not stern. "If you head north from here, um.. Oh, there is a tavern called the Evan's Breath." He turned from me and pointed down a snow-covered street. It was almost dark—

the sky was overcast—but I saw where he was pointing. Even the small building seemed worn and tired, much like the guard. Smoke billowed out from a chimney set upon the snowy rooftop. "There is a little street behind the tavern. You'll find it sits there. That is the street to avoid, and by the looks of it, it's getting late." He said while peering at the sky.

Jumping off the slow-moving sleigh I thanked the man for the ride and the guard for the information. "Don't go looking for trouble now, you hear? Stay clear of that monster house." He shouted after me, but I was beyond caring. I just wanted to return home.

As I ran through the snowy streets, I forgot how icy its surface was, and slipped. The ground rushed at me as I fell face first towards its frigid surface. Suddenly a hand reached out and caught me. "Whoa, little honey bun, It's really icy today. Perhaps you should take it a little slower." A smooth male voice said as I brushed a few renegade snowflakes from my face. For a split second, the hair on my arm seemed to stand straight up.

The man who held me seemed Elf-like, his high cheek bones, and subtle features gave him an almost angelic look. While his body indicated he was very muscular, lean, and well fit. Shoulder-length black hair hung over his face, and into mine. He was so close his lips nearly touched my cheek. The scent of cedar wood, cherry blossoms, orchid, and sandalwood filled my nose. I stood stunned, almost spell like, as his piercing blue eyes gazed into mine.

The need to leave suddenly filled my mind. A gentle pull of magic was coming from this man, as if he was spelled. *He might be who I'm looking for.* However, if I stayed I might reveal myself.

As I stood upright and brushed the remaining snow off myself, I smiled at him. "Thank you for the help. I'm not used to all this snow. Where I come from it's much warmer than this."

The man nodded as he backed up and ran his eyes over me, "Just be careful. We don't want your pretty face to get messed up on the ground now, do we?" He laughed slightly, before leaning forwards. Kissing my cheek, I heard him breathe deeply, taking in my scent.

I stood stunned, in a sense he acted like many of the drunken Vampires in the streets around The Keep. Always calling girls pretty, trying to seduce them, or buy them drinks. I had never been in the situation, even though I had seen it many times before. I never thought I would have to worry about it.

"What's the matter, my little sweet cheeks, cat got your tongue? Don't worry, I'm not going to bite or anything. Have a nice night." He said casually as he walked off towards a nearby building.

For a split second, I stood and made sure he was inside before I proceeded. I disregarded the man and quietly walked down the dimly lit streets towards the mystery house. Meandering slowly, I took my time. I didn't want anyone thinking I was planning anything. Shortly I found it—the old guard was right. It was the only two storied stone structure on the block that was a house. Turning, I saw that the bar's small back entrance stood directly in front of it.

Quickly I scanned the streets to see if anyone was nearby. When I was sure no one would see, I carefully approached the door and laid a hand on its smooth surface.

Summoning my magic, I used it to scan for any power, and it found quite a bit. It tingled across my hand and down my arm. It felt familiar but strange at the same time, like something I was supposed to know, or had learned and forgot.

A surge seemed to radiate from the door and for a moment I felt a connection to it. The amount of energy that coursed through the house startled me. Never before had I felt such a strong magical source. Reaching out mentally to investigate further, the house itself suddenly lashed out at me and zapped my hand with a magical bolt. My mind exploded in a bright array of blue dots, dancing across my vision in various hues. Pulling away, I fell backwards onto the ground, narrowly missing a second bolt of lightning that seemed to have come from the overhang above. It struck the ground with such a force I was sure someone heard.

Looking around, however, told me no one was coming. The streets were still bare and everything was quiet. A few snowflakes began to fall quietly from the sky.

When I was sure the house was done, I investigated my hand. It was in working condition, no marks or anything, it just stung slightly. I would have to be more careful while looking for the owner. I was sure he was one of the Ancient races I sought.

The Magic User ~ Raihanna

I circled town too many times to count, and found nothing out about the person living in the two story stone house. I knew that whoever it was had come from Aeralain; the house was composed of old magic. Rounding the corner near the bar again, I was beginning to wonder if I was ever going to find them. No one reported anyone strange in town and, since Balone was large, it was not uncommon to have visitors coming and going.

I had taken a room in the bar just south of the house, insisting on a window that faced it. I waited and watched out of the old dirty glass. There wasn't even a single hint of a disturbance. Even going down and listening in on the main level of the bar revealed nothing. I was beginning to think that this might be a lost cause and that I was going to have to move on.

Going down, and taking a seat near the barkeep, I began to ask him the same old questions he had heard the last few days. "I know the answer is probably no. But you haven't seen anyone new, have you? Or heard anything about the house behind you?" I asked while the barkeep poured me a cup of mead.

His gruff red beard and full, stout features bent down and spoke quietly. "As I have told you, no. There is nothing new going on in town, and no one seems to know a thing about that house. If I were you I would stop asking. That house makes everyone nervous, and these folk don't care that you are poking your nose where it shouldn't be," he said, before turning and attending another customer.

I sipped the mead and frowned, it tasted like warm cat piss. The barkeep sighed and turned back towards me. "Why do you want to find this person anyway?" He asked in a gruff but casual voice.

I hadn't really thought of what I planned on saying on this subject. "He's just a friend." I said, wondering afterwards, why I said that.

The barkeep looked at me questioningly. "If he's your friend, then you're not from around here either, are you? It would explain your behavior." His tone became hushed.

I felt the hair on my arms rise momentarily. My hand instinctively went to my dagger at my waist. Slowly I leaned in further. "So what if I'm not from around here, I need to find my friend so I can get home." I said trying to feel out the situation.

The man stood upright again, and turned to clean a nearby cup. "I don't know what you are exactly, I have my suspicions, but truthfully I have never seen your kind before. However, I know a little about those magical houses. Those are the sort you hear about in Aeralain, aren't they?" He questioned me while placing the cup down beside him, and picking up another.

For a moment, I was unsure how to answer. Instead, I silently nodded my head. "I thought so," he said as he came closer again. "I don't remember the war much but I remember hearing talk about the Ancients fleeing to Aeralain. It was all because of the Vampires, they say."

I looked at him questioningly. I had heard about this but only in part—other races blamed our race. But I knew it was the Werewolves who started the war.

"Nah I'm sure you don't want to hear about it. I'm old, not too old to remember the beginning, but still. It was nearly over when I was born. My mum was one of the last slain, and she remembered the beginning." The man turned as if to walk away and clean further. I looked around for a split moment and realized that another barkeep had come in, and began taking care of the other customers.

Quickly I grabbed his wrist before he could get out of my reach. "No, tell me. What did your mum tell you about the war?" I asked suddenly interested in what this man knew.

The man looked at my hand on his wrist and sighed. Grabbing a nearby chair he took a seat near me. Resting his head on his hands, he began to tell me. "My mum said the war began because of a silver-haired Mystic. She said the Vampires slaughtered him because of his deception. You know Mystics aren't allowed to toil in worldly events? They can suggest things, but as far as going out and killing whom they please, they can't do that. If they did the natural course of things would change. In a sense, they are like Demigods. Well, this Mystic did; he did as he pleased, and died for it." I looked at the barkeep now thinking that maybe he was a little crazy.

"After this, the Vampires immediately blamed the Werewolves while the Shadow Walkers blamed the Vampires. This was at the time when they all lived together. To keep them quiet, the Vampires began to slaughter the Shadow Walkers, who they had made peace with. The other Ancient races came to their aid. This only created more of a mess. Slowly the other races began to fall victim to the Vampires. Drakar, Mystic, and even Demons were slaughtered for their blood. The Vampires even sent soldiers to the Werewolves. It was bloody, my mum said, the Ancient races tried to take on the Vampires, but there were too many, so they left. Even the more basic races Giants, Elves, Dwarves, Dryads, and Fae left; none of the full-blooded ones stayed. They let the Vampires and Werewolves fight each other because they had greater numbers. There was talk about having aid from Aeralain, but after the ships left with the Ancients, the remaining ones were set aflame. Alecien was on their own and the Ancients wanted no hand in our mess." He shifted uncomfortably for a moment while looking around as if others might be listening.

Breathing out deeply he went on. "It's all because of those wretched Vampires we all ended up in the mess we're in now. If it wasn't for them, we would still have our wits. We wouldn't have lost so much history, and magic to nonsense. Those Vampires are ruthless, and I don't blame the Ancients for leaving us half-breeds. Vampires really are an abomination to the land. They should have never been created."

I reached for my dagger, and began to draw it. I wasn't going to sit here, and listen to an ignorant old drunk say it was our fault the war begun. Or that our race was an abomination. Swiftly I began to pull it upwards, but before passing the bar top, a hand reached out. The hand quickly placed the dagger back into its sheath while another pulled me out of the chair. Looking up, I gazed up into the crystal blue eyes of the man who had kept me from falling.

"You know I have been looking everywhere for you? Come on, let's go have a seat, and catch up before moving on." He said as he placed a golden coin on the bar top.

Stunned, somewhere between confusion and relief, I allowed him to guide me to a secluded table.

"Sit, and we will talk." Swiftly he pulled a chair out. Taking a seat I watched the strange man.

He walked around the table and took the chair across from me. From within his cloak he pulled out a bottle and turned two cups on the table over. "So, tell me, what brings you to Alecien?" He began to question as he poured some dark-colored liquid in the cups, and handed one to me. "I'll tell you this, I am surprised at how primitive this land is compared to home. I mean everyone seems so surprised to see a house that's magically made. Not to mention I had to change my clothes when I got here." Pausing momentarily, he emptied his glass and waited for me to answer. "So what about you, Mystic?"

I looked at him questioningly. *How did he know what I was? And why was he acting as if I wasn't from here?* "It's your house behind this place? I knew it was crafted of magic, I just couldn't place who had created it. Your house sort of tried to zap me. Plus I could ask you the same thing. Why are you in Alecien?" I said in a calm voice, trying to match his wits as I took a sip of the liquid.

It tasted like wine, an exquisite blend of berries and herbs, but it was different. It slightly burned as it went down, causing me to cough a little. The man looked at me curiously, raising an eyebrow as if I was acting strange. Quickly I finished the rest of the wine as he did, and placed my cup back on the table.

For a moment, he looked around, "The name's Howl Wilder. I'm just visiting for a while. I need to forget some things, and have some fun. Do you like the Darah wine?" He asked as he placed his chin on his hands.

Unsure how to answer. I sat and pondered what I should say; before I thought of an answer, he carried on. "You're right, it's weak. I couldn't bring the stronger stuff over here without issues. But since you're here, give me your hand." He said as he placed the bottle in the center of the table, and held out his hand. I didn't think he would do anything to me in front of so many people, so I placed my hand in his.

Swiftly before I could react, he pulled it across the table and ran his dagger over my finger. A few drops of blood fell into the bottle. I pulled my hand back outraged. "Calm down, sweet cheeks. Haven't you done this to Darah wine before?" he asked, as he sliced his own finger, and let a few drops of blood fall into the wine bottle.

Suddenly the bottle gave off a soft blue hue and faded back into a darker color. Howl seemed surprised and happy by the bottle's reaction. He refilled our cups as I looked at him nervously. Howl took a sip of his and placed it back on the table. "Wow, that's better." He said with a surprised look.

Taking the cup carefully into my hands, I sniffed its contents. It smelled almost metallic. Slowly I took a sip, and the liquid felt cool and tasted almost like drinking magic itself, it seared as it went further. I coughed from the feeling, and Howl slightly laughed as he took another sip.

"So again, why is a Mystic like you in Alecien?" He questioned.

Raising an eyebrow to him I took another sip of wine. "Just collecting some spell components." I said casually.

Howl finished his cup of wine and poured himself another while he spoke. "Strange that you're here for spell components, couldn't you find them in Aeralain anywhere?"

Shaking my head, I finished my own wine, and Howl poured me more. Already my head felt fuzzy from the potency of the wine. Howl was an interesting creature and was indeed from across the Silver Sea. He even suspected I was from Aeralain, which I found funny. "I tried, but I didn't have much success as you said these people are more primitive. That makes it easier to find certain items." I replied to trying to sound normal.

Lips pressed together he nodded before he downed another cup of the wine. "So I also saw Vampires make you mad." He said casually. "I couldn't agree more. And plus he's right anyway. The war wouldn't have even begun if it wasn't for them and their heartless ways. Abominations don't even come close to what they are." Howl said as he drank down the wine, and poured more for the both of us.

The room began to spin around me slightly as I drank the cup of wine down. Suddenly all the talk about the Vampires being beyond an abomination, didn't bother me. I was more curious about these accusations.

"So why are they so hated anyway?" I asked hearing my speech slur slightly. The wine was much stronger than it appeared. "And how in the world is this stuff so strong?" I asked while laughing slightly, and inspecting the cup.

Laughing in reply, Howl explained. "The wine is Darah wine, blood-spell wine." He said casually. "The stronger the magic users who charges it, the more potent the wine is." Howl smirked as he took another drink. "And, girly, I know you are one strong Mystic. We don't see your lineage in Aeralain anymore, but I remember they are a force to be reckoned with." Howl stated slowly as if he was taking his time with each word.

The room carrouseled around once more. "Really I can't be that strong. And plus how did you know I was a Mystic anyway?" I asked slowly.

Howl leaned forward as if he was about to tell me something no one else should hear. As I leaned forward, he reached out and poked my nose. "Your eyes change color. I knew when I first saw you that you were Mystic. I followed you around town after that." He said as he leaned back and finished the cup of wine.

He poured himself more before filling my cup. That's when the bottle seemed to of run out. "I thought you said it never ran out?" I questioned suddenly less concerned about the conversation.

Laughing Howl stood up. "Charged Darah wine runs out. Not the regular stuff. It will refill itself, and be back to its normal dull wine in the morning." Howl said as he pulled me to my feet.

The very air seemed to crackle at his touch, and my balance seemed to fail, I felt myself fall into him slightly before I caught myself, and was able to stand upright.

"Whoa, my little honey bun." Howl said deviously as he caught me from falling once more. "Let's go back to my house, and I will show you something." He finished his cup and led me towards the door. Finishing my cup and placing the empty vessel on the table, I let him lead me towards the door.

Silently we slipped into the freezing weather. Snow blew around us but didn't seem to touch us. Howl led on as we rounded the building, approaching his home. Momentarily we paused on the step in front of the door, the snow silently fell, and I watched it melt inches away from our skin. I felt in awe of this strange new power, and the effects of the wine.

Muttering Howl spoke in a strange language, the words seemed magical by themselves. Afterwards, he opened the door and led me into his den. I felt myself stumble over the threshold, and I reached out to grab Howl for support. Howl and I both tumbled to the floor, laughing. Stumbling, and rolling I eventually found my feet. Reaching down I offered Howl a hand helping him up.

Smiling he winked, and went to shut the door while I looked around the simple room. Chairs, a pillowed bench, a cabinet, and a small table surrounded the fireplace while various closed doors dotted the room. A small kitchen lay towards my right, and bookshelves lined the left wall. A soft warm blue glow suddenly illuminated the room before fading. I looked at Howl as he turned to face me, smiling mischievously.

"Let me grab another bottle of Darah wine, and we can go back outside to talk some more." He entered the kitchen and opened a cabinet. He pulled out a similar bottle to the one he had earlier.

I watched him curiously, unsure why he wanted to go back out in the cold weather. He walked from the kitchen back to the door, and as soon as he opened it, I was stunned. Outside was no longer Balone; instead it opened onto a grassy knoll, with small white flowers, glowing in what appeared to be a newly awakened sunset.

Glancing at Howl, I went outside. Lush green forests surrounded the knoll, and far in the distance you could barely make out the sea. Howl came to stand by me as I tried to take it all in. Something seemed to awaken inside, something that I had never felt before; a magical pulse seemed to begin beating deep within.

Almost trance like I found myself kneeling in the grass, running my hands across its soft surface, and smiling. It was a sensation I had never felt before and one that frightened me to the core. Magic seemed to dance across the grass, and react to my very touch. I felt like I could summon the wind to dance across the knoll if I wanted, or call rain down from nearby clouds. It was a power I was not used to, and one that I marveled in.

Sitting down next to me, Howl brought my attention to the bottle. "This shall be interesting, I think," he said as he ran his dagger across his finger, letting a few drops of blood fall into the wine.

Reaching towards my waist I brought my own dagger across my finger before returning it to its sheath. My blood fell, and mixed with his in the wine. Again the bottle seemed to glow blue in color, before fading.

Pouring the wine into cups, he offered me one with a steady hand. Smirking, he quickly drank his, which I noticed was fuller than mine. Shrugging I tossed back the wine, and finished it just as quickly.

Pain and stars erupted across my vision, I heard Howl momentarily say something before my body felt on fire. I felt like I was falling apart that something deep inside was trying to break free, but couldn't. For a second I felt myself slip into darkness, Howl pulled me upwards. A buzzing noise filled my ears, muffling my world. My vision hazed, Howl's worried face crossed my vision before I fell into total unconsciousness.

Reasons & Memories ~ Alkin

With the runes completed, I found myself wandering. The girls were being cared for by Nora, so I had plenty of time on my hands. Tonight I was wallowing in my own self-pity, and I had found myself in the lower den, with a bottle of my specially brewed Darah wine in hand.

Usually I avoided the typical lifestyle of a Mystic or Ancient, but, with Raihanna gone I had time to relax. Sitting in one of the crimson plush chairs, I sat back and looked at the ceiling. *Where had things gone so wrong?* I asked myself thinking back to the original plan.

In a way it was funny, I had found Raillyn first, when she was five years old. Well before Drameon even found her. Later, he had yelled at me for not telling him.

She played outside a large two-story blue house; an older girl with brown hair and hazel eyes watched as she danced and twirled in the summer heat. Her bright golden hair caught in the sun's rays and shimmered in fiery hues.

Laying eyes on her made me smile. It had been well over two hundred years since I had last seen her, and it was by chance I found her then. It took all my strength not to go to her, and scoop her into my arms, relieved. Wanting to watch I climbed high into a tree, and positioned myself comfortably on a branch. I spent the remainder of the day there as Raillyn chased bugs, and butterflies.

She went from one activity to another, she ran after a butterfly that flew by, then stopped, and turned to throw rocks into the nearby lake. She was just as active as I remembered, and it made my heart ache. A few stray tears ran down my cheek as I watched her collect flowers, and present them to her adopted parents. I was sad but relieved, my little poppet was safe, and well care for, since her removal. She was being raised by someone I knew. Chaimh, who worked for my father, Delron.

Finally, the sun set, but still her parents let her play. Chaimh watched protectively as the two girls ran after iridescent fireflies. Wanting to take a chance and speak to him. I jumped down from my tree branch and risked approaching.

The forest floor was dark, the moon was but a sliver in the sky. Chaimh and Lillian had small magical orbs near the house, but that was the only light. Carefully, I went to them.

Raillyn was the first to spot me. She froze, her ever-changing eyes met mine. Whining, she ran to her mother just as Chaimh stood and approached.

"It's been a long time, friend, how are things with your father?" He asked me, reaching out and shaking my hand.

Smiling, I addressed his question. "Things are well. I was just checking in. I see you have been busy," glancing around him towards the girls who seemed to relax after hearing their father talk casually to me. Raillyn was still as brave and curious as ever. She let go of her mother, and ran around us full circle, laughing, and chasing more fireflies. Chaimh half smiled as I heard Raillyn giggle, and a warming smirk spread across my face.

"Lillian and I have two girls of our own. We took Raillyn in two years ago, but we don't know who her parents are. It was a rainy night, and someone stood on our porch in a concealing black cloak. They handed her to me as soon as I opened the door. Then left immediately through a portal without a word. She had a note with her, but all it said was her name, age and to raise her as our own. You, by chance, don't know who she belongs to, do you?" He asked curiously, knowing we were both Mystic.

I knew, I knew exactly who she was, and who she belonged to, but there was a reason she was with Chaimh and Lillian. I was sure the Gods placed her here, and I was not going to rock that boat. At least, not until I was given permission. I was already taking a chance by being there.

"I have no idea, I'm sure she probably belongs to one of the Gods. You know how they are, not raising their own." I said matter of fact. "They have their reasons, and it seems you are doing a good job caring for her." I said, hoping he would stop his questions after hearing that.

My father had sent me a call at that moment, so quietly I removed myself and bade them goodbye. That short visit left me happy but sad; I still wanted to see her again.

Delron told me that I could watch but not interfere, and to let them raise her. So I hid in the shadows and watched. Slipping into her room on the rare occasion to sit next to her bed. I think Chaimh knew, even then, before we started working together to get Raillyn home.

However, as she got older, those days became rarer. The last day came just after she turned twenty one. Winter was cold that year, and the nights long. Sitting in a nearby tree I watched as the moon set, and Raillyn dimmed the magic lights. Minutes later I slipped in unseen.

Like a cat jumping away from water, I leapt out of her room. The scent of vanilla, thyme, honeysuckle, and the tall tale alluring aroma of almond hit me like a boulder. Shakily I held onto the roof as I sat, and tried to collect my thoughts. I couldn't think. Her scent seemed to follow me, it clung to me, and it drove me crazy.

My body felt like it was catching on fire, and this wasn't even the full effect of her cycle. I knew if I touched her it would only get worse. My breathe seemed to freeze in my lungs as my heart stuttered out of rhythm.

Leaning back and closing my eyes, I knew I had to leave. But I couldn't, not until I saw her one last time. So I sat along the shore and waited till dawn. I was exhausted, angry, and hurt that even if I went to her it wouldn't make a difference. She didn't remember me, didn't know I had been her protector when her parents were away. It sucked, and pissed me off further. There would be no more contact with her after today, it was just too risky. The need to touch her was too great. *Gods I loved her already...*

Hours later she and her sister exited the house. Again I sat high above in the trees, watching. Listening, I caught bits of conversation.

"You look exhausted... Didn't you sleep last night... Aren't you cold?" Alihandra asked Raillyn.

Raillyn should have been cold, she wore short brown pants, and a thin shirt. The only seasonal thing she had on was her tall black boots. Her pale leucistic skin was red from the bitter weather. *She should be dressed better than that, brooding or not, she's going to get sick.*

"No, I didn't sleep well, I feel feverish, but I'm not running a fever. I woke up last night, and discovered I had left my window open... Going to mother, she said it was the effects of my first cycle... I hate it... My insides feel like their shaking, and I keep having waves of heat radiating through me. It's almost as if I keep getting submerged in hot water then thrown into an icy river. So, no; I like the cold right now... I just never thought my first blood would be like this. You and Aurielle never seemed to have it this bad. The only thing that seems to help is walking in the forest. I love the smell of pine. It always makes me feel better..."

Their conversation drifted off as I caught a whiff of her scent, again it beckoned to me. Telling me to grab her, and leave. My head hurt, static filled my ears, my breathing was choppy at best; I had to leave. Calling a portal I went to the only person who I knew could help me.

Celeste brewed a potent poppy seed dragon fruit concoction for me. It was the only thing powerful enough to dilute the magic and insanity within my soul. Still, for almost a week, the energy in my body raged on. Years later, the Gods called upon Drameon, Chaimh, and I. They gave us detailed orders that would one day bring her home.

Afterwards, Drameon apologized for previous events over two hundred years ago. He then yelled at me about Raillyn. Telling me how idiotic I was for sneaking into her room as she grew. As well as not leaving when I first knew she was cycling.

After my own apologizing, we began meticulously planning on how we would set her on the correct path. The Mystic path, one that would engulf her in the lifestyle she was meant to live. It took years before we got everything in place. Originally we had planned on acquiring Raillyn by singling her out.

As part of the plan, Delron summoned her father away to assist him in handling the undead. With both sisters no longer in the picture—one married to the Shifter King, and the other turned Vampire—there would be no one she could turn to.

Soon Raillyn would be delegating the Council meetings by herself. Newly appointed and lacking the authority and respect her father once held, she would be vulnerable. We knew it was only a matter of time before Raillyn would call on someone for assistance, just as her father did in times of need. Even still, throughout this she was supposed to remain neutral, just as Chaimh had.

However, a hatchet was thrown in that plan. I was to subdue her magic and mind, bringing her to my father's realm and, in turn, Drameon. There we would explain the situation in detail, teach her, and begin to introduce the Mystic way of life and magic. I was so sure of myself when I saw her hiding in the treetops, waiting, and watching me and my comrade. She wasn't frightened of me at all, in fact, she seemed curious. Probably because of all the time I spent with her while she was young.

Recounting that day, I had gone into the woods, not only to speak with Quinn, one of the Elite, but also to get Raillyn. We had heard she'd been assisting the Shifters in their fight against the Elite, and their soldiers, and was going out to find allies. Before things got further out of hand, since she was not remaining neutral, I was to bring her to Drameon.

As she hid in the trees, and tried to remain out of site, I gathered a ball of energy in my hand. Firing it at her, I intended to knock her out of the tree so I could confront her face to face. As she fell she steadied her balance, so she would land on her feet. Standing directly in front of me, I saw how much she resembled her real father.

We had specific orders: kidnap her, and tell her the truth about everything she was, ensuring she knew what Mystics really were. Suddenly I could feel another power move elsewhere, coming closer, closing in. *Wolves,* I thought to myself.

She was young and cocky. *Catching her thoughts, and remembering our last meeting, should have been warning enough.* Believing she could defeat me, I sensed her wanting to attack before the Wolves arrived. One heartbeat, then two, quickly she summoned her magic to pull me into Death's Realm. *Foolish girl,* I thought; my father ruled that realm, and I would not be taken there against my will.

Calling my own magic I encased her in an orb of light, causing her to falter the spell. Quickly I grabbed her wrist, intending to take her with me, but that single touch, changed everything.

Everything stopped, time, my breath, my heart, every-thing, and in turn I faulted my spell. It brought tears to my eyes as my mind surfaced momentarily realizing what the feeling meant. Never had I thought this feeling would be so forceful. It caused a deep rift to open up in the depths of my soul. In that moment I knew, the time I had spent with her when she was young was for this moment. For her not to be fearful of me, and to already have an unconscious bond with me. Her unconscious mind seemed to recognize me, even though her conscious one couldn't place the familiarity.

In that instant I knew if I took her to Death's Realm it would be for my own selfish purpose, and even then I realized the plan was not going to go accordingly. I saw it in her face, she felt our magic recognize each other, even though she didn't know what it meant. I did.

Then Lord Drake came, and slashed his weapon down between us, narrowly missing both our hands. It angered me, I wanted to lash out, but I was disoriented from the way Raillyn's magic, and mine had twined together, so perfectly, so in sync.

After losing her, we discovered another flaw. I should have known a part of me would've woken inside her, and in turn her inside me. Something only the Ancients dealt with. A deep raw power that drives a stake into ones soul, forever linking two together.

To make things worse since we connected, she began to brood. When she came to me in my home in Silvertine, I was slightly surprised. Even more surprised when she took initiative and came to me, laying her hand on my cheek. I couldn't think, and was lost in the overall sensation of the magic from her cycle. When I realized what had happened it was already too late.

Raillyn was marked, and claimed as my mate; in addition we had shared blood. However I skipped a crucial step and still to this day curse myself because of it. I never bound her to me.

Not understanding these newfound emotions and feelings, she left. She assumed the source of these feelings was somehow connected to some dark spell that I had placed upon her. In a way, she was right. *And why should she think anything else? After all, I was a Demon, the enemy. At least, as far as she knew.* For weeks, I worried about her and paced the halls of the Silvertine palace. There was a possibility she carried my child, and I feared for her health.

When I finally received word, it wasn't what I wanted to hear. Taking a Werewolf to bed with her wasn't anticipated, and hearing she carried the Wolf Lord's child angered me.

However, I wouldn't abandon her to walk the Mystic way of life alone. It was too dangerous and without my help she would have perished. So using the familiarity she had with me, I snuck into the Den, and assisted where I could. In the end, she figured it out but still...

Still I keep the truth from her, so many secrets I have to keep locked away. So much of the typical Mystic lifestyle I have to hide from her. Things would have been much easier if I hadn't faulted my spell on that day, or if her oldest was mine. So much wouldn't have gone astray.

Even now I felt that rift in my soul, and deep down I knew she felt it, as well. However, she was Raihanna now, never faltering, never wavering, and never loving. So different from the Raillyn I had known, and watched growing up.

Home ~ Raihanna

The smell of smoke, and the sounds of a fire crackling was what I was aware of first. I could feel its warmth coming from my left, and I felt a soft surface of my makeshift bed on the nearby bench. Looking around the room revealed I was still at Howl's, and it must be late, the magic lights above were dark, and the fire was growing dim.

Slowly I sat up, unsure of where he was. My head exploded, and I winced in pain. I had to pause for a moment before moving further. In front of me, on a small table, lay a cup of water, a spoon, and what appeared to be a pouch of yellow powder. I had never had a headache like this in my life. I knew that there were herbs which were often ground into powder and added to water to help the effects. Leaning forward slightly I mixed the ingredients, and drank its contents, believing that this was what Howl intended me to do.

Sitting back on the bench seemed to relieve most of the pain. Slowly I looked around the room for Howl, and found him asleep in a nearby chair. Sighing I stood knowing what I had to do. I withdrew my dagger, and the empty wineskin I had on my back. Filling the skin with the blood of an Ancient was the whole purpose of tracking down Howl. As I stood over him readying a numbing spell, I suddenly felt remorse, something that caught me off guard.

Cursing quietly I turned around. Already the effects of the potion chased the pain in my head away. Turning back to face Howl once more, I knew what I had to do. *I will never get another chance,* I told myself, and knelt beside him releasing the spell across his arm.

Carefully I brought my dagger across his palm. His ruby red blood steadily ran from the wound, and across his hand into the skin, filling it. I called my magic again, and allowed the faint blue glow of a light healing spell to close the wound.

Hearing the door, I stood swiftly and quickly placed the skin back behind me. A man stood at the door. He had long wavy black hair, and deep honey eyes that stared at me curiously. Tipping my head slightly, I pushed my way past him and out the door. The man didn't try to stop me but instead I heard him awaken Howl.

Quickly I grasped at the red pendant around my neck, and tried to open a portal to go home. I felt nothing. The magic in the pendant seemed dead, and glancing at it seemed to tell me the same thing. The pendant no longer held the gentle glow it use to; instead it was dull, and black.

Desperately I tried to call the magic once more. I pictured The Keep with its cold empty walls. I tried to imagine the hall just outside my room on the second floor. Suddenly I felt a gentle pull of the magic around me and a darkened portal opened up before me. Hearing Howl, and his friend approach, I quickly went into the portal. Their voices called out from behind.

The cold stone wall of The Keep appeared before me, its empty hall, and my chamber door lay in front. Closing my eyes I thanked whatever Gods decided to listen at that moment, and went through the door happily. Alkin sat in the main den reading a book as I came in.

He met me at the door before I even had it closed. "Thank the Gods you're back." He said as he embraced me gently. "Were you able to get the blood?" He asked releasing me.

Reaching behind my back I pulled the skin out and handed it to Alkin. Immediately he opened it to inspect the contents, he smelled it, then gave me a confused look. Bringing the wine skin to his lips he tasted it. I gaped at him. I don't know why this surprised me.

Even before he said anything, I felt his response. Shocked he quickly closed the skin. "Where did you get the Drakar blood?" He asked in a hushed tone.

Puzzled I replied. "I went to Balone, and found this magic infused house, eventually I found its owner, and after a few drinks he fell asleep. That's when I was able to acquire it. I didn't know he was a Drakar, so I don't see why it matters, or why they are so special." I replied as I took a seat in one of the red padded chairs.

For some reason, this seemed to confuse him further. Alkin brushed his dark hair back as he took a seat next to me.

"Drakars are people born with Dragon blood in their veins, they're Ancients, like us." Alkin began. "And what is this about an infused house, and drinks? Like wine drinks? With a Drakar, I can only imagine what spirits you drank." Alkin said as he got up and paced the room for a moment. I knew he had more to say, so I waited.

"You didn't go to Aeralain, did you? Tell me you stayed on this side of the Silver Sea." I could see worry in his face as he asked.

I reassured him. "Yes the spirits were interesting, he called it Darah wine. And when we went to his house in Balone, he reopened the door and we were on some grassy hill overlooking a large forest. I don't know where we were, nor do I care. I'm here, and that's all that matters." I said, beginning to become agitated. I had performed the task and retrieved the blood. The steady flow of magic I felt on the grassy hill had ebbed away. Leaning back in the chair I felt the room spin momentarily.

Alkin took note of this and quickly rushed to my side. He placed his hand across my forehead, gently. I felt his magic run through me, searching. His worried eyes met mine, changing to understanding. "He took you to Aeralain and you're having issues readjusting to the lack of magic in this land. You didn't seem to spend too much time there, so it should fade shortly. Now the Darah wine, he infused it with his blood and your own, yes?" Alkin questioned, less worried since he knew my condition.

The room continued to spin, and the chair seemed to shake as I sat on its soft surface. My head began to ache again once more. Suddenly the pain subsided as Alkin sat on the edge of the chair, his hand lay on my shoulder. I looked at him questioningly as I felt a steady flow of magic pass into me, and relieve the sensations.

Allowing his power to work its magic, I replied. "Yes, the Darah wine was imbued with our magic. We finished one bottle in Balone before he took me to Aeralain. The bottle in Aeralain was different. I don't know why, it smelled the same and looked the same, but it was too much. I felt like something was trying to tear me apart, and the darkness consumed me. I felt guilty, Alkin. Deep down, I felt like I hated myself for what I was doing, for taking his blood. For everything!" I stood, throwing a ball of energy towards the pile of logs in the hearth. It burst into flame immediately.

"Why? Why did I feel that way? Since I first ran into him, I felt this strange connection. He's different than anything else I ran into in my life. When he took me to Aeralain, I was shocked at how it felt. The land itself seemed to sing, and dance with magic. It beckoned me to reach out to it. That place is so strange, it's frightening…" I trailed off as realization crossed my face.

"He knew I was a Mystic, and he said I was strong, stronger than he was used to. He said our race was not allowed to slaughter people, and not allowed to have a hand in major events, that essentially we were Demigods. Is that true? Are we playing out the very things our race isn't supposed to do?" I asked trying to sort all the information out in my head.

Alkin stood to meet me, closing his mind, and eyes to me momentarily. I knew he was not telling me something, something very important, something I should know. "I think he's a bit mistaken," he said as he tried to calm my fears. His mind remained closed giving me doubt to his words.

Shaking my head, I stormed off towards my room, "Fine, I guess you're right. It was probably the wine anyway. Take that to Hunter so we can get on with opening the portal." I said as I closed my large door behind me and leaned against its hard surface.

Something was going on, something that he refused to tell me. Possibly Hunter was instructing him on a new plan, and he wasn't allowed to tell me yet. Sighing, I went back to the den only to find Alkin gone along with the skin. I hoped he was taking it to Hunter as I instructed.

Alkin

Still stunned that Raihanna had acquired a Drakar's blood, I opened a portal to pay a visit to my true master, before going to Hunter.

Upon entering the large den, I looked around the bookshelves, and past the beautiful artwork hanging on the walls. Drameon was not here, so I decided to take a seat in one of the various deep-red chairs laying around the large mahogany table near the fireplace.

Running my fingers across the Dragon-carved leg made me smile slightly, Raihanna had run into a Drakar, and went to Aeralain. Drameon was going to be thrilled to hear that. Carefully I sent out a call to my friend and master, summoning him to his house for a little chat. I was hoping it would go over well, and we could proceed forward. As I waited I pondered how I would explain the current situation.

The black fog from a portal opening broke my thought; Drameon entered the room, silver hair shining, and ever-changing eyes meeting my own.

"Hello my friend, I'm surprised to see that you called me this time and in my own house, to say the least." Drameon said while smirking, "So, tell me how Raihanna is doing. Everything still going according to plan?" He questioned me as he took a seat in a deep red chair around the table. "Was Raihanna able to acquire the blood of an Ancient?"

I felt my eyes react and change purple, a typical color when debating ones choices. I knew I could not, nor would not, hide any of my emotions or deceive him in any way.

"That's what I wanted to inform you about. Raihanna did acquire the perfect blood for the spell. In fact, I think she did beyond that. She collected blood from a Drakar. Which brings me to the issue, he took her to Aeralain."

Red flashed across his eyes momentarily before he closed them to compose himself. Sitting back in the chair he waited for to me carry on. "Raihanna had no idea that the Ancient's house could do that, and I didn't think she would have had a chance to find a Drakar. Regardless, it awoke something in her. I can feel it; the construct body tried to reject her spirit. I believe it was the Drakar who stopped it and saved her." I said nervously as I awaited his reply, defending her.

Drameon was pondering what I had said, I could feel he was upset at this recent event, but he seemed to understand something I failed to see. "Perhaps you're right, a Drakar would never allow a Mystic to die if it could be prevented. Did they share blood of any kind during this little excursion?" He asked as he closed his mind to me.

Biting my lip, I looked at the fire that always burned in the hearth. "He imbued and shared Darah wine with her, before and after going to Aeralain. Raihanna drinking it in Aeralain caused the construct body to try and reject the spirit. She said the darkness consumed her and she woke up inside the Drakar's home."

Drameon stood rapidly and slammed his fist onto the table. I didn't have to look at his eyes to know they were red with rage.

"Dammit, Alkin, we cannot afford to lose her. I knew Hunter should have sent someone else. I'm sure the Drakar knows what she is, and if he doesn't then he knows something is amiss. We must keep things under our control, the moment they slip from our grasp all will be lost. Gods forbid, the Drakar know this most of all." Drameon said as he began to pace across the exquisite rugs lining the floors of the den. Reminding me, as if I didn't understand how strenuous the situation was, I knew better than anyone what was going on within her.

"Thankfully the Drakar stopped the constructs destruction or else we would have failed, spelling our end." Drameon was furious, the carefully laid out plan that had been set in motion was too close to the end to have it fail now.

I knew what it meant if we failed, chaos would never be controlled; instead it would swing back and forth, and eventually fall to the darkness Alecien was falling in. Already it had lost too much of its magic to support most of the Ancients. It was only the stronger races that could even survive this side of the Silver Sea anymore, and they dared not return, because of the Vampires. It was both an advantage, and disadvantage.

The Vampires in Aeralain were well managed by the Shadow Walkers; they were not tolerated and eliminated on sight. Alecien was different; our land had become accustomed to their race, and wasn't attached to the old ways because they had been forgotten. It was our own downfall when the Shadow Walkers withdrew. Their race was well skilled in annihilating the Vampire race, and held no qualms about intervening as other races had.

Drameon had paused his pacing and stared at me in thought. "Continue with the plan but imbue the totem with your combined blood. I know a blood bond cannot be created without physical touch but ensure she drinks enough of his blood to form a semi-bond. I feel this will help with coping in any ill effects from her trip." Drameon said as he leaned against the mantle of the hearth and gazed into the fire. "Ensure you still bind it to The Keeper. We will just make a more powerful item to use later, a God weapon if we must." Drameon said as he waved his hand dismissing me. "Leave, you have brought much for me to think about. Do as I say and make sure it's done correctly this time, else we shall need to have a little trip to discuss it further." He said as his eyes lit up purple in color as he grinned at me. Nervously I bowed, and opened a portal back to The Keep.

The Portal Created ~ Raihanna

As Alkin and I walked the black tunnels, and went down the stairs towards the cellar hall, I noticed they were clean this morning. Even so, at times I could hear the screams of victims from the cellars deep depths. A rune-marked totem lay across Alkin's shoulder as he led the way.

Quietly we approached the magic wing. Alkin stopped at one of the warded rooms and held the door open for me. These specially guarded rooms, left over from the days of the Shadow Walkers, were used for casting violent and destructive spells.

A giant magic light sprung to life as we entered the room, brightening its brown walls. Old blood splattered a portion of the stone slab, giving it an almost black appearance. A small table and cabinet lay to the left of the door, and various rune marks were drawn on the surface of the walls, and floor. These special symbols kept any magic contained within the small space.

"As you know, Hunter wants us to imbue the main totem. We have to ensure it's done so with our blood, as well as the blood from the Drakar you encountered." Alkin said.

He secured the room and brought the totem up to eye level. The object was no more than four feet tall, a short staff made of white ash. Small dull runes were carved skillfully into the soft wooden surface. Alkin was meticulous, making sure every rune was perfectly placed, and correct.

"Hunter gave me this to imbue. He wants us to place it on top of the totem." Holding out a Bloodstone, he attached it to a hollowed-out area near the top of the totem. Alkin had done his job well, white ashwood glistened as he turned the totem in his hand. Already it held strong magic despite the stone not being charged.

The runes could easily be seen on its surface. Uruz, for strength and power, would overpower a weak opponent that tried to tamper with the portal. Raidho would ensure safe travel, Hagalaz's brute magic would slaughter and attack those who had no business there. While Tiwaz would mark the totem as the main link and Ansuz tied it to Daes, our God. Each rune was not only powerful but deadly in unison.

Alkin approached, stopping so he was directly in front of me. The skin containing the Drakar's blood was clenched in his hand. Smiling slightly he poured some of its contents over the stone, covering it in red liquid. Next he brought the skin up to his mouth, and drank deeply, then withdrawing he held it out to me.

He nodded towards the skin as he held the totem, blood already running downs its length. Taking it carefully into my hands I swiftly brought the skin to my lips and drank the remaining contents. My pulse quickened, the steady beat I had felt on Aeralain seemed to once again pick up. Alkin took note, drawing his dagger from his waist, he grabbed my hands running the blade across the surface of my open palms. Swiftly he did the same to his own hands as he began chanting the spell.

Together, and in unison, we called the dark arts to imbue the bloodstone. The totem lay in our hands, and the stone began to glow with a pure and wild magic. The magic in the natural wood responded, lapping at our hands with tendrils of pure bright energy; each pass slicing at our skin and taking with it a larger blood price. Sensing from the degree of magic the stone seemed to soak it up, it was immense and more than I expected.

Tendrils of magic whipped across my body. Its rapid pulse was picking up speed, distorting my vision of the dimly-lit room. In a single shift, the light which had at one point been coursing wildly began to unify, undulate in a watery liquid motion. Looking around everything seemed murky and bright. The colors in the room began washing out, fading into a grey hue. The brightness began to burn cold, and I felt as if someone had pushed me into a frigid river.

A gentle pull was felt deep within my soul, tugging me through the watery light. It was a separate strand of magic, faint but unyielding. All the while Alkin, and I continued paying the blood price, but physically I felt as if I was drifting somewhere else.

Losing focus and finding yourself adrift upon a wave magic isn't ideal in this scenario. Yet, I sensed the pull didn't come from the magic spell itself but from a familiar source, though I couldn't place it. Somewhere between light that runs cold and the floating sensation that has taken over, I begin to move into a state of total awareness. Magic from the imbuing spell is surging through me, enhancing my senses. I'm able to separate a whole body of enchantment from a single blue tendril of magic whisping its way towards me. Tugging at me gently. For a moment I take in the unique sensation before curiosity wins, and consciously holding onto the current spell, I reach out momentarily to explore this foreign strand that's weaseled its way in.

It wasn't a what, but a who. I was feeling Howl. The intensity of the magic surging through me made it possible to feel the small threaded lifeline linking me to him. Ignoring the increasing power of the current spell, I instead used it, manipulating it to seek out Howl. In one small instance, I knew exactly where he was in a physical sense. Just as if I'd been standing there beside him. I knew him like he had a personal familiarity.

He was located in a large city called Silvertine, somewhere in northern Aeralain, in the Turbid Still. I could see his face, and he mine. Lost in my surroundings, I didn't even notice the magic building uncomfortably inside me. Reaching out to touch Howl, my body was now in two places at once.

A room dotted with various pillowed chairs, benches and seats, decorated in green, red, blue, and white, came into view. Howl stood in front of me, his long black hair, and piercing blue eyes met my gaze while he smiled mischievously. The sensation was strange, I still felt connected to Alkin, and the room I had left, but at the same time I was standing with Howl.

Suddenly the magic peaked, like alcohol being cast into a fire. The air was gone from my lungs. I had an overwhelming feeling that I was drowning in my own spell. A wave of panic encompassed me, inwardly I was splitting apart. The pressure welling up inside my body was at a bursting point while once again I was all too aware of spell searing my skin.

The room began to spin as I doubled over in pain. Unable to focus, the room itself turned a searing shade of white. A sharp pain erupted somewhere in the back of my skull, and I clenched my eyes closed to shut out the light.

My mouth began to fill with a warm coppery liquid, blood I realized. It went into my lungs, and up my nose, I was choking, no wait, I was drowning. I couldn't see, I couldn't breathe, so I began lashing out fearfully. The air felt heavy, my arms restricted, and unyielding. *Why couldn't I move my arms?*

Blood gushed down the back of my throat. Reaching out I could feel hands grasping my forearms, holding me upright. I was asphyxiating on my own blood. Swallowing I let my tongue slide over the roof of my mouth. More blood trickled over my lips washing over my teeth, going easily down. My eyes flew open meeting Howl's piercing blue gaze, anchoring me as the spell threatened rip me apart.

"I really didn't want to do this, but I know you're spelled and not yourself... Heck, who am I kidding? I really did want to do this. Being bound to a Mystic like you may have its perks." Howl said. Realization struck me, my mouth encompassed his wrist, it had been Howl's blood all along.

Slitting my wrist he pulled it to his mouth. The feeling of being consumed seemed to subside. Slowly control returned, and a relieving sensation took over.

This time it was my magic that created a physical pull. It was instinctive. Like a lifeline, fine tendrils of magic sought their way across Howl searching and binding itself to a portion of his. The more blood exchanged, the stronger the force seemed. At the same time, his blood eased the magical strain on my body. For a moment, I was aware again of my physical body. The spell with Alkin was drawing to a close, and my magic seemed to have found what it was driven forth to find. Quickly Howl ran his tongue across the wound closing it as I felt my mental mind and body that was still caught in two places at once, recede back into the warded room where this all began.

The spell drew to an end, Alkin and I sat on the cold stone floor, covered in blood. Cuts lined the front of our bodies. The stone now shown bright crimson fully charged with the completed blood price.

My right shoulder, and arm suddenly burned with a sensation of pure magic. Removing my shirt I saw pale blue lines creeping over my skins surface. The tiny lines seemed to follow an Ancient pattern as they drew across my shoulder and down my arm. It was a mark, similar to the one from Alkin that lay on my other shoulder and across my chest, but smaller. His eyes met mine in a manner of indifference as he pulled me up and towards the cabinet near the door. Stumbling slightly, he pulled out a couple bottles of blood. Breaking the cap he handed it to me, and sat to my left.

This blood seemed powerful, but sweet, and tart at the same time; much more potent than Howl's. Any residual effects caused by the spell were gone. Since blood was used to heal, I can only assume this was specifically used for healing.

"Your magic summoned the Drakar didn't it?" Alkin said as he looked down at the bottle in his hand. "He must have given you his blood already when you were in Aeralain, and there was still enough in your system to summon him." Pausing for a moment I could see him staring intently towards my shoulder. It seemed almost to bother him, a look that was there only for a moment. "Well, the good thing is you're safe, regardless of the mark. At least we have a new ally in this mess."

I wasn't sure what to say or what to do. Howl said he had known I was under a spell, he also said he didn't care if he was bound to me. What had I done?

Exhausted, my body sagged, and I found myself sitting on the floor with my head in my hands, my shirt forgotten. I was now bound to an Ancient of Aeralain. *What did this mean for me? What did this mean for my people? What had I done?*

Alkin felt my thoughts as I continued to worry. "Yes, you are bound to an Ancient, but so is the totem, which means it's stronger than we had anticipated. And this makes it nearly impossible to be destroyed. We still need to finish the spell, and imbue it with The Keeper's magic, making it unbreakable." He said helping me to my feet, placing my shirt into my hand.

Pulling it over my head I stumbled. Alkin gripped my hands tightly guiding me into a portal. We now stood in the icy waters of Death's Realm. My body was still a bit fatigued, but I couldn't allow it to become a state of mind. I'd have to push through the weariness, and regret.

With no time to worry about the bond I had created with the Drakar, I fashioned a blackened blade with my magic and reached into a pouch on my belt. Pulling out demon root, a magically imbued herb which Alkin charged for me, I rubbed it along its edge. This would poison anyone, in case we ran into trouble.

I knew what I had to do, this was not the first time I used the river of death to strengthen a magical items. I dipped the totem into its icy waters, and the blood stone glowed beneath its surface. I could feel the undead around us, the water carrying them towards their final resting place. These undead avoided the stone, and us as if we burned the water. The light of the stone dissipated, before completely going out.

Now all that was left was to imbue it with the magic of Death's Realm. This was the hardest part. There were only two people who could do this, and one would not interfere in this matter while the other, the Keeper of the Gate, would never be willing to accept our terms. So we walked towards Death's gate that sat below the whirlpool, and under the entrance area. Deep below, through water and caves, lay Delron's world. A world all its own.

"Let's go, there should be a lesser known cave just beneath the gates. If we travel its tunnels, we might just be able to find The Keeper." Alkin said as he grabbed my elbow, and pulled me along for a moment.

We walked in silence unsure of what we might stir up if we talked. Upon reaching the large whirlpool, Alkin silently spoke the spell that would create a golden staircase. The vine like tendrils of magic shot out from the top where we stood, forming a golden spiraling staircase down into the waters depths.

As we walked the stairs, spirits that were going to sleep spun around us, their sleeping faces emotionless. It would be easy for a necromancer to reach out and take any spirit they choose, bringing it into the living to do their evil deeds and work. But these were lesser beings, ones that would die too quick in battle. If a spirit were going to be brought back into the living it would have to be much stronger.

At the bottom of the stairs was an entrance to a small cave. Our feet touched its smooth surface, the walls were equally smooth, only strong magic could create this. I felt the very cave sing as we walked quietly though it.

The water from Death's River carried on into its own underground tunnel. Alkin and I followed magic lights, illuminating us in an orange glow. The tunnel spiraled downwards towards the exit, and the entrance of Death's true world. It's an interesting place. Exiting the cave led us to a waterfall, spilling into the bright world beyond. We stood for a moment searching with our magic. Death's Realm was silent, and still as if it sensed our plans.

Walking down the stone staircase and onto the grassy rivers edge below gave us a better view. Death's Realm was similar to Alecien; it was a world all its own, with grass, trees, animals, and a bright sun lighting the sky.

In the dark forest beyond, birds chirped and bushes rattled, the sweet smell of pine lingered in the air just along the riverbank. Carefully, we followed the river, knowing it would go near another cave system. This is what we wanted. Inside these caves was where Delron and Chaimh often worked, the dead waiting to be reborn slept here.

As we approached the caves, we left the river. It carried on into the final gate, a place that only those with Gods blood could survive. As we stood near the gate along the edge of the river, we sensed a disturbance. Chaimh was inside the caves doing some work with his magic. This was promising for us. Chaimh was Delron's assistant, and Keeper of the gate. He had given up his own magic so he could wield Delron's power for his job. We hoped to provoke Chaimh into casting magic towards us so we could harness it within the Bloodstone, imbuing it with Delron's own magic. This would ensure us that no one living could break the new totem.

We crept into the caves near the gate. We knew they were a labyrinth of tunnels, created to confuse any who did not know their way. Crystal coffins sat in rows in large caverns, connected to the main tunnel. Within lay the dead waiting for their new life. Masses of what appeared to be bright fog swirled and danced within. The thought disgusted me.

So many worthless souls had already been reborn. It would be easy to shatter the coffins, causing a true death to all in the room. The thought was tempting but I decided against it. It would spell trouble and Delron would more than likely kill us for such an act. So we kept going, staying as quiet as possible. We walked down the tunnel towards the lower levels where the shadows slept, creatures which necromancers had created.

Mentally I spoke to Alkin, I knew Chaimh and Delron could sense the magic we used to communicate. I mentioned about awaking a shadow to guard the totem. Alkin smiled in response, indicating he agreed. We sensed Chaimh in lower levels. In this maze, we would become lost if we proceeded beyond the main path in search of him. Instead, I decided to draw him to us, by awakening a shadow.

Silently I walked around several crystal coffins, searching for a one that would work. Finally, I found one, a black cloud like substance lie within, indicating it had lost much of its humanity long ago. The creature inside was full of absolute chaos. It was perfect. Alkin took the totem from me, and stood guard keeping watch for Delron or Chaimh.

I began casting a necromantic spell; it would force the coffin to open, summoning the shadow to me. I felt my power pour out across the coffin. Impetuously it clicked open, and the shadow within began pouring out. I felt Chaimh's attention swiftly shift, and suddenly he stood before us.

"What are you doing here?" Chaimh asked as he readied a spell to attack us.

I smiled as I grabbed the totem from Alkin, holding it as you would a staff, so no suspicions would be thought of about its origin till it was too late. Chaimh released the spell, its power shot out in a ray of blinding red light. It was meant to bind us to his magic, we jumped away almost simultaneously. Alkin landed towards Chaimh's left, and me to his right. The blacked shadow we had released quickly took its leave and flew up the tunnel towards the living world. I jumped once more, and called upon my blackened blade. With it, I proceeded through the air, ready to attack.

We needed a strong spell for the stone, not a minor binding spell. As I jumped over Chaimh, Alkin charged him head on, wielding his own black blade. Mentally Alkin told me to not miss, and that he would folly on purpose. I nodded smiling as I flew through the air.

I reached Chaimh without trouble and brought my blade across the front of his shoulder, and around his back. My feet landed on a crystal coffin just a few feet behind him. Alkin smiled as he saw Chaimh falter slightly. Chaimh was already feeling the effects of the blades potent poison.

A call was sent out, Chaimh was calling Delron to come in haste, and cast us out. He didn't try and hide it, he was hoping we would leave on our own accord. As Chaimh waited for Delron, he gathered his magic, an Ancient spell that upon contact would kill and dismantle. This was the spell we wanted, we had to handle the next part with a bit of finesse. The spell was meant to annihilate, leaving nothing left even to be reborn. We had fully angered Chaimh.

God magic swirled around Chaimh as he summoned the power for the spell. His body was hidden behind a veil of red smoke, which marked the destructive magic. I looked at

Alkin, and nodded hoping he was as ready as I was. When the spell was released towards me, I quickly blocked the main sphere of magic with the Bloodstone.

It erupted in a array of red hues. I could see Chaimh smile beyond the rays of red magic, and then just as suddenly as the magic appeared it dissipated into the stone. In an eerie glow, it seemed to mix with the natural red that bloodstones held. It sparkled, and shimmered from the red Death magic of the destruction spell.

I slightly laughed out loud, just as Chaimh realized his mistake. Delron appeared next to him. Before we knew what was happening, Delron cast us out of his realm, and we found ourselves thrown into a field near The Keep. Rolling across the ground, I embraced the totem tightly. Finally, I stopped and held the eerie glowing totem up to my eyes, smiling, knowing that no one in Alecien could interfere now.

Necromancers ~ Drake

As Briar, Saibal, Drameon, and I walked the woods near the eastern border of our land when a portal spell was felt opening in front of us somewhere.

"Did you feel that?" I asked. They nodded in response. We proceeded with caution not knowing what might lie ahead. Upon approaching a meadow area, we spotted two children, one was no older than six, the other around three.

The oldest stood shocked, her golden hair shone in the sunlight while her emerald green eyes and Elven features looked around frantically. She wore black leather clothes and matching black boots that stood out against her stark pale white skin. She grasped the younger child around the arms in a gentle embrace and comforted her.

The youngest child stood facing the other, her black hair and pale skin shone in the light as she hid her face against the older girl. Something was familiar about them, but their smell indicated something dark. Both held the wretched stench of vampirism and decay. I started to precede forward to go to the children when Drameon stopped me.

"No, Drake, these children are Necromantic children and we are too close to the Vampire lands to not proceed with caution. It seems as if these girls just left Death's Realm, the stench of the river rolls off them." Drameon said, while placing a hand on my shoulder. "Let me go first."

The children sat down in the meadow, the oldest still held onto the younger one. A bewildered look covered her face as if unsure of where she was or what to do. As Drameon left the forest edge and entered the meadow, her eyes quickly met his gaze.

"Who are you?" The oldest asked as she stood quickly, putting the younger child behind her back. Her small hand went to an red amulet around her neck.

"Relax, child, my name's Drameon, I'm a Mystic, and I know what you are." As Drameon spoke, Briar, Saibal, and I left the edge of the woods and stood behind him.

"If you two need help perhaps my friends and I can assist you. What are your names, and where do you live?" I asked the oldest, hoping she might let us help them.

The youngest child peeked around to look at us, her ever-changing eyes. Elfin features met ours—a Mystic child. The oldest just shook her head and backed up further, pushing the youngest back with her.

"I don't like how you smell, I don't like you." She said with a snarled look on her face, much like the Vampires gave when they were provoked. "Alkin! Alkin! Please help me!" She yelled while grasping her red necklace even tighter.

As she spoke it gave off a bright red glow. Suddenly a black portal opened up just behind the children. The Demon we had not seen in many years appeared, the very Demon who had worked with the Elite. He reached down and picked up the youngest child who had run to him eagerly. His ever-changing eyes mirrored her own.

The oldest ran to his side. upset. "I did not mean for this to happen. We were cast out; he was furious at me." She cried as Alkin gently brushed her hair back protectively.

"Alkin," Drameon said with an unhappy tone, interrupting the child. Alkin looked just as surprised to see him.

"Ah. my old friend Drameon," Alkin said in response. "What are you doing here with my children?" he asked.

"Your children?" Drameon questioned. "They ported into the meadow while we were exploring the woods." Drameon appeared to choose his words carefully. "Plus this is the Wolves territory, and you have been working with the Elite. Why?"

"Hahaha," Alkin laughed. "Yes so I have, but that's none of your business now, is it?"

Drameon made a small action as if to cast a spell but paused. I picked up the action and readied a spell instead.

"Ah, Ah, Ah," Alkin said to me. "I don't think you want to hurt innocent children Wolf Lord, Now would you?"

I halted my spell, he was right—the children were not doing anything. They were so young and probably unaware of the larger situation.

"I will take my leave I apologize for my children's inconvenience of their spell." Alkin said while creating a portal behind him, and walking backwards into it with the children in tow.

"You know him?" I asked Drameon after they left. Drameon nodded his head. His eyes fixed on where the portal disappeared.

"Years ago we had worked together on another land, but we had lost contact after a while. I had other work to return to." Drameon said, lost in thought. "He used to be a decent Demon if you can call him that, only because he's not a Demon, he's a Mystic." Drameon said. "I have a feeling that those children are being molded into becoming Elite, their power was strong and wild."

I had wondered about Alkin, and now that we knew he was a Mystic brought more questions rather than answers. What were the Elite planning, and what part did this Mystic, and his children play in the bigger picture?

Looking at Drameon I wanted to question him more about this subject, but I could see it on his face. No more would be spoken about it currently. We turned to return home to the castle, instead of answers we were left with more questions than when we left.

Raihanna

That night we returned from placing the main totem, and released the shadow to patrol the perimeter of the new portal location. Sleep was the best it had been in a while, the welcoming darkness helped clear my thoughts and allow me to awaken rejuvenated. In the morning, I found Deestan and Callina in the den reading away at a new book.

"What happened to the brown book you were reading a few days ago?" I asked as I went to pick up a nearby brush and tackle my hair.

"I read it already," Deestan said, seeming to not care about it or its contents anymore. "I've started reading this book about the Werewolves and it's pretty interesting." Deestan said, while she turned the page and scanned its contents.

"Do you think you could get us an item it talks about in here?" Callina asked hopefully, her ever-changing eyes glowing as she asked.

"What item, sweetie?" I asked, intent to please my daughters since I was normally away on business. The means of bringing them items to further their education was one of the only means I had to love them.

Deestan flipped through more pages before stopping. "This item." She said proudly, pointing to a small statue of what appeared to be some Goddess. "It's a symbol of the Lunar Goddess, and it glows during the full moon. We want it for our room."

Callina nodded eagerly looking up at me "I think it would be interesting to have an item that glowed!" She said while smiling.

Taking the book from Deestan I scanned the page myself. The statue appeared harmless, and upon reading further in her book, it was harmless. It was just an idol to a Lunar Goddess. Unless a Werewolf summoned her it remained dormant, but it still gave off light during the moons phases.

"Alright, I will see what I can do." I said while Deestan and Callina both jumped up giving me a huge hug and saying thank you more times than I could count. I smiled as I kissed their heads, before turning to finish my hair.

I had to leave that morning, yet again for an unbeknownst time, Hunter gave Aurielle, Ash, Thierry, and me another job with Alkin. A child lay hidden in a wolf village to the north. The village was so small that Lord Drake never visited it. From what I was told, the child was a Shifter delivered there at a young age. Hunter had said it was time to retrieve her, and bring her back to The Keep.

Walking the halls towards the stables I caught wind of something strange. Aurielle and Ash were talking in the hall about the girl Raillyn who my uncle had told me was the reason we were in this whole mess.

Remaining behind the corner unseen I listened in. "I can't believe it's been over six years since we took care of her." Ash said while he stood, and spoke to my sister.

She laughed slightly. "Yes, I know; that bitch really put us in a terrible situation, befriending the Wolves who destroyed our portal. It only put us further behind and I want to be done with this mess as soon as possible." She said, irritated.

I heard Ash take a big sigh. "I agree, and I'm thankful she's gone. Raillyn always claimed she was a neutral force but even Hunter proved to us that she wasn't. Not once did she meet us on neutral terms as she did the Werewolves, nor did she offer our people any help, as the other races were offered. It's irritating that someone who claims so much never was able to hold up their end of a deal. I'm glad we're at odds with the Wolves again. Filthy creatures of nature; we're better off without them…" He said as Aurielle interrupted.

"Yes I couldn't agree more, but Hunter did say we needed to remain on decent terms with them. That's fine with me because even the thought of draining their blood sickens me.

Tasteless dirty blood that leaves the bad mud taste in your mouth—blah I say to them." Ash and Aurielle continued talking about blood as they walked down the hall further away from me.

Standing there listening stirred feeling of curiosity on Raillyn. I had heard about her. She was the traitor who had claimed to work for both races, helping where she could, but not once had she helped the Vampires one on one. Instead, she aligned herself with the Werewolves and became mates to Lord Drake, hence acquiring Deestan after her removal. If need be, she was meant to be used at a ransom for any future plans.

The thought of Raillyn made me sick; she was a turncoat, a horrible person who was selfish, and a do-gooder. She never saw the opposite side of the coin, never seeing that bad things had to happen for the good of all. I was different from her, I knew that for good to happen evil things needed to occur, and I was pleased to be the one to do the evil the world needed.

The population of the world had grown exorbitantly out of control, and our race had become so hated and ostracized that it required a full overhaul to fix the wrongs. But we would do more than that. We would make those who despised us pay, by using their blood as food and fodder. *Delron smite Raillyn,* I thought to myself. We would ensure that we controlled the races in the world while also ensuring that evil was allowed to reign free instead of allowing good to remain in tow.

Fire and Ashes ~ Raihanna

Adorned in our armor, we headed off to the small village of Isha. A small brigade of soldiers joined us. It was just before midnight and the cool night's air smelled of the oncoming dew.

I didn't care, though; the only thing on my mind was to find the child even if we had to destroy the village. Hunter had told us to do as we pleased and, since the Captain of the Werewolves eluded me weeks ago, I would take my revenge on their village.

We rode hard and fast; hoods, and helmets adorned blocking our face from any bystanders. Mentally I asked Alkin to keep an eye out for the idol our children sought. He assured me he would do so.

My mind drifted to what Hunter had said about this child. She was part of the council, even though she was only a child. Hunter had left her here in hopes to keep her hidden from her father who had threatened to kill her. But with her father now dead she could be brought back to The Keep. She possessed not only Shifter blood but Elven blood, as well.

Darkness enveloped us as we rode into town, the sky was starless tonight. Everyone lay soundlessly asleep, dreaming of the new day ahead. They didn't realize that their silence was about to be broken, and their village destroyed by me and my party.

"We have to wait for midnight—that was the plan." I said to everyone. "I will send the signal letting you know you can begin."

Ash looked at me, and I smiled eagerly. *Soon,* I thought to myself, *soon, and they will be sleeping forever.* Ash led our party, only allowing two troops to stay by my side as my guards.

Finally midnight came, and the moon peeked in the sky, I grabbed a torch from the man on my right and threw it onto the closest house, setting the roof ablaze. This was the signal for the others to do the same and to allow the destruction to begin. Within seconds, the house was engulfed, the screams of the people resonated within. One even made it out but fell to the ground in a pile of burning flesh before me. As the man's body continued to burn I noticed that the whole town had been set ablaze, and people were running and screaming on all sides. Ash interrupted my thoughts. Danzine had found a small child and they were bringing her to me. As I saw Ash and Danzine approach, I dismounted my horse. Danzine carried the unconscious child as Ash walked on, seeming pleased that this would not be as hard as we had thought. After glancing at her, this was the child we sought, her elfin features, and high cheekbone stood out even in the moonless sky.

"Ash, I want you to accompany Danzine and leave with the child. Take her back to Hunter so she is safe. I will allow our men to finish their fun before returning." I said, while Ash nodded and left with Danzine through a portal just outside town. As I watched the portal fade, I noticed a dark shape rise up from a nearby tree, not yet aflame.

A man took out his sword and brought it down across my left guard's head and chest, leaving a blood dripping corpse to fall off a horse, now running for the darkness. My own horse bolted in unison following my guards. I was infuriated by this, and looked around to see if I could spot where the man went. My remaining guard began to circle me on his horse.

Just as suddenly as the first, my other guard was stuck down. This time the assailant crouched down low on the ground, and brought his sword up through the horse's chest, killing my guard in the process. He moved fast and I wasn't able to keep up with him. I suspected he was a half bred Elf or something.

I was frustrated that I was left alone on the edge of town with no horse and no guards, and a crazy man running around killing my men. Then the presence of another jolted my thoughts and forced me to look behind me. I saw Qian, a Demon we had summoned years earlier, appear through a portal. He stood on the other side of the flames watching.

I drew my blackened blade, readying myself for a fight. Looking around I spotted the mystery man, and rushed him at full force. He saw what I was planning, and moved quickly aside. I had missed my opening, and my sword dug into the dirt instead. The man drew his own sword swiftly down across the back of my leg. Pain shot through me, and felt like burning embers. I felt myself stumble for a moment. Shrugging it off, I charged again, less careless this time. Finally I landed a hit, I sliced open his left arm, but little did I know that, at that moment, I was making my death wish.

He retaliated swiftly and circled around with a different blade, a blade of pure energy, similar to my own black blade. I jumped back sword in hand as Quinn suddenly appeared to my left, and charged the man's right. I took note and charged the other side. I would not allow a cut on my leg to slow me down. As I did so, I called Death's Necromantic magic to take us to his realm beyond the veil.

The man who was attacking appeared to suspect what was happening and quickly jumped out of the spells range just as I released its deadly magic. As Qian and I entered Death's Realm, I took a moment to allow the river's magic to cool my leg, which began to feel like it was on fire. Then I prepared for returning to the battle in the living.

One, two, three heartbeats, was all the time we spent there. Delron was still on alert after us infiltrating his tunnels, and I sensed his attention turn to Qian and me. We made haste and left in one fluid motion before more problems arose.

As we entered the living world, the man was prepared as if he knew where we would enter. He charged us from behind, and as I brought my blade down across his arm he did the same to me. We both cried out as the magic ripped at our skin. His blade was poisoned just as my blade, and we both stumbled backwards, realization sinking in.

The poison that entered my body was just as strong as the poison on my blade. The man was a Necromancer who worked against the dark arts, and he had fought our kind before; hence the poison now coursing through my veins. Fever started to set in, a fever that would consume me, and slowly kill me the longer it stayed. This battle was over; if I was to survive and live, I had to leave now. I opened a portal behind me and fell backwards into it, just as I saw the man do the same.

Recovery ~ Drake

When I returned to the castle, I heard Garion had arrived back from his scouting days before. He was to bring more troops to the castle in preparation for any possible attacks from the Elite. From what I had heard, he was wounded badly and lay unconscious in the infirmary. Drameon, who had been helping heal our men, when he was able, was gone, so we were left to hope he healed quickly on his own accord. It had appeared that he had run into an Elite, where or how many, was unknown. I hoped to find these answers, as well as others soon.

My people had been gathering information on the Vampires; they were appearing more often, and more attacks happened, just as before. I began to suspect another portal was created or would be going up somewhere. We had to find out where and fast.

When I made it to the infirmary, Garion had already began to gain consciousness. Saibal and Briar had accompanied me. As I walked into the room, I noticed Garion's skin held a deathly grey look, nothing like his normal luster it typically held. I sat beside his bed and hoped he would pull through.

"Don't look at me like that, Lord Drake," he said, while smiling. "I brought this upon myself. I decided to take advantage of the situation and go after the lone Elite. I killed her guards, and singled her out the best I could, but a Demon helped her." Garion continued, coughing slightly.

"Where did this happen? Was it Alkin that you speak of? How did you know the Elite was female?" I questioned, realizing I was asking many questions a once.

Garion shook his head. "No, it was a half-breed Demon, one I had not seen before. I was in Isha and there appeared to be three Elite there. They burnt the village down and began to slaughter everyone in their path. I could not allow that to happen. So after the Elite came out of the fire carrying a young child and left through a portal, I attacked." Garion went over the events of the attack including how the remaining Elite tried to take him into Death's Realm.

"When they came out of the realm I readied my blade and attacked again. It was spelled, just as before, to poison the Elite, but I didn't realize her blade was poisoned as well. They play the same game we do. We both struck, and hit true at the same time, I heard her cry out. So I knew she was hurting, but I knew I had to leave, and she knew she did too; we both left simultaneously." Garion said, closing his eyes to rest. "At least we know one of the Elite is female and is not one to be taken lightly. I thought I could take her, and I was wrong I don't think I would have gotten away so easily if I had not landed that first blow, slowing her down."

I nodded in response and talked further about the events, Garion did not get a good look at the child they took. Nor did he know what happened to the other Elite and the remaining troops.

"Did you get a look at the breastplate she wore?" Saibal questioned.

"When I attacked her," Garion paused deep in thought. "I thought it was odd that it glowed slightly but that was all." He said, bewildered.

Garion shook his head. not able to recall any more details; a slightly glowing breastplate did not give any more information that we already had. We left trying to discover how we could acquire more on what the Vampires planned to do next.

Raihanna

My head was pounding when I awoke. I didn't know what time it was nor how long I had been out. The taste of blood was on my lips and mouth. My eyelids felt like heavy shutters—refusing to stay open—but I managed, and saw Alkin, Hunter, and Ash standing around me. It felt like someone was taking the hilt of a sword and bringing it down repeatedly on my head. Squinting, my eyes drifted along each of the faces before traveling down, catching sight of my shoulder. It was swollen up to the size of a small citrus fruit. The top layer of skin was turning a jaundice shade of brown. Underneath the skin, broken blood vessels mingled in angry colors of red, purple, and black. Yellow pus was seeping out of boils along its edge. Waves of searing hot pain radiated inside the mass.

Alkin moved in closer, his tone was soothing yet his words muffled, and disconnected. Trying to focus on his face made it worse, everything hurt. I watched his mouth move wordlessly before slipping back into a state of unconsciousness.

Alkin

As Raihanna lost consciousness, Hunter seemed to sweep into action. "Ash, give her your blood so we can get her healed." He commanded, shouting Ash into motion.

Quickly he did as he was told and ran his dagger over his wrist while approaching Raihanna. It displeased me to have him give her his blood. It was not something I wanted for her, but I was powerless, having been told by the Gods to not intervene but to be their eyes in this situation. His blood ran over her chin, and down her throat, suddenly I felt Raihanna's body begin to shut down.

It was a heart-stopping feeling that my own heart reacted to. "STOP!" I yelled at them. "You're making it worse, the poison is now coursing stronger through her system. You must drain her, and carefully." I said, while Ash withdrew his wrist and waited for Hunter's order.

With a wave of his hand he indicated what he wanted done, Ash was to drain her, and I prayed he would not kill her in the process. Already I knew Hunter played a deadly game, Ash was not a regular Vampire, nor was he something that should be here. Rather, something that should have left. I knew Hunter had formed a blood bond with Ash, so I prayed they were not scheming about turning her.

Keeping a close watch on Raihanna, I mentally I kept tabs on her mind, desperately wishing I could use a stronger magical connection that the Ancients used to heal. Irritably, I sat and watched. It was like watching two half-wits with oily greased-up fingers try to fix a delicate tapestry meant for seamstresses.

For a split second something happened, Hunter and Ash made a decision, I could sense it from the energy in the room. Ash began to drink her blood at a rapid rate, he was determined to kill her. And knowing that he had already given much of his blood to her prior, it might in turn, change her. Hunter suddenly smirked as he knew I came to this conclusion. "Do not turn her." I said between clenched teeth. They walked a deadly path, and for Rai I was willing to barter with Delron himself to keep her alive.

Hunter ignored me, and so did Ash. Once more I reached for her; a calming sensation began to sweep across her mind. Ash did not stop, nor falter; instead he tried to take every last drop into him. My mind went blank. If I stood here and didn't stop them, she would die. If I interfered too much, I had a chance of being punished for disrupting natural events. *"Faen with natural events!"* I thought to myself. As I called my magic to me, I used it to lash out red waves of energy.

Hunter was thrown backwards into the wall and held in place as I used the power to smack Ash away as you would a bothersome fly. "Do not make this a fight. Leave and I will attend to her wounds." I said, knowing my eyes burned a bright red.

Ash seemed furious, but didn't budge when I released him from my magical hold. Hunter stood his ground momentarily before leaving the room. As he opened the main door, Aurielle stood there trying to question him. He yelled at her. "That damn Mystic will handle her," was all I heard coming from the hall as Ash followed.

Using my magic I allowed it to slam the door behind them, before turning my attention to Raihanna. She would be furious if she learned Hunter had intended to kill her and turn her.

Her breathing was ragged, and her lips blue from lack of oxygen. Laying down beside her, I reached out to her soul through the bond we shared. It went deep, deeper than anything else. Securing it, I used my own dagger to slice my wrist, and let my blood fill her mouth. I knew she would heal much faster with it than anything else I had on hand, and I didn't want to leave her alone to retrieve the bottles I kept hidden.

Drowsy from blood loss, I laid there with her until I was sure she had enough to survive, I would worry about myself later, knowing that only Raihanna's survival mattered. My eyes felt heavy, and I felt the gentle tug of sleep. It felt so pleasant to lie next to her like this. Even though she would never admit it, I knew she felt the same. I could feel her body relax as I laid there, promoting her to heal faster, and sleep deeper.

Sleep, it's what we both needed. Turning onto my side I cradled Raihanna in my arms. Kissing her forehead slightly, I allowed myself to fall into a deep healing sleep.

Raihanna

Hearing was what returned first, I could hear the birds chirping outside my open window. Laying there for a moment, unsure of what had happened, I slowly opened my eyes. The pounding was gone, and my senses were all back to normal. Alkin sat beside my bed, seemingly deep in thought.

"Hey." I said, slowly sitting up. I felt pretty good, given the situation that I was severely poisoned. "What happened?" I asked as Alkin handed me a glass of water.

"You were out for almost two weeks. I was unsure if you would wake up. Ash gave you blood, but the poison just coursed through your veins stronger. For some reason, the poison only affects their blood. We had to drain you down to almost nothing just to get the poison out of your body." Alkin said while I gave him a curious look. "After you were nearly drained, I gave you my blood, and that seemed to do trick. You started to recover." I looked at Alkin questioningly as he got up and walked towards the door. "I will bring you something to eat." He said as he left me alone to think.

I had had Alkin's blood before, and the blood I tasted in my mouth was not his. It was different, potent; strong like raw power. Not like the blood I had after imbuing the totem. I wondered what Hunter told Alkin to do in order to keep me alive, and to what length they went to do so. At that moment, I knew Alkin was hiding something.

Instinctively, I brought my hand to my unaffiliated shoulder, gentling rubbing the faint blue lines that still dotted its surface. It was the blue marks that appeared after I'd created a blood bond with Howl. For some reason, this brought me comfort. Lying back down on the bed, I tried to relax. I wondered what Alkin was not telling me. *Had Howl been right, was I spelled, and if so what was the extent of it?* Too many thoughts crossed my mind at once. Yawning, I allowed sleeps gentle embrace to engulf me.

Over the day I felt better and better. I was finally able to leave my room and carry on with my daily life. I sought out Callina and Deestan in the courtyard, playing with a new little friend.

The Courtyard was a large enclosure inside The Keep itself. It was our private area. Being on the second floor, only the Elite and Hunter had access to it. Trees, shrubs, flowers, and various rocks filled the large grassy area. It was a small bit of our woods within The Keep. The courtyard was left over from the Shadow Walkers, who once used the area for performing earth spells with druids. Those days were long gone, but areas still marked their existence on Alecien.

The girl who they played with was the one from the village. She smiled at me as I approached, and her yellow eyes met mine. She was indeed a half-breed; her narrow face, long ears and high cheekbone marked her Elven while her eyes gave away her Shifter nature.

"Hey, girls," I said, entering the yard. Deestan and Callina ran towards me and gave huge smiles.

"Mommy! I'm so glad to see you up. Alkin said there was nothing to worry about but I was still concerned." Callina said, giving me a worried gaze.

Deestan laughed a little at her sister's serious tone. "This is our friend Leeda, Hunter told us she can stay and play with us from now on." I smiled at her, and she smiled back.

"Oh and, mommy, Alkin brought us the idol you found in the village. Thank you so much! It lights up our room just right, we love its silver glow!" Callina said while giving me another huge hug before taking Deestan and Leeda's hand, leading them back to their game.

I smiled and went back towards the halls where Alkin stood leaning against a pillar, watching them play.

"Thank you for taking care of them while I was ill." I said smiling and standing next to him. I watched the girls jump about the courtyard, up and down the various rocks dotting its interior. Brightly colored flowered vines hung from the trees around them as they jumped out to reach them in play.

Alkin smiled in response. "It's my job; I have been raising Deestan as my own for over six years now. And Callina, well… There is no need for any thanks, and you know that. Hunter however did in fact release Leeda into our care. She rooms next to Deestan in our chambers now." Alkin said while smiling at me. He knew I hated it when he claimed my chambers for his own.

"You know you have your own chambers." I said tartly, even though I knew the only reason we stayed near each other was because our magic called to one another. Mystics enjoyed the company of other Mystic's, our magic and emotions feed off those around us, it was comforting and satisfying being around one another.

Alkin knew I thought this as he turned to walk away. "Yes, I know, but if I stayed in my own chambers you would be bored and not get anything done. Now wouldn't you?" He said mocking me.

I followed him as he entered the main hall. "That's not true. I get quite a bit done when you're not around. I just find it comical that everyone thinks we spend so much time together because we're more than business partners." I replied as I stuck my tongue out at him, and skipped off towards my sister's quarters. I figured it was best to speak to her about some of the recent events occurring.

Alkin and I were nothing but friends, partners in our duties to Hunter and that was it. Neither one of us wanted anything more, that's what made our Mystic relationship so much better. We could stay in the same proximity as the other with no strings attached. It pleased my Uncle that we worked so well together and that our magic was stronger together, as well.

Alkin shook his head, smiling as he walked past while I entered my sister's chambers. Aurielle's den was similar to my own. A fireplace stood along the left wall, and a staircase winding down was in the corner. While my chairs were red, hers were yellow. I heard her down the hall in her room, so I sat in a chair while she finished her task.

"Hello, sister, I expected you would be here before too long." Aurielle said as she came down the hall to join me. Her auburn hair hung to waist, and she braided it as she came to sit next to me.

I smiled, knowing she had chosen to keep her hair long while I kept it much shorter. It was hard to fight with such a mess braided around, and up all the time.

"Yeah, I figured I would pay you a visit. It has been quite some time and now that the girls have a little playmate I had some extra time." I spoke matter of fact while looking at the colorful ornate silk tapestries which hung from my sister's walls.

Aurielle had finished her hair and began wrapping it into a bun. "I've heard they have a new little friend. It's crazy that the kid's a Shifter, but at least she doesn't remember that life. Hunter said she was so little when she left them." Aurielle sighed. "So what about you, have you taken any little friends to your chambers lately? You seem so stressed."

My sister enjoyed this subject, she lived in her chambers with her mate Ashoten, also an Elite. They still brought their victims here when they needed to feed. "No, Alkin's the only visitor who has been in my chambers lately." Like my sister and her mate, it was typical for most Vampires to bring people to their chambers; the other Elite even did this. Since most Vampires needed blood to survive, doing this made things easier. But I was not a Vampire, and out of all the Elite I was the only one who did not follow this.

Aurielle shook her head. "Oh well, your cheeks are so rosy and bright today. Must be from all the blood you received. Hunter told me that he had to be careful not to turn you and that Vampire blood failed anyway. I'm glad Alkin gave you his blood." Aurielle said as she finished up and tied up her bun.

I looked at her questioningly. "How close did they get to turning me?" I asked worried. I had no desire to be undead and did not want to be a Vampire at all.

Aurielle thought for a moment. "Hunter didn't say exactly, but he made Ash stop giving you blood and drain you instead. Alkin seemed on edge about the whole situation. Only Ash and Alkin were allowed to work with you. I had stopped by to offer my assistance, but Hunter had me leave." She said matter of fact.

I made a mental note to ask Alkin about this later, I didn't want risks to be taken, and an accident to happen. Call me old fashion, but I would not forgive anyone who turned me against my will. I stayed and talked with Aurielle for a few more hours before leaving.

As I entered my chambers, I noticed the light on in the lower den downstairs. All was quiet as I walked down the spiral staircase, and pushed open the already cracked door. Alkin sat in one of the red chairs reading a book.

The smaller den was like a tiny library, bookshelves lined the whole room while star charts were strewn out on the ceiling. Seven fluffy red chairs sat around the room and the table in the center, while a small fireplace lay along the southern wall. A door met the stairs and could be shut if need be while one high window opened out into the courtyard's jungle-like view. This was my haven and my quiet place. I had often found Alkin in it reading and using it for a quiet place, as well.

I smiled at him as I walked through the door, but my smiled faded as I went to sit in a chair next to him. He looked at me questioningly and placed the book down on a small table next to his chair. "You're troubled." He said concerned. "What's wrong?"

I sighed, I didn't want to be angry at him, but I was. "I'm a little upset with you at the moment." I said slowly, controlling my tone, even though I knew he felt my anger mentally, and my eyes would not hide it either. "You didn't tell me that Ash nearly turned me." I said outright, and direct to the point.

Alkin closed his eyes and sighed himself. "I figured your sister would tell you," he said. "I didn't say anything to you because it didn't happen; you were safe. I would never let them turn you," he said carefully.

He spoke the truth, but he still hid something from me. Alkin and I rarely fought. Usually it spiked our power and caused a greater tension on those around us. "No, thankfully it didn't happen, but Aurielle also said you were tense through the whole process. And just so you know after Ash drained me and you said you gave me your blood, you lied. You gave me different blood didn't you?" I asked eager to know the answer. "It was a more potent mix than the one you gave me after imbuing the totem." Even thought I was angry for him not telling me. I was madder because he was not telling me the full truth.

Alkin paused when I mentioned the blood, almost as if I had caught him off guard by the comment. "Who told you about the blood?" Alkin asked cautiously.

I looked at him questioningly, knowing I would find out the truth behind this. "No one, I tasted a difference, it wasn't your blood. It was similar blood from the magic wing, but much stronger, rawer power." I said in response.

Alkin shook his head in understanding. "After I had given you my blood, you began to get better, but it was a slow process. To speed it along I gave you some bottled blood I had." Alkin said matter of fact like. I just stood there looking at him questioningly waiting for him to go on. "Hunter didn't care as long as you got better. We had no time to waste in a lengthy recovery. The blood was from someone much stronger than I am."

I gasped in response, shocked, and angered further. I knew Hunter approved the speedy recovery. I had nothing else to say tonight about the subject, so I bowed to Alkin and took my leave to bed, still furious.

Spells and Light ~ Deestan

Leeda, Callina, and I played together often, and studied together as my sister and I had before Leeda joined us. While my mother and Alkin were away, we began looking over the spell books, and were eager to try one in particular.

"Leeda, we can't let anyone know were doing this." I said while locking the door to the lowest den, below our mother's room. She had gone once more in search for more materials for our Uncle Hunter and would not return for a few more days.

We were in the care of Alkin and our maid, but they often left us alone for a few hours in the afternoon. Callina grasped the Lunar Goddess statue in her hand, and handed it to me as I came to stand next to her. I placed it on the table in the center of the room while Leeda joined us.

"And we have to make sure we don't go into Death's Realm." Callina said, hushed, as if the man named Delron could hear us speak of him. Leeda and I both nodded in agreement.

We had told her days ago what had happened when our mother was away in Fellshores. Callina and I had read a necromantic book, and it contained a spell that Necromancers used to get into Death's Realm. We were curious to test it, and see if it would work for us. Everything went extremely well. We were able to cross the veil into his realm with ease. But no sooner did our feet touch the icy waters beyond did Delron appear, and start questioning us.

He asked who we were, and what business we had in his Realm. I had explained that we were just experimenting, and trying to see if we could even get to his Realm. Delron was not happy, and cast a spell that threw us into a meadow in the Wolves' territory.

Thankfully Alkin had saved us from the Wolves who had found my sister and me, and took us home. Afterwards though we were punished and told not to try spells such as that again. He said we were lucky to just gotten thrown out of Death's Realm since he could have just taken us to the gate forever.

Alkin also told us not to mention it to our mother since she would be furious about us performing Necromancy. He said she was scared of the consequences that we could endure by performing such magic, and afraid of what Hunter would do if he found out.

So with great care I had studied this next spell in detail, I knew nothing bad would happen from it. The only thing that might happen would be that we might be able to speak with the Moon Goddess we were about to try and summon.

"Deestan, are you sure about this?" Leeda asked me while Callina lit candles around the room.

I nodded in response. I was itching to perform this as if I was drawn to the spell. After the candles were lit I drew my dagger out of its sheath from my belt. "Ready?" I asked them. Leeda and Callina both nodded as I cut my palm, and passed the dagger along.

Leeda and Callina both followed my lead and together we laid our bleeding palms on the statue, and closed our eyes. Silently I spoke the spell to summon the Lunar Goddess. I knew she would probably not come. None of us possessed Lunar magic or had Werewolf blood. Regardless, I felt I had to try.

Suddenly I felt a sudden lurch of power from the idol as if it was suddenly awoken with awe. A sudden trance like feeling took over, and a whispering voice entered my mind.

"Ah, my child, you have found your way back to me." The voice said. "And I see you have brought Leeda with you." She continued.

I was shocked I did not expect a response. But the Lunar Goddess was speaking to me. "Who are you?" I said mentally. "And how do you know Leeda?"

"My child, I know you well, I have known you since before your birth. Deestan Marien Pendragon," she spoke the name with power and purpose. It stirred something inside me that had lain hidden for many years. "You called me, and I came in response, just as you asked." She said.

I was taken aback, I had called her but why did she respond to a child in the Vampire's Keep? As I thought this, I felt her brushing my mind, hearing all my thoughts as Callina often did. "Lunar Goddess, I'm confused, and now I feel utterly lost." I said with a plea, and fear in my voice. Leeda and Callina sat next to me quiet, I had called the Goddess, not them, and I knew Callina was not going to talk unless she needed to. I felt myself pulling away from the Goddess' magic, unsure of what to do myself.

"Do not fear me, child; I would never hurt you, your sister, or your friend." She stated. "I have been waiting patiently for you to come into your magic and discover you could summon me. It has been many years since I have felt your presence, but I would never forget it, Princess." At that, I felt even more confused and lost.

The trance-like state had taken a stronger hold on me, I no longer felt my physical body, all thoughts feeling, and emotions were purely mental.

"Yes my Princess, you have a title. And Leeda holds the same position, just differently." The Goddess had chosen her words carefully. It was almost as if she was unsure on how to impart the information. "If I may I would like to lay a spell on you." She said with tact. "The spell will make you sleep, and dream. You will hear me speak to you in the dream, and I will tell you the story that you have missed, and of who you are. But if I do so I will in turn place another spell on you. Making it so only the three of you can speak of the events unveiled here. If others discover them on their own, that is fine, you will be able to speak freely to them, as well. This will further protect you in Hunter's world."

"Hunter's world?" I thought. "What do you mean by that?" I asked confused.

"Time is running out, child! Hurry; fast, do you grant me permission to cast the spell?" She said with haste. Suddenly I was aware of my physical body again, and sensed someone was unlocking the den.

I agreed, just as someone grabbed my shoulder, and pulled me backwards. I felt the spell take hold, immediately I fell into a deep sleep.

A song filled my head; dancing music and a fast beat drum that sounded entrancing. It was the beat of the forest, of nature itself. I felt it course through my body, awakening magic that had been locked away years ago. Images of a village, and various people filled my mind. My dream was from that of an infant, and I was being showed memories of my past which I had long forgotten.

I was born in one of the many Dens around Alecien. My mother was Raillyn, a Mystic. This meant my grandfather was Chaimh, Keeper of the Gate, in Delron's Realm. My father was Lord Drake, ruler of the Werewolves, who recently had taken up the position of upholding peace in the Council meetings. Everything seemed like a whirlwind of emotions, and memories. My mother and I were visiting my grandparents and Delron, when we were taken away and brought into the Vampire's world, by Hunter—and Alkin.

My very own friend who I thought was an ally. Alkin had been the main person performing the deed of kidnapping us. I felt devastated; torn between the love I had for him since he was like a father, and the anger I felt for him for taking my mother, and I away from our life.

Lord Drake, the very person I had met in the field after Callina and I were cast out of Death's Realm, was my father. I felt the magic weaken and felt myself breaking the surface of the Lunar Goddess' spell, I cried myself awake, startled by what I had learned. Callina sat beside my bed reaching out to comfort me.

Business ~ Raihanna

Acquiring components for Hunter was at times tricky business. He had sent us out to get half-elf blood, Wolfsbane and a new bloodstone from the lower mines under the Wolves' territory. The blood was easiest to acquire.

We rode into a small half-elf village on the eastern edge of the ocean, surrounded by mountains, trees, and well away from the Werewolves and Shifters. This location was so secluded and rarely visited I doubted we would have any issues—our whole reason for targeting this village.

Their village resided not only on the ground but spiraled upwards into the five nearby trees. Wooden structures dotted the tree trunks, large twisting staircases. Bridges tied each structure together, made of vines and wood.

I sent out my troops who accompanied us to round up a handful of them to be drained. I told my men to leave no one alive. I would allow my troops to have their fun with them while Ash, Thierry, and I did the draining.

I had to be diligent and careful killing them. I didn't want to spill all their blood over the forest floor. We had to bottle up enough to take back to Hunter.

Thierry rounded up and used magical ropes to hold five of the half-elves that the troops had brought over. I could tell by their tone that they pleaded for their lives but did not speak the common tongue. All around us their kin were dying; slaughtered or played with just for the fun of it. To me this was nothing; let the troops have their fun. We served Hunter and I cared not what destruction they did as long as we got the job done. I was focused on the job at hand not what my troops cared to do with their food.

One by one the half-elves were released from their magical bonds by Ash and held in place. Raising my blade, I brought it across their necks, spilling their blood and filling bottle after bottle until they were all filled. They had bled out leaving nothing but an empty shell behind. I had felt their spirits enter Death's Realm and escape the torture they endured, but I cared not.

As I looked around from my task I noticed blood lay splattered all across the forest floor; leaves and trees were marked with their blood. Their small village was being burned so any remnants would be wiped out. Ash, Thierry, and I stood in the middle of the slaughter. The trees were alight around us as the sun began to sink below the treetops.

I smiled as I walked away from the blood and fire. I wanted to relax before moving onto our next destination, so I found a nice cool tree to sit beneath while the troops finished their fun. Ash and Thierry walked the woods while they waited.

I closed my eyes and thought about the next step. It would be tricky because we had to move silently through the old mines under the Wolves' castle. Wolfsbane would be easy to find along the walls and tunnels of the mines, but finding the stone would be harder, and we could only hope we did not run into any trouble, being so close to the Wolves.

As the troops finished their fun, and the half-elves were disposed of one by one. The fire consumed the village and the remaining incapacitated bodies. As we walked towards the mines, screams could be heard above us as the upper part of the village slowly burned, leaving no escape from its flames.

Bloodstone ~ Raihanna

We had dismissed most of our troops, and kept only two alongside Ash, Thierry, and me as we made our way further east. The entrance to the mines was along the southern cliffs near the ocean shores. Carefully, we maneuvered down the slippery slopes towards the safest opening we knew.

Water sprayed our path as we descended the treacherous cliff. Ash tried to reach out, and steady me as we went down, but I refused his help pulling back from his grasp. He seemed slightly angered by this display but said nothing.

Finally we reached the bottom. Heavy moss grew outside the tunnel entrance and the tunnels reeked of a musty scent. The darkness seemed to go on forever, and held no light. I let Ash and Thierry lead the way. They created magic lights to guide our path, following closely behind them; our two troops brought up the rear.

Silently, we walked through the tunnels, for what seemed like days. Down the deep shafts we trekked, seeking out the stone. We knew traveling in the Werewolves' territory could spell our end if we were not careful; and just a hundred feet or more above us they were going about their day.

As we walked, rats scurried away from our light and bats hung silently from their roost on the ceiling. I felt on edge, unsure what lie around the next corner. We had no idea if Lord Drake's royal guard patrolled these tunnels or not. By the appearance, we suspected not often, if ever.

We turned a corner and our light reflected something shining in the distance. We crept on and entered a large crystal room. Pausing momentarily, the room seemed to come to life—magic lights illuminated the caverns clear blue surface. Crystal and wooden tables sat around the room; various bottles books and what appeared to be alchemy items were laid out on the surfaces. As soon as I entered the room, I felt an immense power vibrate from the crystal itself. I felt sure I could cast a locating spell to track the stone we needed. The room seemed to hold Ancient magic.

"Ensure the room is clear." I said quietly to the men around me.

They nodded and went into the room's vast space, searching all corners, ensuring nothing lay in darkened areas. We found nothing, other than the items I didn't care for at the moment.

Standing in the center of the room, I drew upon the natural magic around me. Manipulating my power to create a ball of pure energy was easy. I pulled—like pulling a rope—and brought the magic to me, gathering it into a ball. This would seek out and find the stone my Uncle sent us here for. The blue ball of energy glowed dimly before appearing nearly invisible, nothing but the outline remained. Then it disappeared down a corridor in search of its target; an answer could take a few hours.

As it searched the empty tunnels, for the stone's location, I walked the room. The smooth surfaces of the crystal tables were interesting to me. They seemed to have been carved out of the very crystals that grew in the cavern. Various objects lay on them, most unimportant and only a few interested me. One particular item held my attention, a small golden ring with a turquoise stone on it. I immediately picked it up, and turned it over in my hand; pure magic pulsed through within. A slight vibration was being emanated from the blue surface. It felt odd, almost healing like. I disregarded it as Ash approached me. Quickly I placed the ring in my pouch, so I could inspect it later.

"Find anything of interest?" He asked as he tossed a few skewers around on the table. His black hair had come undone in the mines and hung around his face.

I shook my head. "Nothing; it seems to of been abandoned years ago. There is so much dust on the tables and books. No one has touched them in years." I said while touching a book written in the Werewolves' language, its brittle page crumbled from the slight weight.

Ash's red brown eyes followed my every move while Thierry sat lazily in the corner where the troops stood. I hated being sent out on tasks without Alkin, it put me on edge since I could not sense others' emotions. To me, sensing Alkin's emotions had become normal—so much that I felt myself missing it. I wondered what Ash was thinking. I had known the Elite were paired by rank, and those they worked best with. Aurielle and her mate Ashoten were paired, just as Thierry was typically paired with his mate Lily.

Recently though Hunter had been separating the bonded pairs because of the issues they created. It made for sloppy work and equally sloppy down time. Ash and I had no bond between each other until recently, but we were still not a pair. Not in the sense of my sister and her mate, and I had no interest in him other than a partner in leading the rest. If anyone was my mate, it would be Alkin.

Suddenly a chime was heard echoing through the room. The orb found the stone's whereabouts for me. I saw the path we needed to take in my mind. I also saw that the stone was being guarded by a large blue Dragon.

I closed my eyes so I could better remember the path, allowing the spell to imprint the directions in my head. A great beast that I had never seen before, and only heard of in fairy tales, filled my mind.

"Wonderful." I said out loud as the image disappeared. How were we going to get it away from something as old as time, let alone something that should not be here at all?

Ash and the others looked at me, confused. Ignoring them, I began to pace the room, thinking of a solution.

"What? Where is it?" Ash questioned as he came to stand in front of me, blocking my pacing.

"I found the stone, but we have a problem; it's being guarded by a large blue Dragon." I said with authority. "So..."

Thierry, who was lounging in a corner, opened his eyes at this news. "Are you sure?" Ash questioned as he approached me, placing his hand on my arm.

I walked past Ash, his hand stayed on my arm as if he was ready to stop me. Pausing, I looked at him questioningly, ready to fight if need be. Emanating a low growl, I pulled my arm away. I did not like how he was acting.

Thierry stood up, unsure of what was about to happen. Even the troops looked tense. Ash, realizing the situation, withdrew; he seemed angry at himself for the act. I walked on disregarding it, knowing we had worst matters to deal with. I would trouble myself with Ash's strange behavior later.

"We go." I said as I walked quietly towards the tunnel, following the directions. I knew if anyone was going to get the stone away from the Dragon it was going to have to be me. I was the Mystic and the only non-Vampire in the group. I doubted that Dragons liked the Vampire race since they were the oldest living beings on Auran.

A musty acrid smell lingered down the caverns, and the temperature wasn't quite as cool as we traveled further in. Following the mental map given to me by my orb, a gut feeling told me we were getting closer, just by the change in atmosphere alone. The air became muggy, and the smell became stronger. *Is this what Dragons smell like?* We knew we had reached the Dragon's nest just by the stench alone. A strong sulfuric smell permeated the air.

Carefully and silently, we entered the lair in which the Dragon resided. The smell in the cavern itself was overwhelming. The back of my throat was starting to feel sore as I drank in the hot air from the room.

It was a large cavern, full of treasure from old and new. Gold, jewels, gems, and armor littered the floor and walls. Magic lights hung from the ceiling from what appeared to be a strange kind of black moss. It was rope-like but also vinery and thin, making it appear more like black cobwebs. Perhaps it only grew around Dragons, seeing as how this one seem to radiate its own climate.

Laying on his large bed of riches, slept the dragon. The creature was barrel-chested with muscular limbs and heavy-set claws. Each was the length of my arm, and seemed to glisten in a sweaty substance. His scales were like the caverns themselves, crystallized, and a dazzling shade of blue. The color was rich and deep. Yet, it would have been perfectly camouflaged if it hadn't been laying atop its piles of assorted treasure. The sweat beads seemed to reflect its treasure trove, like tiny mirrors. We were lucky that it was asleep out in the open.

The animal breathed in deeply, flaring its nostrils. Its body expanded and shimmered like a glittering mass plucked from the night sky. The vision in front of us was enough to make us forget about the smell. For a small moment in time, we stood in silence, our mission momentarily forgotten.

Suddenly I felt myself almost instinctively reaching for the mark left behind from Howl. For some reason I knew I would be able to retrieve the stone if the others distracted the beast. There was no way we could kill the Dragon for fear of it alerting the Wolves on the surface—nor did I think we could handle a force such as this. Relaying this information to Ash mentally, he nodded his head and told Thierry.

Silently, I crept towards the beast. It was seemingly simple. The closer I got to its body the hotter it began to feel. Even the coins felt warmer. Peacefully, the Dragon slept on, emitting a low, thundering rumble as it exhaled. Carefully, I climbed onto the Dragon's hoard, trying not to make a sound. Gold and gems vibrated beneath me under each powerful breath. None of the loot interested me, only the Bloodstone near its right paw.

Nearing the stone, suddenly the Dragon awoke. Protective lenses that covered the eye peeled back exposing one huge iris, severed in the middle by a narrow slit. I froze, swallowing. The back of my throat tingled with a burning sensation. For a moment, all I could do was stare. With one gigantic eye, he watched me right back.

Somewhere down the length of its body came a deep drumming growl that rippled up the length of its neck. The sound seemed to take forever to get to its head. The beast's lips curled back, exposing large white fangs. It lifted its massive head' coins dripped down from his chin, landing musically on other bits of treasure. One mistake and I would become his next meal.

Mentally, Ash told me to "Stand still."

"You think?" I responded sarcastically.

The Dragon seemed to not be sure why I was there, and so he refrained from doing anything else. A strange feeling began to flow through me and the mark on my shoulder itched. I, slowly, inch by inch, kept reaching for the stone. As I touched its smooth, cool, surface, I felt another force enter my body. I felt almost cold while the air around the Dragon felt like a hot summer day. My shoulder glowed slightly with a blue hue; I glanced at it before glancing back to the Dragon.

As soon as the light lit up, it faded. Slowly I closed my hand around the stone's wide berth, never taking my eyes off the Dragon. Again a low growl erupted from his throat as I backed up slowly. In one fluid movement, its neck whipped forward, teeth snapping at me, missing my hand by a hairline. Jumping back as fast as I could, I scrambled to meet the others at the small entrance.

The Dragon lurched forward. For a large creature, it was surprising graceful in movement, not lumbering like I'd imagined. Heavily-clawed feet hit the ground with a traumatic thud. There was a clash as money could be heard being thrown to the side of the walls. Quickly I ran back into the tunnels beyond, following the others closely. The ground began to rumble and shift beneath the dragons large weight. The sound of heavy claw grinding on crystal echoed along the cave walls.

Then, everything went still. The dragon had stopped, too large to fit through and unable to follow. He bellowed angrily from his lair.

Jumping, and leaping through the narrower corridor, the sound of rocks falling from the ceiling behind us could be heard. The temperature began rising, a bright light filled the cave. I glanced over my shoulder to see fire racing towards us, flooding the sides of the crystal caverns. The once blue rocks glowed as bright as the moon as they were heated by the flames.

Ash and Thierry were in front of me. I could hear them turn down a different tunnel, but I lost sight of them when I turned my attention back. A hand grabbed me and pulled me in a new direction. Our troops who followed me were not so lucky and died in a bright blue, fiery blaze; their screams, were short lived as the searing heat consumed them.

"Are you ok?" Thierry asked as I stared in disbelief at the dissipating fire.

Ash held my arm as I took a deep sigh, and shook my head. Thankfully he had pulled me aside fast enough. As I did so, I noticed a change—the fresh scent of pine filled the air. Light beamed in from an opening a few feet away. Stunned, I looked at Ash and Thierry. Voices emanated from outside. That's when I realized our folly, we had taken a wrong turn, and now we were close to the Wolves' village.

Exiting the tunnel proved true, we stood on the outer edge of the forest. The musk of the trees, moss, plants, and more filled our noses, as well as the smell of the Wolves. *Filthy, dirty, creatures*, I thought to myself. Hastily we created a portal and went through it.

Disturbances ~ Drake

Briar and I sat in the throne room, taking the daily petitions. Recently I found it difficult to sleep. Hazy dreams filled my head, and the scent of lemons tickled my nose.

It was always the same dream. For six years now, the silhouette of a shadowed woman with pale skin, hazel-crystal eyes that always changed, and silky hair haunted me. In a way, I felt it was Raillyn calling to me from her prison, wherever that may be. To this day I still suspected Hunter, and seeing Raihanna just made me surer she was in The Keep.

This morning the woman was crying, and even now that I was awake, it bothered me. My heart ached, and hurt from the sound of her tears. My throat tightened at the memory. That's when a group of my village guard came in, bowing swiftly.

Silently, one bowed his head to whisper in my ear. "Sir, we have had a strange sighting, Vampires were near the lower village today and left swiftly through a portal." The guard said, breaking the lingering memory.

I looked at Briar before standing up. "I am sorry, but I will have to leave Chancellor Droggen in charge of the rest of the petitions. Please continue." I said, getting up worried about what I might find. "Briar, please accompany me."

We quietly walked the halls towards the tunnels leading to town. As we approached the training grounds, I silently gathered Saibal to accompany us. The fewer people who knew the better it would be for everyone.

As soon as we arrived at the area I could smell them. Several Vampires were here, possibly the Elite. I followed their trail; backtracking it to the tunnels, just south of town. The entrance was hidden in the woods and behind a large rock.

We carefully entered the tunnels to ensure everything was safe. It was troubling that the Vampires were so close. After hours patrolling the tunnels nothing seemed to be out of place; we exited the system near the castle town entrance, not wanting to take the guards with us into the deeper sections. "Guards, I want you to double the watch tonight. Briar, Saibal, and I are going to explore further." I said, sending the guards on their way.

"You sure we should go back in there?" Saibal asked while brushing his hair behind his ear.

Briar nodded. "We have to. There are too many secrets and items that lay in those tunnels. If one is stolen we might have a big problem." Briar said as he headed towards the tunnels.

We once more entered the tunnels as the near-full moon began to rise. The smell of Vampires was strong in the crystal room under the Dancer's Den. *Why had they come here?* I thought to myself as we walked about the room ensuring nothing was stolen.

"Nothing appears to be out of place." Briar said as he too shared similar thoughts. "I wonder why they were here."

As we traced their scent back into the tunnels, we began to follow a familiar path, one that we had not taken for many years. The path lead to the Dragon area where a horde of Dragons had made their dens and slept.

Briar and I came to this area when we were in need of magical items, or out of sheer boredom. They had taken refuge here, refusing to leave. We had been told their power was the only thing old enough to keep the magic in the land itself, so we often left them alone.

The scent stopped just outside a large Blue Dragon's room, the walls of the tunnel seemed hot and charred. It held a sulfur scent. The Dragon within slept in the center upon his large horde. This was even more puzzling, I wondered what item was in this room they so desperately needed. I also wondered how many had died in this endeavor. Most of the Ancient and more deadly weapons lay further in the lairs.

"What was in this lair that was so important?" I asked out loud knowing I would awaken the Dragon as I did so. They only spoke to those they choose, and I was hoping he would tell me what had occurred here.

Saibal nodded towards the Dragon, I had awoken him. He let out a growl of unease. "Why do you disturb my sleep?" He spoke mentally.

"We have been following a trail and it lead here." I replied, carefully choosing my words. "Was anything taken from you?" I asked while walking forward to meet the Dragon, my hands in front of me so he knew I meant no harm.

The Dragon calmed down and laid his head back on his horde. "Just a simple Bloodstone, but that was all. I would have been more angered if it was my gold. I charred a few of them when I lit the tunnel ablaze, anyway." He said protectively as he withdrew from his mental communication.

We took that as our cue to leave and quietly walked back along the tunnels towards the castle. "Why take a Bloodstone?" Saibal asked. "They hold no purpose to Vampires. Only Shadow Walkers and Mystics can wield them."

That made me pause as I remember the meadow and the conversation with Alkin. Drameon had said he was a Mystic. In addition we knew Raihanna had Mystic blood. "Alkin and Raihanna are Mystics, though." I said. "We need to call Drameon and find out what these Bloodstones do."

We made haste as we went back to the castle, and to the small den which had become our meeting area. Drameon had answered our call rather quickly this time. "I am sorry it has taken me awhile to check on things here. Many things are happening in many places, and it keeps me busy," he said, cautious of his words.

Nodding in response, we caught him up on the events being played out. "How are Bloodstones used by Mystics?" I asked after relaying the details of what I could only suspect as the Elite in the tunnels.

Drameon thought for a moment, "Typically they are imbued with blood magic and are attuned to one specific spell. The spell's power would increase tenfold due to the blood price that was paid during its creation. This could mean any spell they wish from a simple fire spell to a destruction spell. If they plan on a subtle approach, then I don't know what they plan on using it for." He said while pacing the floor, shaking his head.

I too thought about what spell they could be planning on casting with the stone.

Pure Magic ~ Alkin

Having just returned from acquiring more agents from for Hunter. I noticed he had acquired a strange old book recently, and had been trying out some new spells. It was quite irritating since it had nothing to do with the portal, and everything for his own leisure. I was not his pet to control and send off for menial items, I was a Mystic. My father was Delron the God of Death. I couldn't wait until our task was done and life could return to a new normal without Hunter.

Out of sheer curiosity I stopped by our chambers to see if Raihanna had returned from her own little trip. The dark den indicated she was still away, and that the girls were out with Nora, their nursemaid. She probably took them to the dining room or the library to study while we were away. I was not concerned, so I went back to attend to other tasks.

Entering the hall once more, I made my way towards Hunter's chambers. The maids and servants kept their heads down as I walked the desolate halls. Upon reaching Hunter's chambers, I paused to knock before entering. Hearing him bellow inside indicated he was home. "Enter," he said.

The logs burned brightly as the only light in the room. He sat sprawled out on a nearby bench, fresh blood on his lips. "I am glad to see you this evening," he said, sitting upright and smiling at me. "Saves me the trouble of tracking you down. Did you get the materials I sent you out for?"

Walking to stand in front of the bench, I pulled the pack off my back, and I noticed a young girl lay dead and naked on the floor. Hunter looked up and smiled at me as I tossed the bag at him in disgust. Shaking my head, I turned to walk away.

However, he had other plans. "I need to discuss something with you before you go." He said, standing in one fluid motion, and coming to meet me. "We have a little issue, and only one way to resolve it. You see, I am in the process of acquiring a staff of great power. One that will be able to summon creatures of not only pure darkness, but pure evil. With the staff, and portal, we will be unstoppable. Sadly, we need the pure energy of Delron to do this. His magic is the one true power that governs these creatures." Hunter said while smiling at me once more.

Pausing, I listened to his words carefully. He was up to something and, if he had a staff that could do such a thing, he was right it would be governed by Delron's power. Only his realm possessed such creatures of darkness and decay. Possibly he found another way to acquire undead, a faster more efficient way. *Ancient magic*, I thought, standing my ground, waiting for him to go on.

Turning back towards the fireplace and bench, he continued. "We both know I possess knowledge from the days of old. I have had the privilege of finding a reliable source. It was the whole reason I had wanted Raillyn—well, one of many. Regardless, you and Raihanna are both Mystic, and you told me you were Delron's son. This creates a perfect situation for what I need." Hunter said deviously, as he came to stand in front of me once more.

Returning his smile, I had enough of being quiet, I was beginning to get the feeling of what he was suggesting. "If you are suggesting Raihanna and I have a child so you can use it for imbuing this staff of yours, it won't happen. Raihanna and I have no interest in each other in that aspect. Plus I doubt any of us could talk her into such a thing at this time. We are too close to opening the portal to have an eight or so month delay." I said while crossing my arms in front of me.

"I thought you would say that, which leads me to the other choice." Hunter said while turning towards the darkness of a nearby door and snapping his fingers. Out of the pitch black adjacent room came Aurielle, in front of her stood Callina in a trance like state.

My muscles tensed for a moment, and I had to close my eyes to hide the anger and anguish I felt. Hunter was playing dirty, using my own daughter to get to me. Because he had her, I had a feeling he would discover the truth about her if he hadn't already. "So tell me, this child is Mystic? Raihanna had told me that when she went to Issia she met up with the girl's father, another Mystic. Do you by chance know who the father is? Or even what his lineage is to the Gods?" Hunter asked while smiling at me, his wild eyes met mine.

Pausing, I knew I would have to choose my words carefully. "No, I don't know who the child's father is." I said cautiously. "I had known she was Mystic, and that her father was Mystic, but who or what lineage I don't know." I was trying to bluff, and I hoped that Hunter would fall for it. Even though I had a sinking feeling, he would not.

Shaking his head, Hunter turned back towards Aurielle and Callina, who stood silent in her trance, almost doll like. "I am surprised that did not bother you. I guess you wouldn't mind if we fixed this error, and have you and Raihanna correct it, now would you?" Hunter said while he nodded his head.

Swiftly Aurielle pulled out a dagger and brought it to Callina's neck. Red dots began to well up on her pale skin. "Stop!" I yelled, outraged and shaking. "If you kill her, what makes you think Raihanna would be happy to give you another child to torture?" I asked hoping this would stop his insane plan. I was prepared to use other powers and remove Callina from this realm if need be; taking her to my father and away from this chaos.

Hunter held up his hand, and Aurielle stopped. Callina stood unaffected, in her deep trance state. "No, I don't believe so. Raihanna wants the same thing I do, and so do you. We all have to work together to accomplish this goal regardless of how we feel." He said menacingly. "And unless you tell me otherwise. This child is useless to us." He said as he snapped his fingers once more.

Again Aurielle started to run the blade over Callina's neck, this time much deeper. She would die if I let this horror ensue. "Fine!" I yelled at them as my energy momentarily burst out, indicating my anger. "Let her go, and I will tell you whatever you want." Now I knew why Drameon made the choice he did so very long ago. In that moment my hatred was so out of control, I wanted to end Hunter and Aurielle, and remove my family from The Keep, but I knew that was not an option. The Gods wanted us here, and we had no choice but to follow.

Hunter was thrilled that I was finally agreeing, and I knew I was left with no choice. I just prayed he'd asked simple things. "Good now tell me. Who does Callina belong to? Who does she acquire her power from?" He asked me forcefully.

Closing my eyes once more I knew he would not take *I don't know,* as an answer. I would have to tell him Callina was mine. Suddenly his eyes went wild, and he turned back towards Aurielle. Before he could do anything further I answered him. "Callina is my daughter!" I told him determined to keep her safe.

Hunter paused as if I startled him. His eyes turned to meet mine, he looked surprised but happy. "Really?" He said as he approached me with a sly look on his face. "And how did this happen?" He asked suddenly interested.

Letting my breath out I met his eyes. "Raihanna told me if I didn't help her she was going to travel to Aeralain. I couldn't let that happen since they would have either killed or kept her depending on who found her. You know that. So I told her to leave to Issia, and I would meet her later. After you sent me out to retrieve her, in fact." I said sarcastically. Now that Hunter knew the truth he would not hurt or at least kill her, hopefully.

Anger flashed in his eyes. "Damn you Mystics!" He yelled as he grabbed a nearby bottle and threw it against the wall, shattering its glass against the stone walls surface. "I hate the games you play! All of you! You Mystics and the Gods themselves! I can never get a straight answer from any of you!" Hunter ranted on as he paced the room, before finally coming to stand near the fireplace deep in thought. "Thankfully you and I Alkin have a similar desire. Daes must be released into this world. His chaotic nature is just what we need." Hunter said madly. "Aurielle! Get that dagger away from the child's throat! Give her back to her father! Now!" Hunter yelled as Aurielle did as she was told, tossing Callina into my arms. "I expect she does not know she is your child. Let's keep it that way, at least for now. It will make things easier when I will need to use the child's magic to imbue my new toy." He said while turning to leave.

Leaning down to check Callina's wounds, I resisted the urge to pull out the healing salve from my belt pouch, one of many the many items I carried that I needed to ensure was kept out of the Vampire's hands. Picking up her limp trance-like body, I carried her back to our chambers. I had expected Hunter would want to use her power. It was only natural for him to think that. He abused everyone else's power and blood; why not a child? He was becoming more erratic by the day. I hoped we would not have to linger much longer with the children; I wanted them safe and not enduring this abuse.

After returning back to our chambers, I placed a light healing salve on the mark, thankful it was not deep and it would heal fast. Calling my magic, I allowed a red haze to envelop the mark, healing it, and erasing its existence. Then I channeled my magic through her body to release her from the trance-like state. Slowly my magic sought out the Vampire spell Hunter had cast on her. My magic devoured the spell, and in one swift moment, Callina returned to her normal self, no longer in the trance-like state.

As her eyes met mine, I couldn't just stand by and not do a thing. I took her into my arms and held her close; she sensed something was amiss and that I was upset. "Alkin, what's wrong?" She asked suddenly frightened.

Shaking my head I held her tightly. "Nothing's wrong, baby, nothing at all. I'm just glad you are safe." I said as she put her arms around me, and hugged me in return.

Blood Magic ~ Raihanna

Upon arriving back at The Keep we met with Alkin who dismissed Thierry and asked Ash and me to follow him to Hunter's chambers. Quietly we walked through the halls; the maids scurried here and there carrying various items to and from rooms. As we approached the door, Ash and Alkin led the way inside.

My Uncle was bent over an old book, he seemed eager to read the information within. "Did you bring the items?" He asked, lifting his head to meet our gaze.

I nodded in reply as Ash handed him the bottles of blood and the Wolfsbane he had grabbed sometime during our excursion. I pulled the Bloodstone out of my pouch and placed it on the table in front of me. Hunter smiled as he placed the bottles of blood onto the table and held up the blood stone.

"Good." He said in a joyous tone. "Raihanna, I have a task for you and Alkin to perform, two actually, but Alkin can fill you in on the other task later. Let's just say we need some pure magic for summoning Daes and I expect you to provide this." Hunter said while I looked at him questioningly. I knew not to interrupt him. I did not want to anger him and suffer a punishment again. So I stood and listened as he went on. "For now I want you and Alkin to go to the lower chambers and charge this pretty little stone." Hunter said as he handed it to Alkin and waved us on our way.

I nodded in agreement and followed Alkin out the door. We spoke as we walked. "I have been told by Hunter that you are to be sent on a special mission." Alkin said, hushed, choosing his words carefully as we walked towards the lower chambers. "Hunter said he did not want to know the details of this mission nor did he want to discuss it with you personally, for fear someone else might find out. So he sent me, I will be your go-between for any information on this, and I do mean any." Alkin said with precise authority, he seemed stressed and forlorn at the same time.

I nodded my head; I knew Hunter was very busy. "What does he mean by needing pure magic?" I asked hoping Alkin could shed some light on that. I knew pure magic existed, but it was primarily in nature, untrained people and objects. Alkin just walked in silence, anger crossed his face, and mind.

As we walked the black tunnels and went down the stairs, we turned away from the cellar hall and went towards the warded rooms. I remembered back to the last time we were here. Alkin and I charged the staff, and Howl and I had formed a blood bond. I still had to ask Alkin more information about that.

Entering the room we locked it so no-one would be the wiser as to what was happening. The giant magic light sprung to life as we entered the room, brightening its brown walls and rune marks, dotting its surface.

"As you know we have a council meeting tomorrow. This job has to be done then. Tonight is a full moon and this is the only timing we have to make this right." Alkin said as he ensured the room was secured. He pulled out the Bloodstone and a Moonstone. "We need to imbue this with not only my blood but yours also. The Moonstone will be used afterwards." Alkin said, holding out the Bloodstone we had taken earlier from the Dragon, he placed the Moonstone on the cabinet.

"What is this job, Hunter wants me to perform?" I asked again, eager to know what this secret was.

"I will tell you after we have finished the spell. There will be no denying the mission or spell, I am to see it goes that way." He said as he approached, stopping, so he was directly in front of me.

I nodded, and we began the spell. Together and in unison we called the dark arts to imbue the Bloodstone with our magic. Once again the Bloodstone's pure and wild magic responded and lapped at our hands with tendrils of pure bright energy. And again I could tell the price was great, much greater than the last blood price.

I felt myself stagger, but Alkin held my hands still as the spell went on. I knew afterwards I would need a great deal of blood to heal, and was not thrilled about that. Just as darkness threatened to overtake me, I felt the stones magic release its hold. The blood price was paid, and Alkin and I were huddled on the floor together. Alkin smiled as I looked up at him before he stood and pulled me over to a nearby chair. Opening the cabinet he pulled out a couple bottles of blood.

Alkin and I were both drained from the spell, darkness tried to envelop me once more. At that moment, I was thankful Mystics could drink blood to replenish lost magic and energy. One of the similarities we had to Shadow Walker's.

This blood was the same kind that I had when I first awoke from the poisoning. I chased those thoughts away; whatever it was, it helped. I finished the bottle and felt much better. Finally I felt able to get to my feet on my own.

"Now, for the next part." Alkin said as he picked up the Moonstone. "I will draw a magical circle on the floor in which you will stand in the middle. I will be the one to cast the spell, and you will be the one to break the stone, ensuring the spell will take hold." Alkin said as he used his dagger to slice his hand open, and draw a circle in blood on the floor.

I nodded in agreement. The bottled blood was spreading through me, an affect that made me slightly dizzy. I stood in the center and wondered what spell we were preparing.

As soon as Alkin was done completing the circle, he began. The spell he murmured was spoken in our native tongue, the Mystic language. I knew it, but Alkin spoke too fast for me to register what he was saying. I suspected this was due to the no-interference or choice I had in this matter. Suddenly he slowed down, and I was able to hear what he spoke.

"Pulse and wield, course and bind, blood, body, soul and mind." Alkin stated. "Wrought iron, Mithril bind, Wolfsbane power, nature's might, I call the Lunar light."

Dizziness continued to plague me. *A strange spell,* that's all I could think, I wondered what this would lead to. Suddenly I had an uneasy feeling about it. An image of the full moon appeared on the circle around me, strange new magic ran through me, I was powerless against it. I entered a trance and was unable to hear Alkin's words any longer. I could hear his muffled voice and knew what was going on around me, but I felt mesmerized by the moon and the power it gave off.

Suddenly Alkin shouted to break the stone, still in the trance I followed his command, and broke it against the stone floor. The image of the moon became blood red and disappeared from view. The circle itself became a whirlwind and spiraled around me as it filled me with the magic of the spell.

When the wind faded, Alkin stood next to me, kneeling before me meeting my eyes. I was still in the trance but could hear clearly again. "You shall never speak of this spell to anyone other than me. You shall never mention the Moonstone. You will know all the details, but you will do as I say now regardless of your feelings towards the situation." Alkin said with what sounded like spite. "Your job is to attend tomorrow's meeting, and upon its close, you are to get Lord Drake alone and form a Mystic bond with him. Place your mark on him before the moon's magic wears off." Alkin said with authority. Suddenly I felt the spell lock into my very being, binding me to do its bidding.

As the spell faded and the trance feeling left, I became furious. "This is not what I had in mind." I yelled at Alkin as I paced the floor. "Why? Why does Hunter want this? Those Werewolves are disgusting, why would I ever bind myself to one?" I asked, hoping for some answer to this insane plan.

"Because!" Alkin yelled. "I cannot impart those details, but that is your job, and you must do it." Alkin said while walking to the door, opening it and waiting for me to follow him.

He walked with me to my chambers. "Regardless of what you want, that is what will happen." Alkin said once more as he closed the door to the main hall. We were still not done discussing this, and as he left to the small den I followed him.

"What else does Hunter need? What is this pure magic he needs so badly? Does it have to do with this deception I must perform?" I yelled, angered still from the events of earlier. I felt my magic rise in response.

Alkin shook his head, he was angry as well—at what I was unsure, he kept that from me. I closed my eyes to try and steady my racing mind.

As I did so I felt something tear apart deep inside, like shattered glass, I began to fall apart mentally. "I can't do this." I whispered quietly as went to my knees placing my head in my hands.

I felt Alkin grab my arm and pull me upwards. "You are Raihanna Whitervan, Hunter's most prized Elite. This task will be the hardest you have ever faced. Do not say you cannot handle it, I know you better, you can and you will. Through this task, Hunter will be able to harvest pure energy." Alkin said as he pulled me into his arms and into a tight embrace.

Alkin was my closest friend. I didn't have to keep my complete and utter composure around him, he took me for who I was and treated me how I wanted. Not once did I have to worry about how I acted around him, he accepted me for me.

Still a dull ache resonated through my soul and brought tears to my eyes. For one single moment as I pulled back and looked into Alkin's eyes I wanted more. I wanted him as my mate, and wanted a life with him forever. He was my anchor, and forever would be as long as I lived. His emotions were blocked, but still I could feel an emotional battle raging on within. Almost cautiously, he leaned down and stole a kiss. The dull ache subsided but also boomed deeper within my very being. I was thankful for this, for him, at times he kept me sane in the insane madness that my Uncle recently brought.

Council Deception ~ Raihanna

Leaving the girls that morning was harder than anticipated. I was afraid something would go wrong and I would not return to them. Before leaving, I crept into their room and sat by the bed, all the while praying that all would go right. Callina snuggled closer to Deestan in the bed they shared. I brushed her hair out of her face before leaning down to kiss her cheek.

After kissing Deestan's head, I returned to my room. I adorned my breastplate under my armor just in case something went wrong. Afterwards, I stood outside the girl's room, watching them sleep. Alkin was the one who had to pull me away and assure me everything would be fine. Carefully, he took me into the crook of his arm as we left to the council.

Entering the room, realization began to dawn on me, Alkin and I were becoming closer, regardless of what we had planned. It was steadily becoming harder to not act like a bonded pair, or as typical mates did in public. Still in the crook of his arm, he led me to my seat; his hood was drawn but he sat next to me, staying close.

Looking around the room, I scanned the people who were attending. Most of the lesser races had left, leaving only the main races. I saw the Shifter King and Queen, as well as Lord Drake and Briar. Their chancellor was not in attendance, nor did I see the man named Drameon. Lord Drake and Briar sat exhausted from the full moon's magic the night before. I suspected that was the reason for performing the spell now. They appeared either drunk or just magically exhausted.

The meeting went pretty smooth in the beginning. It wasn't until territory was mentioned that Lord Drake became furious and accused Hunter of breaking that agreement and allowed his Vampires to run rampant in his tunnels.

"I heard about that. Regardless I want to assure you that they have been punished." Hunter said sternly. "They were seeking a stone of some kind and lost it in the aftermath of escaping the tunnels. The Vampires who did that were children at best." He assured everyone. I could tell Lord Drake and Briar did not believe my Uncle, but could not prove anything. So they sat quiet.

As the meeting wrapped up I could sense that Lord Drake and Briar were merely walking in a trance state from the magic that possessed them. It was all part of the plan. The spell that danced within me would do its job in this state. As they descended the stair I overhead Lord Drake tell Briar to go on without him. That he wanted to inform Darris and Alihandra on recent events. Gently Alkin nudged my knee indicating it was time to act.

Going to stand beside Hunter, I kept watch, noticing, Darris and Alihandra both glanced my way on more than one occasion. I pretended I didn't notice and just kept my ground, eventually Darris and Alihandra left and Lord Drake seemed to be slightly confused. He staggered slightly and placed his head in his hand, shaking it slightly to clear his thoughts. I wouldn't get a better opportunity. Entering the hall I prepared for my attack, knowing it had to be fast and sudden, and port us away from the area on contact.

Soon as the door closed behind him, I grabbed Lord Drake by the shoulders and did the only thing I knew would catch him off guard; I laid a kiss on his lips as I teleported us away.

As we ported the spell took effect, I felt it grasp not only myself but Lord Drake, as well. The magic poured out of me and over both of us. Neither was immune to its effects nor could we stop the spells forceful energy. Its power was mind numbing, and before I knew what was happening I was already sheathing my dagger, his wrist to my mouth and his blood ran down my chin and tasted oddly sweet.

Lord Drake seemed drunk off the blood I had given him, and slowly I felt him slip into a magically-induced sleep. Carefully laying him onto the ground, I wiped my chin clean. Looking down at him I couldn't help but think how easy it would be to kill him. But looking at my hands I knew I wouldn't. The Mystic mark of a celestial image dotted my wrist and hand, nearly translucent in color, sealing the bond. Irritated at the task I quickly called a portal and returned home.

Unease ~ Drake

As I awoke, I was unsure of why I was near the lake in the old Shifter territory. I had no recollection of how I had gotten here, and had lingering dreams about the girl again. That I had chased her through the woods before she disappeared in a puff of smoke. Because everything was foggy, I wasn't too worried, and figured it was probably due to lack of sleep. I shrugged off the thought, and returned home where I met up with Briar and Saibal.

"There you are." Briar said to me as I walked the main hall. "I was wondering where you disappeared to for so long after the meeting," he said, patting my back as we walked.

Shaking my head, still in the moons trance, "No more drinking the day prior to the full moon and a council meeting, I'm getting too old for it apparently." I said jokingly to Briar as we to meet Saibal at the Goddess statue.

As we entered the tower, we received a blessing from the priest and went up the white spiral staircase. As we entered the small room that overlooked the lake, the Goddess statue stood opaque against the wooden table. Saibal went and peered out the window before nodding and returning to the door standing guard. I knew no one would disturb us.

Briar and I went to the statue and knelt before it. We performed the same ritual so many times. I drew my dagger and ran its blade across my hand as Briar did the same with his blade. Then laying our bloodied hand upon the statue I called the Moon Goddess.

"Goddess please hear our call." I started off saying. "Recently there have been many unsettling events. The Elite are once more coming into power, and that means a new portal might be opened somewhere. I do not know what to do or how to stop this and fear that if we do not act fast our world might crumble all together." I said worried, before adding. "In addition, I am getting antsy waiting to see what Hunter will do; there has to be something we can do. Still I have this strong feeling Raillyn lives, and I want her back." I admitted. I felt Briar's reaction and I knew he too agreed. I was hoping for an answer.

Quietly and whimsically, an answer came. "I know your cause for concern, my child, but do not fear. All is being played out accordingly. In addition, there will be more unsettling events to precede this that will cause more alarm. I cannot do anything about them, nor can I predict their outcome." The Goddess said. "We are at a turning point in Alecien's history and one wrong move could mean utter destruction. I cannot give any more information other than that, my child, please forgive me." The Lunar Goddess said as she left.

Sighing in response, I was hoping for a more secure answer or at least an answer which could give us a direction. At the same time, I was angered. The Lunar Goddess told that Raillyn might return on her own but that we had to wait. I was growing tired of waiting.

The moon's magic still rolled off me mixing with my emotions, angering me in a way. I walked back to The Keep determined to accomplish something today. Briar and Saibal kept pace, and I entered the small den south of my chambers, where I tried to summon Drameon.

Grasping the blue amulet in my hand and sending out a mental call, I hoped he would be able to respond. Instead I got nothing; he was not in Alecien at the time, meaning he was unreachable.

I closed my eyes and walked towards the fireplace. "I grow tired of waiting." I admitted to Saibal and Briar once more. "Hunter is beginning to get out of control, and I say it's time we take action against him." I admitted Hunter had gone too far indeed; more and more his Vampires were on our land and more people ended up missing or dead. I would put a stop to this myself if I had to.

"Are you sure you want to do that?" Saibal asked as he took a seat next to me. "If you attack Hunter then he will have even more reason to lash out at us, or even Raillyn if he has her. But, yes, I agree I am growing tired of waiting also. The Vampires have been encroaching on our land more and more recently. I think it is time to take action." Saibal said in agreement.

Briar nodded, agreeing as well.

I was tired of Hunter's games. There had been no sign of either Raillyn, or Deestan for six years, and I would not stand by while he tried to conquer Alecien. If Raillyn, or Deestan still lived I would storm The Keep and try to go after them, even if it was the last thing I did.

Betrayal ~ Drameon

As a Mystic, I had little hand in the events that were playing out in Alecien. The hand that I did have was through other means and other beings. It was a dangerous path which I tread, with dangerous pawns that helped along the way. This was the life of one with God blood. Something that most of the races on Alecien forgot; instead they started calling some of us Demigods and others Mystic. I couldn't wait until my pawns realized the truth.

"I'm pleased to see you, Alkin," I said as he came through the portal behind me. "Is everything in motion on your part?" I asked, hoping the tides would soon turn.

"Yes, my friend," he said in response. "I have placed the spell on Raihanna just as directed; she cannot speak of it, other than to me," he said with a subtle tone. "Soon we shall find out if the spell performed its true purpose. In addition, Raihanna has formed an alliance with a Drakar, the very one who took her to Aeralain with him. I have yet to find out the details, but he was able to call her to him and they formed a blood bond. So I believe things will be turning our way much quicker than anticipated."

"He was able to summon her to him?" I questioned, deep in thought, knowing that only a Drakar of her power could do this so easily.

Alkin nodded in response. It seemed that the situation was turning even prior to these recent events. Very soon we would have the power needed to finish this task. "Ensure the task Hunter has put before you and Raihanna is completed before she becomes too aware of the situation." I told Alkin before waving my hand to dismiss him.

Next time I met with my friend I had hoped more good news would be brought with him. I was pleased to hear, all our hard work was hopefully not in vain.

Raihanna

After the events of the morning, I felt I needed to drown my thoughts in some much needed mead. Even though the local stuff was tasteless and bitter, I knew if I drank enough I would forget a little of the situation at hand. In addition, Ash and Thierry often visited the tavern after council meetings, so I walked the dusty road, hopeful for some company. While most people avoided me, some stood to the side, bowing as I went by. Vendors asked if I wanted to stop by their shop. I ignored them all and walked on.

Crossing the center of town, the fountain stood tall and proud with its gleaming black surface. The tavern was just on the other side, next to the woodworkers little shop. As soon as I entered I saw Ash and Thierry at a small table in the back of the tavern out of sight of most of the local Vampire's. I went to join them.

The dark atmosphere and smell of sweat, blood and God knows what else tinged the room. As I walked towards the darkened corner where they sat, I watched my step. The floor was filthy, littered with broken bottles, covered in blood stains and various other items. A few unworthy victims lay on the ground amidst their own stench. Most were dead, but the few that weren't looked around with eyes that never seemed to focus; they would die soon.

Last time I had visited the tavern I had an issue with one of the Vampire patrons. He decided to try and get a little too friendly with me and grabbed me as I walked by. He realized his mistake too late. I pulled my dagger out and plunged it into his heart, severing his life source and killing him.

Today I didn't seem to have that issue, and as I walked I saw Ash look up and meet my eyes. He smiled slightly as I went to take a seat next to him. "God, you stink." Ash said as I sat down, "Where did you come from?" he asked in disgust.

Turning, I looked at him irritated. "For your information, I had to attend the meeting and I tried to take a nap afterwards; but that wasn't happening, so I came here." I said, knowing I could not reveal any events of what really happened. "I need something hard, to chase this awful feeling away." I replied as Ash looked at Thierry smiling.

"Well, if that's the case, I guess I could share my personal stash with you." Ash said as he played with a bottle in front of him. "It's the best you will get since the tavern wouldn't be able to match its potency." He smiled as he poured some into a glass.

Looking at Ash questioningly, "So why is Thierry not drinking what you have?" I asked suspiciously, noticing he had a different colored drink.

Thierry laughed at this and replied. "I hate the taste of whatever is in that wretched stuff. The blood is fine, but the herbs or spices used..." He portrayed a grimace of disgust. "No, thank you."

Ash nodded his head. "He just can't appreciate the taste like we can, Raihanna." Ash said, filling his cup once again. "Drink up. You did say you wanted to drown the feeling you had," he said, finishing his cup again.

The red liquid seemed to resemble black blood, but the smell told otherwise. "What is it?" I asked, swirling it in the glass looking at its texture against the sides. I had my suspicions.

"Something I made and prize myself over. It takes a long time to brew." Ash said proudly. "Being what you are, you should be able to stand a few glasses of that before it affects you." Ash said, knowing that even though I rarely drank, it always took a while to get drunk off the tavern mead.

Shrugging, I tossed back the drink, finishing it in one fluid motion. Ash seemed thrilled by this and poured me another glass. The berry-tasting liquid was indeed mixed with blood, it was sweet and at the same time slightly burned, as if magic infused its very essence. It was just like the Darah wine from

Howl, except it wasn't as potent and didn't have the same spices or herbs.

Giving Ash a curious glance, I looked at Thierry. "Hey, why don't you go grab me some water?" Hoping I could get him to leave for a moment or two.

Thierry sighed and stood up before placing his glass on the table and going over to the bar. While he did so, I looked back at Ash. "Hey, can I see your hand?" I asked him while holding my hand out to him. Already I had a dagger ready, I wanted to try something that I had only seen, but was sure I could mimic.

"Sure," Ash said as he placed his hand in mine, before glancing towards Thierry who was already returning. Quickly I brought the dagger across his finger and allowed a few drops of blood to fall into my glass. Ash pulled his hand back swiftly and stunned, just as Thierry put the water down in front of me. "What's the matter, Ash? You act like she tried to bite you." He laughed as he took his seat once more.

Running the blade across my finger, I spoke the same words which I had heard Howl say to imbue the wine. Something was off and I was determined to figure it out. Suddenly my glass glowed blue in color before dying down. Thierry looked surprised while Ash was shocked. "Oh it's nothing, just a little trick I picked up when I went up north." I said, smiling at Ash.

Ash was hiding something; his blood was able to imbue the Darah wine, something which Vampires would not be able to do. "So tell me, how did you do that? What did you do? I guess is the question." Thierry asked while he finished his drink.

"She charged my home-brewed Darah wine is all." Ash said as he drank straight from the bottle. "Where did you learn to do that little spell, I wonder?" I felt Ash reaching towards my mind as if I would relinquish the answer, but my mind was blocked and he got nothing.

Smiling, I replied. "As I said I acquired the little spell from a friend up north, he was visiting from Aeralain and invited me for a drink. I couldn't refuse, since I needed his blood for the totem, now could I?" I said in a mocking tone. "Ash, I'm going to be blunt with you." I started making sure he was listening. "I don't know exactly what you are, but I sure as hell know you are not a Vampire. First off, I know for a fact Vampire's cannot charge Darah wine. Second, you have a bottle that never drains. And lastly, you're one of Hunter's top Elite as am I. Hunter doesn't keep his typical lackeys around for that job. No, instead he keeps people who are unique and special. So what makes you special, Ash?" I said while Thierry looked at Ash, then myself and back towards Ash. I sipped the wine which I had imbued, my heart picked up pace for a moment and felt like a drum.

Red flashed across Ash's eyes, a similar red which Vampire's eyes held in blood lust. I could tell he was contemplating his answer. Before I was able to react, he moved and in a flash and knelt beside me. "Because, love, it keeps things interesting and I couldn't do this to you." Ash said as he laid his lips on mine.

Grabbing my glass, I slammed it into the side of Ash's head. I felt it shatter on impact. Warm blood covered my hands as I finally broke free and ran towards the door. In the streets I felt confused, my heart raced, and my head ached. Somehow I found the entrance to The Keep and raced inside. I was lucky I had found the eastern entrance because I was able to quickly slip up the stairs and to my room without being stopped. Slamming the door shut behind me I slid to the floor and took a few steadying breaths. I sensed Alkin in the lower den, and quickly tried to compose myself.

As he ascended the stairs, I ran into his arms and buried my head into his chest. His scent, which I had never noticed so strongly before, smelled so sweet. Evergreens, mingled with the pungent nature smell of dirt, and moss seemed to pour off him.

"Did you know that Ash has a bottle that never runs out, and it's filled with a home-brewed Darah wine?" I asked, looking into his eyes before he could question me on my whereabouts. "In addition, did you know his blood charges the wine to make it more potent? What the hell is he, Alkin?"

I released him, startled for a moment over my behavior. Turning, I paced the room, my head spun slightly from the charged wine, and I was feeling giddy inside.

I could tell Alkin was trying to sort out the events in his head before he answered. "What do you mean, Ash had Darah wine?" He asked and stood looking at me waiting for an answer.

Pausing for a moment to calm my thoughts I tried to explain. "Ash had Darah wine in the bar this evening. He poured me some, he said only I could appreciate it like he did. I even charged it because I had a feeling something was up. It charged, Alkin; I charged the wine with his blood and mine. It was just like with the Drakar's but different." I said as I leaned against the fireplace, trying to steady my racing heart.

Alkin came and took me into his arms again, trying to calm me down. "Did you drink it?" He asked, suddenly concerned.

Burying my head into his chest and taking in his scent again, I shook my head. "I only had a taste before Ash made a rude comment, and gesture at me. I bashed him in the head with the glass and remaining wine. Then I left to come here."

Sighing, and scanning my thoughts, Alkin took a seat in the nearby chair. "You know Hunter isn't going to be happy that you two are not getting along. This is going to complicate things in the Elite." Alkin said, putting his hands in his lap.

I was shocked, this was all he had to say after everything—that Hunter would be upset that Ash and I had a disagreement. "What the hell? Really? Ash kissed me, and all you can say is that my Uncle is going to be mad." I felt a strange new sensation building up inside me. My body burned, and my power flared with my anger. "Ash is not a Vampire. He's hiding something from us, and regardless of that, we still have not talked more about this Drakar I am bound to. The Darah wine or the effects it brings upon me. What are you not telling me, Alkin? I can feel you're hiding something from me. So what? What is it? Does this all have something to do with the spell I have placed upon me?" I raved on furiously as my power only grew.

"Where did you hear that crazy talk?" Alkin asked as he quickly stood up. Startled, he walked towards me.

As he placed his hand on my shoulder, I felt myself begin to calm. Alkin was pouring his energy into me to calm my racing mind. I threw his hand off and stormed towards the door. "I'm going for a walk, do not follow me." I said as I opened the door slamming it behind me.

Lost in Information ~ Raihanna

I was not sure where to go or what to believe anymore. After leaving The Keep I found myself wandering the woodlands south of the council. After a few hours, I finally decided to take a chance, and try finding Howl. He was the one who had pointed out the fact that I was spelled in the first place, so maybe he would be able to tell me more about it. Concentrating on the easiest location I could remember, I opened a portal knowing it would take me back to Balone.

As the portal faded, I found myself just beside the rear of the inn, directly in front of Howl's house. It still stood tall and quiet, against the smaller houses of Balone's older city section. Carefully I looked around—it was late, and no one was about. Slipping from the shadows, I approached the door and put my hand on its surface. The familiar magical vibrations danced across my hand. Suddenly it stopped and a new sensation took over, a welcoming sensation.

Laying my hand on the intricate handle I pushed the door open, and went inside. "Howl?" I shouted as I closed the door behind me. All was quiet, and I received no answer. "Well, just my luck." I said to myself as I sat down on the pillow-covered bench near the fireplace. "I wonder when he will be back?" I asked as I leaned back to relax for a moment.

No sooner had I closed my eyes than the door burst open, and in walked Howl, along with the man who tried to stop me last time. I had a feeling I was going to have to explain myself, and a few things. Quickly I stood and faced them, unsure what to do or if I should speak first.

"Howl!" was the only thing I could bring myself to say. I was upset at myself, for doing what I had done, and the feeling of guilt at seeing him tried to take over. In addition, the shock of the day had pushed me nearly over the edge. Howl's

Elfin features and piercing blue eyes gazed at me. He seemed crossed between concern and anger at seeing me. Howl's friend stood slightly taller than him, his long, wavy black hair, was tied, and deep-honey eyes gazed at me with suspicion.

His friend was the one who spoke first. The words were unfamiliar to me and yet familiar at the same time. Like something, I had heard many years ago. Howl noticed my confusion and translated for me. "To what do we owe this visit? Back for more blood?" Howl repeated as his friend looked at him and spoke the strange tongue again.

"No, she doesn't." Howl replied back. His friend had a surprised look on his face to this response.

"I have no idea what he said, but I was hoping you could forgive me, and shed some light on my current situation." I said, hoping he would feel my sincerity and forgive me enough to help. His friend seemed suspicious as he took a seat in a chair behind me. Howl stood still facing me crossing his arms in front of him. "What situation?" He asked standing his ground.

Closing my eyes I tried to regain control, the wine still beat at my head, and I felt like I stood on rocky ground since I had argued with Alkin. Emotionally I was unstable, and it was beginning to show. "Well, recently I have discovered there was an Ancient working for the Vampires this whole time. He's one of the Elite even." I began suddenly unable to keep silent on who I was, we were bonded there would be no hiding from him now. "I discovered this because he was stupid enough to be drinking Darah wine in the local bar outside The Keep. I was even able to charge the wine, after watching you perform the spell. I was furious and returned to my chambers, where I argued with my Mystic friend. I mentioned that you said I was spelled, and he seemed to freeze up and shut me out. How am I spelled? What does this mean and how do I get rid of it?" I asked almost hysterically as tears roll down my cheek.

I felt more sincere with Howl than I had ever felt in The Keep where I always had to keep myself in line. Sighing, Howl walked around me and directed at the pillowed bench.

"Sit." He said subtly as he took his own seat. Carefully rounding his friend, I sat on the bench and looked into the fire that seemed to come alive only recently, as if awaken by his presence.

"I think first off we need to know where your loyalties lie before I say anything about this predicament. Tell me about this Elite who had the Darah wine." Howl asked as he leaned back nodding towards his friend. I felt they were having their own personal conversation mentally. It made me wondered when Alkin and I spoke mentally if others felt the same way.

Sighing, I told Howl about Ash, his features, his personality, and how he reacted to me charging the wine. Finally I ended with his behavior towards me, and me smashing the wine glass against his head. Howl seemed amused by this, and smiled slightly. "Alright, sweet cheeks, now tell me are you bound to any of the Gods?" Howl asked carefully.

Looking at him curiously I replied. "What do you mean?"

Howl's friend was the one who responded. "What he means is this. Where do your loyalties lie? You're a Mystic, which means you have God blood. So what God do you serve? Why did you need the blood?" He asked as he looked at me, chin in his hand.

Even before I looked at Howl, I could feel his anger. "I don't understand." I said while Howl got up and leaned against the fireplace. "I don't have any loyalties to any God. I've never even seen one. If what you mean is which God I worship, I follow Daes." I said, trying to think of what he meant.

This seemed to of taken Howl by surprise, and he turned to face me. "You follow Daes?" he asked, while he thought. "You are working for the Vampires and yet you follow Daes?" Howl said as he began to pace.

"How did you..." I began to question before Howl went on.

"Yes, I know who you work for, Raihanna. Your Uncle is none other than Hunter, current leader of the Vampires in Alecien. This Ash fellow I believe might be a Shadow Walker, by what I have seen, and how you described him." Howl was talking as he paced the room. Suddenly I felt even more lost than I had before, and Howl sensed it. "When we exchanged blood, and you marked me, you left your mind open for me to read. While you did not take advantage of the situation, I did, and read most of your memories and thoughts on what you were. That is why I decided it would not be a terrible thing and how I knew you were spelled."

Howl's friend stood at the mention of Shadow Walker. "If he's a Shadow Walker why is he in Alecien, let alone why is he helping the Vampires, unless he's gone rogue. The Vampires killed all the Shadow Walkers who stayed behind." He said as Howl stopped pacing.

"Yes, that's true; unless they spared him in exchange for his assistance, or like you said he went rogue, which is more likely the explanation. As far as the spell you are under, that is much more complicated. It seems like you are in a construct body, but at the same time it seems that you are created from your original body, hence why you were able to have Callina. If that's the case whoever created your body did so precisely and perfectly. The bad thing about this is that construct bodies tend to fail when exposed to large amounts of Ancient magic, and you have been exposed to Aeralain, the very land which breathes of old magic. Also..." Howl trailed off as he glanced at his friend and closed his mind to me.

Fear erupted inside as I felt his response before he was able to contain it. "If I can't find who spelled me, and have them reverse it, I'm going to die." I said quietly as I felt Howl reopen his mind.

Tentatively he replied. "Yes. You see constructs are created to perform tasks by Necromancers. They are created from the soil, plants, blood, and flesh. Once the task is completed, they are usually released from their imprisonment and allowed a true death. However, in your case this was not done by a Necromancer. It's a blood spell and it's not taken lightly when used with living beings. Whatever you did to get yourself in this predicament I couldn't see. But I'm already sure your body is beginning to fail and return to the elements that it was created from." Howl said as he walked over towards me and turned my hands over. "Does anything feel strange or off?" He asked as I sensed he was going to remove my boots and examine my feet. "Claude, my friend here, is a healer in the Shadow Walker town of Zian. Can he examine you with his magic so we know how fast you are deteriorating?" Howl asked as he placed my feet back onto the floor.

I nodded, my head still shocked about all the information I was receiving. Claude came over and leaned in front of me. "This won't hurt a bit, you might feel warm or tingling, but that's all." He said as he closed his eyes and began to quietly murmur a spell in the same strange language as before.

Suddenly a green ball of light appeared in his hand and seemed to jump out and enter my body. Immediately I felt a warm sensation where the light went in, and I could feel it moving around stopping now and again.

Finally, what seemed close to an hour, Claude opened his eyes again and looked at Howl, who had sat back down in the chair. "She seems to be doing okay. Like you said, whoever crafted her construct body did so meticulously. They put a ton of time into it ensuring she could function in a sense like she was in her own body. They made it possible for her to bear children as if she was in her own body, as well. Meaning none of the construct cells were connected in any way to the child Callina; instead it was the original cells from her real body. Her toes are where the wear is beginning to slowly take hold. Possibly in a few months you could visibly see the damage, but for now I believe as long as she stays away from the old magic, she should be fine." Claude said as I heard Howl breathe a sigh of relief.

After standing back up, Claude turned and spoke to Howl in the unknown language. Howl was slightly disturbed by the information that he had learned, and I got the feeling he knew who he should speak with about my condition. I was getting irritated by more secrets. "I'm tired of you talking in that tongue, I don't understand you at all, and I want to know what's going on!" I demanded, trying to compose my natural persona that I felt was beginning to slip away from me.

Howl glanced at Claude before speaking. "Don't worry, sweet cheeks, if we manage to break the spell then I will make sure you learn the language. For now though, is it safe for her to remain in my home?" Howl questioned Claude who shook his head yes. "Good. I say this. Stay here relax and enjoy a little peace. I have a few old friends who I feel I need to speak to about this little predicament you're in. Follow me." Pulling me to my feet, and towards a door, that opened up to a staircase going down.

We went down the stairs. Slowly, I followed behind him. "This is my library, feel free to venture around and read anything you find interesting." Howl said as he mentally shared the location of several books I might find interesting.

The library looked like an old stone cellar. Nice, comfy chairs surrounded a fireplace along the south wall. In the center, a large oak table sat, intricately designed with Elf carvings. A blue celestial rug lay underneath, magic seemed to be everywhere in the home.

Howl led me back to the stairs and back to the main level as he spoke. "I will say this; if you stay, you will not be able to leave. Claude has a room upstairs, through that door." Howl said, pointing towards one of the closed doors.

"You can have this room." Howl opened the door beside him and revealed a small quaint room, with a simple bookshelf full of spell books and maps, a bed and small table and desk. A fireplace stood in the corner, and a washroom was through a small door by the desk. "This is an extra room. My room is off limits, only certain people are able to enter there." Howl pointed towards a door with another intricate handle. "Don't even think about opening it, it's spelled with Drakar magic, and it will burn you. Also, there is a small workshop downstairs that I forgot to show you. If you get the urge to try any spells while I'm away you can find the ingredients there. As I said you will not be able to leave. I will lock all portal entrances to my house and have it remain in its normal location." Howl said while he picked up a bag from the nearby table. "I also keep my kitchen full of food, so feel free to help yourself. Any questions?"

I stood again lost in information. Howl was going to go, and talk to a few friends while he allowed me to reside in his house. "Why can't I leave? And how long will you be gone? I have to get back home." I stated suddenly concerned about how long I would be missing from The Keep.

Howl leaned in towards me before speaking. "That I would not worry about; I will be gone a few weeks, tops. Meanwhile, catch up on the history that was lost to Alecien, or even read about your race. Since you seem to have no knowledge of what a Mystic really is, I think it would do you some good. Plus, this will give me time to see who becomes agitated and begins looking for you, which might reveal who created your construct situation." Howl said as he went to the door and left. I turned towards Claude. suddenly unsure of what I had gotten myself into.

Predicament ~ Alkin

Raihanna had been missing for the past few days. I hadn't seen nor heard from her since our argument, and Hunter was beginning to question me on her whereabouts, which I had no clue about. Frustrated at myself for the situation that happened I walked the marshlands south of The Keep in hopes that I would receive some word on Raihanna.

Just as I turned to go towards the river, a chain blade whizzed past my head nearly missing my face. Several strands of hair fell towards the marshy floor below as it was pulled back towards its owner. Slowly I scanned the surrounding trees for the attacker's location.

"After examining Raihanna further, I had my suspicions you were behind it. Plus I smelled your scent on her." A voice said from the treetops.

Cursing to myself, I recognized the voice, and I double cursed myself for not asking Raihanna more about the Drakar she had found in Balone. "You can come out, Howl. I'm not going to fight you." I said to the treetops.

Howl jumped down from a nearby tree and landed ready to strike if I tried to attack. I knew from past experience that Howl was deadly with his chain blade, so I stood as still as possible. "I know you're not going to fight me. But you are going to tell me why your little poppet is spelled in a construct's body." Howl said, twirling the blade around in circles at his side. "You're also going to tell me why you of all people are working with those bloody Vampires." Howl said as he spun the blade faster.

Closing my eyes, I knew I would have to answer the questions in part if I was to discover where Raihanna was. Howl seemed to know more than what he was letting on.

"Where is Raihanna?" I asked as Howl approached me, still spinning his blade.

With precise speed and precision Howl caught the blade by the handle, stopping it in mid spin. He ran the chain across his other hand ready to start its deadly spin at a moment's notice. "I know where Raihanna is, and who she is. So don't you worry about her. I will release her after I help her situation. As for you, tell me what you know about the spell she's under." Howl demanded, as I shook my head no in response. I could not give out the information he sought else we might lose the upper hand we already had.

Howl sprung forwards grabbing my neck and pinning me against a nearby tree, his chain blade was in hand raised to slice my throat from ear to ear. "What are you hiding, Alkin?" He said as he slightly pressed the blade against my throat.

I knew I could easily attack him, but if I did I had a feeling I would not see Raihanna again. "If you kill me then Raihanna will die." I said knowing he would release me.

He pulled the blade back and stepped away, a slight trickle of blood ran down my neck where the blade had dug into my skin. "You did this?" He asked deep in thought. "Is Drameon in on this also?" He asked suddenly more aware of the situation. Thankfully, he thought this was the case and not what was really behind those words. I didn't reply and stood my ground, unsure of what Howl would do.

Years ago we had been friends and allies who worked together for Drameon and his mate, but that was long ago and much had changed.

"He is, isn't he? Delron smite you both! Hasn't enough happened because of him?" Howl began recalling the previous time we met face to face. "If I had half a sense, I would take her far from you and the troubles you two are bringing her yet again! But I can't do that since you're the only one who can break the spell!" Howl's piercing blue eyes met mine. His magic fluctuated with his emotions. *So like his lineage...*

"You need to tell me more about this situation and what I have gotten myself into. In return, I will tell you this.

Raihanna currently resides at my house with Claude. I'm sure she is studying the Ancient lore and magic Alecien lost. So tell me why have you, of all people, done this to her?"

I was taken aback for a moment. Howl gave her the very items Drameon feared she would discover. I was suddenly nervous on how she would return to us after this little endeavor.

Hesitant, I replied, "Drameon knows more of the details than I do, I'm just following his orders. All I know is that the Gods have their hands in this mess, as well. It stems back to the beginning of the war, maybe even before. That's all I know, I just follow orders." I said flatly hoping he would believe me and release Raihanna.

Howl seemed taken aback by this information. I could tell he was deep in thought by how he played with the chain. "I think I'm going to pay Drameon a little visit," he said as he opened a portal and disappeared.

Damn Drakar, I thought. The only other race aside from Mystics who had the ability to use portals without other means were the Dragons and their blooded kin.

Drameon

The swirling portal opened behind me as I scanned the nearby bookshelf. I anticipated it was Alkin until I sensed the energy, and I prepared myself for a possible attack from the assailant. As the portal closed, I slowly let my guard down. Howl stood before me; his same long, black hair hung in a mess around his face while his fair Drakar features gave an almost Elf like appearance. But his piercing blue eyes could never be replicated by any normal race and told an entirely different story. They were like blue ice, imbued with fiery magic that could pierce your very being.

Relaxing slightly, I turned back towards the shelf, and continued to try and find what I needed. "Hello, Howl. How many years has it been?" I asked, finally finding the volume I needed and pulling it from its resting place.

Howl did not seem happy to see me and I couldn't blame him. The last time we had stood face to face was under strenuous circumstances.

"I'm not here for small talk, Drameon." He said as he pulled out a nearby chair, which surrounded the carved table adorning my library. "I'm here because I have been fortunate to acquire a little bird temporarily." He said, smiling at me in a mocking way.

Curiously, I sat down across the table to hear him out. "Oh, how so? And what little bird could this be?" I asked. I was used to playing these games and so was the Drakar.

Pulling out a small red amulet, he placed it on the table; the once red stone shone black in color. It was Raihanna's amulet, the one that Hunter had given her for using portals. "Oh, I think you know what little bird I have and if I'm not mistaken, I know who she is. Am I wrong?" He asked in a curious manner.

Deep down I knew that the knowledge would get out, Raihanna was all too important—or should I say Raillyn was all too important. For over two hundred years her identity had been kept secret, since the very beginning of the war, when the Gods ferried her away. I was as surprised as anyone when I saw her at Chaimh's so many years ago. I had asked many questions that night before I made the conclusion to her identity myself. Still it was years until Alkin told me he had been following her since she was a child, and it still bothered me in a way.

Slowly, lost in thought, I nodded my head. "Yes, you are right. And if you have her that means Claude is with her, isn't he? And she is residing in your house currently, yes?" I asked, knowing how Howl worked and the precautions he took.

I knew he would have sealed every portal of his house but the main one, and even then it would be spelled so no one would enter or leave. It was in a secluded location of Aeralain that few ventured, far to the north near the Drakar city of Silvertine. If I trusted anyone in Aeralain with information on Raihanna and Raillyn it would have to be Howl, and his partner Claude.

Regardless, I was still hesitant because of the tender situation. This complicated things but at the same time I felt made them slightly easier. Howl, on the other hand, was proud of his new-found knowledge. "Yes, and Alkin said I shouldn't be letting her learn from the old texts, but I feel if she has no knowledge of the deception the Vampires in Alecien wrought, than she would not be careful of them while she resided in The Keep. Yes, that being said, I will release her. I do not plan to keep her hostage regardless of her reputation." Howl said while smiling and continuing. "Who all knows about her?" He asked hushed as if speaking the words would bring the Gods down upon us.

"Only a few, and it has to stay that way until she does what needs to be done. Go ahead and teach her a brief history of the beginning of the war. It's no secret to the Gods that she was involved in it, one way or another. Teach her to be wary of the Vampires. Do what you do best, Howl, and guide her if you want but you must return her to The Keep. Her construct body cannot handle the magic in Aeralain. It's the one place I have been trying to keep her away from since the beginning. I suspect you know that already since you have Claude helping you." I said as I went to stand next to the fire.

Many of the events which lead up to this moment flashed across my mind, much had been lost, and great prices had been paid and were still being paid. It would take centuries before the balance was restored again, but I knew we were on the right track. We only had to keep Raihanna where she was supposed to be, so Raillyn could return.

Howl seemed pleased by this answer. He stood, bowed, and left in a portal of smoke. I prayed he would do as he was told, and return Raihanna to Alecien.

Lost History ~ Raihanna

The history of the Mystic race was simple—the Mystics were born from the Gods themselves, children of the Gods, or ones of God blood they were often called. They were the first children of the world of Auran. They were Demigods. Next came Dragons that were created to be protectors, and assistants to the Mystics. Hand in hand, they would work together to serve the Gods themselves and ensure peace and prosperity in the world. Only children born directly from a God was born with the Mystic blood, or children who were born out of a union between two Mystic born.

If a Mystic had a child with any other race that child was a half-breed, and did not have the typical traits of the pure bloods. Half-bred children would take after their non-Mystic parents. Their eyes would be a set color and their magic would equally be set.

The only time this was ever different was when the first Mystics took Dragon mates, in human form. This resulted in the Drakar race, breeding within their magic lineage. The Gods planned on this, and made certain they had mates between both races, allowing the blood to mingle accordingly for both Mystic, and Drakar offspring.

A Mystic child had the distinct features of an Elf with ever-changing eyes, and the ability to cast all forms of magic. Mystic children tended to become bonded to their God lineage. Half-breeds were free from this burden. It was a flip of the coin to which lineage the child would follow, either their mother's magic, or their father's, but one would prove true.

Mystics were raised to learn to obey their parents, respect the Gods, and follow the simple rule of not disobeying and changing the natural flow on Auran. This meant that they were able to have say in events, but could not actually have a direct part in the outcome. They could not outright lie for an outcome of their own personal choice. They were not allowed to take the lives of anyone who was not threatening their own immediate life. Only in a life and death situation was taking a life acceptable.

All Mystics had to play their cards carefully if one got to out of line their God lineage would reprimand, or punish them. As long as they did not interfere too much with the nat-ural events of the created races the Gods placed in Auran the balance would keep steady. But with peace one must remem-ber chaos is a needed aspect as well, for good cannot live without evil, and even in Auran justice does not always win.

The beginning of the Alecien war was similar in this as-pect. Yes, the Vampires did a great unjust but so did an An-cient. Over two-hundred and fifty years ago the Vampire race had been experimenting with a powerful blood magic spell, they had taken and drained several Ancient races but the blood they retrieved was always too weak, and was never po-tent enough to accomplish their task. Somehow they ended up capturing a Mystic, who they brought to The Keep, tortured and drained. Her blood was the key to the power they sought, and with her blood they were able to resurrect Demons and dead things from the depths of Death's Realm. These were the first troops the Vampires used in battle.

At first the Gentry, and the Vampires in the high council said they had acquired this skill as a gift from their God Delron, but after he came they changed their story. The Vam-pires were careless and in killing the Mystic woman brought the wrath of her mate down upon them. Even though he knew he should not play a hand, he still had attacked and slain the Vampires who had a hand in her death.

The Vampires on the high council, that consisted of the oldest and wisest from each race, first blamed the Mystics. Saying they had revolted against the Gods themselves and should be slain. This caused the first wave of death which spread across Alecien. Many of the Mystics who resided in peace had now been killed because of the attack. The Shadow Walkers, Drakar, Dwarves, Dragons, and other Ancients came to the aid of the Mystics. Knowing their Death would spell the end of their world.

Many were slain by the Vampires, and their monstrous creations. Not long after, the Werewolves got involved, it was discovered that it was their Den Master who was drained, the Mystic who first died. With the High Council now in shambles, war running rampant, and many races fleeing, it was the Gods who intervened.

They commanded the remaining Mystics to leave Alecien, to allow the Werewolves and Vampires to fight their war because this was what should have been. While amidst the bloodshed, a Drakar discovered an issue. As the healthy Ancients left he stayed behind to aid a mortally wounded friend.

The last adult Mystic of Daes' blood line, the two allies, were able to battle through the Vampire lines and attack the remaining High Council members, who took the true knowledge of the war to their deaths. It was the Mystics final task from his lineage God. After his Death, the Drakar was taken from the midst of battle and placed in a safe haven but not before discovering that Daes' Mystic line was not dead.

One single child remained, and the Gods themselves whisked her away from the bloodshed and chaos. Her little mind could not handle the strong emotional toll of her mother's death and her father's slaughter. Even the war taxed her emotions. So in an effort of preserving the nature of Daes and his Mystic child she was placed under a deep spell, unable to awaken till she was able to be released.

In the end, the Ancients who remained in Alecien died, and with them the true cause of the war. Only those who remained across the Silver Sea remembered what really occurred so long ago. The war lasted over two-hundred years because balance could not be restored, would not be restored. It was as if the very land itself knew Daes' last Mystic kin, was gone from the world, and it was thrown into total anarchy.

The Werewolves fought the Vampires and their creatures with the aid of the Shapeshifters, and one necromantic Elven family, who the Gods themselves asked to remain and assist.

The magic of the land died from the lack of Mystic contact, the Dragons all but forgotten, slept deep underground from the dissipated magic that once traveled through the land. Alecien had become a dying continent.

Finally at the end of the war, not only was history lost, but the natural flow of magic, the balance of the land, and knowledge of their very creation was lost, as well. Anyone remaining on Alecien had become fearful of Aeralain, and their old ways. It seemed almost barbaric, or taboo to be able to have a house with several portals that opened up to several different locations, really anchored elsewhere. It was unheard of to have bottles of wine that would seem to never empty and always refill, hours later. So those who had escaped across the Silver Sea were never truly welcomed back.

Howl had drilled this information into my head since the moment he arrived home, saying I only had the rest of the week before I was to return back to The Keep. Now that I had learned this information I was beginning to be unsure of who to trust anymore.

He even told me the story of how the Vampires were really created. That a rogue Shadow Walker had stumbled into Death's Realm using blood magic and was in a sense cursed by Delron. The information was informative, and in a way frightening. I was a Mystic, one of God's blood, this much I knew.

Sadly, I was lacking in other areas, I didn't know what my lineage God was or what my purpose was being in a construct body, or if it had to do with the Gods themselves or not. Even Howl was unyielding to these questions regardless how much I pestered him. So many of my questions had been answered but at the same time so many left untouched.

Howl paced the room in front of me. "I would ask your Uncle more about this Shadow Walker on the Elite. I think if the Vampires wanted you dead they would have done so long ago. They obviously need you alive for something." Howl said as I grabbed my cloak, tossing it over my shoulders. "I wouldn't worry too much just do as you've been doing. The

Gods don't seem to care, and you are still alive." He said trying to be comical.

I nodded my head as I fastened my cloak around my neck. For a moment my hands lingered by my neck, my necklace was gone. I had given it to Howl when he stopped in briefly last week. Howl had said I didn't need it any longer for using the portals. All I had to do was call the magic around me, and picture the location in my mind, a Mystic ability.

Howl went over to the door, and altered the location it would open out into. The door was able to link to several different places, but only those trained, and bonded to Howl could use this. I was untrained in the spell but watched as he performed it, knowing one day I might have the skill.

When he opened the door, I walked out into the snowy streets on Balone. Turning to Howl I bowed and said goodbye. He had told me he would not move the location of the Balone portal for his house, so if I needed him or just wanted to go and study up on more books, I was more than welcome. No one was behind the bar at this hour, so I was able to sneak into the shadows quietly.

Concentrating on The Keep and the halls of the second floor, I silently opened a portal and walked through its shadowy embrace. The cold stone floor and equally cold walls came into view. Few servants wander the halls on the other side of The Keep, away from my chambers. I was sure though that one would tell my Uncle I had been seen.

Quietly, I spoke the spell to unlock my door and slipped in silently. All was quiet, and the girls were nowhere to be seen. Even the lower den was empty; I wondered where Alkin and the girls were at this hour. Suddenly a knock sounded. Ascending the stairs from the dark den below, I had a feeling I would not be happy with who came to fetch me.

Opening the door revealed Ash, who gazed at me with suspicion; his bright brown eyes seemed to glow with energy. "It's so good to see you home, Raihanna. Your Uncle would like a word with you about your disappearance." Ash said while turning to walk towards Hunter's quarters.

Quietly I followed him. "So where is Alkin?" I asked unsure what events were happening since I left weeks ago.

Ash glanced at me as if surprised. "Hunter sent him out with the others to lead a mission. He should be back after this evening's meeting." Ash said as we rounded a corner.

I nodded in understanding. I knew with my absence that Hunter would resort to sending Alkin out to lead missions in my place. "Why do you reek of Drakar?" He said pausing about ten feet from my Uncle's door.

Glancing at Ash, I could tell he knew where I was, and it was obvious he did not care for it. "Why do I need to tell you, Shadow Walker?" I said in a mocking tone. "It's none of your concern, and just to inform you, I was gathering information."

The silver hint of Ash's blade caught my eye seconds before he could strike my chest. Calling my blackened blade I parried his attack and jumped back to strike, catching him off guard I tore his shirt and inflicted a gaping wound on his bicep. Ash cursed before coming at me again. Our blades let out an ear-piercing clash as they met, the crackle of the charged blades nearly threw us backwards from the blow. Jumping back I prepared another attack, Ash was quicker, and as I went high, he went low. His blade tore into my leg.

Steading myself, hands forward on the floor, I heard my Uncle's door suddenly open. "Raihanna! Ash! I will not have my top two Elite fighting in the halls. Get in here this instant and tell me what this is all about!" My Uncle shouted as I dissipated my blade and Ash sheathed his. "And, Ash, I told you to retrieve my niece, not to wound her." He continued as Ash walked into the main den of my Uncle's chambers. Slowly I stood and inspected my leg. Thankfully it was nothing more than a scratch and would heal fast.

Going into the den, the black shades were pulled shut, and the large table was littered with various books and items. The large magic light glowed from its resting place on the ceiling. Many empty blood bottles littered a smaller table near the fireplace. Taking my place beside Ash, my Uncle rounded the table before turning towards us.

"Now tell me, Raihanna. Where in the Death's Realm have you been? I have had Alkin, Ash, and many others searching for you, but it seemed that you just disappeared." My Uncle said, rounding the table once more to stand next to Ash and I.

Glancing at Ash I answered Hunter. His greasy brown hair was slicked back in a messy way, revealing a balding spot. His teeth had become a rust-like color as he smiled at me. "I was gathering information, about the portal and its ability to summon and call various Demons and dead creatures from Death's Realm. I was trying to find something that might assist us more than what we already have." I said trying to bluff about the information I had learned during my time with Howl.

My Uncle looked at me, unsure if he should believe me or not. "Alright, good. I'm glad you studied up on that subject. I was wondering the same thing if there was anything we could do to summon stronger Demons to us. And you, Ash?" My Uncle said as he looked towards Ash.

Glancing at my Uncle he went over the events. "We just had a disagreement is all." He said while looking at me.

I would not sit by any longer about this. "No, he's a Shadow Walker." I said while pointing towards Ash.

My Uncle just looked at me, not surprised. "Yes, I know that. And, unlike you, he has stayed here serving me and hasn't run off in search of his own personal information or other affairs, as I recall." Hunter said, angered. "Plus he's rogue, he hates his kind and what they stand for. He is loyal to us and our cause. What about you, my niece? Why is it you return to us reeking of Drakar?" He asked as Ash backed up and Hunter closed the gap between us.

Before I could react, Hunter grabbed the back of my head and slammed me down onto the table, smashing my nose and lip against its hard surface. "I would say you are having loyalty issues, child. Now tell me why you reek of Drakar? And the Gods help you if you say it's another one of your abhorrent plans." Hunter said while pressing my face harder onto the table.

Every bone in my face hurt, I knew my nose was broken, and lip was split. This would not be a quick heal unless Alkin had more of the stronger blood around. As Hunter pressed my face harder, I felt bones bend, and fracture, finally I couldn't take it any longer. "I went to speak to the Drakar who I acquired blood from. That's why I smell of Drakar. He was the one who told me that I could summon stronger creatures with a stronger portal structure." I cried out in pain.

I felt Hunter grab my hair and toss me backwards onto the floor. "And where were you during this little chat? Why was no one able to find you? Give me one good reason why I shouldn't punish you further." He asked as he pulled his dagger and put its blade against my cheek.

I shuddered in fear for a moment. It had been years since I had been chastised like this, and I hated the treatment. Usually he was easy on me, but with Ash here I knew he wouldn't let me off like usual.

As the blade pressed against my cheek, I told him where I had been. "I was in Aeralain, I don't know where. I have no idea, just that the house resides in Aeralain, and there was a portal in one of the northern towns. The Drakar found me because I went north to search for any older lore." I said in my half-truth. "And you won't kill me because you need me! If I die then the portal that has been erected will crumble and you will never get the chance to mix such blood again." I cried out and met his eyes.

Hunter withdrew the blade and placed in back in his belt. "I'm glad to see you're not lying to me and equally glad to see you learned that bit of information. It means I don't have to caution you to proceed carefully from now on. Now go get yourself cleaned up, you have a council meeting to attend!" He yelled as I got up off the floor and went to the door.

Carefully, I walked the halls. I would not show any weakness here where I was watched. However, upon entering my chambers, my solid composure fell apart and tears ran down my face.

Howl was right; the Vampires wouldn't kill me because they needed me. I was still confused about one part though, something Howl didn't explain. Why were the Vampires summoning Daes, the God of balance and harmony? I knew during our wayward history the old God Delron was lost to the Vampires because of his believed ways. Daes was adopted afterwards because of his chaotic nature, but with his chaotic nature came harmony at the same time. The Vampires forgot that though.

As I thought this I knew I had to hurry. I didn't want to suffer any more of my Uncle's wrath tonight. So I stood up and went to the washroom. Even using a light healing spell couldn't do much to help my appearance; it only made the wounds look old. Eventually, after doing the best I could without the aid of strong blood to help heal, I went to the meeting.

Subtle ~ Raihanna

In many ways, as I walked the corridors towards the council room, I feared what events might unfold. The meeting we were attending was a simple one. Land agreements would be signed while harvest and vendor trade purposes were brought forth. My face hurt and was an ugly color, I was sure I would get a few curious looks.

Walking through the doors, I took my seat on the lower level and noticed the Shifter King and Queen were present but the Wolves were not.

"We are sorry to inform you that Lord Drake and his people are unable to make the meeting this morning. We are sitting in to relay information to them in their place." Darris said to Hunter, who had noticed their absence as well.

I sat in silence and listened, thinking about the events that had been happening around me. All the events that had lead me to this moment, and what I should do about them. Who could I trust anymore? And what should I believe....

As the meeting finished up—most of it I had missed due to my own thoughts—Hunter finished with his closing state-ment. "In addition to this meeting, if you and Queen Alihandra could inform Lord Drake of the signing. Since they did not attend I can send some peace representatives to get the papers signed if he wants to do it on his own ground and terms." Hunter said while King Darris and Queen Alihandra both nodded.

"We will let Lord Drake know and inform him of your offer. I'm sure he will send word about it later." Darris said as the meeting wrapped up.

Aurielle and I went on our way. She accompanied me to my chambers. As we walked, she asked what happened and if I was punished by Hunter. I kept quiet. I was not as outspoken about my punishments as my sister and instead nodded my head silently.

As soon as we entered my chambers, she sat in one of the comfy red chairs which adorned the den. My fireplace was burning brightly and had warmed my chambers nicely.

"I still can't believe Hunter smashed your face and didn't give you any blood. He knows Alkin is with Ashoten and Thierry and can't assist you. Plus most of us are not good at healing." Aurielle said casually and solemnly, unsure of what to do.

I shrugged, "Personally I don't care." I replied "When Alkin returns I'm sure he will have something to speed the healing process. I just wish I studied more healing magic while I was away." I sat laughing to myself before having to catch my breath. As we sat and talked, the door to my chambers opened.

Alkin walked in and stood in front of Aurielle and me. "Hunter has received word from Lord Drake and he wishes for you two to be our peace representatives to meet with him at his castle." He said, before looking at my face. I felt his response and his magic reach for me. I knew he would not speak freely in front of my sister. She often was a rat and told Hunter everything.

Chasing concern away for the time being, I looked at him questioningly, curious to know why I was to go. Especially after the events that had happened. But Alkin continued before I had a chance to say anything further. "He wants to see you before you go. So, please, follow me." I felt Alkin struggle internally with what he was told to do and what he wanted to do. He wanted to help heal my wounds but was commanded to hurry and retrieve my sister and me. Knowing this, he tried his best to do as Hunter wanted so we wouldn't suffer his wrath anymore. Alkin walked to the door while Aurielle and I followed not far behind. We walked the halls in silence as we went to Hunter's den.

Entering the room, I felt the stares of the other Elite. Ash was slouched against a corner, speaking with Thierry. Hunter was hunched over in his usual spot, looking over the various items on his large table. My blood still stained its surface.

When we shut the door behind us, Hunter stood up. "I'm glad Alkin found you so soon, I was wondering what else to do if you were late." He said, smiling at me maniacally as he walked around the table handing me a sealed document. "You and Aurielle are to be my peace negotiators. You are to go to Lord Drake's castle on peaceful terms and get him to sign this document." Hunter said sternly, "That means you will not cause trouble of any sort. If I hear of an ounce of trouble, you both shall suffer my wrath." Hunter said before he turned back to his work.

"Why us?" I asked, rather upset because he chose us. "Why not someone else?"

"I choose you two because I know you work well together. Plus I figured you would jump for a moment to redeem yourself, Raihanna." Hunter stated tartly, waving us to move on while he pressed his nose back in the book. Pissed off, Aurielle and I entered the halls, leaving the others behind.

I was getting tired of this endeavor, tired of the lies, and tired of the secrets.

Returning to my chambers, I left Aurielle as she went to gather a few items of her own. We were told to dress normally, and to appear subtle and peaceful. I still felt uneasy and adorned my Elite chestplate under my regular clothes, I hoped I wouldn't need it. However, this way if something happened, I would still be somewhat protected. Before leaving I grabbed my red cloak and tossed it over my shoulders. Entering the hall, I felt like a blazing ball of fire, my temper was getting the better of me, and I wasn't going to deal with anymore bullshit today.

Uneasy ~ Raihanna

Nearing the castle, we dismounted and walked. My temper had cooled somewhat during the ride, and I was thankful. I was wanting us to appear as harmless as we could. So all blades and weapons were left at home. The Werewolves would know that didn't mean anything though, we could still use our magic. Lord Drake and Briar had already seen some of what I was capable.

Aurielle and I walked in silence. unsure of what we should say to one another in the land of our enemies. Not long after approaching the village near the castle, we were approached by what I assumed was the Captain of the guard. It was the same guard from the Northern Peak; his dirty dishwater blonde hair shone in the sunlight as he approached us.

"My name's Captain Saibal and we're to accompany you to the castle. But first we must search you for weapons and ensure you will not cause us trouble." He said as two female guards each began patting us down. For a second, he noted my face but said nothing.

"All's clear, sir." One said as she backed up and took her position next to the captain.

"Same here." The other guard replied. Captain Saibal nodded and turned to leading the way to the castle. The female guards waited for us to follow, before bringing up the rear. They were taking no chances with us. They held no trust for us or our kind. Aurielle and I felt the feeling was mutual and just hoped to get back home alive.

A lush green forest surrounded buildings, shops, and houses that lined stone streets. A large, black onyx fountain lay in the middle of it all, gleaming in the sun. The townspeople stared at us as we walked. Most had not seen a Vampire and those that had wondered what we were doing so close to the castle. Ignoring them, we neared a giant stone cliff. In the cliff was a cave. Two more Mythril armored guards stood beside the entrance, each wore the Wolves insignia on their armor.

Nodding politely to the other guards, we entered the tunnel. It seemed to be used frequently. Unlike the deeper tunnels, this one was well lit, and less musty. *It must be the main passage between the castle and village below.* I thought to myself as we left the caves and walked along a balcony and through a door. Everything seemed to be happening so fast, they gave us little time to dilly dally too long in one area.

The halls of the castle was lined with a plush red carpet running the length of its golden walls. Various artworks hung, and I glanced at them momentarily as we walked on; they seemed to be various scenery paintings. One of the guards coughed behind me. I suspected she thought I shouldn't be so curious, so I kept my eyes forward and walked on.

Finally we stopped, a large door lay in front of us. Captain Saibal opened it and led us into a giant throne room. Lord Drake, Briar, the Shifter King, and Queen, and their Chancellor sat at a large wooden table. The room had elegant Mythril walls trimmed in gold and white paint that matched the floor. Various tapestries hung from the walls. Several had the royal crest, a wolf's paw print. Large white pillars stood dotting the immense room, holding up the exquisitely sculpted ceiling.

Immediately everyone at the table stood, and Lord Drake looked us over. He too seemed unsure about my face but remained quiet. Through the bond, we now shared I could feel he was concerned and unsure about the situation. Fortunately he was not able to utilize the bond effectively; only Ancients could utilize it properly.

Quickly he looked at his Captain. We stood in silence for the moment. "They're clear and carry no weapons." Captain Saibal said to Lord Drake and the others. "They only had this, which was found during the search." The Captain said while handing Lord Drake the documents Hunter told us to have signed. Aurielle had been carrying them, and in my distraction I hadn't noticed they were removed.

Being the one to lead the Elite on various outings, I took charge of the situation. "We were instructed to come and ask for you to please sign the documents. That is all. We mean no harm nor will we cause any trouble." I said calmly and politely, hoping not to stir up any trouble. I could sense unease from everyone in the room. They did not enjoy us being there anymore than we enjoyed it.

Lord Drake took the papers and glanced over them. Afterwards, he handed them to his Chancellor to look over a final time. While the Chancellor looked over the documents Lord Drake looked us over more thoroughly. I could tell he was debating on saying something about my face. He was not the only one that seemed to want to say something.

"These are the exact documents which you signed ten years ago, my Lord. Nothing has changed in them other than updating the information. It is safe to sign." The Chancellor said while handing the documents back to Lord Drake who took them and signed them.

Aurielle stood beside me looking at Queen Alihandra, smiling. "So, sweet sister, I'm glad to see you are doing so well." Aurielle said to Alihandra trying to make small talk as Lord Drake signed the papers.

Queen Alihandra gave a cocky smile and replied harshly. "A much better choice than you made and mine was not done by deception!" Queen Alihandra said with spite. "Now what are you doing running around with some beaten Vampire?"

I was highly angered by this comment and rage started to boil up inside. It would be easy to call up a spell to silence her or better yet dispose of her. But I was told to behave, and I knew if I called any spell it would possibly mean my death. I could not risk such a thing.

Aurielle seemed annoyed by the Queen's response as well. I felt her begin to draw power, for a possible attack.

"Aurielle, you will not do anything!" I said sternly, taking a step towards her, staring her straight in the eyes. Aurielle quickly let her power fade, and she stood quiet once more.

King Darris quickly grabbed Alihandra and pulled her back. "I knew this was a bad idea right when I saw them walk through the door. Excuse us, and I'm sorry for her words and actions." King Darris said as he pulled Queen Alihandra out of the room, back towards the halls.

The Queen was obviously upset, but she allowed her King to remove her without much fuss. King Darris nodded towards Lord Drake apologetically as they left the room. Lord Drake nodded in understanding before turning back to us.

"Sorry for that outburst, but I do find it strange that you are injured and still you were sent to us." Lord Drake said to us while he held out he documents, the situation calmed a little.

He seemed understanding of my sister's anger and accepted my reprimanding of her. I took the documents from Lord Drake and replied to the comment since everyone in the room seemed just as curious for an answer of some sort. He was truly concerned by my appearance and anticipated asking if I was abused.

"Well, that's none of your concern, now is it?" I said while in turn handing the papers to Aurielle.

He gave a half nod response as if he expected no more answer than that "Let me escort you to the main entrance." Lord Drake said while leading the way.

After exiting the main halls, we entered a courtyard. The whole castle seemed to gleam an onyx color. Whether it was man made or made by magic, I didn't know. Silver ran in streaks across its black surface. It made me wonder what material was used in its construction.

The courtyard was full of stalls and various buildings. Ahead of us laid a large gate, and as I looked around I paused for a moment next to what appeared to be an armor stall. A chestplate hung from a wooden dummy, gleaming in the sunlight. Lightly I touched it before the guards detoured me back to Aurielle's side. Lord Drake equally gave me a warning look.

Walking on, I thought about the armor. It seemed familiar in many ways, it felt like it lightly gave way as if it was flexible. Its soft surface was cool to the touch, almost like metal. I made a mental note to look into this further later.

On the other side of the gate lay a large lake, its iridescent waters sparkled as we walked on. Ahead I could see a large bridge leading to the forest beyond, on the other side I saw our horses waiting casually in the field. "This is where we part ways. Thank you for taking the time to bring me the documents." Lord Drake said as he waited for us to proceed.

I bowed slightly while my sister went on ahead. "Our pleasure." I said before following her.

As I mounted my horse, I noticed he still stood on the edge of the bridge, waiting for us to depart from view. *Wolves are such an untrustworthy race*, I thought as I pressed my horse onwards towards home.

Chestplate ~ Raihanna

After arriving back at The Keep, I had my suspicions about the item I had seen in the Wolves' castle. We had reported to Hunter and gave him the documents. He asked us to draw a map of where we went. Even though it was small, it gave us a semi-view of the castle itself.

When I returned to my own chambers, I noticed a light from the lower den, figuring it was Alkin, attending to business. I quietly went about my own, still unsure on who to trust.

After I removed my outer clothing, along with my chest plate, I placed it on the bed and examined it closer. At first glance, it appeared to be leather, but when placed in light it shined as metal, even the temperature of it was metal like. It was even extremely flexible. Alkin had told me it was made of Mythril and Hunter wished to acquire more.

Going to the window to inspect it further, I sat under the moon's light, it looked no different. So I unclasped the sides and turned it inside out, even the clasps seemed similar to the one I had seen in the Wolves' castle. I wondered if Hunter had acquired this from them and if that was one reason as to why I was sent as a 'peace representative'.

As I was looking it over further, Alkin came quietly into the den. Lost in my thoughts, I had forgotten he was in the lower den. Surprise crossed my face momentarily as I realized I barely had any clothes on. Pushing that thought aside. I didn't let it bother me any longer.

"What are you doing?" he asked as he sat next to me, catching my thought momentarily and smirking at it.

I had become so accustomed to Alkin I no longer cared what I wore or did around him. He would never do anything I didn't want and respected me fully, so it mattered little to me what he saw. In addition, it wasn't like he hadn't seen it already.

Carefully he removed the chestplate from my grasp. Turning it over and looking at it as if something was damaged, before placing it aside and looking my face over. I tried to shrug him off not wanting to show how much it bothered me.

Sighing Alkin stood up and walked down the hall towards his room. I looked back at the chestplate as I heard him looking for something. Before I could inspect it further, he returned, carrying a bottle of blood with him.

Breaking the seal he handed it to me. "Here, this will help you heal fast." Alkin said before taking a seat again next to me. Leaning back, he lounged casually as I slowly sipped at the bottle. It was the same powerful, bitter-tasting blood that held strong magic. I knew this would heal my wounds by morning.

Looking back to the breastplate, I knew I had to press this matter further. "Where did Hunter get this chestplate?" Before meeting his eyes, "It's Werewolf made, isn't it? From Lord Drake's people?" I asked, more direct.

Alkin picked the chestplate up and turned it over in his hands. "Hunter wants to keep it quiet. As I've told you, he wants to get more of these and if anyone finds out where it was acquired from, all of the Elite would be after them. You, being his niece, were the first to acquire one. Plus, since you hold more authority over the others, you needed it." Alkin said matter of fact while setting the armor aside and relaxing into the chair once more.

His emotions shifted and I felt myself wanting to lay and relax with him. Even this far away the scent of a mossy forest filled my nose. Averting my gaze I looked at the chestplate, I knew he was right. It was extremely difficult to get anything like this.

His hands reached out to me and carefully pulled me to him. Gently he laid my head on his chest, and I could hear the steady beat of his heart. Casually it picked up pace from my touch. "Hunter told me you returned last night. He also informed me you were punished due to your disappearance. I know you went to speak with Howl because he paid me a little visit." He said holding me lovingly. "What did Howl teach you?" Alkin asked curiously as he played with a loose tendril of my hair.

Howl hadn't hid the fact that he paid Alkin a visit, I had known all along. It was the information exchanged between the two that I could not access.

"Not too much, he did tell me that the real reason the war broke out was because a Mystic sought revenge when he shouldn't have. That he disobeyed the Gods, who were already handling the situation of a drained Mystic, his wife." I said while relaxing further into him. Already the effects of the blood made me feel better. "He said I had access to his home anytime I needed it."

Alkin nodded in reply before leaning down and gently laid a kiss on my hair. Snuggling into him further I smiled. It had been a long day, and I felt myself so relaxed with him that my eyes felt droopy.

"Sleep, my love." He said into my hair as he too relaxed deeper.

Alkin

Rai and I slept in the den chair overnight. It was so perfect to have her lay against me, true for once to her emotions. We had become so comfortable with one another. Already I saw the construct body begin to fall apart before my eyes. Her demeanor was shattering and Raihanna was falling away, revealing Raillyn.

It made me smile, and my heart warm, the spell really was working, and she was returning to normal. Even though it was slow, I saw the subtle effects. Brushing away a few stray strands, she snuggled closer. Again I kissed her head lovingly, Gods, I loved her. I would miss this most in the end, when I had to return her to the Wolves. But I knew what was right and what the Gods planned for her, and I would not disrupt things further. I only prayed she would find her way back to me.

Sighing I knew I had put off visiting Drameon for too long, and decided it was time to pay him an unexpected visit. So not to awaken her, I carefully moved her aside and stood up. She stirred slightly before returning to sleep.

Before leaving I grabbed a nearby blanket and tucked it around her. Leaning down, I kissed the top of her forehead and brushed away a few loose strands of hair, carefully tucking them behind her ear. Standing, I called upon my Mystic magic to create a portal that would take me where I needed to go. As the mist dissipated I looked around my surroundings seeking my old friend out.

Standing in the center of the large den, the ceiling was sculpted with exquisite rafters. As equally beautiful artwork dotted from the walls. Bookshelves stood everywhere as deep red chairs were spaced perfectly between them. Walking around the large mahogany table which stood in the center of the room and glancing by the fireplace, Drameon was not in the room.

Sighing, I walked towards the door leading into a hall-way. Deep brown and gold carpet lined the hall and led to a smaller den, at the bottom of several steps. Here, I found Drameon relaxing in a chair next to the fireplace. Book in hand, he turned as I entered the room. I bowed slightly to him before descending the stairs.

Closing his book, he stood; a worried look crossed his elfin face. "What brings you here unannounced?" He asked softly, perplexed by my sudden appearance.

"For the most part all is well." I assured him, feeling extremely calm after sleeping next to Rai last night. "I wanted to catch you up on recent events is all, since it has been quite some time since we last spoke." I said calming his worried thoughts. "I had a little situation, and I'm sure he has already made that apparent. Howl had taken Rai into his care for a few weeks but has released her. He did fill her in with some lost history and information." I said getting the important part done with.

My old friend smiled at this remark. "Yes. Howl paid me a visit. He told me he had planned on teaching her to be cautious around the Vampires. I hope he has done his job." He spoke, nodding his head.

Smiling in return, I went on. "I do have to say Rai is suspecting something is out of place because of her recent visit. But I think it will do her some good. Hunter punished her for leaving. I knew he would but still I believe it fueled her fears." Here, I allowed my anger to show.

He was not pleased to hear this. "Ensure whatever she finds out that Hunter is kept out of it all." He said while pacing the floor. "You and I both know he will not kill her, he can't unless he doesn't care about his portal. We will take care of the situation on Rai soon."

I nodded in agreement, and could tell we were done. I had my job to do. I would ensure that whatever suspicions she had were kept between the two of us. I still was angered at having to involve Callina, but I knew this was planned. Bowing before taking my leave I opened a portal back to The Keep.

The Plan ~ Drake

We had received word from Drameon that Hunter would be outside The Keep with his entire top soldiers for several weeks. Where they were going was unknown, but I felt this was a perfect time to stage a distraction so I could investigate further.

Even after six years, I still held strong thoughts that Raillyn was still alive along with my daughter Deestan. If only I could get inside their most guarded place, I believed could find them. This was what I had hoped, even if I could not accomplish anything other than knowing they were alive; that was all I needed.

So secretly I worked with Drameon and Saibal. I did not want Droggen to find out what I was doing since it was a mission that could end me. Saibal spoke with his troops to see if there were ten that were willing to accompany me to The Keep, knowing they likely would not return.

They would cause a distraction for me and allow me entry during the chaos into The Keep's walls, hopefully giving me free access to the main level. I had hoped from there I could use my sense of smell to track what I wanted.

Before leaving, I wrote a note indicating to speak with Captain Saibal if I had not returned in two days' time. Saibal was left with specific instructions, as well as a documented decree stating Lord Briar as heir to the throne. I said a silent prayer to the Moon Goddess, hoping it would not come to that, but I wanted to be prepared.

Leaving the castle was hard. I hoped to return that night with good news or at the very least some indication to my family's whereabouts. Whether I returned with Raillyn or Deestan didn't matter, I just wanted to know they still lived. My heart ached as we rode in silence. Things should have never gotten this out of control. I still didn't understand why Hunter would do such a thing, or what he planned.

Upon reaching the outer wall, all was silent; the Vampire's main town and Keep was well guarded behind large black walls. The only entry point was the massive gate in front. Once more I said a prayer before sending my troops to storm the entrance. All I needed was a few seconds where the guards were away from their post, so I could slip inside.

Before I sent them to what probably would be their deaths, I thanked them. "I am grateful for your assistance tonight on this mission. I hope you will be safe, but as you all know I cannot guarantee that. If you wish to leave, then do so now. Know if you die now that it is not in vain, your death will be avenged." I said as I looked at each man, no one left, they waited for me to give the signal.

Closing my eyes I waved my hand. Taking cue, they charged the gate just as directed. We wanted this to appear as if it was a revolt from villagers so none of my men wore armor or any indication they had come from the castle. As blows were made and a few cut down, I pulled my black hood over my face and slipped past the guards who gorged themselves on the blood of the fallen while others continued to fight. Slipping through the gate was easy. I had dressed in all black to appear as if I was one of them and in hopes to not raise more alarms than needed.

As I made my way throughout the streets, it had seemed to be working. We had planned for the attack to be made on a new moon when my magic would be weaker and less detectable. Since most of the village people had not, I assumed, ever seen a Werewolf I was able to slowly walk freely, avoiding any guards I saw along the way.

Nearing their castle Keep, I knew I could not enter the front and proceeded to trail the wall from a distance looking for a way in. As I did, I could hear muffled cries as I came around the tower.

One of the guards was busy with a women, they were too distracted to hear the bushes I was hiding in make noise. Suddenly, a horn was heard off towards the main gate. They must be calling backup, to dispose of my last remaining men or to alert something else.

Raihanna

Since I had been gone for several weeks, I took Deestan, Callina, and Leeda out for a little walk to see the new wares. As we strode through town, we picked up little knick knacks along the way. We had stayed out late tonight and it felt great. Just as we prepared to head back to The Keep a horn blew in the distance. Its shrilling sound told me all too much of what was happening. Wolves were spotted and were at the entrance of the gate. Our people were calling for more troops and to lock down The Keep from any entrance or exit.

Quickly, I grabbed Callina and lead the older two along. We ran towards our normal entrance in hopes that I could get to the door before it closed, but I was too late. I knew the door behind the guard was closed with magic and would not open until the spell was lifted. Even using a portal would be useless; cursing to myself, I lead the girls along.

"What's going on, mommy?" Callina asked as we turned from The Keep, and I thought of another place to hide the girls.

"Please keep quiet for a moment, I need to think. Bad things are happening, and you girls need to be safe and out of harm's way." I replied just as I saw my answer.

A dancer was running towards the Den from the main street. Quickly, I followed her, trying to stop her before she got too close to the Den, and I would be forced away.

"Please wait!" I called to her as she ran. Seeing the children, she paused for a moment.

"What do you want, Elite?" She questioned, her blood-red eyes examined me. The Elite were not permitted into the Den because of their violent nature. The dancers knew who all the Elite were, and she was wary of my presence.

"Take the children." I said with a plea in my voice. "I know I am not welcome in the Den, but they are just babes and it's not safe out here." I said hoping she would do so.

She gave me a weary look just as the horns blew again, louder and more demanding. Sighing she took Callina from my grasp and herded the older two along. Into the darkness, they went, towards the one place I knew they would be safe from all harm.

It was hard to let them go, but I had no choice in the matter. Slowly, I turned and began to retreat towards the barracks, a place where I would at least feel comfortable if something more were to come of this skirmish.

The Barracks were on the other side of town and there were only two ways to get there, I knew my luck with the main roads. They would slow me down, so I chose the deserted side streets. Running swiftly, I followed the outer wall to my destination. Calling my black blade to my hand, as I went, I prepared for a possible attack.

The moon was black and gave little light to guide me. I ran through the shadow-lined streets. The horns blowing could only mean one thing that the Wolves had nearly broken through the front gate. Speed was essential. If they made it any further, the horns would again below three times from both towers and the barracks.

Suddenly, before I had time to think, I was grabbed by the arm and thrown down face first onto the ground. I felt a blade pointed at my back through my chestplate.

"Don't move," said a familiar voice. "Or I will drive this blade through you faster than you can react," he said. I felt the anger and hatred fill his mind. It was Lord Drake.

I had failed to sense this threat. "Okay," I said quietly. I had no horn, nor did I have any means to alert anyone. I had chosen to take the most secluded route during a battle. I was on my own.

"Stand up," Drake's voice said. "And turn around slowly."

Slowly, I stood and turned, allowing my sword to dissipate. My cloak hung around me concealing my chestplate underneath, but not covering the remaining Elite armor. As soon as I met his eyes Lord Drake knew who and what I was.

It was not an uncommon site around The Keep for the Elite to wear their battle gear. In fact, it was quite common. I wore my whole attire that night as I usually did when I went into town. Now Lord Drake could pinpoint one of Hunter's most important Elite.

"I was right, you're an Elite." He stated, blade to my throat. I sighed knowing when Hunter found out he would be furious. There was no choice but to try and take out Lord Drake.

Arms to my side I silently prayed and called upon my blade once more. Quickly, I jumped at him, smacking his Mythril sword away from my throat. Ducking back I charged him once more, hoping to catch him off guard. He seemed surprised but quickly recovered from the diversion and jumped towards me. His sword swung swiftly around, nearly missing my midsection. Twisting sideways I narrowly avoided the blow.

This was not a battle I had wanted, nor did I feel it was a safe choice, I was still healing from the injury Hunter inflicted upon me. Blade in hand, I swung it around brushing his Mythril armor. That's when it occurred to me, that I would have to strike under the shoulder or below it. There was a clasp, like mine, just under the armpit.

After twisting out of reach, I immediately stopped and turned to face him. This surprised Lord Drake' he expected me to back off again and charge. I had a single moment to attack, and took it. Blade in hand, crouching low, I thrust it up. Before he could pull his arm in, blocking the soft spot underneath, I hit. His blood ran over my face and down my front, but it was just a glancing blow. Drake jumped back, diverting my attack. Instead, I got the backside of his bicep.

Smiling as Lord Drake advanced on me again, I was left with no choice, but to duck under his blade and hope I would not be hit. He had placed me between the wall and himself. As I ducked I felt his body shift; instead he kneed me into the wall and hilted my face, ripping my cloak off in the process.

My body lurched in protest. As I fell I saw him raise his blade and strike.

I knew it would be the final blow unless by sheer luck, he missed. I was too close for it not to be a deadly blow. As his blade made contact, I felt my armor block the brute force. The screech of metal was ear piercing even for me. Blue sparks flew from both armor and blade while a blue symbol appeared on the front of my chestplate.

Eyes open with fright, I suddenly found myself in Alkin's arms; he must of teleported in and grabbed me. Lord Drake stumbled, his wild eyes met mine and Alkin's. Crying out in pain, I felt Alkin's anger boom and become a raging inferno. He wanted to make Drake pay for what he had done.

Please.... I mentally said to Alkin. Closing my eyes he teleported us into The Keep's inner walls. I was alive, but I hurt.

Hope ~ Raihanna

Upon entering my chambers, I found myself swamped with pain, my chest hurt from the blow. I knew I suffered a broken rib or two, my stomach hurt equally with immense pain. I had to be bleeding internally, each breath was agony.

I barely heard Alkin speak to me. "Faen! I have to get this damn armor off you." He said cursing as he cut its bindings. Breaking free, he lifted it over my head and threw it aside. Alkin began coursing magic through me, trying to stop the internal bleeding. I felt a sudden onset of more pain, my belly burned, and my head felt like it was exploding. Blood poured from my wound, and as I looked down at my now bare stomach, it was turning an ugly shade of purple. Alkin stayed with me.

Alkin

She fell into unconsciousness just as I reached out to hold onto her soul. I was no healer, not the kind she knew, and I knew the one healer who could help her refused to enter The Keep. So I was left to help her differently, using our bond and my blood to keep her alive.

Securing her soul to me, I drew my dagger and ran it over my wrist, at this moment I didn't care about any repercussion that this could bring about. All that mattered was that Rai would live. Bringing my wrist to her mouth, she unconsciously fought against my blood flowing into her. Her construct body was not meant for the bond or magic we shared between each other and I knew it was only killing her faster. Still, she was in danger and bleeding internally; this was the only help I could offer her. I couldn't even mix my saliva, and magic with healing herbs to help her, like normal Ancients. I knew it would only kill her faster.

Using the mental link we shared, I willed her to drink. Taking hold of her mind, and abusing the link we shared once more, I forced her to listen to me. Her mental mind seemed to shut down as her soul realized what was happening. Mentally her mind wanted to fight, but physically she knew this was the only thing that would save her. Finally she relaxed in my arms, and I felt her mouth began to suck at my blood. Shuttering momentarily I had to fight my instincts.

Mystics were like Shadow Walkers and naturally laid claim to their mate with blood and magic; making the Mystic mark, she already carried over her heart and chest, larger and more visible. Her scent would change, and her body would naturally carry my scent for all time, and mine would carry hers.

My instincts fought me, encouraging this bond to be placed upon her, wanting her to only respond to me, her true mate. Even though she was mine, I knew I couldn't mark her though. Her soul belonged to Rai, but her body was still a created mass of nature. It was agony as I laid there healing her and battling my inner demons. Tears of pain and hurt filled my eyes. I hated myself for having to be the one to inflict such torment on her.

Thankfully she was unconscious, and it allowed me to be in control, I feared having to heal her this way when she was aware of what was happening. Even though she was Raihanna and was ruthless that demeanor was fading, and naturally she found herself wanting to be around me. A situation like that would carry heavy mistakes, knowing her magic would twine with mine so perfectly and in sync that we both would be powerless to its effects.

Lost in thought I felt the gentle release of my wrist. Rai no longer in pain, relaxed in my arms. Her mouth covered lightly with my blood, I found myself leaning down, placing a kiss on her sweet lips.

Instantly I knew it was a mistake. The smell of her blood mingled with mine, along with the sweet scent of honeysuckle, vanilla, and thyme. Her scent nearly sent my mind careening over the edge. I needed to leave, I needed some fresh air, and space before I did something I would regret and Drameon would be furious over.

As every natural instinct in my body cried out against it, I opened a portal and left to Silvertine, the only place I could relax; but not before I sent a healer to properly check on her. Stepping out of the portal I found myself exactly where I wanted to be, in one of the small rooms in the Silvertine Den.

Celeste, Lyth's mate, sat in the corner talking quietly to him. Bright golden hair and Elf-like features turned as her vivid green eyes met my ever-changing ones. She was an Ancient, a Drakar and so was her mate who sat beside her. Lyth's crimson waist length hair, tranquil blue eyes, and well balanced muscular face smirked as the portal behind me faded.

Only once had I called on Celeste and her help, while in The Keep. That was when Callina was born. This was due to the dangerous nature of childbirth, in fact she had been there for both girls. Already Rai knew who she was, but knew little about her, and I wanted to keep it that way. She didn't need to be tangled up in the affairs of Aeralain sooner than needed.

"Celeste, I would like to ask you to check in on my mate for me." I said stating claim on her so by the old ways she was protected. I was tense, and she could tell. I moved stiffly, taking deep breaths trying to calm myself. "She had an unfortunate accident, and I have healed her all I dare. Please check on her, but leave before she wakes up."

Smiling Celeste stood and walked towards me. She was one of the Goddess Destiny's Drakar, a well-educated renowned healer of her race. I knew she would not deny this request, because of who Rai was.

"I will check on your mate, Alkin, but I still don't see why you don't lay claim to her and bind her to you. Things would be so much easier if you did." Celeste said as Lyth stood and put his arm around his mate, gently laying a kiss in her hair. "Even if you just bound her soul, I know you can't bind her body till she overcomes the construct task."

Yes, things would be easier if I did so but at the same time things would be utterly disrupted, as well. Alecien had already seen enough chaos to have more erupt within its folds now. I knew I would have to sacrifice, and in turn Raillyn, to keep that balance in check. At the moment, her construct body couldn't handle the effects of a binding. It would kill her. *Already we were racing against the clock, against her cycle. When it hit, her body won't be able to handle it, the rush of Ancient magic that will course through her... Will kill her....*

"As I already said, it's complicated, and it cannot be done at this time, regardless of how convenient it would be." I said bothered.

Celeste shrugged and smiled as she left the room. Standing with Lyth I knew she would do as I asked and take great care of Rai while I tried to relax and regain some control before returning.

Deestan

My mother had handed us to a dancer who pulled us into the darkness towards the Den itself. I wanted desperately to protest and stay, but I knew that was not a choice for me to make and I had to obey.

In silence, we ran, the lady was quick and smelled strange almost like the Vampires but also almost like something else. Upon reaching the door to the Den, the dancer spoke quickly and harshly in a strange language to the person who opened the door. He nodded and quickly pulled us inside as she disappeared into the crowd.

It was dark. Other than a great fire burning in the center of the room, there was no light and the sound of its crackling embers was the only sound. People gathered quietly as if listening and awaiting news. Most appeared to be Half-breeds, Elves, Human, Fae, the normal races of Alecien. Some were Vampires or like the first lady, Vampire-like. I wondered why so many different races lay within the Den here at The Keep? With great haste, the man led us to the other side of the large room and pushed into a smaller room, where two ladies stood.

One was a rather tall woman with olive skin, beads, and feathers braided in her long black hair. The other was a fair-skinned lady with long red hair. Both looked at us rather perplexed as we were shoved into the room.

The male dancer who brought us here spoke quickly in a tongue I barely recognized, the Werewolves language. I knew it from my studies with Alkin. Remembering back to one of Alkin's lessons, he mentioned in passing that Mystic's naturally recognized and spoke many languages. So I was sure Callina understood. But, I couldn't make out a single word, they were speaking too fast. Distracted, I almost didn't see the dancer grasp hold of my little sister's hand and begin to pull her back into the main room.

"No, what are you doing? Callina stays!" I shrieked loudly.

The two women and the man paused for a moment. Callina reached out grasping my hand tightly. Tears began to streak her face as she screamed. For a moment, her body began to become hot, and a red haze clouded around her. "Hush, child." The olive-skinned lady spoke, saying something again in the Werewolves language, too fast for me to make out.

Then the man leaned down and spoke to us. "Don't worry, she will be safe. These two ladies wish to speak to you. I'm just going to take the little one to get something to warm to drink. To calm her a bit. I promise, she won't be far." He said softly. Hugging my sister, I patted her head.

"It's okay, Callie, go with the Denmate. I will see you soon." Kissing her head, I let him gently pull her out of the room.

Leeda stood beside me, she did not study as much as I did. She was not interested in learning about the Werewolves. But knowing what I was, as I stood before people who spoke my birth language, I was frightened. The thought that they had been so close for so long, and yet so far, equally worried me. I was even more uneasy about where they had taken my sister, but tried to put on a strong face.

As they talked between themselves, my composure faded. Slowly, I sat down, shaken, unsure of what to say or do. I stared at them, concentrating and trying to figure out what they were saying. The fair-haired lady called the tall one Stasha while the lady named Stasha called the black-haired lady Yumi.

They talked about the attack on The Keep. They were nervous and had locked down the Den during the event. Everyone was quiet. Saying some spoke in hushed tones, wondering whether, or not they should make a hasty escape through the tunnels below.

"Tunnels below?" I asked in their tongue, almost too quiet for anyone to hear. Leeda looked at me, surprised and shocked that I had spoken in their tongue. The lady named

Stasha also noticed and placed a hand on Yumi's arm, stopping her mid-sentence.

Stasha knelt down and spoke directly to me in their tongue. "Who are you, child, and how do you know this language?" She asked slowly so I could understand better. Yumi looked on curious, as well.

I didn't miss a beat and replied. "I studied it while in The Keep. Alkin taught me. I also have a Goddess statue in my room." I said matter of fact.

Stasha reached into her pouch and pulled out a small statue, "That's it." I cried as she turned it over in her hand.

Grabbing my wrist, she placed the sharp end of it in my hand cutting me slightly, causing me to cry out. The statue let out an illuminating glow as my blood touched its surface, the cut healed quickly with the same silvery glow the statue held.

Briefly I felt the presence of the Lunar Goddess as she spoke lightly to all in the room. "You are safe, Princess." She said as I met Stasha's eyes.

"Deestan." She said in a whisper as she grabbed me off the floor, hugging me in her arms.

I was shocked and happy at the same time. She knew who I was, and I couldn't help but cry as she held me. "We thought you were dead, what are you doing here?" She asked placing me back on the ground.

I looked at Yumi and was unsure of how much I could say to them, I didn't want the Vampires to know, and take me away or punish me.

Yumi sensed my tension and reassured me. "It's okay, child. Nothing you say will leave the walls of this room. Even though my Den is inside the Vampire's Keep, we are a law of our own and have been slowly trying to help create peace in the world, similar to how our Den has peace."

I nodded trustingly, knowing I had no choice. I quickly went over the events that lead me here along with events that I knew of my mother. I figured if this lady knew me then she probably knew my father, and could tell him. Leeda sat quietly beside me, unsure of what to do.

As we talked an uproar suddenly erupted from the main room. Stasha and Yumi quickly opened the door, and headed out to see what was going on. Lord Drake, my father, was walking towards the main stairs that spiraled down on the outer edge of the main room.

"What in the Lunar Goddess' name are you doing here, Drake?" Stasha said while storming over trying to stop him from leaving, he paused momentarily.

"Do not bother me right now!" He shouted as he descended the stairs quickly.

Stasha quickly glanced back at Yumi and us. I could tell she hesitated on whether to just take me or leave me in the Den. Yumi helped her make the decision and told her to go and that she would not let us go.

So Stasha disappeared from view and went after my father down the stairs, probably back to the Werewolves castle, and my real home.

Utterly Lost ~ Drake

I walked the streets towards the Den, confused and shocked. The lady who claimed to be Raihanna was one of the Elite, and on top of it she wore the Mythril chestplate I had given Raillyn. It had to mean something. Either Hunter had, in fact, killed Raillyn or something else had happened to her, and Raihanna was the result of it. I was leaning more towards this option since we had not seen Raihanna prior to Raillyn's disappearance. As I walked, dazed and confused, I felt sure that we had to do something, but at the same time I didn't know what.

Somehow I had found the Den and walked in, startling most of the members. It was a mixed group like always, and the only difference from ours was that they had more Vampire members. Ours had more Wolves in our Den, but in the end all the Dens were alike, and held their own personal law. They lived like a small world inside a larger one operating on their own accord.

Quickly so not to stir up more trouble, I made my way to the stairs, thankful that most Dens had the same layout, and I could find my way back to the tunnels that would lead me home. I walked in a daze. I was completely and utterly shocked from this information.

On top of it, I had nearly killed Raihanna in the process of discovering this information. I barely registered the fact that I had shouted at Stasha and she was in the Vampire's Den tonight. She followed me as I ran through the tunnels, jumping and going as fast as I could giving myself time to think and no time to explain. I did not want a confrontation with her yet, I didn't want to have to explain myself tonight.

It must have worked because upon entering the castle and proceeding to my chambers, Stasha did not follow. I knew I would have to go to her the next morning and speak further about this subject. For the time being though I had time to think. I went to seek Droggen, the one person who I believed would be awake at this hour and who might be able to assist me in this situation.

I found him in the great library reading up on his finding of interest. Upon seeing me, he knew something was deadly wrong and immediately told me to sit down.

"Why do you come to me at this hour with the look of dread on your face, Drake?" Droggen asked me as he took a seat directly in front of me.

"I have done something I cannot change, but in turn I am happy I did so." I said quickly going over all the events which lead me to sitting here this night.

As I finished I could tell Droggen was furious with me. "You went to the Vampire's Keep!" He yelled at me, "This is so irresponsible of you! And for what? In hopes that you would find something out? Thankfully you did or else I would have killed you myself." He said in anger.

"Yes, I know." I said. "But if that means Rai is there then I bet Deestan is also." I said while placing my head in my hands, feeling defeated for the time being.

Droggen nodded in agreement, "I think you should go and rest, there is nothing you can do about this situation further tonight. You look pale and not well, go and sleep we shall talk about this further in the morning." He said.

I agreed it was late, and I would not get much else done till morning. So I went back to my bed chambers hoping that when I went to Stasha in the morning, she would be able to share more information on this subject.

Upon awakening, I quickly readied myself and headed out to the Den to speak with Stasha. Luckily she wasn't hard to find, and was in the Den itself this morning.

"I've been waiting for you." She said as I closed the door to one of the smaller rooms off the main Den.

"I know. I'm sorry about last night." I said while coming into the room. She too was quite stunned. Before she could say another word, I quickly went over the events of last night.

She sat subdued. The shock had died down and gave her time to think.

"So, you see, if Hunter in fact did something to Raillyn then I believe this Raihanna is the key to it all, and that gives us a good chance of possibly finding my daughter." I said while walking the room.

Stasha smiled as I said this, "Drake I have something I need to tell you, and with the events you have just informed me of I am glad I made the decision I did last night. Yumi, the local Den master of the Vampires has your daughter. In fact, one of her dancers acquired her and two other children last night through Raihanna." Stasha said, making me stop mid-stride.

"Yumi has Deestan?" I asked knowing I had walked through the very Den that she was in. "And two other children?" I pondered this thought, *Who could the other children be?* I felt weak in the knees, knowing it had been over six years since I had seen her, and knowing I could have seen her the night before.

"Yes, and I believe one is the Shifter's child, Leeda. The other I know for a fact is a Mystic child who I have placed in the care of a distant friend." Stasha said carefully, "I cannot be sure yet, but I know if we speak with her today, you could see Deestan, and we could probably find out more information on this subject." Stasha said causing me to smile. I was eager see my daughter who I had not seen since she was an infant.

Before Stasha left to try and retrieve Deestan she asked if she could have the signet ring that was meant for her. I had been wearing Deestan's ring around my neck since her disappearance. Unclasping the necklace I carefully allowed it to fall from the chain and into Stasha's hand.

Safe ~ Raihanna

As I slept I dreamed, I saw a girl that looked much like myself, but with different hair and features, I could tell she was a Mystic and the one who Hunter had called Raillyn. I knew her history, but I found it strange that she wore the very chestplate I wore.

She held the chestplate in her hands while a golden ring with a large blue stone lay on her finger. Raillyn murmured a lunar spell that awoke magic in the metal, an inscription was revealed. It read, "To my love, and treasured mate, may this protect you from darkness.–Drake–" Suddenly everything went black, and a healing darkness consumed me.

When I awoke, Alkin was nowhere in sight, only a maid was there to assist me. I looked around my room for my chestplate. It lay on a nearby, chair. Grabbing it I quickly went down the hall. The maid was coming to check on me, and bowed slightly as I descended the stairs to the lower den, I locked the door behind me.

Going over to the window I sat down in a chair. The words from my dream came easy, and I spoke them fluidly. Suddenly blue lines danced across its surface, and the same words adorned the metal. The chestplate I wore was Raillyn's, which she had gotten from her mate, Lord Drake. I leaned back for a moment, unsure what to do next or even how to proceed. Everything felt like a jumbled mess, and I was in the middle of it.

Suddenly a thought entered my mind. I had given the girls to the local Den last night, a Den who had full access to the Werewolves. If there had been word about the attack be-tween Lord Drake and I, what would they do about my daughters? I feared where they might be. So I got up and left back up the stairs.

Running to the Den, I didn't care if I was an Elite or not I needed to get my children back, and now. Lord Drake knew who I was, and I was sure if the Den knew what I did to him, word would get around and reach Lord Drake that my daughters resided in a Den, and he might use them to get to me. I reached the Den in breakneck speed and pounded on their door demanding access. Suddenly it opened, and a man stepped out. Long crimson hair hung braided waist length, and his Elvin features and bright icy blue eyes felt like they pierced my soul. His emerald green pants billowed as he partially closed the door behind him. Firm muscles rippled across his chest as he stood guard.

"You are not welcome here, Elite." He said.

"No, you don't understand. I need my girls back now." I said, hoping they would be released back to me.

"Your children are safe, but I cannot allow them to leave until Yumi gets back."

I knew Yumi was the Den Master, "When will she return?" I asked hopeful. If I wasn't dealing with the Den and their own laws, I would have stormed in and took the girls myself, but I knew I had to be cautious. Placing my hands on my waist, I felt around for the pouch that held the same golden ring Raillyn wore in my dream. The man shook his head, he didn't seem sure when Yumi would return, and then turned to enter the den.

"Wait." I said, pulling out the ring. "Give this to your Den Master." I said, hopeful he would grant me access. As my hand touched his, a spark snapped between us, like electricity jumping from one lightning bolt to another. Momentarily I stared at him shocked, my magic flared, and my eyes flashed blue.

Smiling, he nodded in agreement. "You will receive word from us as soon as Yumi grants their leave." He said as he disappeared back within the Den, leaving me speechless.

I sighed defeated and returned to The Keep, I found Alkin sitting in the main den. He looked concerned that I was not here when he returned. "Where did you run off to?" He asked. "And where are the girls. I know with the chaos last night I sort of lost track of them."

My Mystic blood pounded at me as a whirlwind of emotions swirled in my head. I felt like a mess, nothing like my normal demeanor. I nodded and agreed, I was having a hard time, I didn't know what I should tell Alkin or how much.

I tried to keep it simple. "After the horns alerted everyone of the attack, I tried to get back to The Keep, but it was already sealed. I had to get them someplace safe and I saw a dancer going to the Den. I asked her to take them till things calmed down. But since I'm Elite I have to wait for permission from the Den Master to get them back." I said trying to not sound too alarmed. I heard my voice crack slightly, I was upset, and never was I this distressed about anything before. I didn't know how to handle myself. I felt tears well up in my eyes.

Alkin's eyes got wide when I mentioned this. He blocked me from his mind so I could not read his emotions. I expected he was beyond mad at me.

"They're at the local Den?" He asked as he slightly laughed. "Oh, Hunter will love this one. If we're not able to retrieve them before his return, he will have our heads." Alkin continued. "You know the Den is tied to every kingdom around Alecien, and on top of it they don't follow our laws. They do their own thing." He said, upset. He circled the room outraged. Reaching out he grabbed the small table near the fireplace, and overturned it in his anger.

"You gave them the Princess! You just handed her to them as our Keep was being attacked by Werewolves, the very people who are aligned with the Shifters!" I regretted my choice now, Alkin was mad, and I had lost my daughters for an unknown amount of time. "What do you think will happen if they deny their leave and keep them? All the plans Hunter put in motion years ago will fall apart." He yelled. Then on a lighter note added, "If I were you I would pray." He said as he stormed out of the room, leaving me standing there alone.

I closed my eyes, on the verge of tears. Nora, the maid came into the room. "Out!" I screamed at her. "Leave me now!" I said as she quickly ran towards the door, running from my wrath.

Trouble ~ Drake

As I waited for Stasha to return with Deestan from the other Den, I received word of trouble. I figured this was probably in retaliation to me infiltrating their Keep last night and I felt obligated to go.

Frustrated I walked the halls of the castle hoping it would not take long at all. I sent a message to Stasha explaining the situation and informing her that I would let her know as soon as I returned. It was turning out to be a long day already.

Deestan

Stasha lead me through the tunnels below. Some contained rooms of crystal while other lay dark and dank. A strange smell emanated from within the darkened tunnels, I stayed near Stasha, unsure what it was. She had told me that morning that my younger half-sister was safe and taken to a friend while Leeda remained behind in Yumi's den. Finally, we reached the other Den, just before noon. Stasha lead me into one of the smaller rooms on the lower level.

The room was simple, furs were piled into a bed in the corner while a simple table and a few chairs sat around the room. An orange magic light sat on the table blazing, illuminating the room in an amber color.

Stasha picked up a bag laying on the table and opened it. She pulled out what appeared to be a small dancer's outfit. I stared at its pale ice-blue pants and matching top, adorned with matching beads.

"This is for you, child." She said as she handed it to me.

I turned the outfit over in my hands amazed. "Can I wear it?" I asked hopeful.

Stasha smiled. "Of course you can, child. You need to wear it before we leave the room." She said as I began removing my clothing.

Once on, it fit wonderfully and I spun around in a circle while the small beads jingled against my stomach. I felt at home already, I was happy and it felt so good.

Stasha attached a small silver anklet with ball shaped bells on it to my ankle. She tied a dark blue sash with the dancers Den's charm on one end around my waist.

"This will mark you as a Denmate. You are safe as long as you wear the sash, no one shall harm you. It is our symbol and no one would strike down a dancer for fear of retaliation." Stasha said as she pulled out one last item.

It was a small insignia ring with the Werewolves royal symbol on it. The cool metal made me smile as I placed the insignia ring on my finger.

"As long as you are outside of the Vampire's Keep you will always wear that. Never take it off, no matter what." She stressed. I nodded in understanding. "It marks you as Lord Drake's child. Though for the time being, I would like you to hide the symbol. We do not want word to spread of your arrival quiet yet." Stasha said hushed, unsure of who might hear.

I nodded in understanding, it would be terrible if word spread that I had returned, and worse if that word got to my mother and Hunter at The Keep.

As I thought this the door opened and Yumi walked in to meet with us before our leave.

"It seems that Raihanna visited us this morning," Yumi said to Stasha as she closed the door behind her. "I did not grant her access to the girls, but before leaving she gave Lyth this." Yumi said as she handed a small, golden ring with a turquoise stone on it to Stasha.

"This used to be Raillyn's." Stasha said as she turned it over in her hand. "She acquired it the night Deestan was born from one of the gemcrafters below. I wonder why she had it?"

From what I could remember, I had not seen the ring before and wasn't able to shed light on the situation. I wanted to see my mother desperately, but I also wanted to see my father. I waited patiently as Stasha caught Yumi up on what was happening.

Just prior to leaving, a knock was heard at the door, Stasha answered it. It appeared to be a messenger, he held a letter which he gave to Stasha and closed the door. She had a troubled look on her face while looking it over; she closed her eyes and sighed while closing the letter.

"It seems that there is trouble near the Vampire's borders." Stasha said while looking to Yumi. "Perhaps you would like to see the village for a while?" Stasha asked as she noticed my concerned look.

I smiled with delight. I was eager to see the village since I had only read about it in books. Stasha walked over to me and reached down taking my hand in hers. She made sure the ring was turned around so the symbol would not be visible.

"For the time being, child, only show that to guards and only if you end up in trouble." Stasha stressed again. I knew I was in unknown territory and agreed to proceed with caution. "You are very important, and I hate having to leave you like this, but I feel I need to go assist in this matter." Stasha said as she led me through the door and into the main room.

Canopies of different colored silks hung from the ceiling and furs of many kinds hung on the wall and were strewn around the floor. A large hearth burned in the center of the room while women, men, and children of all ages sat and talked, danced or sang. It was as if the building itself held a tiny village.

Stasha called over a dancer who was standing near the hearth. She had olive-colored skin and waist-length brown hair that was kept in a long braid. She wore a brown dress with a yellow wrap around her waist that had a golden charm at the end of it.

"Can you entertain my little friend here for a little bit until I am able to return and retrieve her?" Stasha asked, hesitating on what to exactly say.

She smiled at me as she responded. "Sure, is she a Den child?" She asked while looking at my outfit.

Stasha nodded in reply. I think it was easier to leave it at that then to explain the real situation. "Child, this is Nyrene, she will stay with you until I return." Stasha said as she turned to go, not once speaking my name.

Nyrene led me down the small path into the village. She had not seen the insignia nor did I mention it. Since I was dressed as a dancer and wore their seal I was looked upon as a Den child, and that was all. I was told this allowed me free passage nearly anywhere, and the ability to claim sanctuary at any den. It meant I was free to come and go as I pleased, even as I got older.

Nyrene and I wandered the village, I could tell she thought I had grown up there, and nothing was really new for me. I was ecstatic as I looked around. We passed the black onyx statue, and I gazed at it in marvel. It was so unlike The Keep where things were always quiet and hushed. I didn't have to fear here, no one was going to try and hurt me; for once I felt free.

We stopped at shops and looked at little trinkets. I was in awe over the art and skill they had. It was similar to the Vampires but more magical and held a special sort of tune for me. Nature itself seemed to be imbued in everything they made. Everyone was nice, and Nyrene often stopped and talked about small things to many of the people. No one was surprised to see me walking about.

"Oh you have such a lovely companion tonight, Nyrene." A lady said while we stopped at a bookshop. "Den children are always darling." She went on as I picked up a small book about local lore. The lady took note. "Go ahead, child, take it, the book is yours. Call it a gift to a Den child." She said smiling.

I smiled in return, eager to read it. As dusk approached, and Stasha was still missing. Nyrene sighed.

"I am due to dance at the square shortly; would you like to join me?" She asked giving me a choice I had not expected.

I shook my head. "No, I can find my way back to the Den if need be." I said as she leaned down and kissed the top of my golden hair before leaving.

As I stood near the Goddess fountain in the middle of town, I looked around for the castle. I had found it south of me, and headed in its direction. No one stopped me or gave me a second look as I passed; this was so different from life in The Keep where it seemed as if everyone had their eyes on me all the time, following my every move. Of course, no one knew who I was here.

Upon reaching a large cliff, I saw a cave where guards stood. I could only assume that the tunnels lead to the castle high above. Casually I walked in; the guards didn't even budge nor care.

I smiled, giddy with joy and ran through the tunnel, laughing as I went. All too fast I was excited, two additional guards stood, they nodded at me as I walked on. I realized I was on the top of the cliff, on a balcony. I lean over the edge and heard the village below. Here, I could easily see the setting sun start to descend from the horizon, it was beautiful. Rays of pink, blue, purple, and orange danced in the puffy white clouds above.

As I stood there looking around, one of the guards who stood watch at the tunnel stopped me momentarily. "Are you lost, little dancer?" He asked me.

I smiled and casually. "No, I was just on my way to meet my father." I said while he nodded and returned to his post. I smiled and went on my way.

As I walked on I spotted a door and went inside. The floors of the hall where lined with red carpet. Everything was so big, and random art portraits hung along the stone walls, most were images of woods or the sky. The lighting in the halls came from large yellow magic infused lanterns that hung from the ceiling.

There were many people coming and going here. Since I had no true sense of where I was going, I walked the hall randomly, looking around at the various artworks as I went.

I was not able to get too far before getting stopped. An older man with dirty dishwater blonde hair approached me. He had the same wolf emblem on his armor that I had on my ring, and he walked with authority. I tried to keep calm, remembering Stasha's words.

"Excuse me child, but what are you doing here?" He asked.

I was unsure how to answer him. I didn't want to lie to him if he was important, so I stood in silence for a moment. "Don't be afraid of me. My names Saibal and I'm captain of the guard here and friend to Lord Drake."

I smiled at this knowing I could half tell him my mission. "I'm here to find my father, but I seem to be lost." I said hopeful I had a chance of just being taken to my father by the captain.

He took my hand and led me down the hall, "Let's see if we can fix this then. We will go back to the throne room and see if we can find him there." Captain Saibal said as he led me through another door and into a larger hall much similar to the one we had left.

As we walked the maids and people in the hall slightly bowed their heads, Saibal bowed in return. Finally, we reached a large oak door and entered the throne room, the main place where everyone met. A group of people stood in a makeshift like line. The captain led me straight towards the front of everyone and to another man who looked equally important and older that Saibal. He looked skinny, and had chocolate colored hair, which he wore in a tight braid along his back.

"Chancellor Droggen, I seemed to of found a young dancer looking for her father. Have you seen any of the male dancers this evening? He questioned while looking towards the crowd.

The chancellor looked me over and looked around at the people nearby. "Not recently; there was a group here earlier who said they would return later perhaps he is with them." The chancellor said while looking around, once more. "Why don't you sit with Lord Briar and I? We can wait for him together." He said smiling, patting at the chair next to them.

So I sat and joined them. I looked at Briar who had light brown hair, and bright blue eyes. He had the very insignia ring I wore. They were taking care of the small happenings of the castle while my father was away. The man called Briar looked at me with his crystal blue eyes and smiled, I smiled back. He seemed very interested in me and asked many questions between townspeople.

"So you're a Den child?" He asked while smiling.

I nodded my head. "The Den's amazing, everyone was dancing this morning, and those that weren't sat around the hearth and talked about what the day would bring." I said relaying the events I saw that day. "So what are you doing? Helping the townspeople?" I asked curious.

Briar nodded. "They come here to ask for help if they are having problems that they cannot handle on their own. We try and help them when we can, making sure we treat everyone equally." Briar replied while Droggen gave him a stern look. Briar didn't seem to care and rolled his eyes at Droggen's response.

I pulled my book out and began reading. I had been carrying it around and figured I would spend some time with it. Briar eyed me and smiled again as I began reading.

While Droggen was addressing a merchant he spoke to me. "So tell me more. How old are you?" He asked matter of fact like.

I paused momentarily and smiled at him. "I'm six, almost seven." I said proudly. "My mother said she would start teaching me magic when I became seven, I can't wait!" I said happily.

Briar smiled in return. "Your mother sounds like a wonderful lady." He said.

My smile faded. I was unsure how to answer. "She's a great mother, don't get me wrong, but she is always very busy with work." I said quieter.

"What kind of work does she do?" Briar asked curious to know more.

I pondered a moment unsure of how to answer. I knew I couldn't tell them she was an Elite. "She's very powerful and servers an equally powerful man. Her work often takes her away from me and my sister." I said trying to keep it simple.

Droggen had finished addressing the matter at hand, and Briar turned back to take care of a new issue. I went back to reading. Lost in the book I began quietly singing to myself, unknowingly in the Mystic tongue.

At the next break Briar listened in, I stopped when I realized he did so. "So what are you reading?" He questioned after a while.

"A book about the Wolves' history during the war." I said casually, not realizing I had said, the Wolves instead of ours, like I should have. I looked at Briar who seemed to notice, as well.

He leaned down and whispered into my ear. "You need to watch how you speak, child." I stared at him unsure how to answer. "Are you visiting from another Den?" He questioned equally quietly.

Shaking my head no, I suddenly felt frightened. I looked around briefly; no one else paid me any attention. I couldn't decide whether I wanted to cry, or run. Then I looked back at Briar who just looked at me awaiting an answer.

I put my book down and did the only thing I could think of. Quietly and carefully, so no one else would see, I opened my hand with the insignia on it, palm up, revealing the very ring Briar had on himself.

His mouth fell open as I looked at him silently. "Don't you agree, Lord Briar?" Droggen said, drawing his attention away from me.

Briar quickly composed himself so not to seem shaken. "Sorry, what was that?" He asked as they continued their conversation.

Before I went back to reading, Briar glanced at me and smiled, shaking his head back and forth, before returning to his work.

As evening began to fall, I grew hungry and tired. "Briar, if my father doesn't come soon, is there a way I could get something to eat?" I asked hopeful.

Briar tried not to laugh about the situation. "Sure thing, little dancer." Briar said while Droggen seemed displeased with the idea. "Oh come on, Droggen, she's a kid, and I'm sure if her father doesn't come for her soon Stasha will." Briar said while patting Droggen on the back, smiling.

Chancellor Droggen sighed knowing he would not win. I was led out into the halls, Briar stayed close by me as Droggen led the way.

Missing ~ Drake

As I thought, Stasha had come to inquire about the problems of the Vampires. She had told me that she left Deestan in Nyrene's care but did not inform her of who she was.

"Nyrene has the child; everyone is calling her little dancer for now. No one knows who she is, and I knew you trusted her." Stasha said as we went over the details on the Vampires.

A small group had attacked the village east of the castle, out of spite for the attack on their Keep the night before. The group was not experienced and by the time I had arrived most of the soldiers were disposed of. When I arrived I was informed that a man with black hair had been attacking the Vampires prior to my troop's arrival. He now held the last remaining soldier who I wanted to question.

This man, who had assisted us seemed strange, I had never seen anyone like him before. His high cheek bones gave him an Elven appearance, but I had never seen eyes such as his. They were a piercing blue color that seemed infused with magic. The man seemed to take the authority of my troops well, and followed orders. Since he was not a threat, I was going to have to speak to him later. For now, I would allow him to assist us.

One of my guardsmen knocked the Vampire on the side of his head. "Who sent you?" They asked. He was determined to not answer.

"No one I swear!" He yelled as they hit him again.

I had my doubts. Hunter would not have left The Keep unattended with no one in charge while he was gone. My guards were treating this Vampire better than they would have treated us. A mere beating was nothing to them. If the tables were turned they would torture, cut, and drain us as if it was nothing.

"I know Hunter is not at The Keep, so who sent you?" I asked again hopeful he would answer to my authority. "Why did you come? To just slaughter my men for no reason?"

Another blow to the head from my guard let loose a spray of blood. The Vampire coughed slightly before speaking. "It was the Mystic, the Demon one." He said. "He's in charge while Hunter is gone. He sent me." The Vampire said while his head hung low, blood ran down his head and face, dripping onto the ground.

I walked over towards him. "Why did Alkin send you?" I asked, hoping I spoke the correct name. The only one who was labeled a Demon that I had seen with the Vampires was Alkin. But I didn't know if another was residing there.

The Vampire looked at me, surprised, I had guessed right. He laughed slightly but spoke nothing. The strange man's ears seemed to perk up at the mention of him, I was equally curious to know more. I looked around wondering if Alkin had accompanied them. The rustling of leaves from a nearby tree alerted us to another possible oncoming attack.

Alkin leapt out, sword in hand. With a great burst of speed, he lunged forward, bringing the sword down across the Vampire's head, splitting it open before jumping away.

The strange man and I drew our own swords as Stasha began to call magic to her, just as he landed a few feet away.

"He speaks too much; I can't have that going on." Alkin said while he turned smiling. "I believe you have something I seek, Lord Drake." Alkin said while he dissipated his black blade and approached me, hands in a friendly gesture, before looking at the black haired man. "And why are you here?" He asked him.

I allowed Alkin to approach. My guards stood ready in case he attacked. The strange man with blue eyes made a motion forward. Raising my hand, he paused and relaxed. I sheathed my own blade and stepped in front of Alkin to meet him face to face. "And what do I have that you could possibly want?" I questioned as I stopped in front of him.

Alkin cocked his head to the side. "I lost something to the local Den last night. Since word travels fast between them, I think you might already know what it is." He said spitefully.

Understanding suddenly crossed my face, he was seeking Deestan. "I don't know what you mean." I bluffed.

He looked around me towards Stasha. "No, but I bet she does." Alkin said addressing Stasha. "Tell me, Den Master, where are my girls?" Alkin said while pulling out a small token that lie hidden on a loop of his belt.

Recognizing the symbol, I turned to look at Stasha. It was the unity symbol all dancers used to identify themselves. Stasha stood eyes closed for a moment. I was sure she would answer to him since he carried it.

Stasha sighed and looked at me apologetically. "We have them, but Yumi's the one who has to release them. I cannot grant them leave." Stasha said truthfully. "When I get back to the Den I can speak with her, though." She added.

Anger flashed across his eyes momentarily. "Even the little one? The youngest?" He asked in a monotone.

The strange man spoke up, his blue eyes glinted deviously. "That one is in Silvertine's Den. Solomn has her."

Alkin's eyes flashed red as he advanced on the stranger, black blade in hand once more. "Blast you, Howl!" He said as his attack was parried.

The man named Howl released a blast of wind and threw Alkin backwards. "Let's not fight about this, Mystic. Now is not the time."

Alkin looked skyward, and closed his eyes letting out a big sigh. "See to it you return the girls as soon as possible. Or else it will be my head and another dancer's," he said, pointing towards Stasha.

Bowing her head Stasha seemed unnerved about the situation. "I understand," she said, while he opened a portal and left.

The whole situation seemed a bit cryptic. Only Stasha comprehended the laws governing The Dens, whereas I only had a vague idea. Was Alkin threatening Stasha? That couldn't be right. If he was a member, he must have known what kind of trouble it would instigate, threatening a Den master. Nor did it seem like he had any real authority among its community. What did he mean by *my head and another dancers*? I knew enough to know he wasn't talking about Stasha. I would have to try talking to her more about it later.

Instead, I turned towards Howl, hoping for an explanation. Stasha gazed at Howl as well. Carefully, he withdrew a dancer's token before continuing. "Yumi passed **his** daughter onto the Fae Den after Raihanna released the girls into her care. From there, the Drakar of Silvertine wanted her because of her heritage. So the youngest was passed to them. I've been in Alecien for a few months now investigating the Vampire activity. I mean you no harm, and I assure you I'm on your side." He said carefully.

She shook her head. "I trust your word and intentions, but I will not speak further of it here. We must hurry back; we have other matters to attend which are more important. Please feel free to accompany us though." She said as she turned towards the castle to leave. I nodded towards my guardsmen, who would stay behind and clean up the mess. Howl and I followed.

Howl, Stasha, and I sought out Nyrene; she was dancing, but no child was near her. Stasha and I quickly approached her about Deestan and her whereabouts.

"Nyrene, where is the child?" Stasha asked with a worried tone as we neared her. I gazed at Howl, still unsure if he should be included in this information, but trusted Stasha and her Den mates.

Nyrene stopped dancing and looked around the Den unsure of why we seemed worried. "I had to attend other things, she said she was okay and told me to go on ahead. I figured she would return to the Den or her family as evening went on." Nyrene said as I felt the blood leave my face. Nyrene seemed to notice, my paleness.

"She's not just a Den child, is she?" Nyrene said, hushed, taking note of our behavior.

Now we had a missing child on our hands and no easy way of finding her. Just great. Stasha, Howl, and I walked the village, Nyrene stayed in the Den in case she returned there. Stasha had told her she would tell her the truth about the child later, and that finding her was top priority.

We stopped around asking local vendors, and shop owners seeing if they might have seen a small child, seeking out places a child would most likely go or end up. The few that had seen Deestan only mentioned seeing her with Nyrene, earlier that day, but not recently. I was beginning to feel more frustrated. She was in my grasp, in reaching distance, here in the city, and I might never find her, yet she was so close to home. Where else she might be? Then as luck would have it, one of the townspeople approached us.

"My Lord, Den Master, I was wondering if the dancer child made her way back to your Den yet?" She asked sincerely.

"Do you mean a small girl, with reddish hair and bright green eyes?" Stasha asked her.

She nodded, "Yes the darling child was so adorable as she sat next to Lord Briar, and Chancellor Droggen while they attended today's petitioners."

Stasha and I looked at each other and knew immediately it must be Deestan. All I could do was thank the lady. Smiling in appreciation and trying to seem as nonchalant as possible, I quickly turned on my heels and walked back towards the direction of the castle. I had to remind myself to walk, not run. I knew I had to keep calm and not let my inner emotions show, I didn't want anyone to know we had her back yet. Perfectly composed on the outside, I was inwardly a mess of emotions. Howl followed us quietly behind as we went through the tunnels and towards the entrance.

Upon reaching the castle, I quickly stopped by the training grounds to grabbed Saibal since it was so near the balcony and the tunnel entrance, I hoped he might have seen her.

He was in the middle of practice but came to speak with me as I approached him. "Did you happen to see a little girl with red hair, dressed as a dancer this evening?" I asked as he looked between Stasha, Howl and I.

"As a matter of fact I did, I took her to the throne room figuring someone would fetch her." Saibal said to me. "Is that why Stasha and this man are with you?" Saibal asked while pointing towards Howl and Stasha questioningly.

"Actually no," Stasha replied, "I sort of misplaced our little princess and she decided to wander off alone."

Saibal had known some of the events of the night before but did not know we had found Deestan, nor did he know she was in the castle unaccompanied. He stood shocked for a moment, before turning calmly and walking back onto the training grounds. Quickly Saibal placed another man in charge of the troops and accompanied us towards the throne room where he had left Deestan.

The hall was silent when we entered; it was late past dinner for most. Neither Briar nor Droggen were anywhere in sight, I thought for a moment where they would go with a child who was lost.

"Why didn't you tell me sooner?" Saibal asked me as I walked the throne room's length.

I stopped and faced him. "I didn't know myself till recently, and I didn't want to alert too many people about it. I didn't know she'd wander off; otherwise this wouldn't have happened." I replied. "I was trying to keep the knowledge secret. Word could not get out that she was back in the castle, not yet anyway." I said cautiously knowing Alkin wanted her back in The Keep.

Stasha sighed, "Where could she go?" She asked.

"If she's here and she was with your friend Briar and Droggen then where would they be at this hour?" Howl asked while leaning against a nearby pillar.

I thought for a moment; if she was with Briar and Droggen then they would probably be in the dining room at this hour. "Droggen and Briar would be eating right now. Let's head there and see if they took her with them." I said hoping we could find her soon. I was growing antsy with anticipation and fearful of Alkin's words.

"Oh my Goddess this stuff is great!" I heard a child say as we entered the dining room. She seemed giddy with joy.

"I'm never allowed to eat this stuff at home!" She said as she danced around in the chair trying different meats that were served.

Droggen and Briar met my eyes as I entered. Droggen seemed rather confused with the child's behavior while Briar sat and laughed hysterically about the situation. My fatherly instincts took over as I went and stood behind Deestan, who appeared to be the same necromancer child we had found in the woods months ago.

"There you are, child. I have been looking all over for you." I said in a concerned but gentle voice. From what Stasha had told me she knew exactly who she was. "You had me worried sick." I said as she slowly turned around in the chair, a look of guilt crossed her face.

"Ah, what do you mean, Drake?" Droggen questioned. "I figured Stasha and this man were with you to accompany this child back to the Den. Or am I wrong?" Droggen looked at Stasha, Howl, and I confused as if searching for answers. While Briar sat in the chair trying to hide his chuckle.

It was Deestan who broke the silence. "Hello, Father. I'm sorry." She said in a quiet, meek voice, unsure of what to really do.

Droggen looked at me perplexed, and Briar smiled, while I reached down and picked her up, giving her a huge hug.

"I never thought I'd see you again." I said while kissing her head and inspecting her hand where she held the insignia. I gently turned it around as Droggen stood up.

"Drake, what is the meaning of this?" Droggen demanded. Briar just laughed, I figured he knew all along, and that was why Deestan was still with them.

"We have been entertaining Deestan this whole evening, and no one even knew who she was." Briar said, laughing more as he stood and patted my back. "This is great news to hear, I must say." He said, retaking his seat.

"Just don't get too attached so soon, she has to go back to The Keep before Hunter finds out she's gone. We have to be careful how we tread from now on." Stasha stressed as I looked Deestan over.

"I do have to go back." She agreed as a few tears ran down her cheek. "If I don't, I'm not sure what Hunter will do to my mother, and Alkin." She said, placing her head on my shoulder, holding me close and taking in my scent.

"How long before Hunter gets back?" I asked her. Deestan thought for a moment. "I'm not sure exactly. He left a week or so ago, and said he would return before the next full moon." She said. The next full moon was still a week away. We had a day or two at most with her before she had to return to The Keep.

"Where is your mother?" I asked her, eager to know about Raillyn's whereabouts. Stasha coughed for a moment as if ready to correct me until I realized my folly. "Where is Raillyn, better yet?" I asked her.

Deestan answered matter of fact like. "My mother is back in The Keep probably with Alkin since the attack happened. But I don't know where Raillyn is. My mother, the lady who raised me, is Raihanna."

I had figured Raihanna was her "mother" and proceeded carefully I did not want to make Deestan unwilling to share information with me, nor break the trust we were building.

"Tell me then about your mother. And more about who Alkin is?" I asked while placing Deestan down on the ground. She seemed to like to talk with her hands and her whole body. Her movement was fluid in doing so. *A werewolf trait,* I thought to myself. She started her story.

Deestan told us who her mother was, that Raihanna was one of Hunter's top warriors, and how she worked for him. She went on missions for him and collected various objects he needed. But recently she had been away without Hunter's knowledge, and Hunter punished her because of it.

Deestan told us about her half-sister, who she adored and spent most of her time with. She suspected Alkin was her father, but her mother never spoke of it. She told us Alkin was the Mystic that took her from Death's Realm as a baby. Deestan shared with us her knowledge of the Werewolves, and that the Lunar Goddess told her about her past because she performed the calling ritual one evening.

She carried on and told us Alkin lived with them and that he had his own room in their chambers. Alkin helped her mother and brought various books for her to study. He had brought her an entire collection of Werewolf magic and lunar books, including the Lunar Goddess statue.

As she told me this, I wondered about who Alkin really was and why he was bringing Deestan items that she should not have. In addition, why did he possess a dancer's token? If Hunter didn't want her to find out who she was, why he was encouraging her to learn about our culture. I was equally curious about Raihanna and the younger child.

"Sweetie, can you tell me more about Alkin? Does he work for Hunter or what does he do exactly? Also tell me about your sister." I said tactfully hoping she could answer. No one interrupted as we spoke as everyone was interested in the same information.

She began by telling us that Alkin didn't really work for Hunter because she noticed he didn't always follow his directions. He actually only followed half of what he was supposed to, from what she saw.

Hearing this indicated that he might be actually working for someone else, and spying on Hunter and his group. In a way, I felt that was sort of what we were doing, with having Deestan give us all this information and then having to send her back. I guessed it was a good thing she could impart and share so much information and no one would suspect her one bit.

Then Deestan started talking about her sister and her mother. "Last year I asked my mother if Alkin was Callina's father since he practically raised us as his own anyway. And she laughed about it. I even asked her if another warrior did it. I'm old enough to know how babies get there." She said proudly with her hands on her hips, before continuing on. "She never really told me who my sister's father was. But I know he's a Mystic." Deestan said while stopping in front of Howl. "Can I ask what you are?" She said looking up at him, her nose twitched. "You don't smell like anything I have ever smelled before."

Stasha met Howl's eyes for a brief moment as if she knew. He did smell odd, and it made me curious as well. "I'm something you don't get to see every day." He said while reaching down to ruffle her hair. "I can say this. You are right to suspect Alkin as your sister's father. He's the only other Mystic who I have found to still reside on this side of the Silver Sea."

At hearing, this Deestan's face lit up. "You mean in Alecien? You're not from Alecien? Oh, wow! What's it like across the sea?" She asked, suddenly eager for knowledge.

Howl smiled as he replied. "Maybe when things calm down a little, and you are able to stay freely in your father's land, I will tell you."

Deestan nodded her head, suddenly concerned before walking over towards me.

Gently I picked her up and hugged her again. "Don't worry, everything will be okay. I love you." I said, reassuring her, while closing my eyes, knowing I had to go to the Goddess statue tonight to seek some more answers.

"She can't stay here," I said wishing she could. "If we don't send her back, Raihanna and Alkin will alert Hunter, and we will never get them back for good." Hoping they heard the strain in my voice.

As I walked, Stasha smiled when she looked at Deestan again. "She's sleeping." She said, walking over and brushing her hair away from her face. Deestan stirred slightly, and I figured we should take this discussion into the den south of my quarters.

After laying Deestan down in her own room, I walked south into the den to rejoin the others. "Deestan said that Raihanna was punished for leaving The Keep for so long by herself. I would have to guess no one knew where she was during that time." I said as I walked towards the fireplace.

Howl smirked at me slightly. "That's how Vampires are." He said. "They can't be trusted, and they don't care if they kill their own kind." He said pausing for a moment before going on. "I know where Raihanna went and why Hunter punished her. When I was investigating, I heard word that she was doing research on the true reason the war began. So in other words she began to poke her nose where it shouldn't be. The Vampires of all people would be furious about this, so I'm betting that's why Hunter punished her. It's what led me to those Vampires on the edge of your land." He said while looking at me. "I assure you I am on your side. I have an idea about what's going on here, maybe we can work together and solve this little problem. I believe I have more information on Raihanna that you might be lacking." Howl said with a gleam in his eye.

Stasha stepped forward to speak with him. "First off, tell us how Alkin knew your name and second, why is Solomn leader of Silvertine involved?" She asked.

I stood and listened. I had never heard of Silvertine, nor their leaders, but believed it was possibly in Aeralain or else-where.

Howl paused for a moment hesitant. "That information I will impart to you if we are willing to work together. Let's just say the Drakars take particular interest in Raillyn and her God lineage. But that doesn't mean much to your people since that information was lost at the beginning of the war. Does it?" Howl said as he indicated he did, in fact know more than what he was telling us.

"How do you know about Raillyn? And how old are you?" I asked him suddenly unsure of what we had brought with us.

Laughing Howl replied. "Much older than you think, I remember the beginning of your war, and how it ripped asunder the land, it was a devastating time. I have returned to Alecien because the Vampires once more are gathering forces and trying to conquer this land. It can't happen, and this world cannot afford that darkness. Too much has already been lost and too many have paid the price. I will not stand by and watch our world fall into darkness. Delron can smite me if the Gods disagree. In this affair I will not stand by and watch this time, nor will I run." He said determination crossing his face. His blue eyes seemed to glow and boom with power, becoming an icy inferno within.

At that moment, I felt we could trust Howl. I sensed he spoke true and would offer a great deal of knowledge to impart to us.

I shook my head "We have to find out the true purpose of Alkin's plan. We know he fights with the Elite and possibly had a hand with the portal's creation. Whatever his purpose is, he has done much damage not only to us but possibly to Hunter as well."

Howl nodded in agreement, standing silent for the time being. "I will tell you more, later, Lord Drake. Preferably just the two of us can talk. Just know that Callina is, in fact Alkin's daughter, and at this time she is in Silvertine, which is in Aeralain." Howl said as he showed himself to the door, nodding his head respectfully before entering the hall. I knew he would not make it far before my guards escorted him the rest of the way.

After he left, Briar and I decided to visit the temple before turning in for the night. Stasha accompanied us to the village and headed toward the Den while we crossed the center of town toward the temple, Stasha left for the Den.

"Just remember, friend, she has to go back soon; she cannot stay." Stasha stressed as Briar and I waved goodbye and nodded in reply.

I agreed. I wasn't sure what to think of Alkin. If he wasn't really working for the Vampires who was he working for? It might make things better or worse for us in the end. I wanted to find out the truth about him and what his true purpose really was.

We entered the quiet temple and walked the spiral staircase towards the top floor. I had left Deestan under Saibal's guard, and ensured that there was only one door unlocked which was the one to my room, where Saibal stood watch.

Entering the top chamber, Briar and I performed the ritual as we had so many times before, I cut my palm and Briar did the same. As I laid my hand on the statue, I couldn't help but remember Deestan telling us she performed the ritual on her own after reading it in a book. I smiled knowing she was already well educated in our ways, and very few things set her apart from our people.

As we summoned the Lunar Goddess, she gave us the feeling that she was glad we had done so. "I am pleased to see you, my children." She said in a whimsical tone. "What have you called me for this night?"

I was hoping she could illuminate more on the matter of Raihanna and the girls. I went over the information which Deestan had shared with us. "It seems like Alkin might be working for someone other than Hunter. I don't know what that means. If it's better he's not one of Hunters pawn, or not. I don't know which would be better." I said, after sharing the information.

I felt the Goddess smile in response. "I cannot share much light on that subject, my child. I do not know what travesties the Vampires are planning, but I care not for them myself. As you know we Gods cannot outright play a hand in any events that happen in your world, we are only allowed to watch and suggest happenings to our children. If we or our kin played a direct hand in such events, terrible things would occur as a result." The Goddess said reminding me of what I already knew.

Anyone that had a connection with any God or Goddess knew this fact. The Gods and their kin could not nor would intervene directly in anything that happened. Catastrophic events could occur if they did intervene.

I nodded my head, "I'm sorry, my child, I cannot help any further in these events. I will say this, tread carefully in the events to come. One false move could spell disaster. Trust those around you and allow new friendships to begin, even if strenuous events occur." The Goddess said as she left us to ponder her words.

Removing my hand from the statue, I sighed, the only other person that might be able to shed some light on this situation would be Drameon. He had said he once worked with Alkin, when we saw him and Deestan in the meadow months ago. I relayed this to Briar as we descended the stairs and made our way back to the castle.

In the castle, I left Briar momentarily in the den south of Deestan's room, I had to check on her and inform Saibal we had returned. Upon entering the room, it was strange seeing her sleeping so soundly in her own bed.

The bright green walls with the forest mural seemed to glow and come alive with light from the tiny green magic ball on her desk, while her deep purple bed looked nearly black in color.

After her being gone for so long, I felt as if I had missed so much. She was no longer a small infant, but a child with her own blooming personality.

I sat by her bed momentarily and brushed a small bit of hair away from her eyes. I found myself thinking back to the time we saw her in the meadow and wondered why I hadn't considered her to be my daughter then. Something must have masked her scent from me that was the only solution. I should have known her scent right away, but she smelled like the Vampires, and I could not smell her Wolf blood at all then. That was something else I would have to find answers to later.

She resembled Raillyn in many ways but held her own distinct features. You could see the Mystic in her with her high cheekbones and bright hair. I brushed her hair once more from her face and tucked it behind her ear, pausing I noticed her ears were slightly pointed as some Mystics were. This made me wonder since Raillyn herself did not have this feature. I shrugged; she must have acquired it through another family member in Raillyn's line.

I smiled as I got up and opened the door to my room. I saw Saibal standing guard nearby. He sat in the chair to the left of her door, and nodded as I entered the room. I closed it quietly behind me.

"How did the temple go?" Saibal asked while standing from his seat.

I shook my head. "It didn't go as planned; she had no more information to give us, and gave us a warning to proceed with caution from now on, but to trust those we are working with right now and not falter."

"Well, you can't help but to proceed without full caution on this. I mean if Raihanna has any tie to Raillyn, it could mean her death. Maybe Hunter used magic and Raihanna is in fact, Raillyn. I've heard evil magic can be used to changed appearance and magic. If that the case, she obviously doesn't know who she is, or she wouldn't be one of his Elite." Saibal said in response to my disappointed mood.

I had to agree. I was beginning to believe Hunter had done something to Raillyn and Raihanna was the result of it. "Stay here and guard her a little longer. I have to finish some stuff up." I said as I left the room and decided I needed a quick reprieve before summoning Drameon.

Walking out to the balcony was refreshing and calming. So much had happened from the events, even just a few moments away would help me think and clear my racing mind. Grasping the necklace I tried to contact Drameon, but he gave a magical response that he was busy with other matters at the time. Going to the rail I gazed up at the bright moon and felt its calming effects on me.

Howl ~ Drake

Just as a chill began to cool the air, I turned, sensing a presence near the pillars. Howl stepped out of the shadows. Nodding his head he came to sit in a nearby chair, I was surprised to see him and wondered how he eluded my guards.

"Sit, Lord Drake, I have much to tell you tonight, and I figured we could share a drink or two while I tell you my story." He said while pulling out a bottle of what appeared to be wine.

Sighing I sat next to him and took a newly poured cup. Smiling he tossed back his drink and refilled it once more. "How did you get out here without alerting the guard?" I asked hesitant of the answer.

After pondering for a moment, he answered. "Ancients don't always need doors to get where they want to go. Even though the magic in this land is weak, I can still utilize it, even more now due to certain events." He said casually before going on. "Alright, let's see. First off, I guess you want to know some information that might tie Raihanna to Raillyn." Howl said as he drank down another cup.

I looked at him curious to know his ideas, I had my own about how the two were tied together but Howl seemed as if he knew. Nodding my head, I took a drink of the wine. Its tart bitter taste slightly burned as it danced across my tongue but felt refreshing all the same. It was a potent blend of herbs and spices that caused warmth to spread in my body.

"I believe Raihanna is a key of some sort. She's in a construct body, meaning she is created, but not just a normal creation. She was put together meticulously and carefully to ensure she would appear and function as normal as possible. Her body consists of natural components found in nature, soil, herbs, gems, and various other items." Howl said cautiously while taking another drink of his wine. "As for her soul I believe she has her normal soul. That being said you know Raihanna is a Mystic, but what you don't realize is what a Mystic really is. A Mystic is someone who is born with God blood. They are what your people call a Demigod."

After hearing this, I paused for a moment, surely he was wrong, but he continued. "It's true, Mystic means child of the Gods or one of God lineage, in the Ancient tongue. The meaning was lost during the war, and your people began using the word Demigod to describe what they could not and Mystic to describe those born here in the world but still had the power of the Gods. In other words, a Mystic is only born when a God mingles with pretty much anyone in Auran. Or if two Mystics have a child, that child would be a Mystic. Any other time, such as your daughter, they are considered Half-breeds and take after their non-Mystic parent. So your daughter is a Werewolf, but Alkin's daughter is a Mystic because Raihanna is her mother. If that makes sense." He said as he filled his cup again.

Slowly I drank some more of the wine, it made my head spin a little, and I couldn't believe he had already drunk three cups. "So if Raihanna is in a construct body does that mean Hunter did something to Raillyn and Raihanna is the result?" I asked, trying to think along his terms, as well as get answers to some of the questions we had.

Pointing at me, Howl smiled. "Here's the thing. Hunter doesn't know a spell to do that, and neither would anyone in Alecien. It's an Ancient art in the blood magic. Only the Ancient races have the power and knowledge to create a true construct body and soul. Alkin crafted Raihanna's body. I'm sure if you got him to talk he would tell you what he did to Raillyn." Howl said as he took a sip. "Raihanna is under powerful magic. She has a task to complete before the construct body can be dispelled. If she fails the task, she will die along with her soul and her real body." I looked at Howl curiously. "Do you know where her real body is?" I asked unsure of the magic which was being dealt with but sure it was tied to Raillyn somehow.

Howl paused for a moment to fill his glass before going on. "I don't know where her body is, nor do I think Alkin even knows. He's working for an interesting consort. An old friend who dates back to many of the issues Alecien has currently." He said with concern in his voice.

Finishing my own cup, I allowed Howl to refill it as I thought over this information. "So who Alkin is working with? And if they are both Mystics why are they interfering with events so much? I thought Demi... I mean Mystics, were not allowed to have a hand in events?" I asked suddenly aware I was acquiring lost information and history our land hadn't been associated with in many decades.

Nodding, Howl answered me. "Yes you're right. Mystics are not supposed to mess in the affairs of the non-Ancient races of Auran, unless the Gods say they can. I believe their God lineage has allowed their affairs to go unnoticed, but for how long I cannot say. And sadly, yes, I know who Alkin is working with. Too much blood has been paid for the acts of the war." Howl began deep in thought. "Before the war Alecien was a peaceful place, even though the Vampires ran rampant over here. It was a land where Half-breeds could live without worrying about their lineage, and discrimination. Aeralain tries to be understanding about Half-breeds, but most of the older races force you to choose which way of life you want to live. Yes, it makes things easier overall except for those who do not wish to choose, and become nomads. Aeralain is dangerous, and nomads often fall victim to rape, death, and dark arts, it's always best to stay in a close knit community, but often Half-breeds don't always feel this way. That's why some left here to Alecien, it offered them a safe haven, and a land where they could just blend in." Howl said with a far off look in his eyes. "There are very few cities where everyone mingles, and usually those that do tread carefully there."

Howl smiled at me before going on. "As far as the war itself, it wasn't until they acquired Daes' favorite child that things went sour. They stole her, tortured her, and drained her. I will never forget how powerless I was when she died. I was sworn to protect her, and I couldn't do anything. The Vampires had poisoned me and planned to drain my blood as well, but Drameon stopped that affair. I felt Calista's death just as I knew he would; he was her love, her mate. Minutes after she died he was already there, storming through the lower levels of The Keep towards the spelled portion of the cellar. In his rage, he killed everyone in his path, only Alkin could break his berserk state of mind. After realizing what he had done, he released me. Calista was gone, we knew there was nothing we could do. Alkin himself went to Delron and begged for her release, but both Delron and her father denied our request. Balance had already been disrupted and already the realm of Alecien began to fall to darkness. Afterwards, I knew Drameon would be punished for his crimes, but what punishment he received I cannot say. Just that I imagine it was a long hard road for him. I haven't seen him since then either, nor heard about him till recently." Howl said as he paused to finish his cup and refill mine again.

I knew shock crossed my face. "Drameon?" I questioned unsure what else I should ask. My mind seemed to go blank, he had been helping us, guiding us and for what?

Howl frowned before speaking. "I won't bore you with all the details now, but I had lost track of Drameon and Alkin after that. I was given another task, which I carried out, but through it we lost the dearest thing Auran had. All adult Mystic's of Daes' lineage were gone. Only one remained, a child and Daes himself handled her. I was told never to speak of it until the day she returned to Auran. You see, during the war they laid a powerful spell upon her. Her tiny child body could not handle the chaos surrounding her, she was used to the harmony Daes' blood and magic brought, and the war was ripping her asunder. It wasn't until recently that I realized the Gods released her from her magical slumber. I was equally shocked to learn they placed her into Alecien. The very place where she was needed, but at the same time the very place that could spell her death. I had half a mind to come to her when she was young, to prevent the Vampires from getting her, but I was forbidden until recently. And the funny thing about all this, she was the one to find me, having the harmonized chaotic blood of the blue Dragon race Daes himself created. I know it in my very being. Raihanna has to be Raillyn." He said pausing as he realized he had said too much.

For a brief moment, our eyes met. "While the Mystics do what they are told they also in turn do what is best for the land. Raillyn was the last lineage Mystic of Daes, she was the child that the Gods stole away from the world to keep safe. In a way, I'm half surprised Alkin didn't grab her sooner, she was his—as you put it—betrothed.... If she dies our chances of correcting this mess will die with her." Howl said as realization struck me. Drameon and Alkin had been working together since the beginning. Drameon and Alkin were taking orders from the Gods and were carrying them out. In turn, Raillyn was a Mystic, a Demigod, and Alkin was her betrothed before she was taken by the Gods and placed with Chaimh... They had to know what happened to her. Did that make me and my people pawns in this game?

Lost in the new knowledge and feeling my head swim from the effects of the wine. I finished the cup I had. I had much to think about and debate over.

Shocked I finally spoke. "Thank you Howl. You have been of great help. And have given me much to think on. If you need anything just ask." Wondering what else he knew.

Matters ~ Drameon

I grew tired awaiting Alkin's response. I knew he had accomplished many tasks I had sent him to do, but one in particular troubled me. I needed to speak with him further about
the matter. I was growing more impatient when Alkin entered
a portal just beside me, bowing while it closed.

"I bring news, my friend. Rai has become apprehensive
about the Vampires, thanks to Howl's lesson." Alkin said
while smiling at me.

I nodded and could not help but smile myself. Everything
was happening according to plan. I only hope that Hunter
would go about his scheme. If he diverted from his plan it
would cause us more problems in defeating him later.

I turned towards a nearby shelf and retrieved a simple
crystal bottle which stood amongst other items. The bottle
was the size of my palm and contained a glowing blue liquid.
I tossed it to Alkin, knowing reflexively he would catch it
with ease.

As he turned the item over in his hand, he gave me a puzzled look. "What is this?" He asked, inspecting the bottle once
more.

Grinning knowingly, this simple bottle would cause
Hunter's plans to fall apart. It would take time but once it began nothing would change the outcome. Daes himself crafted
the powerful potion and only he knew what its full effects
would entitle. While I was nervous about this, I knew had to
be done. "That bottle contains a powerful potion; it's a blood
potion, a reversal spell from Daes. I believe it's time that you
give it to Rai." I waved my hand at Alkin beckoning him to
take his leave.

He seemed to pause for a moment while turning over the
bottle once more in his hand, but decided against whatever it

was he was going to ask. Instead, he opened up a portal and left back to The Keep.

Alkin

After entering The Keep, I couldn't help but pause to ponder Drameon's words. What would the potion do to Rai once I gave it to her? I knew it was a blood potion. The thought of it having been crafted by the Gods made me uneasy. I considered the powerful effects it may have on her and the construct body.

Walking into our chambers I saw Rai on the floor, books piled around her. She seemed to be pouring over more of Howl's texts. Still I smiled, knowing she was on the right path mind wise at least to our goal.

"How goes getting the girls back?" I asked as I sat next to her in the nearby chair. She grimaced at my question.

"I went to get them this morning, but the Den refused me, and turned me away. Hunter will be back before nightfall two days from now, and if the girls are not back with us, I don't know what he will do." Rai said saddened by the mistake she made, even though at the time she was left with little choice.

All I could think of was what trouble the girls were getting into. I knew Deestan was dabbling in the Werewolves magic, I had found her myself after she awakened the Goddess statue I brought her. It left me to conclude that the Den knew who she was. This was the main reason I had my troops attack the Werewolves on their land. It allowed me to speak to Lord Drake, confirming that the Den had them.

Callina was another matter; I had to get her back for the last step in the spell. I cringed at what my daughter would go through, and hated myself for what I had done to deserve this. Never would I try and attempt to kill Lord Drake again, as I had tried, so long ago near the river's edge in my father's realm.

"Well, maybe if I go and speak with them they might change their tune. I know you are not permitted entry, but I am not one of the Elite. Let me try tonight and see where it can get us." I said as I got up and left the room, knowing Yumi, the Vampires Den Master, would listen to me.

As I walked, I thought how I would get Rai to drink the potion. I knew she would not drink it outright unless she was dying. After the recent events, she had become suspicious of everything, at least everything that was around The Keep.

Unconsciously, though, she gravitated towards the bond we shared. Needing nothing that would interfere with these final stages, I knew her erratic power and construct body was going to push us towards another mishap. Her construct body not only was out of control as is neared its death, but it caused her natural instincts and primitive behavior to be unbalanced. Already I sensed her cycle was erratic, matching her unbalanced behavior. The sooner we finished this and Raihanna died the better things would be.

Her magic, emotions, and instinctive behavior would level out over time and fall into the typical three to five year cycle female Mystics followed. I feared her next cycle though. Instinctively, just as before, she would seek me out, like an addiction. It was a dangerous time and one that lead to equally dangerous issues.

Walking the illuminated streets, I looked up at the glowing half-moon and took a deep breathe. We had enough to think about now than to worry about what would happen later.

Soon we would leave this place, but first I had to ensure my girls were safe. Surfacing from my thoughts, I found myself at the white wood doors belonging to the den. Casually I let myself in. Being a Mystic granted me access to just about anywhere, regardless of my status in Hunter's ranks. Another key bit of information that Rai had lacked. I also had the token that marked me as a dancer, granting me permanent access and sanctuary.

Upon entering the Den, my appearance startled many of the dancers, and a few came to stop my entry. As they approached, I drew the small token that lay hidden on my belt. All but one dancer returned to their work, he eyed me warily, and came to see what I wanted.

"What do you want here?" The male dancer asked as he approached me. Like all the male dancers, he wore no shirt and had long billowing black pants with black beads adorning his belt and sash.

"I'm here to speak to your Den Master." I said while smiling. "And as you can see I have access." Nodding towards the charm.

"How do I know you didn't steal it off one of our own after you killed them? That's what your people do, isn't it..." The man began to say as he was interrupted by another.

Stasha, the tall lady with olive skin stood next to Den Master Yumi. "Ralous, don't threaten our guest." Stasha said, causing the man to retreat back to his prior task in the main room of the Den. "Please accompany us to a smaller room where we can discuss this matter further in quiet." She said while holding her hand out towards the room which was behind her.

I had been in more than a few different Dens through my life, and all of them had the same layout. I knew the staircase, was to my left as I walked across the main room. It would lead to other Dens in the area, through a series of tunnels beneath the ground. The hearth burned brightly in the dimmed room. As I passed, its flames reflected my image in as a shadow against the furs and tapestries adorning the wall. Entering the small room Stasha indicated, Yumi shut the door joining us.

Yumi broke the silence. "What are you doing here Alkin? I have asked you not to come to my Den without alerting me beforehand." Yumi said, angered at me for not sending word before my arrival.

"Wait; you know this Mystic?" Stasha asked.

Yumi nodded. "Yes, this is Alkin. He's a friend, I guess, if you can call him that. His adoptive parents rule Silvertine, hence why he carries our token." Yumi said, relaying a bit of my Ancient history to her friend.

"It doesn't matter!" I yelled in an authoritative tone.

Stasha knew who, and what, I was. We had been working together with Drameon and Celleste since we first discovered

Raillyn was pregnant with Deestan. Celleste cast a spell, binding her not to speak about our endeavors, and so far it worked, the Wolves and everyone around her were oblivious.

"What matters is that you have my girls and if I'm not mistaken this has become Den business due to it." I said while pointing to myself, knowing I had an upper hand in this matter, due to my title and family.

Yumi paused for a moment with a look of disbelief on her face, and glanced at Stasha who spoke. "Alkin, you and I both know the truth about what happened in the past. But, why do you claim them as yours? Other than the brief conversation earlier, we haven't spoken since the incident!" She yelled, obviously upset at me still.

I sighed, knowing it would come down to this after what happened in the woods with her. "They are mine because I claim them as mine. The wolf child I have raised as my own for over six years and I convinced Hunter to release Leeda into my care, as well. Making them both mine, regardless of blood. Callina is my own flesh and blood daughter, and they must be returned to me before Hunter arrives home." I said looking at them, hoping I wouldn't have to explain to Yumi what happened.

She looked at me baffled, and knew me well enough to see that I was playing my game. Not wanting to press me she apologized. "I'm sorry, Alkin." She said. "But I cannot just release them to you. They are Den children now. We have given the girls free access here." Yumi said, I could tell she chose her words carefully and tactfully. Playing her own game.

I was enraged by this, furious that if Hunter found out, horrors would break lose. "Do you know what will happen if those girls are not returned before he arrives at The Keep in a few days' time?" I stressed knowing I could speak freely about my situation.

Stasha and Yumi paused for a moment, pondering; they knew I spoke the truth, and I saw a flicker of fear in both their eyes.

"Yes, I know what will happen. Hunter will storm the Den, but if that happens war will break out." Stasha said smiling. "Hunter won't risk that, especially if he learns more about your lineage, and that Silvertine would come to our aid."

Damn that woman, I wished we never had to involve her in our affairs in the first place. Because of it she knew way too much of the game we played. At the time, we had no choice, we needed someone on the inside who would allow us access to Raillyn and who would assist us. Someone who could give her the herbs and blood she needed to survive being pregnant, but who she would never suspect. Stasha had become our double agent in that affair. She allowed us access to the Den, and in turn she blended Celeste's herbal drought with Raillyn's raspberry tea. Helping us ensure her safety. Those old wounds seemed to tear open.

"Return to me my daughter, the Shifter Princess, and the Wolf Heir, and I will leave you now." I demanded holding out my empty hands in peace, trying to calm myself.

Stasha smiled at me again. "I think it's time you tell me why Raillyn is so important to you?" Stasha asked me mockingly.

"You really want to know the truth?" I asked as I saw Yumi shy away. She knew how powerful I was when I was angry and at the moment my power seemed to boom in a haze of red smoke. "Raillyn never belonged to Drake or his people, he took her from me. You remember the day we met, when we asked if you could keep an eye on Raillyn and get her to tell you if she knew who Deestan's father was? That's because the baby was supposed to be mine. Whether Raillyn told you or not, she mated with me first and I claimed her as mine. Drake has no right to her, nor has he. Even before she knew it, she was my—as you say—betrothed. In addition, I was the one who ordered the Elite to capture the Shifter Princess as the portal was being taken down by the Werewolves and the Shifters. In turn, I was the one with Hunter when we took Deestan and Raillyn from the realm of the dead. By telling you this, you in turn know what I am capable of. As I told you, this is the Gods will. So again I am telling you to return the girls to me."

Both had a look of fear in their eyes. I had come out and said what happened, admitted the truth about Raillyn and what infuriated me the most about Drake. As I stood there and realized what I said, I regretted it.

Truthfully, I had come to terms with what happened over six years ago. Taking Raillyn and Deestan, dissipated those ugly, jealous, inner demons. However now that Drake was becoming more involved, I was feeling protective and begrudging again. Neither of them would understand the full truth. What I had given them was truthful in a sense, but only shed light on half the subject. The rest would have to be addressed at a later time. Waiting, Yumi looked at Stasha once more and waited.

Stasha sighed and finally spoke. "I cannot allow you to have Deestan at this moment, she is not here. Leeda is asleep in the lower chambers, but it is late, do not awaken her tonight. As you already know the Silvertine Den has your blood daughter. I assure you I will have Yumi return the girls by nightfall tomorrow at the latest." Stasha assured me.

"Where is Deestan?" I questioned hoping I would be wrong with my thoughts on where she was.

Yumi's wide eyes met mine for a moment as she took a deep slow breath. She knew I would not like the answer.

"She's with her father tonight." She said quietly.

Furiously my magic rose with my anger, I knew my eyes flashed red before I closed them. Both Stasha and Yumi felt my response, and before I did anything irrational Stasha carried on.

"She's a child who wanted to see her father. That is all! I cannot ignore that, regardless of the stupid situation. We have kept everything hush and allowed her one visit. I assure you no one knows who she is other than the select few who will keep quiet. If you are a Den member, then you will understand and accept this as our way." Stasha said with determination.

I was shaking with anger. If word got out that the Werewolf Princess was returned, Hunter would be furious and I did not know what he would do. I did know that his first order would be to have Rai, and me sentenced to death because of our mistake, but Stasha was right as well, it was their way.

Since Rai released the girls into the care of the Den, they acted on their own accord and took the girls as their own; granting them permanent access into the Den for life. I knew that Hunter would not like that information. As long as the people who knew kept quiet there was not much else I could do—or hope for—at this time.

"If you or the ones who know about the girls so much as breath any of the information I just told you to anyone else, I will personally see to your punishment." I said, pointing my finger towards both of them. "You will return to the girls to me before nightfall tomorrow, or I will inform Raihanna that you don't intend to release them." I said choosing my words carefully. I could not act against the Den in this matter since it was their tradition and laws that bound the matter, but Raihanna could.

Turning to leave, I left more furious than I was before arriving, but equally concerned about what was going on with the Wolf Princess since she was in the Wolves' castle tonight. By the Den law if they failed to ensure their end of the bargain I had equal rights to direct punishment upon them.

Curiosity ~ Drake

I sat and waited in the small den south of my chambers, my eyes reflected the firelight as I watched it dance. I had sent out another call to Drameon, this time I felt he would arrive before the night was done. It was frustrating and I was furious. Drameon had to know what was going on, he and Alkin had been working together this whole time and for what? I asked myself as I got up and began pacing the room.

The grey smoke indicating a portal broke my thought. Drameon stepped out and stood watching as I met his ever-changing eyes. "I am highly upset with you!" I yelled at him as I pointed my finger towards him and tried to control the boiling anger I felt inside. "Not once did you tell us that you and Alkin are working together! Or the fact that Raillyn was betrothed to Alkin before she was sent to Chaimh and Lillian. You set all this up, didn't you? Where is Raillyn?" I asked, outraged, my ears and face burned with anger.

Drameon smirked slightly before taking a seat. "Sit Lord Drake. I cannot say everything, but I feel I owe you a little explanation as to what is going on." He said in his calm tone and mild demeanor.

Taking a seat I fidgeted slightly to keep myself from raising my voice once more.

"First off, this situation is much more complicated than anyone had first anticipated. Second, who told you Alkin and I are currently working together? I assume this same person also mentioned the betrothed part?" He asked curiously.

Leaning forward in the chair next to him, I explained. He hadn't done anything directly to hurt me or my people, so I felt I could at least give him that piece of trust, for now anyway. I explained the attack Alkin had lead on the village near the borders and that Howl was there. In turn, I explained a little of what Howl imparted to me about the Mystics and Raihanna being a construct that could only be fashioned by Alkin. Lastly I explained that Howl had said they had a long history that included Raillyn's past and it seemed that Alkin and Drameon were still working together. I was not sure how much he already knew but felt he understood what I was talking about.

Drameon seemed to be deep in thought, and as I grew weary of waiting, he finally answered. "While I cannot say too much I will say this, everything that is happening is happening because the Gods deem it necessary. Yes, Alkin and I are Mystics, and we serve our lineage God, and in turn yes, Raillyn is Mystic. Eventually, she will have to follow her God as well."

I listened intently I was unsure what he would impart to me, but wanting to be sure I understood it all.

"Which brings me to the problem. As you know, Raillyn is much older than you or her originally thought. In addition, Mystics have certain traditions. The Gods made her forget her past before she was taken. So she has no knowledge to her real parents or her betrothal. But you know she's Daes' last Mystic, and if she dies then so does hope for the world to return to normal..." He sighed and gazed into the fire for a moment.

I interrupted, anger boomed in me once more. "If she's so special then why is she with the Vampires? Is there a reason and if so it better be good because I am sick and tired of this game you Mystics play! I want to know where Raillyn is, and I want her home safe! Betrothal or not, she is my mate, and I laid claim to her first!" I yelled while standing and pacing in hopes of calming myself once more. I felt my power rise in response to my anger, and I knew from the past it could be a dangerous mixture.

Looking up and taking note, Drameon leaned back and went on. "Do not think I don't want her home safe as well, Wolf Lord?" He said in a slightly mocking tone. "I have known her much longer than you and, trust me, if I didn't have to place her in The Keep I would've never had Alkin take her. Let alone have Alkin stay in that wretched place for so long!" Drameon stood as his eyes flashed red with anger.

The magic that poured from him was startling, not once had I noticed how much power he really had, before now. "In addition if you are so done with the Mystics, that in turn would include Raillyn! She is in The Keep to do a task. In turn, that task will unlock her memories and magic so she can restore the lost power in the world. Daes himself wanted her there, and I am not going to go against a God to make myself, or her so-called mate happy!" He finished with his burning red eyes meeting mine. "Yes, I know. I didn't make things better by doing what I did, but Raillyn belongs to Daes, she is his, and she will serve him one day just as I serve my mother! If you want her back alive you will have to trust me and let us Mystics do our job!" He said, as he paused to try and compose himself. "I'm sorry, but I will have talk to you again when things are not so heated between us." He said as he began to call a portal to leave.

As the smoke dissipated, I was left wondering. I had more unanswered questions than I started with. I would have to ask Howl sometime about Raillyn and if she truly has no choice. I was eager to learn that she had a chance to return to us, but also I was growing fearful of how she would return. It equally irritated me that I didn't receive any more information on Raihanna. Opening the door to the hall I walked through it to my own chambers. Hopeful that sleep might help clear the fog in my head.

Deestan

Upon waking, I breathed in the scent of the castle and smiled. I could tell I was home. I was in my father's castle and felt better than I had any other time in my life. I sat up and stretched, reaching my hands towards the white canopy that was hung from my cherry wood four poster bed.

Carefully I climbed out. My bare feet touched the beautifully colored rug beneath. I lightly walked to the end of my bed that was adorned with purple blankets and my father's royal symbol. I was in the Werewolves' castle and not the Vampire's Keep. For a moment, I felt saddened because I missed my mother but in turn I was happy and wished she would one day be able to see where I was.

Deep in thought, I walked to my cherry dresser, I hoped there would be something that fit. Sure enough it was filled with many clothes; most of them were dancer outfits. I dressed in a similar outfit from last night, this time it was forest green instead of the icy blue.

I looked around momentarily, my room had several doors, one sat beside a large window, and I could see went outside, probably to a balcony. While the three others went possibly to other rooms or the main hall, standing and pondering I went to the largest door. Walking over, I slowly opened it and peered around the corner. It led out to the hallway, and Captain Saibal stood nearby. He turned and faced me upon hearing the door open.

Saibal walked over and knelt down to meet me. "Glad to see you are up, little one. Your father had business in the Den this morning, and wishes me to bring you there when you are ready." Saibal said to me while smiling.

I smiled in return, scanning the empty hall. "I would like to see my father, please." I said while coming out into the hall slowly.

Captain Saibal nodded and stopped me from closing the door fully. "You need to get your cloak then if we are to go to the Den. We need to make sure no one knows who you are." Saibal said while pointing to a red cloak that was laid out on a nearby chair.

I quickly ran over to it and put it on. As I walked back to the doorway where Captain Saibal waited I reached for his hand. I made sure the hood was pulled over my face as Saibal pulled the door shut, and led the way.

Upon exiting the tunnels, the lady from the day before greeted us. "Captain, I will take your charge from her, so you can return to your duties." Nyrene said, holding out her hand for me to take.

Captain Saibal smiled as I reached out to take Nyrene's hand. "She's a good friend of your father's and a good Denmate. She will take you directly to him." He assured me as he turned to re-enter the tunnels. I smiled up at her knowing she knew who I was now.

Upon entering the Den, I saw many dancers practicing around the large hearth in the center of the room. Nyrene smiled as my face lit up in response to the music being played. It was a fast beat tempo on drums, with the haunted shrill of flutes, and timid lutes. I spun around several times, dancing to the beat of the music to my own accord.

Nyrene laughed and danced around me once before taking my hand once more. "Come on, little bird, we need to take you to the lower levels." Nyrene said as she led me down the stairs to the smaller rooms and the tunnels below.

Laughing we made our way down. Nyrene stopped at a door not too far from the bottom step. Carefully Nyrene opened it and nudged me into the room. Stasha and my father sat at a small table, a magic light on its surface gave off an orange glow.

When I saw my father, I ran to him, removing the cloak as I allowed him to pick me up and hold me in his arms. I found myself nuzzling my face into his shoulder and taking in his scent. It felt good being in his arms once more.

"Did you sleep well?" He asked me. I nodded my head in response. "Thank you, Nyrene, for bringing her here." My father said as Nyrene waved and left the room pulling the door shut behind her.

I looked up at my father, he seemed uneasy this morning. "Is there trouble?" I asked hoping all was well.

My father sighed lightly, and Stasha looked towards the ground, I knew something was amiss. "Nothing too big, but I have to return you to The Keep by nightfall." He said while placing me back on my feet.

I looked up at him saddened by this but also curious as to how these events came about. "How do you know you have to return me tonight?" I asked. I was hoping I could stay another night in the Werewolves' castle.

My father looked at Stasha momentarily as if he wondered how to explain the situation. As he did so I felt a magical presence behind me, it was a portal spell. My father lightly cursed at its appearance.

Whoever was coming out of the portal was strong, stronger than I had ever encountered before in my life. With living in the Vampire's Keep I had often ran into powerful beings, but this one frightened me. I backed up and hid behind my father as I carefully peered around to see who was coming to visit us.

A tall man with high cheekbones and an elegant face which gave him an elfin appearance stepped out. His long silver hair and ever-changing eyes indicated he was no Elf, but Mystic instead. Between his eyes and his power I knew he was something much more than a typical Mystic which I had read about in the books my mother and Alkin had given me. Eyes wide, I watched as he bowed slightly to my father and spoke.

"Lord Drake, Den Master Stasha, I am sorry for the outburst earlier and hoped we could talk on less strenuous terms." The man said as he met my eyes momentarily. I felt my father tense and step further in front of me.

Quickly I ducked behind my father more, and he gave a light chuckle while he looked at me. I was unsure really what to do, and no one was saying anything. I looked at my father, wide-eyed and nervous, for a sign that this man was okay. "It's alright, Deestan, this is Drameon he's a friend of ours. He has been assisting us for some time." My father said while stepping aside so Drameon could see me. He seemed tense but was trying not to show it.

Drameon looked at my father before kneeling down and smiling. "Why, hello, 'little bird', I'm glad to see Lord Drake was able to retrieve his daughter." Drameon said, reaching out to shake my hand.

For a moment I didn't register what he had said, then it struck me; he had used the Mystic tongue to call me little bird, something my mother and Alkin had taught me after my sister was born. Suddenly I felt less afraid and reached out and took his hand. A strange pulse of energy emanated from him and I tilted my head in response.

I paused for a moment unsure how to proceed. "What are you?" I asked carefully the best I could in the Mystic tongue.

My father and Stasha gave us an odd look, but Drameon held up his hand stopping them from asking anything. "I can sense that you are Mystic, but you are stronger than anyone I've met before."

Drameon smiled, and I saw a gleam in his eyes, he casually brushed his silver hair back behind his ears and paused momentarily as if debating on how to answer my question. I noticed when he did so that his ears were slightly pointed like my ears. While looking down, I noticed his hand and wrist held strange white marks.

"I am what you know as a Demigod." Drameon said again in our language keeping our conversation to ourselves.

I thought for a moment, allowing my mind to remember what my books had said about Demigods. In our lore Demigods was often used to identify a child born from one of the Gods. These children held the same status, with magic, as the Gods themselves. They were witnesses to the events occurring in the world, but they could not play an outright hand in them.

Often, like the Gods, they used pawns or people to play out their intended events. If they were to play an outright hand in the events of the world, catastrophe would occur, upsetting the natural balance. I wondered what a Demigod was doing helping my father and his friend, or was he having them play out a plan he wanted accomplished and, if so, was that why my father was acting strange with him?

Drameon sensed what I was thinking and placed his hand on mine momentarily. "Do not fear. child, I have helped your family for many years, and will continue to do so. I want nothing more than to protect everything you hold dear." He said while smiling and tousling my hair. I nodded in understanding as Drameon stood and spoke to my father in the more common tongue.

"So why did you call me?" Drameon asked while my father stood with a puzzled look on his face.

"What did Deestan ask you?" My father asked, slightly angered.

I spoke up addressing the conversation Drameon and I had. "I recognized him as a Demigod and I never spoken to one before. He called me little bird in the Mystic tongue. My mother and Alkin taught me the Mystic language after my little sister was born. That's all really." I smiled proudly that I was able to talk to him.

Drameon laughed slightly at my response. "Yes, it seems your daughter is well versed in the Mystic language." He said while ruffling the hair on my head once more. I was feeling more comfortable with Drameon the longer he was around. He didn't seem to scare me as much. In fact, he reminded me of being home with Alkin, my mother, and sister.

My father seemed content by this response and carried on. "As you already know we had a little run in with Alkin." My father said choosing his words carefully. I looked up at him startled.

Alkin had probably gone to the Den in search of me and my sister. "He was looking for the girls. Were you aware he has free access to the Dens in the area? In addition did you know he has a daughter?" My father asked Drameon hoping for some answers.

Drameon nodded and thought for a moment. "I knew he had Den access, through his adoptive parents, and he's friends with Yumi, the current Vampire Den Master." Drameon nodded. "As far as his child, yes I knew he had a Mystic child, and we have seen her. She was the little one from the meadow when we first saw Deestan."

Stasha stood hoping for more information. "Why would a Mystic who has Den access kidnap a pup and the Queen of the Werewolves, both of whom are Denmates?" Stasha asked.

My father nodded in response. His tone told me he was being careful about what was he was saying, and I was unsure why. "Yes, Stasha, there is something amiss with Alkin. He does not always follow Hunters direct orders." My father said while glaring at Drameon.

Drameon looked deep in thought while pacing the room. "I'd like to say he likely had a hand in whatever ultimately happened to Raillyn. I think you should try and speak to him alone, maybe when you return Deestan to him tonight." Drameon said cautiously. My father gave him a strange look.

I was unsure exactly what Alkin had done to my mother. Raihanna had been the one to raise me and care for me. I knew Raillyn was my real mother. My father and the Moon Goddess told me this, but I couldn't shake the feeling that Raihanna was still my mother.

My father looked at Drameon frustrated. "So Alkin knows where Raillyn is and how to get her back? From what I've been told, I should assume, he knows how she's tied to Raihanna?" He asked sounding hopeful.

Sighing, Drameon closed his eyes a moment. "I think he can tell you more of what tie there is between the two women, and, no, at this time he cannot get Raillyn back. I will impart no more on that subject. As I have said you must let us do our jobs and follow the Gods' orders. Speak with Howl if you want more details." Drameon said, shaking his head.

Looking back at my father he seemed to relax, but was still antsy. I stood unsure really what to do to lighten the situation.

Drameon cleared his throat for a moment and seemed tense before asking. "I would like to ask something of you, Lord Drake." He said cautiously. My father nodded and folded his arms in across his chest, waiting for him to go on.

Glancing at Stasha she stood quiet as if trying to listen to a message behind a closed door. Something was amiss, and I couldn't place my finger on it.

"If I could, would you allow me to place a Mystic mark on your child? This way when she is released back into The Keep she will have a way to call someone if trouble occurs."

My father pondered this for a moment. "Well, what about Alkin?" He asked sarcastically.

I knew what a Mystic mark was and that it would allow me to call Drameon whenever I wanted. It was much like the amulet I had around my neck for calling Alkin, but often times it involved a blood exchange. "At times Alkin is unable to attend to certain matters. I want nothing else than to see your daughter returned to you and have the ability to stay in your safekeeping." Drameon said in a sincere tone. "That is my most truthful wish I can impart to you. Please trust me in this matter. It is for her own good and not to benefit me in any way."

Sighing, my father nodded his head. "As long as Deestan is alright with it. I have to agree it would put my mind to rest knowing she had contact outside The Keep." My father said while looking at me.

I thought for a moment, I wanted a way to call someone from their side if I needed help. "I don't mind having the mark placed on me, my only concern is if others see it." I said hesitant, knowing it would spell trouble if Hunter or anyone else discovered it.

Drameon nodded in understanding. "I can make it blend into your skin. It would be practically invisible unless they knew what they were looking for. A small tribal mark on your ankle, faint and light, that is all. And I can assure you it won't hurt either." Drameon said while holding his hand out.

I hesitated for a moment, I didn't want to have to drink any blood, suddenly I felt Drameon realize why I was so unsure. "Blood is not required for this mark, not for you." He said smiling and putting my fear to rest.

I knew what Mystic marks were. As long as I accepted the magic he pushed onto my body I would feel no pain. If I rejected the magic, the mark would burn and sear onto my skin, causing immense pain. I wondered why we didn't need to exchange blood though, from what I read you couldn't have a mark placed on you unless there was a blood bond.

I slowly reached my hand out and allowed him to take it. He wasted no time and immediately I felt the warm pulse of magic enter my hand and work its way up my arm and across my body. I remained calm as I felt it wash over me, cementing a concrete bond with Drameon.

"Stay calm, child, and accept the magic it will not hurt you if you do so." Drameon said, pushing even stronger magic upon me.

I felt it twining up my feet and around my ankle. It glowed brightly momentarily, then as Drameon finished. The glow died, leaving only a small barely visible mark. The mark appeared like white lines dotting my already deathly pale skin.

Deception ~ Drake

As Drameon released Deestan's arm, I noticed a barely visible mark dotting her ankle. I knew the Vampires would not notice it outright unless they paid specific attention to her. I was still furious at Drameon but remembered the Lunar Goddess words about trusting those around you. In a way, I felt I had no choice and that if I wanted Raillyn home alive I had to trust Drameon a little.

Deestan would be safe with the mark around Raihanna and Alkin, and if what Drameon said was true I was willing to give him a chance. So many questions lay unanswered and I knew I would receive no more answers about Raillyn from Drameon. So after an uneasy goodbye he left through the portal as I prepared to meet with Alkin. I was saddened that my daughter had to return to the Vampire's Keep so soon, but I was anxious for her to discover more information, as well.

I bent over the table and wrote a quick note asking Alkin to meet us in the meadow where we had first seen Deestan. I used wax from a nearby candle and my insignia to mark and seal the letter. Then I handed it to Stasha who would in turn send it to Yumi's people and to Alkin. While we awaited a response, Deestan and I talked more about The Keep.

"So tell me about what you like to do." I asked her hoping she would continue to talk about her life in The Keep, and catch me up on what I had missed.

Deestan pondered for a moment. "Well I love to read. I've been reading for over two years now, and since then I've read anything I could get my hands on. I particularly love to read about magic and history." She said while smiling. "I also love being able to go outside and play. But at The Keep I can't wander off by myself. There are too many Vampires in the village and the Gentry enjoy taking the living, to bleed them." She said in a more hushed tone.

I ruffled her hair to cheer her up. "Maybe once things calm down a little bit you can come here and play outside, with some of the other Den children." I said her.

Her face lit up at this. "Really? I would love to come and play with other kids! Calista, Leeda, and I are the only kids at The Keep!" She said eagerly as she got up and jumped around briefly before sitting again.

Her warm smile melted my heart. I knew she still held me around her little finger even though it had been so long. "Do you like horses?" I asked, thinking she might enjoy riding in the woods around the village sometime.

She thought for a moment as if debating how to answer. "I don't know. My mom took me to the stables one day. I've only seen the horses at The Keep. The horses there are called Death Steeds, they're made with necromantic magic, making them undead." She closed her eyes momentarily deep in thought. "I don't like those horses. After meeting Delron, they gave me the creeps." Deestan said as a small shiver ran up her back.

I was taken aback that she had met Delron when I knew she said she hadn't learned magic yet. "When did you meet Delron?" I asked. "Does your mother know?" I added.

Deestan looked at me with guilty eyes. "No, she doesn't." She said quietly. "Alkin does, however."

I looked at her questioningly and waited for her to continue and explain herself.

"Alkin brought me a bunch of magic books, some of them were Necromancy ones as well as Werewolf books. Just like when I played with the idol I got curious and tried the veil spell. As I stood in Death's River, Delron came. He wasn't happy I was there and cast me out. That's when you first saw me in the woods." She said. "But that was before I knew who I was or that you were my father."

I grabbed Deestan into a tight embrace. "It's okay. It's not your fault; you didn't know. Neither of us knew." I began saying. "We have plenty of time to catch up." I said as we talked about how life was in the castle instead of talking about The Keep. Soon Stasha arrived, interrupting our little talk about Werewolf lore and myth.

"I am sorry to interrupt, but I received word from Alkin." Stasha said as she opened the door and closed it behind her. "He wants to meet with you within the hour; he said he will remain peaceful, but it's urgent to meet sooner than later. I guess Hunter is returning earlier than expected. He said he needs enough time to get our smell off the child before Hunter returns." Stasha said, shaking her head.

Confrontation ~ Alkin

I had to hurry, Hunter would be back any minute, and I was sure Deestan would reek of the Wolves that she had spent so much time with. Already Callina and Leeda had been re-turned and bathed in Sandalwood oil, removing and hiding the smell of where they were. It masked any scent, and I had been very diligent in keeping it on the girls as they grew. I was hoping this would not take long, and I would be able to get Deestan back from Drake quickly.

As I waited I thought about the different options I could use to get Rai to drink the potion Drameon gave me. *So many things to get done in so little time,* I thought to myself while I gathered a bag from the lower den. I made sure extra sandal-wood was within. Dabbing it on her would help hide the scent of the Werewolves until Deestan could receive a proper bath in the oil.

Grabbing my cloak from a nearby chair, I left. Silently I walked the halls and spoke to no one. I was thankful that as I quietly slipped into the streets and left through the front gate towards the marshy woods outside that no one stopped me. And entering the woods would give me the cover I needed to use my magic. Quickly and quietly I opened a portal to take me to the meadow, where we had planned on meeting.

As I left the black and grey clouds of smoke, stepping in-to the meadow beyond, I heard an excited voice, it was Deestan. She stood with her father and his friend Briar, on the edge of the woods. She smiled as she called my name.

"So glad you came." Drake said to me as I flipped back my cloak back revealing that I held no weapons around my belt.

Deestan ran to me and hugged my waist on contact. I was weary of what the Wolves intended of me and stayed alert.

Brushing Deestan's hair back lovingly, and kissing her fore-head, I kept my eyes on the two Wolves.

I knew they felt my unease. "We simply want to talk." Drake said as he showed me he too carried no weapons; he glanced at his friend Briar who in turn showed he carried nothing.

I felt better after seeing that and leaned down to care for Deestan for a moment. "I need to rub some of this on you, it's the Sandalwood oil, and it will mask the Wolves scent." I said hushed even though I knew they would hear me.

Deestan nodded and allowed me to rub her hair, arms and legs with the oils masking the scent from easy detection. As I did so I asked if everything was alright, and where she had gotten the Den outfit,

"I'm fine, Alkin, everything is alright, and I got the outfit from Yumi. They accepted me and will allow me free passage to any Den." Deestan said excited as she spun around, green dancer pants and sash spinning in unison around her small frame. I closed my eyes for a moment and thought. *Yes, this was a great thing, it was what we needed,* but at the same time I was unsure how others would view this, especially Hunter.

Looking at the Wolves once more I knew I was running out of time. "So what is it that you need from me?" I asked subtly, wanting to get back and get some other things under control before Hunters arrival.

Drake casually leaned up against a tree, and relaxed, folding his arms in front of him. "I was hoping you might be able to help me with one thing." Drake said while reaching into his pocket, and tossing whatever it was at me.

Instinctually I caught the object, a small golden ring. Turning it over I saw it had a turquoise stone on it. It was Raillyn's old ring, the one I had given her to protect her and aid in healing. The very one I had removed before carrying her out of Death's realm. I was directed to drop it in the water, in which I had. Why did Drake have it?

"I was hoping you could tell me why Raihanna had my mate's old ring, and why does she have my mate's old chestplate. In addition, why are you and Drameon working together? And what is this betrothal business you have with Raillyn?" Drake said while walking towards me, knowing that something was amiss.

I stood shocked for a moment, I had been unaware Raihanna had acquired the ring. The chestplate, well, that was because I had talked Hunter into letting her keep it. He was going to have it destroyed. Hunter told me he had planned on making Raihanna his most prized Elite. I had spent hours afterwards convincing him Raillyn's old chest plate would be a great item for her to wear. That it would be like a slap in the face for his enemy and, of course, he liked that idea. He allowed her to keep it, lying about its true origin. I was shocked he had heard about my betrothal to Raillyn. Drameon on the other hand, I was not surprised to hear about. Since Howl was poking his nose in places he shouldn't again, I had no doubt that he informed the Wolves of our past.

I smiled at the information he learned, knowing Drake had figured out part of the game that was being played out. "I have no idea." I lied, "I was unaware she had either item. And as far as the betrothal, that's none of your business." I said casually, hoping he would not call my bluff. I knew it all depended on who he had spoken with about this subject, and where he was getting his information from. Howl, I could tell, was on that list but if anyone else was included I was unaware.

Deestan looked at me curiously, even before Drake carried on. I saw he would not believe me.

"We know you don't always follow Hunter's orders, Howl told me that much. He also told me an interesting piece of information—that you knew Raillyn before she went to live with Chaimh and Lillian." Drake said trying to get me to answer something at least.

However, I stood silent waiting for him to go on.

"We don't think you are working for Hunter, but in truth you and Drameon are working together. Is that true? Drameon himself told me to mention this." Drake had come closer towards me, almost within arm's reach. He stood proud, and I knew this was one reason he made a great leader, he was able to handle situations which were difficult.

I debated my choices. No, I was not working for Hunter, but I couldn't tell him that. Yes, I was really working with Drameon. I was not fortunate to have the freedom to actually say who commanded me. My father spelled me to not say. This protected not only myself but Raihanna from torture. Knowing that Drake knew that Drameon and I worked together made me smile. The fact he knew Raillyn and I had known each other over two hundred and fifty years ago almost made me laugh. Drameon and I had a long history of practicing this game which we had become masters at. I paused choosing my next words carefully.

"If you are indicating I am a spy, you are sadly mistaken." I flashed a smile at him, hoping he would drop this subject. I needed everyone to view me for who I was supposed to be. Hunter's right-hand man, or in this case Mystic. Before I spoke a word of my betrayal to anyone, I had to get Raihanna to drink the potion. I had to ensure my family was safe. I could tell Drake was furious with what I had said. He turned back and walked towards Briar before facing me once more.

Anger lit up his eyes as he spoke. "You are a Denmate, whatever game you are playing, I am growing tired of it! You are either with Hunter or against him. And since you took Raillyn, I'm betting you know what happened to her. Don't you? You were betrothed to her at one point, doesn't any of that matter to you?" Drake yelled, he was at his breaking point, and if I pushed further fully hiding who I was it might send him over the edge. I was sure things would get interesting between us after Raillyn was returned. However I wanted to avoid a fight with him since he was Deestan's father.

Thankfully, a bell echoed throughout the woods interrupting my next thought. It was Hunter's way for calling his Elite to his side. Deestan took note to the sounds haunting tone as well, and looked up at me knowing that time was up, Hunter was home.

As Drake and Briar looked around, I took advantage to say a quick word before leaving. "I understand you are mad about this, but I cannot say more at this time. Maybe at a later time we can meet again, but for now I must take Deestan and leave. Unless you want her in danger?" Hoping Briar and Drake heard the stress in my tone.

They nodded as I picked Deestan up and summoned a portal for us to travel through. Deestan waved goodbye to her father as we left, not wanting to speak a sound since we were returning to The Keep. I felt terrible that I had to pull her away so soon, but I knew that before long she would be safe and happy back in her own bed and her home with her own people. I was still unaware what fate lie ahead for her mother and I, but I couldn't think about that now I had more pressing matters to attend to.

As soon as I entered the small den below Raihanna's quarters I took action. I led Deestan upstairs and into the washroom. There, I helped her draw water for a bath and placed a good amount of sandalwood oil into the water. Next I left Deestan to attend herself as I went in search of Raihanna.

She was in her room brushing out Callina's hair. I opened the door wondering if she was summoned, as well. "Did Hunter summon you also?" I asked wondering if I should wait for her or not.

She shook her head, "No, is he home already?" She asked fear filling her eyes momentarily. "Did you get Deestan back?" She asked frantically.

I sighed and smiled "Yes she's taking a bath right now." This seemed to calm her down and she settled back into brushing Callina's hair. I knew there was a lot I had to ask her, especially how she had acquired the ring, but I had to hurry. I said I would be back later after I was done seeing what Hunter wanted.

After sensing the power from the hall, I knew that walking into Hunter's study would be a mistake. As soon as I opened the door, its power overwhelmed me. The room itself reeked of a deadly mix of magic. Magic that was both harmonized and chaotic in nature a terrible mix for anyone to wield, and made for only one owner. I knew where he acquired the item as soon as I saw it. There was only one place he could acquire such an item.

As I closed the door behind me, I looked at Hunter who stood behind his table clenching the large staff. It was nearly as tall as him and had a phoenix and Dragon spiraling up its length meeting at the top. The mouths of the Dragon and phoenix held a rather giant Bloodstone in their grasp. My own father had a similar staff, but this one possessed darker magic than even his. The wood was crafted from the same wood Delron's staff was made. The God-like staff was what reeked of the horrid power which filled the room. Knowing this, I knew he had met with one of the Gods somewhere.

Hunter smiled at me, madness filled his eyes. It seemed as if he was power-hungry, even more so than he had been in the past. Suddenly I realized the destructive nature of the staff in the wrong hands. I feared what would happen if Drameon and I didn't hurry things along.

"Welcome Alkin, I am so glad to see you this evening. Please join us." He said in a subtle tone, trying to portray perfect sanity. I knew with the staff emanating the energy it was that he would not be able to handle its nature, and slowly it would drive him mad.

I nodded my head and looked around at his other Elite, Ash and Thierry stood to my left between Hunter and myself. Lily, Aurielle, and her mate Ashoten stood on my right casually sprawled out on the furniture as if they had been there awhile. The only Elite missing was Raihanna. No one in the room appeared concerned by Hunter's behavior, even though it was more erratic than normal.

"How is Raihanna?" Hunter asked me concerned momentarily. "I had wanted to call her, but after hearing that she was attacked, I expected her to be healing still." He said while eyeing me, I was unsure who had told him that Raihanna had been injured. It didn't matter though, Hunter was pleased she was doing her job, which was staying behind to ensure all was well.

I expected Hunter wanted me to fill him in on the rest. "Raihanna is fine. She lost a lot of blood, but that was it. And

I gave her the bottles you had given me before your depar-
ture." I said lying. I had not given Raihanna the bottles of his
blood. Instead, I had traded these bottles with another blood.

I smiled at Hunter, knowing he would not realize this until it was too late. He smiled back, eyes wild with glee. He
was eager to step up his plan. "Good, maybe I will pay her a
visit later tonight. As for now I wanted to tell everyone that
we are ready to take our actions to the next level. As you see
here, I have acquired a new item for us to play with. This staff
I received from Daes, the God of chaos and destruction. With
it, I will summon him into our world where he will destroy
everyone and everything that he does not see fit. What this
means for us is that our race and like races will reign. We will
be free of the prejudice we have dealt with for so long. We
will enslave the good races of the land, and build a new kingdom under Daes' rule." Hunter smiled as he spoke while the
other Elite in the room nodded their heads and smiled in return.

"Both remaining pieces are in place, all that's left is to
finish. Tonight I will imbue the staff with the wild and free
magic of Alkin and Raihanna's very own Mystic daughter.
This will strengthen it beyond our wildest dreams. I am eager
to finish this and get our true God here once and for all. I am
sure everyone else is equally ready for our new life." Hunter
continued while looking around the room at his Elite.

I could sense that each one was thinking the same idea.
They wanted a world of chaos and destruction. One that the
races of good would be their slaves only kept alive for blood
and labor. This meant that Hunter would be taking out the
other race's leaders in the weeks to come.

Drake and Briar were the biggest issues in Alecien since
he had already removed Breckon from his position years ago.
They had been avoiding the conflicts in Alecien lately, having
their infant Silas to attend to and ensure the throne was safe. I
did not think Alihandra and Darris would fully return unless it
was dire.

I closed my eyes momentarily and smiled to myself,
knowing I had much to do and little time in which to do it.

Yet, the time had come, *things were falling into place perfectly,* I thought as Hunter carried on, giving assignments for gathering Humans for a bleeding.

As he sent his Elite out, he placed the staff down on his table and walked towards me. "Shall we pay Raihanna a visit? I am eager to see her after so long and to see if I may borrow Callina for an hour or so." Hunter remarked while he pulsed with evil energy and power.

I nodded and led him down the hall towards Raihanna's chambers. Regretful that our daughter had to be used as a trigger to bring the staff to full power, only the magic of an untrained Mystic could awaken such an item in the living world. I was fearful what Hunter would do with the item before it could be returned to its rightful owner. It was my sin, another burden to toss onto the already heated fire.

Transmute ~ Raihanna

Alkin had sent me a mental warning even before I sensed Hunter. Nervous about the situation, I was equally worried about how Hunter's behavior would be tonight. Mentally, I reached for Alkin's mind, who kept it open to me momentarily. Hunter seemed erratic, twisted between utter joy and merciless anger. They were coming to see Callina and me. Alkin indicated to keep Deestan away for the time being.

To make matters worse, Deestan insisted on staying dressed as a Denmate. If Hunter found her like this…, well, I didn't want to think about it. I didn't have time to argue with a six-year-old. Barking at her and Leeda to go downstairs immediately, I told them to do something quiet. It was imperative that they not be seen.

After ensuring they were out of the way, I ascended the stairs. Reaching the top step, I heard Alkin open the door. Quickly I went to meet him and Hunter, dreading the events that might occur if Hunter suspected anything was amiss. Walking up the stairs to the main den I felt my Uncle's presence.

The air in the room became frighteningly thick and claustrophobic. It threatened to suffocate me. My gut ached and nausea began to bubble up. A heaviness began to settle in my stomach as if it were filling up with many stones. My head slightly spun from the force of its darkness. Even though a wall separated us, the darkness on the other side of the wall moved with a heavy authority, filling all the empty space. It made me feel like a child.

Alkin surfaced in my mind, feeling how overwhelmed at that moment I felt. *Compose yourself my poppet, we're almost there.*

I hadn't realized that I'd been holding my breath this whole time, and took a few deep, steadying breaths. I allowed my mind to regain a calming composure, reminding myself that the lives of three little girls depended on me. From across the room, the door eased open on quiet hinges.

"Hello, Uncle." I said while bowing and smiling. "I am glad to see you returned safely from your trip. I hope everything went according to plan."

Hunter smiled and pulled me out of my bow, hugging me instead. "All is well, niece, and everything is going perfectly!" Hunter said eagerly.

The touch of his fingertips burned as he held me, but I resisted the urge to pull away. Feeling him up close like this made it worse. The pressure in the air around him could crack glass and was statically charged. My skin turned to gooseflesh. Bitter-tasting liquid crept up my throat, burning its way up my esophagus. I swallowed hard and clamped my eyes shut. His power was much darker and evil. Alkin was also treading carefully around him as he eyed me solemnly over Hunter's shoulder.

"I am glad to see you are doing so well. Alkin had said you lost a lot of blood. I was worried and wanted to visit you myself. I also wanted to see Callina, if that was ok." He asked as he released me from his grip. Hunter seemed unaware that he was a walking affliction. He was delighting in his power with a drunken revelry.

I nodded, backing away. With another gesture of my head, I signaled to Alkin to follow me. Hunter didn't seem to care; turning away, he found a large-backed red-pillowed chair carved out of mahogany and made himself at home.

Looking over my shoulder as we made our way to the hallway from the main den, I could see the happy glazed over expression on Hunter's face as he lounged on the sofa. Closing the door behind us, Alkin leaned close next to my ear. "Please tell me Deestan and Leeda will stay out of the way?" He asked hushed, almost too quiet for me to hear.

I nodded and looked at him questioningly. I felt he knew something that was about to happen that would displease me.

Possibly it was with my Uncle, but I dismissed the feeling as I heard my Uncle question me from the main room.

"I expect Deestan and Leeda were no trouble for you while I was away?" He asked while Alkin and I stopped by the girl's room and picked up Callina, who had been sitting quietly playing with her cloth doll. He held her close before pulling me into an embrace and kissing my head lightly. Holding me close, he took in my scent, then kissed Callina on the head. She looked at us questioningly as any child would look at her parents being affectionate towards each other. Sorrowfully he released me before heading back towards the main den where Hunter sat. For a moment I wanted to pull him back against me, and not let him go, but I decided against it.

Following, Hunter immediately ruffled her hair and smiled. "Do you mind if I borrow her? It would only be for an hour or so. No longer, I promise." My Uncle asked while Alkin eyed me warningly, waiting for an answer.

I nodded my head, knowing I really had no other choice other than to infuriate my Uncle. As I watched the three of them leave, I quietly closed the door.

From the main den, I descended back down the stairs to check on the older two. I was met with excitement. Both girls ran up to me shrieking happily as they expressed their enthusiasm for being welcomed in the local den.

"It was so fun!" Leeda began. "We slept on the floor then in the morning we all got up, and I learned a dance to bring good luck for the day! It was amazing!" She continued.

"I know!" Deestan chimed in. "There's also amazing rooms below the Den, pretty ones where the dancers go practice in. And I got these amazing pants and shirt! I love them!"

The girls continued and even though the situation upset me, I was happy they were able to do something they had dreamed about. Even, if it was unintentional.

Leaning against the door jam, I smiled as I watched them twirl and dance about the room. However, another presence crept into the chambers. Irritated, I turned and made my way quickly up the stairs. *This person better have a good explana-*

tion to enter without knocking. I certainly didn't need whoever it was coming down to the lower level. Stepping onto the main level, Ash stood next to the fireplace arms crossed, looking directly at me.

"What are you doing here?" I asked him, outraged.

Casually he unfolded his arms and approached me. "You realize Hunter knows about Callina? That she belongs to you and Alkin." He said matter of fact like. I shrugged not sure where he was going with this.

"I was just making sure you knew and were okay with it." He said casually.

"I'm not quite sure what you're getting at." I said flatly.

"Well, if you wish to ignore the obvious puppet, who am I to care either?" He said in mocking tone while turning to leave.

I felt no need to stop him and thought it was a little odd he had come. *What was he getting at?* Ash had always been strange, and I probably should be more concerned. Perhaps he was just checking in on things and ensuring that I wasn't causing trouble. Whatever he was going on about, I was relieved to see him go. After a few minutes, I opened the hall to make sure he was gone.

Knowing the older girls would be safe with Nora I grabbed my cloak and went towards the door. I wanted to go to the woods and acquire a few herbs that I had been running low on. Walking the halls was silent, not many lingered while the ones who did were servants; no one stopped me. It was equally calm on the street. Nearing the gates of town the guards regarded me silently. It was best to address them with a quick explanation so as not to run into trouble later. Hunter's eyes were everywhere.

"I needed some items from the wooded marshlands, just let my uncle know." I said without waiting for a response. Passing the gates, I stepped off the road and made for the trees. The bright near-full moon shone down on me as I entered the forest. Its mossy floor gave way as I carefully walked across it, the trees gave off eerie shadows from the moons glow. I felt peaceful as I walked towards the perimeter of our lands. This was the only place to find locust flowers. They grew wildly near the Werewolves' land. I knew that this was the only season I could acquire them fresh, which made a much stronger truth serum.

Cautiously, I approached an open meadow which glowed in the moonlight. Carefully I began picking the flowers and folding the petals inward, so as not to damage them. Slipping them into my pouch to brew later, I continued my search. A light breeze wafted over my back carrying with it the sound of distant voices. Someone had crossed from the Vampire's land into the Werewolves. Quickly I ran to the darkness and peered into the woods as the voices grew louder.

The moon lit the woods perfectly. Familiar voices approached, I recognized who walked the woods. Lord Drake and his friend Drameon walked out of the Vampire's land back towards their own. Curious I decided to follow them. I knew crossing into their lands could cause trouble but at the same time they had crossed into ours.

Hood drawn, I silently crept across the forest floor, Drameon and Lord Drake walked slowly, casually, so it was easy to keep up. The woods seemed hushed as I moved. As if the very trees knew I stalked prey. As we got deeper into the thick of the forest, a twig snapped underneath me. Silently I cursed, knowing they heard.

Drameon placed a hand across Lord Drake's chest, stopping him in his tracks. "Someone follows us." He said, hushed, as he looked around.

Ducking further into the shadows, I prayed nothing else would give me away. Drameon looked around as he walked in the direction of my hiding spot. Looking around, Lord Drake walked the other way in search of the sound. I sat silent as he walked past. I felt I had a moment to attack. If I didn't take this now I was sure they would find me, and at least injuring the strongest one would make it easier.

Swiftly I called my blade and leapt forth, raising it high ready to attack, but Drameon was faster. He whirled around at the sound of my first move, grabbing my throat and throwing me onto the ground while his other hand tore back my hood before he drew his own blade. I felt it make contact just above my heart and begin to dig into my Mythril armor. Realization crossed my face as I knew it could pierce it. He laughed slightly. Then spoke in a strange language, I found my blade hand suddenly empty and looked up at him, knowing I would not win.

"What are you doing here?" He asked as I heard Lord Drake approach. "You know you are on the Wolves land." He said sternly as he put pressure on his blade.

Pain echoed through me momentarily at the pressure of my bending armor; anymore, and it would break. He smiled knowingly, and then I remembered, he was Mystic. That meant he couldn't kill me.

I tested his reserve and applied my own pressure to his blade. Sensing this, he backed off slightly. "You can't kill me, Demigod. I'm a grown woman and it's not like you're my father! You can't tell me what I can or cannot do!" I said in spite, knowing I now had the upper hand.

Drameon seemed taken aback by this, and for a moment was speechless. "Well, if that's how you feel about it, let's see how much damage I can actually do." He said in return, releasing his hand from my throat, and pulling me to my feet.

I saw Lord Drake approach, confused. Drameon kept his sword at my heart. "What do you want to do with her?" He asked Lord Drake.

Drake's face became of mask of authority. "Release her; I don't think she will try anything else." He said. Drameon sheathed his sword and backed up, letting him take control of the situation.

I looked at Lord Drake questioningly. He knew who I was, and he wasn't killing me. I thought it was odd and waited to see what he had planned. Lord Drake approached me and automatically I took a step back, ready to fight. Drake put his hands out in a peaceful motion and stopped.

"I don't want to hurt you." He said standing there. "I only want to ask you a few questions." He let his hands fall to his side. His emotions said the same thing. Silently I stood waiting for him to continue, I knew I didn't have much choice in the matter. Seeing me slightly calm, Lord Drake proceeded. "I was wondering if you could shed some light on how you acquired two items." He said looking at Drameon as if he was unsure how to proceed. "The chestplate you are wearing now and the little golden, turquoise ring."

I looked at him strangely, but I felt that I could at least partake this information to him since it was not unknown where I acquired them. "The ring I found in the crystal room below your local Den." I replied while I smiled. Drake was not happy about that and waited as I went on. "As for the chestplate, my Uncle gave it to me. I expected he had to kill one of your royal guards to acquire it also." I said mockingly. I didn't realize that as I spoke Lord Drake had walked carefully closer towards me. I found myself only an arm's width away.

Snarling in disgust, I backed up slightly, only to find the Demigod behind me, blocking my escape. Suddenly I heard Lord Drake say a spell, the very spell I had heard in my dream barely weeks ago. My chestplate began to glow in response.

Summoning my sword, I jumped forward, grabbing Lord Drake's shirt and pinning him against a tree, blade at his throat. He smiled slightly at me as the light faded.

"You wear my mate's armor, and the ring was hers as well." He said. Nothing, but calmness crossed his mind and face.

Anger built up inside me. I knew he spoke the truth, and if I was going to get the answers I sought, I might have to work with those I did not care for. Releasing my grip on his shirt and dissipating my blade, I stepped back once more and stood silently waiting with my head down.

Lord Drake carried on "Did you know that?" He asked calmly.

The only thing I could do would be to try and bluff my way out of this situation. "No, I had no idea." I lied smiling.

Drake was not convinced, and Drameon was not pleased by my behavior. Swiftly he grabbed my shoulder and pinned me against a nearby tree. "You will answer our questions truthfully, child, or you will not like what happens." He said as he released me and stepped aside. *He was really beginning to irritate me by calling me a child.*

"Tell me." Lord Drake began, "How much about Raillyn do you know? Do you know where she is by chance or what happened to her? Or even that you appear to resemble her?" He asked while casually walking towards me, stopping an arm's length away.

Shocked I didn't know how to answer. "I really never thought about Raillyn, or where she was. To me she's nothing, but someone who tried to stop us, and get in our way. I despise her, even though I've never met her. My Uncle assures me that she's gone, dead for good." My lip curled, and my nose wrinkled as I said the words. For a moment, Drake looked at Drameon and nodded.

Without warning, Drameon grabbed me once more and pinned me against the nearby tree. His hand around my throat, as he began to speak an Ancient spell. For a moment, my breath stilled in my lungs, deep inside something cracked. My reserve was breaking, and so was the construct body, he intended on killing me... Or that's what I thought. Angered he threw me onto the ground, I rolled before regaining my balance and going to my feet.

"What in Delron's Realm was that all about?" I screamed at him, ready to attack again. Like a rock being tossed into a clear lake, my vision scattered.

Statically a vision filled my vision. A large city with red, blue, green, and silver buildings and statues. People with vibrant eyes and booming power walked the streets in elegant clothes, long-sleeved shirts, nature-toned pants, and dancers dressed in bright colors.

My head felt like it would explode. I was nearly on my knees when, a chime echoed through the forest, pulling me out of the vision. Hunter was summoning me. Lord Drake and Drameon took note to this as well and watched curiously as I created a portal, leaving them in the woods alone.

The Staff ~ Raihanna

The portal took me directly outside Hunter's door. My head still hurt but I didn't want to waste any time after such unsettling events. Approaching his door, I could feel the same strong unsettle evil and darkness from when Hunter visited me earlier today. A small amount of fear began to creep up on me as I reached for the door hesitantly. Suddenly it swung open and Ash stood, holding it open for me.

Quietly I walked in, glaring at him as I did. My Uncle stood in front of his table, holding a large Dragon Phoenix staff in his hands. A massive red stone glowed in the grasp of their intricate wings. I had only seen a staff similar to it wielded by the Death God Delron. Hunter smiled as I walked to stand next to the table. Ash bowed deeply before going out the door, closing it tightly behind him. My Uncle seemed overjoyed at my presence.

He came to stand near me while he spoke. The burning feeling I had felt before seared my skin the closer he stood. "I am glad to see you so swiftly. I have imbued the staff with Callina's power." Hunter said as a knock interrupted him.

Slowly I backed away, not fully comprehending what his words. *What was that about Callina?* My Uncle's unusual behavior shoved the thought far from my mind. Right now I was the one in trouble, he seemed possessed. As he reached for the door, I began to feel that summoning Daes might not be such a good idea.

Alkin walked in, bowed to Hunter slightly, then walked towards the nearby chair and took a seat. Mentally he was furious. Physically he looked deathly pale for his skin tone, his bright peach skin now shone, dull, and translucent. My Uncle smiled at him before turning back to me.

"As I was saying." He continued. "All I need is your blood to complete the ritual. Once I have that, the stone will be imbued, and all that will be left is to wait until the perfect time." My Uncle said with a mad look to his eyes.

Trying to distract him I asked about Callina. "How did it go with my daughter?" I said hoping to break the madness swimming in his eyes.

His wild eyes met mine. "Fine, fine. There was only a minor issue, but it worked out." He said to me while slicking back his greasy brown hair. It was in this moment I was beginning to realize how unkempt my Uncle was keeping himself lately.

Once he had taken pride in his image, and dressed as a king, now he seemed to not care about anything else but summoning Daes. Hunter grasped the staff as he spoke, rubbing its crystal. Unsure of what to do I looked at Alkin. His blank face and equally blank emotions gave me no relief. I could tell he had lost much blood. I wondered if he too had to pay a blood price to the stone.

Suddenly I felt Hunter grab my wrist as he called to Alkin. "This will hurt a little, child." He said as Alkin came to stand behind me, holding me in place so I was unable to move. "Alkin, keep her still." He said as a blade cut across my hand and wrist spraying my blood across the room and onto the floor.

A sudden pulse was felt through me, not only the pulse of my own heart but the pulse of the stone's magic, Ancient magic. It wasn't a spell the Vampires could cast, instead it was the staff itself. I felt its power pour over me as I was immediately thrown into a trance-like state. The stone liked my blood, it fed off it like a starving animal. As it did so, a burning began to radiate from my very being.

My body hurt, and I felt as if I was being ripped apart. I was unsure if I screamed out loud or if it was just in my head, but it didn't stop. The pain felt like it was consuming my very being, and the stone sucked more, and more blood out of my body, greedy for its power.

I heard my Uncle laugh in the background. "Yes!" He said in a satisfied tone. "More, more, more. The more blood you take the stronger you become." He said to the stone as it blazed red with power.

I felt myself stagger slightly, and Alkin secure his grip. "I think you need to stop, Hunter." He said cautiously.

Alkin's grip on me tightened as the world around me began to spin wildly. The stone kept taking blood eagerly, and at this rate it would drain me. Naturally I felt my mind reach for Alkin mentally trying to escape the horror being wrought on me and wondering why he allowed it. Weakened by the stone and burning with pain, I let myself fall into unconsciousness to escape the torture.

Alkin

Feeling Rai's pain and shock—she was limp in my arms—I knew Hunter had gone too far. The stone still lapped at her power greedily trying to take in every last bit including her life force. I would not just stand by and watch this happen. If the stone killed her construct body then in turn Raillyn would be lost to us forever. She was too precious to me, I would never allow him to kill her, I would die first.

Angered I drew my blade and knocked the staff out of his reach. It flew across the room with tremendous force, landing on the other side of the table. Hunter stood shocked and angered I had interfered.

Feeling a primitive protective urge well up inside me, I cradled Rai's body against mine, one-handed. My anger was at a breaking point. "I said you have enough." I shouted at Hunter, startling him with my behavior. "You have already made one mistake tonight, do not make another." I said, reminding him of the incident with Callina. The one he addressed as a minor issue, I knew when Rai found out she would be livid about the problem.

Hunter's rust-colored eyes met mine as he seemed to try and regain his composure. He shook his head as if clearing his thoughts. "You're right." He said, angered. "I will complete the ritual, you take her and makes sure she lives." Hunter commanded.

Carefully, I lifted Rai in my arms. Hunter opened the door and allowed me to leave. I dared not take her to her own chambers, so instead I took her to mine. It seemed like a lifetime ago since I had walked into its main room in anger, throwing it in disarray.

The same deep blues and purples hung from the walls and decorated the chairs; while furs lined the stone floors. The mess had been cleared by the maids. I disregarded all of it and instead walked down the hall. Kicking open my bedroom door, I was thankful they kept it clean.

Raihanna's breathing began to become shallower as she struggled with each breath. I was running out of time. Reaching out, I grasped the unique bond we shared together. I felt her soul stir in response, recognizing my touch, she seemed to wrap her magic around my very being. Desperately trying to anchor herself to me and the living world. This was the worst I had seen her since I separated her soul from her real body.

Swiftly I laid her onto the fur-lined bed, and turned to my cabinet that held the last few bottles of blood I had been given, for incidents like this one. If anything was going to save her it was that and our bond.

Popping open the seal released the strange aroma of the blood within. It was potent and stung the nose slightly with a spiced smell. On a few occasions I had a different brew myself, I knew the warm liquid slightly burned the throat as you drank it, it was like drinking pure magic, and its immense power was what we needed tonight.

Slowly I lifted Raihanna up, so I could pour the liquid down her throat. I knew time was precious, and each haggard breath could spell disaster for us. Rai had still not gained her true identity.

Anger built up in me once more, but I felt her soul quiver and pull away from the power welling up inside me. Instead I quickly calmed myself, and in turn felt her relax. With her lips turning blue and her heart skipping beats, I became anxious. I was losing her, my own heart skipped a beat and tears came to my eyes. *Please.* I prayed as my throat constricted. *Don't die on me, not after all we have been through.* A single tear escaped my eye and fell onto her upturned face.

Holding her close, I shakily cradled her closer, still trying desperately to get the unique blood mixture inside. My heart ached, and my soul felt like it was falling apart. *You can't die on me...*

Just as I thought hope was lost and her breathing was ceasing, color began to return. The first bottle was empty, so I turned and retrieved a few more, breaking their seals and giving them to Raihanna.

Finally her breathing steadied, and she once more took deep full breaths. I smiled, elated, gently I kissed her forehead a few times, thankful. Hope was not lost, and we still had a fighting chance. As I tossed aside the third empty bottle, I remembered the vial Raihanna was supposed to drink. Carefully I pulled it from its pouch and laid it on the small table beside the bed. I would give it to her once she woke up.

For now however, I would not be able to pull myself away, and I arranged myself on the bed, covering us with the furs. Gently I lay with her and took in her scent, honeysuckle, vanilla and thyme a sweet combination. Kissing her hair once more I laid back gently holding her close.

Looking around the room for a moment, I realized nothing had changed since the last time I was in it years ago. The same wooden walls decorated with simple tapestries hung in the exact place while the bed lay in the center of the room. The small table next to it contained various books, and the cabinet which held the extra blood sat empty. I had nothing more to give to assist Raihanna in her task and prayed she would be free of the spell she was under soon.

It was up to her now. How she chose to proceed would decide the fate of not only herself but Raillyn, as well. If she chose to keep assisting Hunter, I knew she would be lost. I hoped that today's display would deter her from this decision. Closing my eyes and cuddling her close, I hoped to get a little sleep before the nights end.

The Past ~ Drake

Pacing the small den south of my chambers I was outraged once more. Drameon was being elusive and had to leave
immediately, stating that events had become unsettling else-
where and he had to attend to those matters. As I walked the
floor I could think of only one person who might be able to
shed light on this situation.

Recently Howl had asked if I minded him residing in the
castle while he was assisting us and attending his own business. I saw no need to turn him away and allowed him to reside in one of the many empty rooms on the western side. If I
was going to get any answers I would have to meet with
Howl. I only prayed he was in his room.

It was late, and I was thankful no one was in the hall tonight. Stopping in front of his door, I gently knocked, hopeful.
After a moment or two, the door opened and Howl stood,
smiling, his piercing blue eyes meeting mine. "Hello, Lord
Drake. To what do I owe this late night visit?" He asked as he
held the door open for me.

Entering the room seemed strange, it was not the room I
had given him, and I couldn't help but turn and eye him suspiciously. Chairs, a pillowed bench, and a small table surrounded a fire place, while various closed doors dotted the
room. A small kitchen was towards my right, and bookshelves
lined the left wall.

Howl seemed amused by my surprise. "I hope you don't
mind, I linked my home to the room temporarily while I attend matters here in Alecien." He said casually while taking a
seat in one of the chairs. "It's not permanent, only a means I
use to be at home by use of my magic."

Sitting in a nearby chair, I nodded. Howl was toiling in
magic I did not understand and probably wouldn't. "I guess

that's fine, as long as no one else finds out." I said cautiously, unsure what others might think if they saw what he was capable of. "I'm not even going to try and figure out how this is possible." I said while looking at him.

Laughing out loud, he slapped my knee. "It's simple really. It's just a portal spell that I link to my home. My home stays in one place. It's just the door that travels. Currently I have figured out how to link my house to six different locations, but normally I keep only three active. This helps me get around much quicker instead of using teleportation spells, as they can be draining." He said while smiling.

Meeting his eyes I nodded, understanding the spell a little better. I had to ask, Howl might be the only one who could shed some light about having a normal life with Mystics involved. He seemed sarcastic but at the same time he had been helpful and truthful most of all.

"I spoke with Drameon." I began cutting to the chase. "I know I was furious at him for what's going on, but he assures me Raillyn will be fine. Do the Gods always influence everything so intensely all the time or do they let you actually live your life and leave you alone? Do they ever have their children not interfering?" I asked in a joking, but serious tone.

Smiling, he took a deep breath before speaking. "No, it's not always like this. Normally the Gods keep to themselves unless they have a desire to have children. Hopefully when things calm down, and this unbalanced mess of power is corrected, things will return to normal." He said, leaning forward and gazing into the fire. "You know, it wasn't always like this. Right now it's a necessary evil, I assume."

Leaning back in the chair, I wondered why a Drakar would be so mixed up in this mess of Mystic's. "So tell me, why are you mixed up in this mess and so intent on helping us?" I asked suddenly curious to know more about this man.

"Ah, that? Well that's kind of a long story. The history between Drakar, the Gods, and Mystics goes back hundreds of years," Howl said.

"What's your story then?" I asked.

"My story started off similar to your own, I would guess. Before I met any of the Mystics my life was much more laid back. I will admit I was a ladies man, always chasing the girls and bringing them back here to my place for a night of passion, before leaving them the next day back in their own home, thinking it was all a dream. I disregarded both my bloods at the time. The Shadow Walker side was so attuned with nature and destroying Vampires and my Drakar side focused on serving the Gods and the old ways." Howl said cautiously, as if he was imparting important information.

"Hold up. What's this about 'both bloods?' You're not just a Drakar then? You're also half Shadow Walker?" I asked.

"Was." Howl corrected me.

"How could you be born a hybrid of two races, and then suddenly not be?" I asked, puzzled. These Aeralain's were so confusing. "Did you just decide not to associate with one side of your family?"

"Not many people know my heritage, but since we are working with each other and you are in a position of not being able to trust easily, I will tell you. My mother was a Drakar who made a stupid decision at a stupid time, and my father was a Shadow Walker who had gone rogue. After my mother gave birth to me, she hated me. I craved blood in order to live and function, it was the one thing that restored my magic and put the burning blood rage at rest. If I didn't have it, I would enter a blood lust and go after anyone around me, almost draining them to death. It took me years before I was able to control it." He said, suddenly lost in the past.

"Finn, the village leader of Zian, became obsessed on restoring the Shadow Walkers to power so that one day we could cross the Silver Sea and eradicate the Vampires from Alecien," He went on.

"I like the sound of that," I mused. "How did you learn about Finn?"

"We became acquainted through Claude who, for as long as I have known him, has assisted Finn with keeping the village safe and ensuring laws were followed. Similar to your position. Claude and I became good friends when I was grow-ing up, and he sort of took me under his wing. He was only fifty years older so he treated me much like a little brother. Through a recommendation from Claude, I was able to join the guard as well." Howl said.

"I see," I said nodding. "Please, continue."

"This posed a problem. Our race could not be created, but a spell could be used to turn the Half-breeds with our blood essentially to full-blood Shadow Walkers. It would dampen and consume the other blood. A painful process and one that not many choose to take, I myself did not want it. Finn was furious at my choice. Being one of his top warriors, he felt I needed to be a Shadow Walker and have my Drakar blood eradicated. This was just before the start of the war."

Hearing about the war made me even more curious. "You mean the war here in Alecien?" I asked wondering what he meant.

Smiling he replied. "Yes, that's right, the war here in Alecien. I was here at the beginning; in fact several of us were, visiting friends or family at the beginning of it. This is where things got out of hand."

Looking at him curiously, "How so?" I asked eager to know more.

"At the beginning of the war, I was assisting a Mystic named Calista. She had sought me out because we served the same God, Daes." He replied.

"The war started when Vampires killed one of our Den Masters as I understood it." Recalling the old stories of our race.

"In part you are right. The Den Master killed by the Vampires and Drameon's mate are one and the same. In a metaphorical sense, the Vampires had thrown the first stone." He stated.

My eyes grew wide with understanding. Small pieces of information were beginning to form a larger picture, and just how long Howl, Drameon, and Alkin have been around. Sud-denly I started to feel like a small pawn in a larger game. I patiently waited for him to continue.

"Then what happened to you?" I asked.

"I was brought to a turning point in my life. I was poisoned and while Calista, the Mystic I was sworn to protect lay dying, I knew I had to make a choice, and I was only left with one option. I knew what the poison was that coursed through my veins and no Shadow Walker blood could cure it. I needed Drakar blood. Claude told no one and took me to a red Dragon named Solomn; he's the leader and oldest Drakar in Silvertine. In addition, he's Alkin's adoptive father. While that happened, an old friend came and tried to assist the Mystic I was sworn to guard. As the Shadow Walkers had a spell to bring Half-breeds to be full-blooded, so did the Drakar." He said as I looked at him confused.

I had never heard of any spell which could do this and wondered if it was this way for all races. "What type of magic does that?" I asked, curious to know myself.

Laughing, Howl explained, "It's a type of magic that only some races possess; it's blood magic. Only the Demons, Shadow Walkers, and Drakar hold this power. Mystics have their own type of blood magic, but I'm not going to go into that. It doesn't work with other races. Only the races that drink blood for power, or use it in spells." He said, hesitant, while I looked at him, unsure how and when he acquired blood. "Don't worry." He said while laughing. "I only take from the willing, and I haven't killed anyone by accident in centuries. Plus I prefer to cook with it instead. Anyway, Solomn performed the spell, and I received enough Drakar blood for the change. Later I woke up a full-blooded Drakar. It was a painful process, like someone skinning you, filleting you, and cooking you alive in a frozen tundra. All at the same time, for days on end; until exhaustion wins. When I woke up I was like any other Drakar. I didn't need blood for food anymore but enjoyed it in my meals. It was a source of power just as it was for the Shadow Walkers, minus the terrible blood lust. As long as Drakar cooked with magic and blood they always had enough power. Unless a spell drained them, then of course they would need rest and a good meal to recharge. To Ancients, blood is power, blood is everything." Howl smiled again as he met my eyes. "I will admit when Daes' power left, all the blue Drakar and Dragons felt the unsettling shift as his magic become unbalanced. We began to crave blood for power, needing it, but still never entered a blood lust. Instead, it drove some to lose their minds. Our line had to learn to adapt or die, and dying was not an option. It was so bad that our race had to hunt those that turned rogue, like the Shadow Walkers. Thankfully Solomn, Opal and I had found a way to alleviate the effects." Howl said as he held up the blue amulet from his neck.

"Solomn—you said he was Alkin's adoptive father, right? Was Opal his mate?" I was starting to see how Aeralain was tied up in all this mess also.

Laughing, Howl answered. "Yes Opal and Solomn are mates. They took Alkin in and raised him alongside Opal's daughter, Calista. The Gods do not raise their own and instead find others willing to do it for them; hence why they also had Calista." He said, toying with his necklace.

"Anyway, this little piece was crafted to hold a portion of Daes' magic. And while the last remains of his power were in chaos in Alecien, Aeralain's was still balanced for the time. So before his power faded forever from the land we met with the blue Dragons themselves, the very beings that Daes himself had placed there to keep his flow of magic steady. They helped craft forty or so necklaces before Daes' power was too weak; and they required rest. That is what happened to all the blue Dragons. Even though in Aeralain, green, red, and white ones are still found, if you look close enough. Here, I know they all sleep deep in the earth because the land is in such chaos and magic is so unbalanced. Regardless, after things settled down, I had returned to my carousing way of life. I returned to Zian and explained the situation to Finn and, even though he disapproved my choice, he respected it, as well. So I continued to assist his people. Eventually, life just overall returned to normal. We fought renegade Shadow Walkers, killed Vampires, drank deeply, and played around. I assume much like your own life before the Mystics entered it." He said while looking towards me once more.

Sighing, I knew he was right. My father had lived a normal life, as normal as we could at the time, but still one free of influence from the Gods and their kin. "So, do you think things will return to normal again here?" I asked hopeful.

Standing and tossing a few logs on the fire he responded. "I believe as long as you give the land and the Mystics time, they will right what is wrong and, yes, life will fall back into the boring balance whence it came. Remember it has been in disarray for over two hundred years. It will not correct itself overnight, it will take some time. Let them do their jobs while we do ours here. It's a hard choice but one that needs to be done. Mystics do what they do because they are trying so hard to help the world as a whole, not as a part." He said while smiling and going to the kitchen.

I guess I needed to let Drameon do his job. From what Howl just said he was trying to follow orders. Orders that I knew if he deviated from could spell more destruction. It was the only option I had left. "What about Raillyn? I still haven't figured out how she is tied to Raihanna. Or what will happen to her?" I said hoping for answers to the many unanswered questions.

Sighing, Howl leaned forward and placed his chin in his hands. "I believe Alkin severed her soul and erased her memories. He essentially made Raihanna out of Raillyn using a construct body. Chances are Alkin recreated her memories too, making her much more Raihanna than Raillyn in The Keep. The last time I'd seen her it got me thinking along that path, but I didn't want to say anything if I was wrong. I don't want to give you any false hope, but I'm sure Raillyn's personality has been breaking through. Raihanna was amiss, distraught, not her cool, collected self. From what I could tell, that was very unlike her." Howl said before getting up and tossing more logs onto the fire.

"So what do we do?" I asked hoping we could fix this issue. "How do we turn Raihanna back into Raillyn?"

Shaking his head I watched him bite at his lip with his teeth. "We can't. That is not our job. I believe it's part of Raihanna's task and will break the construct spell that Alkin placed on her. Only Raihanna can correct this issue, only if she remembers. And before you get any ideas, you telling her will not change a thing," he said pointedly. "Well, other than you ending up sliced by her blade. She won't listen to you, let alone anyone else. She's Raihanna, Hunter's most prized—and—fiercest Elite. She's heartless and selfish, and she controls situations and gets what she wants from those around her without regard. No, this is something we need to leave in the hands of the Mystics. They can handle her better than we can. The situation needs a delicate hand but one that is insistent on the correct outcome. If Drameon assures you he is trying his best to bring her home, believe him. He will not lie about those things. I am sure he is trying his best to do what is right in the end." Howl said as he paced back towards the kitchen and pulled out a bottle of wine. Tipping it towards me he asked if I wanted a drink.

"I think I will pass this time my friend. Thank you for being truthful and I guess we will have to wait and see how the Mystic's play things out." I said while Howl took a drink of his wine.

Nodding his head, he smiled at me. "Yes, that is all we can do. Wait and see what happens. I'm glad we have the job we have, instead of the job the Mystics have. I am sure they're all hard pressed in this matter because it affects everyone, everywhere, not just Alecien."

I agreed. This matter had grown from something simple that we believed just affected us to something larger that could spell disaster. Why was Raillyn given up to the Vampires in order to restore her? No doubt Hunter was using her rare gifts to make everyone miserable.

"So, what about this portal Hunter is having his Elite create? The last one was used to bring undead into the world, I can only assume he plans on using this new one for the same purpose," I asked. I was growing tired and knew I wouldn't be able to stay much longer.

Looking around the room, Howl seemed unsure. "Truthfully, it could be just like the last one, or it could be different since Alkin, and Rai have a hand in it." He said as he tossed back the rest of the wine.

Hearing him say Rai's name made me smile. It seemed much easier to refer to her as Rai instead of Raihanna or Raillyn, with her being trapped and working in The Keep. "How do you think Rai will return to us? I mean if she's in The Keep and being subjected to Hunter's care and The Keep life, how will she be affected mentally and physically? I don't quite grasp the spell Alkin used to create the construct body but how is her being Raihanna going to affect Raillyn? Lastly what about this betrothal?" I asked, suddenly fearful how my mate would return to us.

Meeting my eyes, I saw him grimace. "That I do not know. As I have said, much has to change in order to fix what is amiss. I'm sure Raillyn's magic will be affected by this. When she stayed at my house to study I sensed she was growing in power. Maybe the Gods have her in The Keep so she can learn what she does not know. She's used to being here with the Werewolves and Shapeshifters but has not had much interaction with the Vampires. Her mother, when she was alive, had interaction between all the races and was never limited to just one. Possibly they are making Rai like this, more understanding so she can do her job right later." Shrugging he leaned back once more. "Truthfully, I really don't know; it could be magic, personality, balance, hate, or just really something simpler. Neither the Gods nor the Mystics will share that knowledge with me. I'm only tied to Daes and his blood line, which is currently only Rai here in the living." He said hesitant. "As far as the betrothal, that's an Ancient tradition, and you will have to speak to Alkin about it. It's not my place to say more."

Nodding, I understood. In turn, Howl only worked for Daes' line, and at this time only Rai since Daes had no power in the world due to the lack of magic from his children dying at the beginning of the war. He was powerless here and could not intervene with anything until his power was restored and balance swayed correctly. "So, how do we help the Mystics ensure Daes' magic is put back into the world? I thought Daes was an evil God, not a good one." Hoping he might know.

Howl shook his head. "No, Daes' power is not evil, it is balanced. He is the God of all harmony and chaos, he understands the whirlwind of emotions that every living creature has, and the constant struggle they endure to keep themselves harmonized. Good cannot live without evil, and that is what Daes' magic is. As far as helping the Mystics, I have asked myself that very thing since the beginning of the war. All we can do to help them is do what we're told, in good faith. At times, I feel terrible that Mystics cannot live a normal life. They are constantly governed by their God and have to learn to let normal things slip by, making a normal life very hard to live. Calista was always that way; she set herself apart from everyone she could. Never risking a relationship, she felt she was unable to love, but she fulfilled her duty and did what she was told without question. Even after she carried Rai, after meeting her mate Drameon, she always followed her father's orders. He was her sanctuary, and I knew why. Her chaotic power often brought times of unrest. During her pregnancy, she had trouble controlling her magic. For Mystics, bringing a child into the world is not an easy matter. I remember it used to bring her to her knees as she fought hard to control the rising chaos inside her. It was only the chaos side she struggled with, never the harmonized power. And her pregnancy made her very unbalanced, often swaying from one extreme to another. I'm sure Rai is slowly getting her power restored, and she will more likely be like Calista was for a time while she learns to control her unreliable magic. We will get answers soon. I have a feeling this spell is coming to a close and when it does we will know what to prepare for and what is expected." He said as I nodded.

Howl was right, at this time we could only speculate what we needed to do. Rai was Rai to me, regardless of what she was. I only prayed the Gods would return her to me in one piece and that when they did so, she could live peacefully. At least for the time being.

Enough ~ Raihanna

Opening my eyes, I awoke—unsure where I was. Soft furs lined the bed and warmed my skin. A white canopy hung high above my head. The walls were decorated in simple blue and red tapestries; symbols of nature, trees, vines and saplings, Elvin symbols lay on them. Next to me was a small dark wood table, books were strewn across its surface.

The room smelled like Alkin, but he was nowhere to be seen. I closed my eyes momentarily, my toes burned, and I felt so tired. The weariness of Hunter's spell had completely overwhelmed me both physically and mentally, my magic was drained. And I was beginning to feel less than myself. Somewhere past the foot of my bed a door clicked open. Alkin entered the room and quickly came to my side.

He took my hand in his, kissing it as he did so. I felt concern wash over his mind and fill his eyes. "I am so glad to see you are alive." He said genuinely, coming to sit on the bed next to me.

Confused I looked around once more. "Where am I?" I asked in a haze, my body began to burn again as I remembered the recent events. I had a feeling Howl was right and I would be able to visibly see the deterioration happening.

Alkin grabbed a blue glowing bottle sitting beside his bed. "You're in my chambers. Hunter got a little carried away last night, and I didn't want to concern the girls, so I brought you here to heal." He said as he uncorked the crystal. "Drink this, it should help." Even though I hadn't spoken to him about my construct body, Alkin seemed to understand my concern. I was beginning to wonder if he actually knew more than he was letting on about this particular spell.

Looking at its contents suspiciously, I wondered how it would taste. I hated drinking concoctions, even if they would help me. Hesitantly I put the crystal bottle to my lips and drank. A sour tartness danced on my tongue and into my stomach. The room became cloudy, and I felt light.

A strange magic seemed to stir within; it was like the subtle beat of a drum echoing deep in my soul. The steady beat placed my mind in a deep trance. Mentally I found myself in what I could only interpret as a Den. Dancers walked around a centralized hearth while various silks and colors decorated the ceiling and walls. Everything appeared fuzzy, but I still made out objects and people.

The vision pulls me in closer, but I can't see any colors. Judging by the circular shape of the cavern, it has to be underground in some sort of cave system. I can tell the cave is well used, the floor is smooth like a paved road. On the ceiling disembodied lights, conjured out of magic, light the path. At that moment a woman walks past me, her presence seems familiar. I notice her skin is a darker tint than my own, possible a rich olive color. A thick silk sash hangs at her waist. The woman's pants flow loosely as she walks barefoot down the tunnel. At her side is a child. Deestan holds her hand as the woman leads her down a flight of stairs that lay on the outer edge. Deestan's clothes are very similar to that of woman's. Down they go, and I follow at their backs. At the bottom is a small room. Then the scene shifts and I see a dark room, with only a slight glow from a fireplace. Two chairs sit around the fireplace and Deestan is sitting with Lord Drake.

The room is quiet and subdued. The two of them together are talking. Deestan's words are hushed and rather fast-paced as she talks her words run together, and I'm unable understand a single syllable. Drake's replies are quiet and soft spoken.

A single word slips from Deestan's mouth, and there is no mistaking it. Again she says it; she says it over, and over. I can hear it now. It's the only word I can make out. She is calling Lord Drake Father. I can't ever recall a time I've seen her so happy. I simply sit watching her laugh and spin around.

Shifting again, I now stand in a dark green room with a forest mural dotting its walls. Lord Drake sits watching

Deestan sleep in a deep purple bed, her small frame so tiny in its large blankets. He sits brushing her hair behind her ear before leaning down to kiss her. My heart holds an odd mixture of heaviness mixed with happiness for her.

I can't help but notice that Lord Drake has similar facial features as Deestan, she can indeed pass for his daughter if you look close enough. Realization begins to sink in as I try to remember how I acquired Deestan. Hunter had told me she was taken from the Wolves but who she was he never said. I understand now; Deestan is Lord Drake's child, the one who had been taken along with Raillyn from Death's Realm. I am equally sure then that Leeda is the Shifter Princess who had be abducted and spirited away during the fall of our last portal. I feel hopelessly lost, not only do I have Raillyn's items, I also have her child and niece. I feel a deep crack vibrate throughout me as the construct body protested.

Deestan

I knew Hunter had my sister Callina, and Alkin was on his way back as well. I could feel Alkin's presence coming down the hall, he seemed very displeased. I felt another presence with him. *Ash,* I said silently as I ran to my room. Leeda had already gone to bed, tired from the morning's events, but I couldn't sleep.

Quietly I peered out, watching as Alkin and Ash walked into the hall in silence. I gasped in shock. *What had Hunter done?* I thought to myself. I knew my mother would be furious when she returned.

Alkin led Ash down the hall and into my mother's room, I opened the door slightly to peer down the hall further. I could hear Alkin and Ash talking but couldn't make it out what was being said. Suddenly the door to my mother's room opened up as they stepped back into the hall.

Quickly I jumped back into my room, closing the door behind. They passed my room in silence. "I'm sure when Raihanna sees she will be on the warpath." Ash said to Alkin in a hushed voice.

Alkin crossed his arms. "Yeah, I know. I wonder if Hunter realizes how bad he's made this situation with this mistake." Alkin said in return, shaking his head.

Ash crossed his arms as well "Well, I know that it needed to be done, so regardless, we have the energy now and shortly we can summon Daes. I'm sure when that happens Raihanna's anger will die down. She's just as eager as we are to get this done since we have been at it for nearly a decade." Ash said while he smiled and walked out the door, Alkin went with him.

As soon as the door closed, I ran down the hall to my mother's room. Callina lay sleeping amongst the blanket, her face no longer that of an innocent child, something was different; it seemed more hardened as if by a great distress. Her hair, no longer dark in color, now hung silver around her small frame, giving her a Fae-like appearance.

A sudden fear gripped me. Quickly I ran to my room and opened my chest at the end of my bed. Tossing its contents frantically on the floor, I found it, lying inside my leather bag. The Goddess statue glowed slightly, and since Hunter's return I keep it hidden for safety. I took the statue with me as I went back down the hall towards my mother's room.

Carefully I drew my dagger out from my belt and took my sisters hand in mine and ran its blade across her tallest finger, she didn't even stir, exhausted from Hunter's spell. Her blood dripped down and across the statute as it slightly flared in response.

After adding my own blood, the statue flashed brightly, and magic danced across its surface as I was pulled into the same trance-like state as before. I heard the Moon Goddess speak to me whimsically, as a gentle spring breeze. Tears ran down my cheeks. Even though I couldn't sense my body, I knew I wept both inside and out. "My Uncle hurt her." I cried, unsure of what to do.

Mentally I felt a light touch across my cheek. "It's okay, child, she is not in pain." The Goddess said as she began to sing a calming song soothing me and my racing mind.

Hearing her whimsical voice made me sleepy, I fought the urge to close my eyes, but the power of the song was too strong as I slipped into a gentle slumber. "Sleep, my child, soon you will be safe as well." She said as darkness consumed me.

Raihanna

This time I awoke in Alkin's room, startled. I remembered my dream but dared not think of it at this time. I had to check on the girls, something was terribly wrong. Quickly I got up and went to the door. Carefully opening it revealed that Alkin was not in the main room, and sensing with my magic he was not in The Keep either. Silently I left, down the hall towards my chambers.

As I walked through the door, all was quiet. It was late, and I figured the girls slept. Quietly I crept towards Leeda's door and checked. Leeda slept under the large blue quilt, but upon looking into the other room, Deestan and Callina's bed lay untouched.

Quietly I walked down to my own bedroom and silently opened the door. Deestan was on the bed, snuggled close to her sister. Her once silken brown hair lay tousled about, now silver, fear was on her face. While a bruise high on her cheek tarnished her creamy skin, her eye was purple, as well. Hunter had beaten her.

So not to awaken Callina I lifted Deestan off the bed, carefully taking her into my arms. "Baby, I need you to wake up." I said carefully, while I brushed her hair away from her face. "Deestan, sweetie, please wake up." I said as she began to rub her eyes sleepily. When I knew she was awake enough to respond, I went on. "What happened when I was away?" I said with concern.

Deestan turned in my arms and looked at her sister. "Alkin and Ash said there was a mistake in the spell." She said as she woke up more. "Ash said you wouldn't care because now you could summon Daes now." She said as I brushed Callina's hair away from her eyes.

Ash was deadly wrong, and I was going to stop this now before it got out of hand any further. Anger brewed inside as I remembered Hunter briefly mentioning a slight error in his spell earlier. I was furious and wanted to make sure Hunter felt my wrath. Quickly I grabbed Deestan's arm and took her into the hall.

"Go wake Leeda." I said rushed. "Tell her to get her dancer attire on." I said as I turned to go into the main room, locking the door as I did so.

Deestan had followed me into the main den instead of going to fetch Leeda. "What are you doing to do, Mommy?" She asked in a frightened voice as I placed a ward on the door, ensuring no one would hear us.

I knew she had been through a lot recently, but I had to do something to protect them from more harm. Hunter's behavior was becoming too erratic. He had almost killed me in his quest for power and hurt my youngest. I was through with his games.

Angered and upset I yelled at Deestan. "Do as I say, get Leeda this moment." I shouted as she jumped, stunned, and ran down the hall to retrieve her. Suddenly I felt terrible for yelling, I was near tears again as I went on in a more gentle tone. "Also grab any of your most prized possessions and put them into a bag. You will not be returning here again so be quick about it. We don't have much time." I said while sitting down in a chair to calm myself. "Grab Callina's things as well." I added.

Adrenaline rushed through me. I was so angry at Hunter for his recent endeavors. At the same time, I couldn't help but shake out of fear from my decision to correct it. I saw Leeda and Deestan emerge from one room and quickly rush into Deestan's.

Leeda's flame-red pants, top and sash blazed behind her as she followed Deestan, who wore a matching ice blue outfit. *Fire and ice,* I thought to myself, smiling for a moment before they returned to the den. Both had black cloaks on and carried a small pack. Leeda's yellow eyes met mine in fear, neither knew what I had planned and as I got up they moved aside so not to upset me further.

Silently I guided the girls down the hall towards my room, keeping the door open as we went in. I reached down and took Callina off the bed. She was limp in my arms but still breathed steadily. The girls looked at me questioningly. I knew I was running out of time. I had to do this and fast, before I changed my mind. I knew the maids would be making their rounds soon and I wanted the children gone beforehand. Silently, I hustled them back down the hall and out the door in silence.

The main hall was empty, I was thankful we were on the second floor and many stairs lay about to get to the lower levels. I guided them in silence to the closest stairs. No one emerged from the nearby doors or walked the halls as we entered its darkness.

"Where are we going?" Deestan asked silently as I led them down the dimly lit staircase.

Instead of answering I shook my head. I dared not speak about it until I reached our destination. As we emerged into the village below, I quickly hustled the children down a nearby street and out of view. Three Vampires staggered nearby as they dragged a woman along, one caught my eye but quickly looked away as he recognized me. Turning back towards the girls, I pushed them further along into the darkness of night towards the one place where I knew Hunter would never be able to touch them again.

Finally we emerged and entered a well-lit area of town, a large ball-shaped building stood in front of me. The girls eyed me, knowing where they were, and fear flickered in their eyes. I took a deep breath and pushed them forward towards the light brown door.

Sighing momentarily, I pushed it open. The girls ran quickly in front of me as I entered its interior and closed the door swiftly behind me. The large hearth I had seen in my dream burned in front of me as dancers lay sleeping amongst the floor on various furs and brightly colored blankets. The dancers who were awake eyed me, shocked, and a group came towards me, angered. I held Callina tighter against me as the girls stayed close to my side.

"Why are you here, Elite?" The man with fiery red hair and piercing blue eyes asked.

I opened my cloak that was closed in front of me to reveal Callina sleeping in my arms. "I am not here to cause trouble. I will not enter your Den any further than I am, but I bring you these Den children." I said feeling a pull at my heart at what I was about to say. "Please, I release these children into the care and the safety of your Den. Return them to their parents, but please take them." I said desperately.

The man looked at me shocked, staring at me in disbelief.

"Be sure Lord Drake gets his daughter back and ensure that the Shifters get Leeda. As far as my youngest, please keep her safe and allow no harm to come to her. She has already been through a lot." I said as I handed her to him and turned to leave.

As I did so, the same lady from my dream, with olive skin, entered the main Den from a small room beyond. Her eyes met mine as she called for me to stop. I knew though that I couldn't do that. I wanted to alert Lord Drake that I had released his daughter into the Den's care. Swiftly I made my way through the streets and out the front gate. I summoned my magic and created a portal. I knew I could not appear in Lord Drake's castle, so instead I went south of their village to the woods near the caves.

The moon still shone high as I emerged from the black mist, and into the crisp air. I stood amongst what seemed like thousands of glowing purple locust flowers in a decent-sized clearing facing the castle; the lake was at my back. The whole area seemed enchanted.

As I stood there, I noticed a figure walking along their edge towards the castle. Immediately I recognized Lord Drake. Closing my eyes and looking skyward I thanked whatever God or Goddess that had allowed this to happen. He paused suddenly as his eyes met mine.

Standing in complete silence he seemed to wait and see what I planned on doing. I looked around, checking to make sure no guards or anyone else was around before slowly making my way towards him. I tossed my cloak back casually, revealing I had no weapons. As I got closer, he crossed his arms and waited.

I closed my eyes, knowing that I was not only going to suffer Hunter's wrath but also Alkin's because of this. I didn't care anymore. If Hunter was going to kill me I would ensure the safety of the children, and take him down a few steps while I was at it.

"I came to tell you I released your daughter into the care of the Den. She should be here by morning." I said calmly and quietly.

Concern crossed his face as he shook his head in shock. "I don't understand. Why are you helping us all of a sudden?" He asked thinking it was a trap.

I shook my head. "Never mind why I did it. It's done. She's yours." I said as I suddenly felt a portal open up behind me. I turned, frightened, to see that it was Alkin who stepped out of its shadowy mass.

His ever-changing eyes meet mine. He looked at me confused and concerned, he had not discovered the children were missing, or he would be fuming. "Rai, what are you doing here?" He asked unhappily as he reached out and grabbed my wrist.

Something cracked further inside me. Suddenly I felt a deep connection to him, something that ran to my very soul. My eyes widened, and my nostrils flared. This was not me, I thought as tears built up in my eyes.

In retaliation, anger built up inside as I decided to create a portal and flee. Yanking my arm free upset him more. Going through my portal, I sensed Alkin create a new one to follow. I was on a suicide mission, only caring about the damage I could inflict upon those that hurt me and who I could bring down with me. I knew I wouldn't make it far, and as my feet touched the carpet of my den, Alkin was beside me. He grabbed my arm and threw me into a chair.

"What is the meaning of this?" He yelled at me furiously.

Staring back at him fiercely, my blood began to boil and I was feeling hot under my collar. I found myself beginning to hate my Uncle as well as The Keep, and everything we stood for.

Either the blood spell with the staff or the blue liquid that healed was stirring up changes inside me. Contemplating my next move gave me a slight twinge of fear. It didn't matter, anything I did now was going to be reckless, and I no longer cared about the consequences. Already I felt my construct body break further, and I knew I had little time. I accepted the fact that my Uncle would punish me, lashing out in a possible beating, or worse a draining. Either way I was going to die. Shaking my head to clear my thoughts Alkin shouted at me again.

"You will tell me why you were with Lord Drake and what is going on." He said in a hushed voice. He placed his hands on either side of the armrest, pinning me down in the chair.

I turned away from his gaze. His anger and magic was already mixing with mine, and everything turned into a whirlwind of emotions. I felt something deep inside shatter. A rush of magic hit me, my eyes suddenly flashed blue in color. Closing them I tried to regain control of it, but couldn't, instead I looked up into Alkin's deep red eyes.

As soon as his eyes met mine they changed. He took a step back, unsure of what to do or say. His mind went blank momentarily as I stood to meet him. This power felt more right than anything else in the world, it was the driving force behind my decisions, and my fate.

Suddenly I felt that as long as I let it lead me, it would not lead me astray. Carefully I explained. "I went to Lord Drake to tell him that I released his daughter into the Den's care." I said quietly waiting for an answer or a possible blow to my face.

Alkin seemed stunned. Turning away he silently went down the hall, checking to see if I spoke the truth. He returned to the main room stunned. Just as I felt myself fall back into a steady rhythm of power, my eyes returned to normal as I was able to control the raging emotions inside myself.

Composure took over once more. "I am sick and tired of this game he plays." I said while pointing to the door as I indicated to Hunter. "He lies to me about so many things. About my armor, his plans, and even my own daughter. I will not tolerate this any longer. The children are with the Den now, he cannot touch them again!" I said angered. I didn't care what Alkin chose to do to me or if he would go straight to Hunter and tell him. I stood waiting an answer.

Suddenly the door to my chambers burst open, slamming against the wall, and Ash walked in. Anger lit his eyes as he walked to stand in front of me. "Where are the girls?" He asked between clenched teeth.

I felt his anger and knew even before I spoke what would happen. I cared not. "I said I released them into the Den's care." Ash's hand struck my face.

The force from the blow was enough to knock me to the floor, and onto my side. My head banged against the floor as Ash reached down and sunk his teeth into my neck. I heard Alkin gasp.

Ash removed his mouth and pulled me upwards grasping the cloak around my chest tightly. My blood ran down his face, covering his mouth and chin. Still I cared not and felt a fury of power rage through me once more.

Once again my eyes flashed blue in color, I felt on the verge of being out of control, a feeling that left me very uneasy. "I should drain you for your frugal thoughts. Instead, I will take you to Hunter and let him decide what he wants to do with you." Ash said mockingly as he pulled me out into the hallway and down to Hunter's den.

Alkin followed closely behind, I knew he could not intervene now that Ash had done so. It would ultimately be Hunter's decision on what my punishment would be now. Ash tore open the door and tossed me onto the ground forcefully. My bright blue eyes met Hunter's as he stood behind the table where his staff lay. Grabbing it, he walked around to meet

Ash and me. "What is the meaning of this?" He asked while Alkin closed the door.

Ash stood angered. "Raihanna has released the girls into the Den's care." He said, pulling me up and slamming me into the nearby wall. The bookshelf beside me rocked in protest to the blow.

Hunter's eyes went wild with rage as he approached me. Setting the staff down on the table he walked over and stood beside Ash. As he looked into my eyes something changed, I tried desperately to try and control the raging power inside and felt my eyes try and return to their normal ever-changing color, but a strong force was willing my magic to remain erratic.

"Release her." He said. "And leave, Ash."

Ash did as he was told and released me, backing away before bowing and going out the door. Hunter took control of the situation swiftly. His red eyes met mine as he spoke. "Is this true? Did you release the girls into the Den's care?" He asked me trying to control his anger.

I shook my head in response, not daring to say anything for fear that I would say too much. I briefly saw Hunter reach out. Quickly he grabbed my hair, taking a handful into his grip before he brought my face down onto his table. Pain erupted across my face as blood sprayed from my nose and onto its surface. I felt bones crack, and break, swiftly the swelling set in.

My eyes caught sight of his staff laying a few feet away from me. *Maybe I can grab it...* I thought as I felt a sudden flare in its power. "Do you forget why we have them?" He asked slamming my head onto the table again

I gasped in pain as my head struck its surface several times. My eye was swollen, and my face felt broke. "You wouldn't even have those kids unless I allowed you to have them." He said spitefully. Hunter made a motion to bite me, but Alkin spoke up.

"Wait." He said cautiously. Opening my good eye just a slit, I saw that he placed a hand on Hunter's shoulder.

His wild eyes spun to meet Alkin's. "What is it?" He said while sprays of saliva flew from his mouth.

Alkin smiled in response, and I could tell he had a plan. "Perhaps this situation can be remedied." He said while Hunter loosened his grip. "You have the staff already charged. All is set to summon Daes, other than the execution of Lord Drake and Briar. Why not have Raihanna perform that task? You said yourself that you had wanted someone who had seen the Wolves' castle to do it. Well, she's been inside the castle, and personally I don't think Aurielle could do it alone. The less Elite you have to send out to perform this task the better it will be. Think of it as her redemption for causing so much trouble." Alkin said tactfully.

Hunter released his grasp from my head and stood up, smiling at Alkin. Slowly I stood as well and touched my face. Everything felt swollen, but the bones were all in place. Overall my injuries included another bloodied nose, a cut on my cheek and head near the hairline, and a swollen lip. Thankfully, the rest of my face seemed intact other than bruises.

Hunter looked back at me. "Go get yourself cleaned up and meet me back here before daybreak, and do not think about leaving or I will storm the Den and kill your children, before killing you." He said going back to his desk as if nothing had occurred.

Alkin went to the door and opened it waiting for me to follow him. Shaking with fear, I saw Hunter grabbing an old book from behind his table and grab his staff. A wild smile crossed his face as he flipped through the pages. Quickly I ran through it and down the hall. Alkin followed closely behind me, we had about five hours before I was expected back.

My chambers were quiet as Alkin closed the door. Going to the red chair next to the fireplace, I sat and tried to collect myself. Alkin went down the hall, returning with a small bowl of water, and a rag. He sat next to me and began gently wiping the blood from my face.

"Now tell me what happened?" He said lovingly as he wrung out the rag in the now bloodied water.

I shook my head, still dazed and upset. "I'm tired of Hunter not telling me the truth. He said there was a minor issue with our daughter." I said baffled. "She looked like he beat her and her hair! That is not minor!" Alkin nodded quietly in response as he began wiping the blood from my neck and hair. I felt his reaction; he was furious as well but was keeping his emotions under control for my sake.

He stopped momentarily to meet my eyes. "I think you need to tread carefully for the rest of today. Your magic is very off, and I fear what Hunter will do to you if you do not follow orders. It's probably your cycle, I smell it, faintly; it will probably hit sometime next week." He said looking at me closer. "You don't appear to have a concussion but anymore beatings like that, and you will end up with Vera." He stressed as he went to dump the bowl. I wasn't surprised, I had felt this way last time also.

The thought of having to deal with Vera during my more vulnerable time, made me shutter. She was The Keep's healer and she wasn't very good at attending the living, or understanding the workings of a female body. It was almost like she forgot when she became Vampire.

Nodding, I got up and went to my room. I took my blood-stained clothes off. Looking down, I couldn't help notice that my legs were ashen in color. Already my construct body was failing me, and was returning from whence it came. I wondered how long I had left... Knowing the girls were safe I shrugged it off and adorned my armor instead. If Hunter was going to have me slaughter Lord Drake then I would need it. As I left I paused momentarily and looked around my room, a feeling of finality overwhelmed me.

We had accomplished every task, but this; it bothered me that I was the one who had to perform it. Lord Drake was the father of my child, and I was feeling conflicted on what I should do. I didn't want to trust Hunter any longer—he had hurt me too many times already. At the same time, I had nowhere to run. Hunter would hunt me down and slaughter everyone I cared for along the way. Even if I took the girls and went to Howl, Hunter would eventually find me and even then

I knew I was slowly dying. Sighing I closed the door and returned to the main room. This was it, I felt it in my very being, time was running out, my construct body was shattering, and this was the end. What lay ahead I could only guess.

Alkin sat tensely on the cushioned bench near the stairs, his chin rested on his knuckles as he leaned forwards slightly. He watched me with unwavering eyes. I felt a sudden pull towards him, much like the pull I had felt earlier. Slowly I went to stand next to him, and he pulled me onto his lap and into a deep embrace. Leaning against his chest, listening to his heartbeat made me feel safe, I closed my eyes.

"You know if I could stop Hunter I would." He said quietly. His magic danced across my skin, sending waves of comfort throughout me. Nodding I felt a crack in the deepest region of my body. My throat tightened, breathing deeply I met his eyes. They were saddened and hurt. I knew he felt my body falling apart, as well.

"Why do I have to kill Lord Drake?" I asked, knowing I had no choice.

Alkin lovingly kiss the top of my head, not hiding his emotions any longer. They were a whirlwind of love, terror, and sadness. Deep inside, my soul cried out, and for the first time I felt myself wanting to soothe him, to chase those fears away from his mind. Reaching out I brushed his chestnut hair behind his ear and kissed his forehead.

"It's the only way you can survive in this world." He said quietly in return. "If you want to win Hunter's favor once more and avoid a worse punishment, you will inflict a killing blow." He said, looking at me lovingly.

I had always felt that Alkin had truly cared for me, but I would not allow myself to be pulled into a relationship. Living in The Keep, like that, just became more difficult. I couldn't risk having more loved ones hurt, or used as leverage.

Our eyes met and locked, sweeping me out of reality and into a tidal wave of emotions I was not used to. Gently he pulled me closer. I knew I shouldn't, but I didn't care any longer, our lips met. Gods, he was sexy. Dark, dangerous, caring and in a sense untamed all at the same time, just below the surface. A sudden burst of emotions tore a hole in my heart.

Its steady rhythm picked up pace, as a flare of magic lit up my eyes, blue in color once more. Deep down something shook inside me, an overwhelming pull that gave me the impression that if I continued on this path, I would lose something dear. I did not know what that was, but I felt at a turning point. *Gods I loved him, never before had I loved anyone the way I loved Alkin. If only I had given in a little, I would have given him everything I was.*

His grip tightened as I felt him kiss me back and shift my weight. His mind momentarily pulled back as if he was going to stop, but then it changed. He didn't care either, and wouldn't trade this little moment of peace for anything in the world. Again his emotions flooded my mind, how much he cared for me, and loved me, going to great lengths to keep me safe.

Our breathing picked up as he feverishly kissed my neck, I felt his hands on my armor, removing it. I knew where this would lead, and I didn't care. For the first time I wanted him to know how much I loved him that I didn't just see him as a tool. Opening my mind up to him, I left myself vulnerable. Like an open book I was easy to read for the first time since we met, so very long ago.

Alkin truly had become my world, he protected me, respected me, treated me as an equal, and he never hurt me. *What did I do in return?* I hid from him, distrusted him, and his purposes, and never returned any of the love he gave....

Yes, we fought and argued at times, but that was to be expected. For years, I had been running from the truth, and now I was ready to accept it. Alkin had always been my mate, and I loved him with all my heart and soul. A tear ran down my cheek, *this might be the last moment I get with him.* It was heartbreaking and bittersweet. I hated the construct body I was residing in and wanted to know the truth, wanted to be myself, whoever that was. But most of all my soul wanted to love him.

Pulling at his clothes, he laid me down on the bench. His hand ran down my leg and paused for a moment, his eyes on my ashen skin. Through our mental link I felt his heart break; his eyes became watery as he pulled me against him, and kissed me once more. Returning his kiss, he pulled out a dagger.

"You need blood to heal if you're going to survive." He said as he ran it across his chest, only thinking of my well-being.

Seeing it welt up and run down his bare skin made me shutter. It was tantalizing and smelled sweet, like berries mixed with honey, smoked over pine wood. My eyes focused on the blood, unable to resist I leaned forward and traced my tongue over his skin to its source. Sweat, blood, and the feel of his skin on my mouth mingled together in a euphoric blend. Placing my hands on his chest, to steady myself as I sucked at the wound.

His blood was like sweet honey, a nectar of all that was him. My soul resonated blissfully as something in my body cracked once more. A deep groan rumbled from his throat as I felt his body stiffen then relax.

As the wound closed, I found myself laying down on the bench, Alkin held his weight up with his arms. Looking up at him meekly I smiled. Smirking knowingly, he leaned forward and rubbed his nose against mine. He understood, he felt how much I cared and that I was sorry for running and hiding from the truth.

For the next hour, he stayed with me, in our own utopia. He was gentle and tried to chase away my fears of what was to come. Kissing away my tears, he spoke softly to me and promised to help make it right. In a way, it was our final farewell; the future was unknown and dangerous.

Waking a few short hours later, I was sad. I shouldn't have hidden from him, or run from the truth. He was my mate, and I loved him deeply. Sitting up and looking down at him made me smile. His face was peaceful and calm as he slept.

I tipped my head sideways, wondering what he would look like if male Ancients grew the facial hair the common races did. The gruff beard of the half Dwarf from Balone crossed my mind. After a moment I was thankful our race didn't. Not that it would make any difference, but I preferred his smooth face.

Without thinking, I reached my hand out and brushed it against his soft cheek. It made me want to curl up against him and forget about the troubles to come. However, I knew that would not happen, already time was running out. Sadly, I didn't have that choice any longer. His lashes fluttered open, and his eyes met mine. He sat up and took me into his arms, kissing my shoulder.

"You should get dressed. I don't know how much longer Hunter will be patient. I am so sorry for everything that has happened, my love." He said, sighing regretfully. "This will all be over soon and hopefully we can live somewhat normal."

Not wanting to get up, I knew he was right and slowly went to gather my items. As I dressed my throat tightened, I didn't want to leave. I was scared. Pausing I watched Alkin, pull his pants up and tie them. Sweat still gleamed between the lines of his muscles. I found myself staring, at the way his chest rippled as he moved. *Was he really mine? What did I do to deserve someone so sexy?*

Letting a tear run down my cheek, Alkin looked at me and paused. Smiling, he finished pulling on his shirt before coming to help me clasp my armor. His fingers tickled my sides as he pulled the leather through the metal straps and tightened them.

"I don't deserve you... I've done everything wrong..." I said as he worked, my voice cracked. Another tear fell from my face. Now that I was letting him in, I didn't want it to end. I was scared of dying and possibly never seeing him again.

Finishing the last strap he sighed and took me into his arms. "No, it's me who doesn't deserve you. I should've stopped him. I should've protected you better, or something." He said as he held me tighter. "When all this is over, I promise to tell you the truth. But, I'm sure by then you will already know. I promise to make this better. You will never be rid of me." Our eyes met as he gently took my face into his hands and kissed me once more.

Nodding my head, he released me. "Ready?" He asked while going to the door. Time was up... Sighing and feeling glum I went into the hall, unaware of the dangers that lie ahead.

Respite and Treachery ~ Drake

As I watched Raihanna and Alkin disappear through their portals, I couldn't help but wonder what was going on. Quickly I ran back to the castle, in hopes that I could find an answer to this madness. I knew Howl and Drameon were in the small den south of my chambers, so before I went anywhere else, I would go there.

Not many of my people were in the halls tonight as most had already retreated to bed. Swiftly I ran down the red carpet with breakneck speed. If what Raihanna had said was true then Deestan was in the care of the Den, meaning she relinquished her claim to her. As I rounded the last corner, I slowed down. I could hear Drameon speaking to Howl within. Despite recent events between us, I couldn't disregard his friendship. I was learning to let it go in hopes of a better future. Drameon had helped us so many times over the past few years I felt we had to trust him if we wanted life to return to normal. Especially if I wanted Raillyn returned to us safely.

The fireplace burned brightly as I went into the room. Drameon and Howl looked surprised. Probably because I was still awake at this hour. I nodded my head as I went to sit in the chair beside them.

Where to start became my problem. Tonight I had seen Alkin and Raihanna. Alkin had seemed on edge while Raihanna was angered by something, was this why she gave Deestan to the Den?

Drameon knew something was amiss. "What troubles you, Drake?" He asked while looking at me.

Shaking my head I answered. "I ran into Raihanna tonight. Or rather she seemed to seek me out." I began looking at Drameon who seemed surprised by this event. "She told me she released Deestan into the Den's care." I paused, looking

into the fire myself. "Before I got a chance to find out anything else, Alkin showed up. He wasn't too happy that
Raihanna was talking to me. They both left after that." I
trailed off recalling the events.

Drameon was nodding his head when a knock was heard
at the door. Howl, who had been listening quietly, stood up to
get it. A messenger stood with a sealed letter, I barely noticed
him as Drameon spoke to me. "I wonder why she did that."
He said tapping his fingers together. "I can see why Alkin
would be upset. Hunter is probably furious. If she keeps it up,
I'm sure she will get herself killed. That's what Alkin was
probably upset about the most." Drameon said quietly.

Howl brought the sealed letter to me as we spoke, I immediately recognized it as the Den's symbol, and nearly
ripped the letter open.

Lord Drake,
We have acquired a special treat for you, actually make
that several. You should have them by nightfall tomorrow.
~Stasha~

Drameon looked at me, waiting for an answer. "Raihanna
was right. She released Deestan and from the sounds of it,
Leeda and Callina as well." I sighed while taking my seat
once more.

Howl seemed eager by the news, as well. "See, things are
turning our way. Hopefully things will be back to normal, before too long." He said while looking at Drameon.

Sitting back in the chair, Drameon just smiled, not saying
a word, but his eyes lit up eagerly. Finally, something seemed
to be going our way. I wondered what was happening in The
Keep that made things urgent enough to cause Raihanna to
give up the girls. I went to bed that night with a lightened
heart and hoped tomorrow would bring more answers.

Again the dark figures of the lady entered my mind, she
seemed to appear and disappear randomly, like a hall with
many doors. One minute she was happy, the next she wept. I
called out to her.

"Who are you?" I asked. All she did was place her finger to her lips as if it was a secret.

Out of anger I felt my magic boom. For a moment I felt on the verge of waking. Instead, I reached out and grabbed her arm, pulling her around to face me. Suddenly an image flashed across my mind.

An open plain, tall brush, and grasses grew everything was green. Looking left, I stood near a large lake; the water shimmered and rippled, like a pebble hitting its surface. Remembering I held her arm, I looked down. Sure enough, I still held onto her.

Whether this was a dream still or not I was not sure, everything appeared so vivid. My eyes traced her ivory skin to her armor, a light brown leather shirt, and deep brown pants. Meeting her face I was stunned, expecting to see Raillyn, instead a petite pixie-like face met mine. *This was the girl who had haunted my dreams for over twenty years.*

Her face was slim and she had high cheekbones, but her ears were rounded like mine. Tousled, black as night hair, hung in loose curls over her shoulders. Bright hazel eyes that seemed to change from blue to green, looked at me, wide eyed.

Squealing, she withdrew her arm, and looked at me horrified. For a moment she seemed unsure what to do, I was still trying to figure this dream out. *Who was this girl?* A look of determination crossed her face as she brought her hand up to my shoulder and shoved. Like lightning I felt a jolt of energy enter my body and shove me away. "I'm so sorry..." I heard her melodic voice chime as I faded back into the blackness of sleep.

Raihanna

I knew walking into Hunter's den would be bad but I hadn't imagined how much distrust we had in each other. As I stood near the table, Hunter leaned over its hard surface reading the old book he had pulled out earlier. Alkin was beside me in the chair and eyed Hunter warily; he hadn't left my side since we arrived. *Be careful,* he said to me mentally. *That staff is not to be taken lightly.*

Hunter broke our conversation. "Since you dishonored me by releasing the girls into the Den, I will make sure you do not fail this task." Hunter said sinisterly as he walked around the table, book in hand. "Thankfully we had already infused the staff with your daughter's power, or else I would have killed you myself. Before I forget, I have a little present for you." He said as he laid the book onto the table and picked up a leather sheathed blade. He avoided the hilt as he laid it in front of me. "Go ahead." He said waiting for me to pick up the blade.

The blade seemed to beckon me to pick it up, and as I grasped its handle and drew it from the sheath it seemed so familiar to me. I tipped my head as I looked at it closer, it was crafted of an unknown material, and had gems lining its silvery moon balance. The blade was slightly curved while a bright blue line ran its sharpest end.

My Uncle seemed to smile manically at the sight of the blade. It glowed and pulsed with magic as I held it, I felt my own magic reacting and my eyes glow blue momentarily. "Good, I'm glad you can wield it." He said trying to sound casual. "Perhaps you can regain your loyalty to me. That blade is a God forged blade, just as this staff is." He explained as he looked down at the book momentarily. "As you know these items can only be wielded by certain people. I can wield the staff since Alkin and you performed the ritual and imbued it with your power and blood. In turn, you can wield it if need be, as well." He said cautiously, giving out information which could spell his end. "That blade can only be wielded by a certain blood; anyone else would be burned by its magic. Alkin, try and take the blade from Raihanna." He commanded.

Alkin stared wide-eyed at Hunter and me, he was on edge and did not care to try and take the blade, but stood anyway. However, to not upset Hunter further, he didn't hesitate. I held the blade out in the palm of both hands, and he took it. Blue static leaped to life across the blade, burning Alkin and causing him to drop it. Hunter stood by waiting as Alkin's hand smoked momentarily from the power.

I dared not show any feelings towards Alkin and grabbed at the blade instead. I sighed knowing I had no choice in the matter. Hunter would have me do as he pleased until Daes was summoned or until he grew tired of me. I knew he often thought of everyone as being expendable. I closed my eyes knowing I had fallen out of his favor and if I wished to remain safe in The Keep I would have to gain it back.

Hunter picked the staff up as he traced some of the text in the book with his finger. "I will give you a choice, Raihanna." He spoke as I looked up meeting his eyes. "Give me your hand. I'm going to perform a spell ensuring you won't betray me again. And be lucky you are my niece if you had been anyone else I would've allowed the other Elite have their way with you already, you know how they treat traitors." His eyes went wild, and swirled with darkness, but I knew he spoke true.

The only reason I was spared death was because I was his niece. So I gave him my hand, knowing as he grabbed a dagger from the table, he would spill my blood once more. As Hunter drew the blade across my palm, it began to pool and run down my wrist and arm. Quickly he grabbed his staff and placed it onto the bloodstone's smooth surface once more.

Immediately I felt the stone's power, it was now directly connected to Daes, as well as Delron and the other Gods. I felt their presence pounding at my mind like a ton of bricks. It was inescapable. My Uncle spoke a spell, the language was unknown to me, but I felt my very being was beginning to be tied to something important. I tried to fight it briefly when another sensation was felt. As this new feeling spread over me, I felt the hold Daes had on me grow stronger.

The surreal feeling took over as images began to flash across my mind. It was as if I was remembering something I had never seen before. A crystal coffin and a sulfate smell swam in my nose. Images of the Den flooded my mind, I suddenly became confused.

I must be going crazy that was the only thing I could think of. And as Hunter's spell began to peak a binding spell was felt, the godly power entered my body once more, locking itself forever in my soul. I knew Hunter had bound me to the task of killing Lord Drake.

Ultimately I was tied to the God of Death, and if I failed the task at hand his magic would consume me from the inside out, killing me in the process. The new power seemed to overtake me, and I knew now this was the end of the construct spell. My decision would either spell my end, or my salvation. I fell to my knees as I suddenly became aware of Hunter's den. I looked at him startled; shocked that he had sentenced me to death if I failed.

"I told you I would give you a choice, child. Now I would get going; time's ticking and I know you don't have long." My Uncle said as Alkin went to my side, my wide eyes met his as I grabbed my new blade, and left out the door.

Even though few people dotted the halls, I fell to my knees outside as I felt the power overwhelm me. My eyes burned blue in color from the power coursing through me. Already it was beginning to work its way into my very being, eating away at it. Even now, I felt it begin to kill me. I had to hurry and kill Lord Drake while I was still could. I knew the spell would probably affect my mind before too long. I was going to need my sanity to get into the Wolves' Castle.

Meeting my eyes in shock, I heard Alkin's voice. "Are you okay?" He asked me as I glanced down at the God blade Hunter had given me. I nodded as more images suddenly flashed through my mind, making me grimace in pain. *The purple locust flowers in the field near Lord Drake's,* I thought. Swiftly I stood and called a portal. Hunter's magic had already begun to burn deep in my chest, I would do anything to rid myself of this horror.

Retribution ~ Raihanna

As I stepped out of the portal and into the purple field of locust flowers, Alkin was nowhere to be seen. I could only assume he had been told to stay behind while I attended the matter of slaying Drake, it was better that way. Knowing I had a troublesome task ahead of me, I needed no distractions to deviate me from our ultimate goal.

The Werewolves' castle lay across the lake, I knew the bridge was nearby and wondered if I would have to fight my way in. A slight tremor began to ripple across my body as the dull burning ache in my chest began to radiate. The spell was fast-acting, and I knew I had to be swift. Already I felt my construct body failing me, faster than before. As the morning sun began to peek over the treetops I climbed up a small embankment and onto the road. The bridge stood in front and as I walked towards it, a pair of guards stopped me.

"What business do you have here?" They asked, slowly approaching me, hands on their hilts.

My hood was off, but I still wore my Elite armor. I suspected the guards didn't know who I was, or they would've killed me on the spot. "I'm here to see Lord Drake." I said hoping for no trouble.

The blonde-haired guard looked towards the other one nodding his head. "We had been informed by Lord Drake to allow you access if you showed up. Please follow us." He said as they turned and escorted me down the bridge and across the open field on the other side.

Upon reaching the castle gate, I had acquired several odd stares from various guards and townspeople. I didn't care. The spell was burning inside me, making me itch, and the pain it brought began to drive me mad. Images of what seemed to be another time flashed across my mind, distorting my vision. It was like seeing through someone else's eyes in a dream. A déjà vu feeling took over as we neared the main entrance. Another image flashed gripped my mind, of someone standing before this very gate with Lord Drake and Briar, years ago.

Pausing, I shook my head as a tremor took me over. The guards walked on not seeing. Regaining control, I barely noticed we had entered the throne room, Lord Drake, and Drameon stood in the center. Each nodded to me as I entered. Seeing Drameon this time stopped me in my tracks as another image took over, playing out like a movie in my head. Drameon was reprimanding Lord Drake and Briar. They stood in the center of a slaughtered human village. Talk of a dark warrior in black armor was mentioned. A tremor vibrated through my body, it made me think of the Elite and the armor we wore.

"Leave us." Lord Drake said to his guards, breaking the vision.

The spell continued to burn inside me, and the visions seemed to come faster, stronger. I was having a hard time distinguishing between my emotions or the feeling from the visions.

"What brings you here?" Lord Drake said, breaking another vision of climbing a balcony. "I thought after you released my daughter into the Den's care that Hunter would kill you." He said as he began to approach me, concern crossing his face. His emotions just added to my already chaotic mind. Drameon grabbed his arm halting him from proceeding forwards.

My head swam as another tremor took over. Reaching up I placed my hands on the side of my head, momentarily allowing the tremor to take hold. As it passed, I slid a hand over my forehead; blood lined my hand as I pulled it away. The pain increased and began to sear inside like a burning ember charring in the center of my stomach. I had to get this done. I stared at Lord Drake with disgust. Killing him would end my suffering and in turn place me in high standing with Hunter. Once more I found myself wanting to please him. Summoning

Daes was the most important thing at this time and only Hunter had the power to do so.

Smiling, I slowly took a few steps towards them, I tried to regain control, to portray total sanity. "I've come because Hunter tortures me." I said not lying, trying to get close enough for a killing blow. "Even as we speak, a spell eats away at me." Taking another lugged step towards them.

A trail of blood ran down the side of my face, to my chin. Dismissing it, I could tell Drameon would not be tricked. He was a Mystic and sensed my true purpose there.

"Do not believe her, Drake. She's truthful about the spell but not the reason for being here." He said as I burst into motion. I was angered he had spoken up.

Sudden bursts of evil power consume me as I drew the God blade and flew at Lord Drake. As I approached he drew his own sword, and prepared himself for my assault. Drameon backed away knowing he could not intervene.

Swiftly and suddenly, my blade slashed down towards Drake, missing him by mere inches. Drake backed away just in time and retaliated swinging his own blade towards my midsection. I parried his attack, nearly knocking the sword out of his hand. Cursing, another vision overcame me—the Wolf Captain fought a girl who eerily resembled me in some training grounds surrounded by Wolves.

I jumped back, trying to regain my composure as another ripple of pain nearly brought me to my knees. Blood seemed to seep from every pore in my body, a sharp pain echoed deep inside. Grabbing my stomach momentarily I jumped back towards Lord Drake. I was done, I wouldn't play anymore I reached for my magic to call the dark arts to end this but got nothing. Instead, a blast of pain penetrated my skull, causing me to cry out, and grasp my head once more. The spell was not allowing me to kill Lord Drake with magic, it had to be a blade. Distracted, Lord Drake took the opportunity to attack. He swung his blade around, landing a blow across my left arm. My blood sprayed across the white floor just as I jumped back trying to escape the next advancing attack.

Shifting my body in midair, I soared across till my feet touch the wall. Immediately I propelled off it, leaping towards Drake once more, my blade twisted meeting his. With a flick of my wrist, his sword went flying across the floor and out of reach. Swiftly I swung my blade back around and hit Drake across the side. His warm blood spray my face, and arms as I twisted out of his outstretched hands.

Jumping back towards the far wall of the throne room, I made one last charge at him. Knowing this would be the final blow. Watching Drake stagger from my attack made me smile, I knew I had hurt him immensely, but I still needed to inflict the killing blow. Drameon stood in shock at the events occurring, not able to stop any of them. He would be my one witness to Drake's defeat.

Licking my lips, I jumped towards him one last time. I knew this would end his life, but as I tasted his blood it sent a whirlwind of emotions through me. A sudden eruption of power and memories poured through me. Flashes of an entire existence with Drake, happiness, sadness, love, and joy, I felt them and saw them all. Instead of just visions now I heard voices. Raillyn, I heard the name clear as day, and suddenly I felt an overwhelming urge that what I was doing was wrong.

Death ~ Raihanna

The visions continued as I neared Drake in mid-flight.
Visions of Deestan and her birth, Lord Drake and his people,
Raillyn's immense rage and hatred for her Uncle, it all poured
through me. I felt crippled as the searing pain of the spell echoed throughout my body and soul; desperately it tried to
dampen the memories flooding through me.

Memories, I thought, these were my memories. The real-
ization hit me stronger than anything else before. Howl had
said I was a construct, but he could not say how or who. As
Raihanna, I never remembered a time where I had seen
Raillyn. Now as I inched closer to Drake, I remembered
Deestan and I had been taken by Hunter and Alkin in Death's
Realm. I felt tears running down my face as I stilled my blade.
My eyes met Drake's in heartache. I opened a portal and fell
through, sheathing my blade as I did so.

My forward assault threw me against the floor hard and
fast. The pain of the spell burned fiercely inside as even more
memories of Raillyn ravaged my body. Alkin was by my side
in less than a minute. Briefly I heard him speak frantically as I
opened another portal, letting it take me through its darkness,
trying desperately to control the power raging inside me.

As I fell into its black depths determination crossed my
face as memories of my childhood exploded in my mind. I
had lived with Chaimh, who took me in as a young child and
raised me as his own. How I met Drameon, just prior to my
first council meeting in the library. Then Drameon rescuing
Drake, Briar, and I as we had ventured into a trap set by the
Elite.

I fell onto the grassy knoll near the entrance to Howl's
home. The magic and pain from the spell gripped me, willing
me to kill Drake, pushing me to travel to him. I couldn't

though, not with the knowledge of being Raillyn, I would much rather die before that happened.

Never would I kill a friend with my own hands. My heart raced at this thought, it felt as if it might jump out of my chest. I was covered in blood, from head to toe, it poured out of me in a heavy sweat. Looking up, I saw Howl exit his house. Not wanting to explain, I threw myself into another portal. My chest felt like it would explode in pain, my breathing became dire with each haggard breathe I drew. I knew it was drawing me closer to the last.

A marble floor met me and a room dotted with various pillowed chairs, benches, and seats, decorated in green, red, blue, and silver came into view as I rolled out of the portal. Suddenly I heard several gasps; through the pain I tried to control my vision. Two ladies with high cheek bones and Elf-like features, the oldest stood with long brown hair and bright blue while the younger one stood with short blonde hair and equally ocean blue eyes. A man stood next to them, tall with black hair Elfin like features, and bright red eyes. The oldest woman leaned down and brushed my hair aside. "Raillyn," she said, as I opened another portal to fall through.

Grass padded my landing as I rolled out of the portal frightfully, and suddenly the pain faded. However, the memories continued. The sight of the red, blue, green, and silver decor triggered it.

Alkin and I walked streets of the same color. Tall, gleaming white and gold buildings stood towering over us, and small wooden stalls lined the bricked avenues. The city was magnificent and emanated power in everything. We paused at one, my mind stuttered, and the memory became staticy. Next thing I knew, Alkin handed me red ice cream in a breaded cone. Looking at him my face beamed as he smiled at me lovingly and took my free hand.

Stuttering again I found myself watching short flashes from a time when I was barely able to remember. I had to of been only a year old, close towards my second birthday. My parents handed me over to Alkin on numerous occasions; he was my protector, my guardian when they were not around.

He played games with me, hide and seek, chase, read to me, and played with me and my dolls. At night, he would stay up late and read stories, or tell me tales of long ago. As a child, I adored him, and stomped my feet in a fit of rage when he had to leave.

My eyes flew open and I laid there staring at a massive starry sky. Another memory brushed my mind, as the smell of herbs filled my nose. A dark room, lightning, and sulfur. Nothing registered in my mind, everything seemed like a jumbled mass of information, like my brain was on overload.

Sitting up, I recognized the scent around me. I sat on top of a hill in the middle of an enormous herb field, a massive river ran a few miles away. The same strange rune pillars dotted its shore as I had seen at the gate in Death's Realm.

A presence was coming. Closing my eyes, a few tears streaked my face as realization was sinking in. Looking to where I felt the disturbance, a grey portal opened up, Chaimh and a young-looking lady with white hair and pale skin walked through. Their eyes meet mine as utter shock crossed their faces.

My mind shattered in pain at the sight of them. Another memory gripped me in its tendrils, one inside a crystal coffin. Alkin stood beside it. "I'm so sorry, Raillyn." He said as he backed away and Hunter came into a room. I felt tears running down my face as I realized it was Alkin who had created the construct body that I resided in for over six years. Only he could release me from this terrible pain and hatred consuming me. I knew what I had to do, and before they could speak a word, I opened my own portal and left, knowing I was going to my death.

When I emerged, the pain from the spell returned in full. I cried out from the gruesome onslaught it portrayed. Clenching my stomach and taking ragged breaths I knew my time was close. I found Alkin beside me once more as another wave of pain echoed within.

Alkin looked shocked and shook his head. "What can I do to help? There has to be something." He begged. Deep down I knew now he would do anything I asked.

Wave after wave erupted within, I was losing the battle, and my body was failing me. Another memory gripped me, a large white oak lay on a hill overlooking a house. Of all the memories coming back to me, this one seemed displaced. Disoriented and confused, the image pulled at me, a deep force in my soul called me to its location. With nothing to lose I grabbed Alkin by the shoulders, tossing us through another portal to the location. We rolled onto the grass beneath the tree. Alkin stood and looked around. I sensed that he knew where we were.

Another tremor erupted through me. I felt like my skin was on fire and was melting off, desperately I ignored it. Instead, I focused my pain into a deadly wave of magic. Firing it towards the base of the tree I blasted a hole in the land itself. Falling to my knees, Alkin looked at me in disbelief.

The blade I thought as I fidgeted at my belt for its sheath. My once nimble finger felt slow and sluggish. Frustrated, I looked down at them. No long was the skin on my supple hands a creamy white, instead the flesh was turning a surprising shade of black. The skin had shrunk back a bit, giving them a bony appearance. I forced myself to ignore it and continued on. Drawing my blade, I pressed it into Alkin's hand as he sat beside me.

Pulling myself to my feet for the last time, Alkin shook his head and tried to hand the blade back. "I know now." I said as I pressed the hilt into his hands harder than before. For some reason, I knew that he had never been harmed by the blade and that it was a farce intended for Hunter.

He looked down on the blade and waited. "You have to kill me." I said. I cried out from another wave of pain.

Darkness threatened to consume me and I began coughing violently, blood splattered the brightly colored grass. Time was up, I would either die from the spell, or Alkin would listen. I had no intention to let the spell annihilate me and prayed Alkin would put me to rest, finishing this spell.

Staggering as the darkness tried to envelope me once more, I felt it. A pain deeper than I had ever felt pierced my heart. As it did so another tremor erupted inside me threatening to send me to my knees. Gently Alkin pulled me back up, holding me close to him. He began whispering in the Mystic tongue before he kissed my forehead, a tear fell onto my burning cheek as the spell ate away my existence. A pull stronger than any magic tried to consume my soul. It was a burning desire to leave, and escape the agony enveloping me. Wearily I looked down and realized that the pain was not from the spell, but the blade. Alkin stood, hilt in hand, covered in my blood as the blade sat lodged in my chest. Pulling it free, his eyes met mine. Like freezing from the inside out, cold erupted deep inside, as his magic, and the darkness of death enveloped me.

Unveil ~ Drameon

I couldn't assist Lord Drake, I knew I had to stand aside and allow the battle between Raihanna and him occur on its own accord. As soon as I saw Raihanna, something did not seem right. Her bright blue eyes and the bloodied sweat running down her face indicated a powerful spell had her in its grasp. She had come to remove Drake from the throne. I knew Hunter wanted the easy way out and taking care of the major leaders before summoning Daes would give him no retaliation later. Raihanna would be his puppet in this display of power and terror.

I watched as they fought with amazing speed. As soon as Raihanna tossed Drake's blade aside I knew she had him. It hit me hard, in that instant, I hated her. Raihanna was winning over Raillyn, and the outcome was looking grim. She had been so cunning and evil that she had tricked nearly everyone in her display of good show by releasing the girls.

As she went in for the killing blow, she staggered—sheathing her blade and falling into a portal instead. Something was not right. Immediately Drake shouted for his guards and hearing his yell, they rushed the room, and sent for Luca. Kneeling beside him, I applied pressure to the wound. It was bad, but not life-threatening, and thankfully he would survive. In no time at all a plump, dark haired lady appeared beside me. She commanded the guards to carefully carry Drake to the infirmary. Stepping out of their way, I decided to stay and help, following close behind them.

Briar had come and brought fresh herbs that would help prevent infection. Leece, Luca's assistant pulsed green healing magic into his body. Slowly the bleeding stopped, and Drake seemed to rest easier. Quickly I filled Briar in on the attack and told him to remain sharp. I was sure another assault would happen since the first one failed.

Knowing Drake had intended on retrieving Deestan and the girls from the Den, I decided I would do so in his absence. I walked the red-carpeted halls towards the town entrance and the tunnels beyond. Guards ran about me and were doubled up at every entry point. No one stopped me from leaving and as I walked down the balcony towards the tunnel, I looked up at the near-full moon. Smiling, I went through the tunnel and across town; it was early and shops were just beginning to set up.

It had been decades since I had walked this path alone. The Den was quiet, many dancers stood near the door, trying to stop everyone's entrance. I spotted a young man with long black hair and billowing black pants. Drawing out the small dancer charm, I explained my purpose. "I am here for the girls," I said. He nodded and said Stasha was in the lower area fourth room down.

So I descended the stairs and knocked quietly at the door. I heard a happy cry within as Stasha opened it cautiously. Deestan sat with her sister, her once dark hair had become silver. A scar was left on her magic from the spell Hunter performed. Hunter had hoped Callina possessed Rai's magic, but he was mistaken; she had Alkin's God lineage, not Rai's. Instead, he abused the child in his madness. Knowing Rai, this was what drove her to remove the girls from his grasp.

"Where's my dad?" Deestan asked eagerly. Stasha looked at me, worriedly. I suspected she had not told the children of the recent activity. They had already heard, hence the additional dancers at the door.

I bent down and brushed her hair behind her lightly pointed ear. "There's been an attack." I said, not lying to the child. "Your father is fine, just hurt. I came to bring you girls to the castle and make sure you stay safe." I said as her eyes widened.

Deestan looked back at her sister, quickly wasting no time. She took her tiny hands into hers. "Come on, Callie. We have to go with Drameon now," she said as she guided her sister towards me.

I paused, tipping my head sideways as she spoke her sister's nickname. "Callie?" I asked, "What a pretty name." I said while smiling.

"It's short for Callina, only I call her that. Have you heard from my mother?" She asked, as I shook my head. I couldn't bring myself to tell her that her mother was the one who injured her father. Looking at Stasha told me that she knew the truth and frowned, saddened by the thought.

Before leaving, Stasha told Deestan to hide the insignia but I stopped her. "No, let it be, Hunter can't touch them here. So let the people know we have their heir back." I said, as she nodded in understanding, allowing the insignia to show.

As I led the children out of the room and up the stairs, Stasha accompanied me. She carried Callina. As we walked, Deestan told us about how her mother took her from The Keep and released her into the den. She was happy about the situation, but frightened because she was not sure if she would see her mother again.

Smiling down at her, I tried to reassure her. "You will see your mother soon. She might be a little different, after everything that happened, but she will love you just the same. It pains her to be away from you girls."

I knew we didn't have much time before someone would recognize the rings. Sure enough, as we made our way through the Den and out the door already whispers could be heard about her. Word would spread quickly, and if Raihanna was still alive after today's attack, I was sure Hunter would kill her.

Walking quickly through the village, we entered the tunnels. Callina huddled closer towards Stasha as Deestan walked ever closer to my side. They sensed the unsettling power emanating from the deeper tunnels below. It was one of the few places where Dragons still resided in Alecien, and the Wolves had been given the task of protecting them. Another lost piece of history on their part...

Soon we emerged from the tunnel, and I led the girls towards the small den south of Drake's room, the safest place I saw fit for them. I had much to do and ensuring the girls were safe was the most important task I faced. If they were lost, I knew we would lose Raillyn for all time. They were her children, her flesh and blood, her heart, and love. She wanted them safe regardless of who she was. However, in turn I had to ensure she was safe, as well.

Alkin

Rai had no knowledge where she had sent us, and as the mist dissipated, I was shocked to find us at Calista's, her mother's, grave. Suddenly her power rose in response to the unlocked memories overwhelming her mind. Knowing I couldn't assist in the spell eating away in her I stood aside as she fired a blast of blue Mystic energy towards the ground, exploding a crater beneath the tree. A sight I hadn't seen in over six years revealed itself. The crystal coffin containing Raillyn's perfect body sat against the darkened soil. The vital spell had let its darkness loose on her, fortunately giving her access to the missing time and memories. The time was coming where she would have to choose, to live or die.

Distracting me, Rai thrust the blade into my hand. Either she figured out it would not harm me, or she had forgotten entirely. Regardless, I was happy she did so, but I had to stay diligent. Gently I tried to hand it back, this had to be her choice not mine. Even though everything in my body screamed for her well-being, I couldn't make this call. Again she thrust the blade harder into my hands. She begged me to kill her. I knew the spell burned at her very being, trying to destroy her and wipe her from existence.

Her once pale skin had been consumed with an ashen death look; her construct body was dying—she would not survive longer than a few moments. It ate away at her body and soon it would devour her soul. Driving the dagger deep into her heart, she fell into me, not knowing if the pain echoing through her was her own death, or not.

Gently I pulled her up and held her close, muttering an apology in the Mystic tongue. "I have always loved you and everything I do is for you; please know that I never meant to hurt you." I said as a tear escaped my eye and fell onto her cheek. The spell consumed its presence as it burned her skin. Her blood covered not only me but her, as well. Looking into her eyes, I couldn't resist but to kiss her once last time, a final farewell. I knew what would happen after this and it was the last goodbye I could give her. The last of my love.

Daes had a plan for her and I was sealing her fate by giving her to him forever. It would be up to her after this—how she choose to wield the power and knowledge she gained, and would continue to gain in the days to come.

Suddenly she staggered, her heart was stopping, and death was approaching fast. Summoning my father's deathly magic, I began the spell. I had to remove her soul and I had little time. As her body died, the spell would continue to eat away at her. Only when she touched the river of Death would the spell begin to wash away. Taking her chaotic soul with me across the veil, it fought fiercely between searing hot and frigid cold. Her magic grew deep within her very essence and fought desperately to break free. Finally, I was able to control it, containing it in an orb.

Crossing the veil, I fell with her into the icy river, praying. I held her soul orb tightly in my grasp, frightened it might slip away, along with her very being. Continuing to pray, I knew if the spell already ate her soul, she would not be complete. It would leave her in a half-life, a vegetative state. Had I made it in time? Did she make the choice correctly? Only time would tell.

The river bit into my skin as it threatened to consume Raillyn's soul, trying to drag us into the depths of its watery embrace, to be reborn. My shoulder burned with such an uncanny force that it felt as if thousands of daggers pierced me over and over. It was the mark, Raihanna had placed on me. Now that her body was dead so in turn was the mark and the bonds we shared.

For a moment, I felt my heart stutter as my body realized once more my mate was dead. Gasping for air, it seemed to freeze in my lungs. Agony exploded in my head as the spell wracked my brain and tried to tell me she was gone forever.

In a way, it made me want to die alongside her, but that couldn't happen.

Instead, I fought it, and pushed the feeling aside; forcing myself to remain callous to what was happening. That only made it worse. My soul fought violently against my body, forcing me to double over in pain. For a moment, I found bile rising in my throat, stinging as it came up. Her soul fought to break free, I struggled with my hold on it. *I was not willing to lose now.*

My body went numb with pain, and my mind clouded, with dispair. Holding onto it tightly, I stood my ground. My father was the ruler of this realm and his power coursed through me, I wasn't going to allow the river to win. Her soul flared black with taint as it boiled the waters around us, searing my hands in the process.

This was the powerful effect from the spell; slowly the color began to wash away, and fade; purple, and red, orange, yellow, to white. As it did so, the temperature of her soul cooled. The orb glowed brightly as if reflecting the full moon's light. Finally, the river released its hold on her soul and myself. I smiled, and knew now was time to slip back into the living.

Time was of the essence. I had to work quickly. The longer the soul remained outside her body, the more she would lose, giving me just seconds before the deterioration began.

Quickly, I jumped into the hole and found the small door atop of the coffin. Brushing the dirt off and pulling it aside revealed the small opening that allowed components to be added. Gently I slipped her soul orb inside, praying I had done so in time.

Rainbow light erupted from within; it lit up Raillyn's body. Her familiar features glowed with a strange bright blue power. Raillyn's magic was slowly returning to her. Waiting, I knew the next step would have to be done quickly before she began breathing.

Now that the bonds were broke, she would return—mind and body—to the way she was prior to our meeting. If I touched her once she lived, it would bring the onslaught of emotions that erupted the first time between us. That was an issue we did not need, I hoped to avoid her—and her cycle—for the time being.

She needed knowledge of how Mystics lived. What it meant and what it entitled. Most of all she needed to learn how to live as a female of our race. I was sure she would be fearful of the information, but it wasn't a choice. It never was for her. We don't choose what we are born into, no one does. We only made do with what we have, and make the best of it.

Just then a sound shook everything around as the crystal coffin erupted and split in an earth-shattering crash. The ground around us shook momentarily from its effects. The crystal's once smooth surface began to fall apart, like grains of sand through an hourglass. No longer did it seem like crystal; instead it looked like white sand slipping away.

Reaching out I took Raillyn from its grasp, her once bright-golden hair fell over my arm as I lifted her unclad body up, and out of the hole. Her elfin face portrayed a peaceful sleep, and as I descended the hill towards the little house, I looked at her hair further; it was now streaked with silver.

Prying the back door open, we entered the house. Walking the length of the large den, exquisitely sculpted rafters hung from the ceiling, and equally beautiful artwork hung from the walls. Red chairs dotted the room, and a large mahogany table sat in the center near a fireplace. The table legs were adorned with Dragon and Phoenix carvings, which spiraled upwards, meeting the tabletop. Bookshelves stood everywhere marking its interior.

I carried Raillyn past the bookshelves and across the ornate rug into another hall. Turning right, several intricate mahogany doors remained shut. I entered the last one on the left. The room beyond held a large four poster bed in the center, a small table, wardrobe and chairs sat along the walls while a white chest lay near a large bookshelf.

Carefully I placed my foot on the bed, using my left leg to balance Raillyn. Holding her up with my left arm, her head lay on my shoulder. Reaching down I pulled the green satin blanket, and sheets back, a symbol of a sapling decorated the surface. Gently I laid her down and pulled the blankets back over her bare form, just as she began breathing.

Breathing my own sigh of relief, I was thankful to have dodged our bond for now. However, I felt the brute force of its magic wrack my brain. My magic knew she was alive; her scent lingered in the air, the sweet smell of vanilla, honey-suckle, and thyme. It beckoned me to reach out and touch her, or run my fingers through her silky hair.

Hair that was once golden now stood out silvered. How-ever, that didn't matter; she was still beautiful to me. Drameon and I had done everything we were told. I prayed that I had made it in time, as well as prayed for my soul. That I would have the strength to deny her and keep away, not only just for both our sakes, but the world of Auran, as well.

The Gods never told us what would happen once she re-turned to Raillyn. Standing up, I went to sit in a nearby chair. We would have to wait and see the final result of Daes' spell.

Looking down at my hands, they were red--bits of flesh hung off my fingers, and pus-filled blisters puckered below the surface. They had been boiled in the river. Sighing, I prayed I wouldn't have to leave and seek my father out for blood to heal.

Almost on cue, a portal opened. Just as I began gathering energy to heal the blisters, Drameon stepped out, a bottle of blood in his hand. Handing it to me, he looked at Raillyn.

"I'm glad to see she lives. How are you holding up, my friend?" He asked concerned.

"Heh, I'm fine, the blood will heal my injuries. At the moment, I'm more concerned with her. She's remembering everything; she's going to hate me when she wakes up. All because she doesn't know why..." Popping the cork, I drank the bottle down as Drameon talked.

"She won't hate you; she's never been able to do that. Like always, she will be angry with you, yell at you, and I'm sure try and avoid you. But, we will see how long that lasts." Drameon smirked at me as I looked at him sarcastically. We both knew what would transpire once she woke, and it didn't look promising.

Retribution ~ Raillyn

Suddenly the pain began to subside—a lady sat rocking a small child: me. She sung a lullaby I had heard before in the Werewolves Den. Someone walked close by, a strand of silver hair trailed behind, leaving my vision. They went and stood behind who I could only assume was my mother.

Then, my father's face filled my eyes, and my child face smiled in joy. He kissed my mother's head, and they spoke briefly. My head turned, to look at them. They were happy and loved each other. My mother laid me in a bed of furs in a small room in what I could only place as the Den. She stayed beside me and sung me to sleep as my father worked at a nearby table.

Then my father and I walked the woods of a nearby village. Elves wandered about, eager for the day. I was filled with joy. My father stopped and spoke to many people, I saw my mother spinning and jumping as she practiced with a silvery moon blade with the-gem encrusted balance.

The vision changed, and my father and I sat in a great library, he read to me for hours. I had often fallen asleep in his arms while he did so. The vision faded from view.

More memories reamed my mind—Delron. I had seen him as an infant. His long black hair hung loosely over his equally black cloak. He had high cheekbones and pointed ears. He appeared almost Elf-like, very young, but his eyes told otherwise. My father often spoke to him and had spent much time in Death's Realm, in the caves below the river.

Then I was in the Den once more, with other children, but my parents and Alkin were not far from my sight.

Anger and sorrow; I felt it before anything else. My father was furious. I felt it in my little body as any Mystic would, his anger felt like a hole was torn in my chest, yet at the same time a great sadness overwhelmed me. My father threw objects, toppled furniture and tossed various vials about as if they were nothing. As I lay on a large pillow on the floor in our house, distraught, he realized my distress and held me momentarily. Then someone came.

Her magic frightened me, it was a force not to be reckoned with, and she used it accordingly. My father suddenly became a statue, powerless. As her silent spell took over, she removed me from his grasp. I screamed louder as she took me outside into the bright moonlight. A large portal stood in front of her.

Somehow my father had managed to break the spell and just before we entered the portal, he stepped out of the house. Furious he sent a deadly wave of God-like magic across the field. It toppled purple locust flowers, killing them instantly. In response to my father's anger, I sent out a wave of my own power. It lashed with such chaos that a human would perish from the effects. The lady who held me was troubled by this. Lips hard-pressed into a thin line, she nodded her head as Delron came and instantly teleported my father away. She turned with me in her arms and walked through the portal.

Pain twisted inside me, similar to the pain I felt in the construct body, and then another memory took hold. The young lady with her Elfin features and white hair rocked me as she cried. "I can't control her." She said between sobs.

Another man with long black hair, tied back, and stunning blue eyes looked at me. His Elfin face was elegantly sketched, and his subtly features tried desperately to hold my attention. His magic washed over me, it was intense and just upset me more. I hurt, the pain inside was too much, and the balance this man tried to bestow upon me only increased my pain. I felt like I was being ripped apart, deep inside I knew my little mind would break, under this stress.

The man took me and held me close; he sung to me and tried desperately to soothe my raging mind. Gravely, I tried to embrace his calmness, but couldn't; my magic wouldn't allow it. "Hush, my child, all is well; you are safe. You are loved, and everything will be fixed, you have to trust me on this." He said in a loving voice as my magic continued to lash out uncontrollably.

Daes himself walked me around the room, frightened that his last child would become consumed by hate. Inside I knew he was right—everything happened for a reason, but that reason was what made me so unstable. Try as I might I just couldn't control my emotions or magic. I continued to scream and cry out; my magic lashed, and reaped anyone around. Like fine tendrils of light, it whipped about wildly. Even Daes and the lady received blows, slicing their skin and tearing the room asunder.

The young lady continued to cry as Daes handed me to her once more. "We have to do it," he said as I heard him speak in the Ancient tongue and draw upon a deep dark magic. "We will fix things after she is safe." He said as the lady held me close. She nodded as she seemed to glow with a green power. Tears ran down her face as she apologized for the recent events. She said they would make it better. Then sleep overcame me. It consumed me in a matter I could not escape, and I allowed the darkness to embrace my now chaotic mind.

Everything I do is for you, even if at times I refused to admit it even to myself, it's the truth.

It was Alkin; flashes of more memories poured through my mind and engulfed me in sorrow. During the years, I spent with Chaimh I always felt someone watching, especially after I met Drameon.

The day I got away from Hunter, it was Alkin who saved me. Later when I found the dead bodies in the woods, after sending Alihandra away, Alkin protected and watched over me. Even later he never did anything to hurt me, or anything I didn't want.

He had given me a ring to help me heal after Deestan was born. In turn, he had been there for me, holding me, comforting me, and loving me regardless of the child not being his. He even apologized in Death's Realm when he had to whisk me away.

I remembered the conversation that I had with my mother hours before I was taken. How I admitted that I liked Alkin, regardless of his darker side. I was comfortable around him, as Raillyn and even as Raihanna. He was the only one I could be myself around and not fear being judged wrongfully by.

Last time I had spoken to him as Raillyn, I knew I had hurt him. Even though in turn he hurt me, it still was upsetting. He was right about my so-called dream, I never said no. I didn't want to, deep down there was a part of me that hoped he would give me what I wanted, a Mystic child. But, my logical side got the better of me and fear took over, and drove me away.

Tears fell from my eyes as I sat up and looked around the room. I had been here before, I thought, long ago. I sat in the large four poster bed decorated in deep green Elven blankets and felt the cool magic pulse in its very weave. Various tapestries hung from the walls, each imbued with magic. Something moved out of the corner of my vision, looking, I saw him.

Alkin relaxed in a chair and met my eyes. Suddenly he got up; approaching me he paused for a moment. "How are you?" He asked as I looked down and realized I lacked clothes. For a moment, I wasn't sure how to act if I should be offended or not. I tried to reach for the blood bond we had and found nothing.

Looking down towards my right breast I saw there was no mark, it was gone, along with the mark from Howl. Even Drameon's mark on my wrist was gone. A twang of pain echoed in my soul, for a moment my breath stilled in my lungs as I felt on the verge of tears.

Alkin walked over towards the wardrobe and pulled out black leather pants and my blue mercenary tunic, tossing them to me, smiling. For a moment, I felt relief wash over my mind. Returning his smile, I stood and dressed, fighting down the tears and grief. In a sense, it was odd putting on the same outfit I had worn years ago, almost as if I needed to wear something else. That this part of me died when I was taken to The Keep; deep down a part of me knew I would never be the same. However, it felt good to finally be back in my real body.

Smoothing the material over my waist and hips felt so right. No longer did I possess the evil-constructed half-body that had been Raihanna's. I gazed in a crystal mirror hanging on the wall and smiled at the sight of myself. My hair no longer pure gold now held streaks of silver. Deep down, I knew I would never escape the horror I went through during my stay in The Keep, it would haunt me forever. *A small price I had to pay.*

Turning from the mirror, I realized I felt more alive than any other time in my life. Every piece in the larger puzzle was now coming together. Smiling I felt a slow stream of Ancient magic pulse through me. Very few questions presently lay unanswered, as I was sure of the path that I was placed on. Even though it frightened me, and made me nervous.

Alkin stood smiling, his eyes following my every move. While in The Keep he had been my rock, now however, I was less sure. In a way, I wanted to go up and slap him for everything he had done, yet at the same time he had treated me so well. In The Keep I had even found myself beginning to love him. My heart ached as I felt on the verge of tears again.

"I want to slap you right now." I said, turning to look at him while trying to lighten the mood between us.

Alkin met my eyes as he approached, "You can try." He said smirking, almost reaching out to touch me, before drawing back.

"Why won't you touch me?" I felt myself say before I could stop myself. Alkin seemed shocked, almost hurt. "You hate me, don't you? Something changed, and you hate me..." I said, shocked at how I was feeling from his sudden lack of contact. My emotions yo-yoed from one extreme to another, dizziness overcame me, causing me to grab onto the nearby chair.

"No, Raillyn, that's not it..." He began before I felt my anger rise as another memory gripped my mind.

It was of my supposed dream that really wasn't a dream. He was so gentle with me, so careful. Even when he dug his claws into my hips, marking me as his, he still tried to chase the pain away with sweet kisses.

In a way, I was still shocked. We had mated with each other then. *Even though our mating wasn't successful, did that make me more obligated to Alkin than Drake? Since he was my first?* I was so confused, and no one had told me anything on this subject. My body burned momentarily at the memory, as the scent of a pine forest after a rainy day, lit my nerves aflame.

This is not what I needed right now… I knew as Raihanna I had been close to my cycle, but did that mean the same for me now, as Raillyn? For a moment, fear gripped me as I felt myself wanting to go to Alkin. *No…* I thought to my-self. *All this was because of a spell, right?* It angered me. *I would not fall victim again to its power until I found more information out.*

"Well, then, what is it? Everything about you drives me crazy. The memory of how you smell and taste, even your looks make me feel like I'm burning up inside. It sets every nerve in my body on fire, I hate it! I hate the way it makes me feel and that I have no idea what it means!" I found myself yelling unintentionally about my frustration on how I felt, not meaning for it to be directed at Alkin.

However I knew that's what happened. I channeled all my frustration towards him. Indicating how irritated I felt to-wards the whole situation, and how it angered me, how being around him angered me. Alkin met my eyes, they were filled with hurt and immediately I regretted my words. No longer did we have the link, so there was no way he could feel my emotions.

Closing my eyes I felt on the verge of tears, and not wanting Alkin to see, I looked towards the ground and stead-ied myself before facing him again. Solemnly he held out a night blue cloak. Reaching out I took it from his hands before carefully securing it around me. Not wanting to hurt or anger him I tried to focus on easier things.

"How long?" I croaked, on the verge of tears again. I wanted to know how much time had passed since my narrow escape from the deadly spell.

Alkin frowned, something I had hoped not to see. "A week... Everything has been kept hushed and calm on both sides, so all is well." He replied, smiling at me.

Nodding my head I cautiously asked the next question that haunted my mind. "Is he alive?" I questioned hopeful that my blow as Raihanna did not kill Drake.

Alkin seemed upset by my question. In a way, I could see why, after everything we had been through, before and even while in The Keep. Still, he seemed understanding.

Things were returning to normal, and that meant I would probably return to the Werewolves. Part of me didn't want to, though. Yes, I had mated with the Wolf King, but in a way it didn't matter. I could never take a throne. Still deep down I felt I was missing some piece of important information. And regardless of it all, I still felt more at ease with Alkin, even after everything that happened...

Alkin nodded his head, "He lives." He said as he interrupted my thoughts. "Are you ready?" He asked smiling.

I smiled at him as I nodded my head. "Let's go." I said as I pulled the hood up on my cloak, hiding my face, I followed him through a portal. I knew where we were going, I slightly feared it but at the same time I wanted to see him. So many questions remained unanswered yet, so many became so clear.

As we left the portals black mist, I saw Drake standing beside the table in the throne room while Briar, Saibal, Howl and Drameon stood around him. I left the hood up, taking in the faces of my friends and family. Alkin, seeing my apprehension, went to address Lord Drake. Even without our bond he still read me like an open slate, and I was happy about it. No one approached me, and after a minute or two the rest joined the conversation.

Drameon stood off slightly to the side and listened in. Slowly so not to alert anyone I walked towards him, his ever-changing eyes met mine. He disregarded the conversation the others were having and looked at me.

Looking back towards Drake and the others I knew what being a Mystic was. It was a hard life, and I was frightened by what it would bring me, but equally I was happy I was becoming who I was supposed to be. This life held hardship, joy, love, and despair. Most of all it held harmony and chaos, a perfect balance of everything. It marked you as different and set you aside from everyone else. It was a life of servitude to the Gods and to the land, a life of hard choices and equally hard situations. This was my fate.

Closing my eyes I looked back up into Drameon's. "Hello Father." I said. As he pulled me into a deep embrace, he spoke, I knew the others heard. "My daughter..." He said kissing my head. "How I have missed you..."

~Symphony of Power – Preview ~

A kaleidoscope of memories, in unrelenting flashes, began pouring into me. My life, the life I was used to, was a lie. I lost my balance when I went to the Wolves. By doing so, I shifted from harmony to chaos, and later back again in The Keep. Now I was finding myself, finding what was lost, forgotten. I never knew who, or what I was, it always escaped me. The significance behind it all was startling and frightening.

All my memories, even the ones that were locked away, were open to me. He kept nothing from me, going as far as showing me his own memories from times long ago. Tears filled my eyes as I realized he had always been there, before Chaimh and Lillian, and even during. Always he had protected me, from unseen dangers, often risking his own life for my own. It was daunting, and mind numbing.

Only now was I able to see, that I was blind, that until I lost it, all of it, I could never be whole. Tears ran down my face and onto the floor below, forgotten. It had been Daes' plan the whole time, to break me, letting me find my center.

Dizziness spread, and overwhelmed me, causing me to fall into him. Eyes open wide in shock, they just kept coming. The moment he touched my face, sparked what I had lost, reawakened in our bond. I couldn't stop it. I didn't get a choice and never would. It was the Gods plan all along. Thankfully, now I knew who I was, what I was, and what it meant. For the first time in my life, I finally felt like who I was born to be.

Symphony of Power ~ Fall 2014

~About the Author~

LYNDIE SWEDERSKY

I was born in California and had the privilege to live in Washington, Colorado, and finally settled here in Indiana, where I met my wonderful husband. During the journey, I attended modeling with NY Modeling company, did theatrical work with Jester Productions (now Dream Alley Studios), and performed in various local musicals and pageants along the way. Needless to say, I was very busy, very young.

Along the way, I developed a passion for writing, but this did not come until my 8th grade school year. Prior to that I will say I hated reading and writing with a passion. It wasn't until I picked up that one special book, enriched with fantasy, that something clicked. After that, it was hard to take a book away from me, and as I became inspired by friends and family, I began to create my own world, and my own characters. Sadly I lost my father in 2002. We often stayed up late watching the stars and talking about all the possibilities the universe held. He had a big hand in the world I created.

Currently, I have two wonderful children and a great husband who supports my dreams of writing. I still live in Indiana and am working on the rest of the Alecien Series as well as a possible Aeralain Series.

www.ingramcontent.com/pod-product-compliance
Lightning Source LLC
Chambersburg PA
CBHW071510260626
47170CB00002B/322